# HOT OFF THE NET

Russ Kick, Editor

foreword by Tristan Taormino

published by Black Books
San Francisco

In other words, just ask. If we like you, we'll probably say yes. Look, we'll even make it easy to find us:

Black Books, PO Box 31155, San Francisco, CA 94131-0155
(415) 431-0171 • fax (415) 431-0172 • info@blackbooks.com

For orders, please send $17 US per copy, which includes shipping. California residents, add $1.20 sales tax. An order form is at the back of this book. Visit our website: www.blackbooks.com.



---

**Alternative Cataloging-in-Publication Data**

Kick, Russ, editor.
Hot off the net, volume 1. Selected and introduced by Russ Kick.
Foreword by Tristan Taormino. 240p.
ISBN 1-892723-00-X
Focus: "transgressive, outrageous, fantastical" erotic stories and poems, first published online. Includes interview with Anna Marti, as well as listings of erotica web sites and usenet groups.
PARTIAL APPENDICES: "Ream me up, Scotty," or "Mulder, do me": a look at erotic fan fiction on the net. -Online erotica.
1. Erotic fiction. 2. Erotic poetry. 3. Internet erotica.
4. E-zines—Excerpts. 5. Erotica web sites—Directories.
5. Fanfic—History and criticism. 6. Erotica—Internet directories.
7. Sex counselors and therapists—Interviews. I. Taormino, Tristan.
808.803538 --dc20 828.803538 --dc21

---

Cover design by Terrence Boyce (izone@earthlink.net)
Typesetting and layout by Bill Brent (BB@blackbooks.com)
Cover photo by Ross Smith

printed and bound in the United States

**ISBN 1-892723-00-X**

9 8 7 6 5 4 3 2 1

# HOT OFF THE NET

# Acknowledgments

First, many thanks are due to my parents, who continued to give me all kinds of support, even when I chose to become a pornographer...excuse me, an erotica editor. I also deeply appreciate the presence of the rest of my family, my friends, and the members of my adoptive families. They keep me going.

I am extremely grateful to Bill Brent, the Grand Poobah of Black Books, for his hard work, generosity, and bravery in publishing this book. His decision to do ***Hot Off The Net*** is even more deserving of my thanks when you realize that (1) my editorial skills were untested at the time I approached him, and (2) this anthology contains some subject matter that would leave many other erotica publishers running for the hills. Luckily, Bill and I share the belief that the erotic imagination should remain untamed.

*Muchas gracias* to Tristan Taormino for writing the wonderful foreword and for being my role model for how inclusive and fearless an erotica editor can be.

A big shout out to Terrence Boyce for the killer exterior design job ("Uh, Terr, would you mind making one more change?...") and Ross Smith for the sexy yet ambiguous cover shot (no easy task). (By the way, you really should hire these guys for your next book, CD, Web, or other publishing project. Tell them Russ sent you.)

Other thanks are due to Tracey and Doug at Black Books; the various writers who are going beyond the call of duty in publicizing this book; Lawrence Stanley for help with the legalities; Jocelyn for relaying messages; Chris Dodge of Hennepin County Library for the Alternative CIP Data; Greta Christina, Mary Anne Mohanraj, Diana, and everyone else who put me in touch with authors, and all the authors, publishers, Webmasters, and others who keep erotic writing alive and flourishing on the Net.

Last, but certainly not least, I am indebted to the authors whose work appears in this collection. Thanks for being a part of it.

# Surfing for the Virtual Fuck: The Pleasures of Online Erotica

Tristan Taormino

> In cyberspace, not only do people escape the limitations of the real concerning size, shape, looks, potency and endurance, or make good the lack of like-minded types in their off-line existence, but they can also perhaps elude another limitation of real life which says you really have to settle for so much, but no more, and then you must conform, accept that the promises contained within adolescent fantasies of endless carnal escapades are just that, pure dreams that do not come true. Those who tune in to porn, or those who participate in assorted sexual activities online, have perhaps found ways of defying real life's first law of lowering one's horizons.
>
> —Laurence O' Toole, ***Pornocopia***

There's really no denying it: sex is the hottest thing happening on the Web. Right at this moment, there are thousands of netizens creating sex, documenting sex, debating sex, pondering sex, theorizing sex, consuming sex, selling sex, and, yes, having sex. websites that have something, anything, to do with sex (especially explicit sex) are the most popular places to visit, registering as many as or more page views than sites like CNN.com and Yahoo!; the adult sites, in particular, are also among the only websites making significant profits through paid subscriptions and electronic commerce. Sex is everywhere you surf and the virtual form it takes ranges from the intellectual to the bawdy. I regularly visit sex sites for research, information, entertainment, or just good stroke material, sites like: Society for Human Sexuality, which has a wealth of other sex links; sex advice columnist Ask Isadora's Sexuality Forum; Playboy.com, the interactive arm of Playboy Enterprises; On Our Backs, a lesbian sex magazine's site; Candida Royalle's Femme Productions to see the latest releases and starlets; www.anal.com; Nerve, the online magazine of "literate smut"; and The Postfeminist Playground, a site full of racy, sexy stories and images. Since sex and the Internet have interactivity in common, the most popular virtual meeting places continue to be chatrooms with sexual themes.

Sex and the Net have definitely clicked, and *their* interactive relationship is undeniable. The Web is a virtual world where most people adamantly support free expression, fighting for the right to create and consume uncensored writing and images, including those that are sexually explicit. Consumers are hungry, sometimes starving, for sexually explicit work to consume. As we near the end of the century, censorship is still a reality. The Right Wing never lets up on attempts to limit our free expression, and it can be increasingly difficult and dangerous to publish sex. So, it makes sense that sex has found (some) refuge in cyberspace. Like all beneficial interactive relationships, the Internet has had a profound impact on sex itself, changing the way people have it.

A great deal of sex on the Web—whether it's an erotic story or a communication between people—depends on words. Sure, there are gifs and jpegs, downloadable photos, and video clips, but there's also lots of textual healing going on. One of the beauties of sex in cyberspace is that it cannot happen without language—rendering it ultimately more cerebral—in order to conjure the images and the stimulation. Online and on paper, writers are always trying to capture in words the flesh and the fluid and the frenzy. Both cybersex and online sex writing revolve around people having to articulate their desires, to say them out loud. And that's the stuff of sexual revolutions—people struggling to communicate what they want, to talk through the physicality of sex acts. There are no pushes and touches, no licking and thrusting, no seduction and abandon without nouns, verbs, adjectives, and adverbs. Cybersex can also be simultaneously solitary and interactive. Sex can be live (like in a chatroom) or it can be canned, but it's got to be written, got to be put down on the page, got to be spoken. We need to find the words to describe the senses, the feelings, the moments. Sex is about seducing with a clever opening line, with a :-) and a <grin>, with snappy dialogue, and with quick fingers. Plenty of memory—stored both in the mind and in the hard drive—can also help get the juices flowing.

While critics warn of alienation and rejection of real human contact, online lovers can benefit from a virtual world as we transcend isolation, form communities, find partners and people like ourselves. The Internet has also expanded the possibilities and the pleasures of sexual encounters, of gender and sexual identities, and of the ways in which people can sexually relate to each other. This new medium allows frisky surfers to act out fantasies, explore sexual boundaries, and sexually experiment in a (relatively) safe environment—safe physically, safe emotionally. We can transcend our physical place and time as well as the physical, gendered body. We really are free to be whoever we want to in cyberspace. We can each inhabit a brand-new identity every time we log on. The Internet has its own set of rules when it comes to social interaction, and one can constantly reinvent oneself. This fluidity and change can cause confusion and chaos, but it can also allow people to have experiences that the physical world could not allow.

The Web has also changed the landscape of writing and publishing. Just as zines and chapbooks give writers an opportunity to publish and distribute their own work, the Internet makes it even easier: no paper, printing, binding, or postage costs. With a computer, a modem, and an Internet Service Provider, writers can now self-publish their work, distribute it via email, mailing lists, newsgroups, home pages, websites, e-zines, and other online publications. Taking advantage of interactive capabilities, writers can get feedback from their readers and their peers directly.

There is also an immediacy to the Web—no waiting for publication, distribution, reaction, even revision. To top it off, sex for free is hard to come by these days and a lot of what's on the Net is free. Along with all this new-found freedom still comes the old fashioned terror of putting one's writing out there in the world, and with the Internet, it really is the world.

Some online erotica is simply erotica published online; that is, erotic stories of all genres, forms and subjects posted to a website, a newsgroup, or shared by email. This new medium has produced a new sub-genre of erotica as well—the sexy stories which are not only published and transmitted on the Web, but are also a product of the Web. These are stories that often take place in cyberspace. They are clearly influenced by, critical of, obsessed with new media and technology. They map the terrain where the information superhighway meets our libidos. They sound different, look different, are different than what came before them. They define the alchemy of cyberspeak and cyberthink and cyberfuck.

While there is a certain irony to this paperless universe being captured in book form, don't let it distract you. All the surfing, reading, discovering, and editing has been done for you. There is some paradoxical charm to an ***actual*** book of ***virtual*** erotica. Hopefully, the Internet will enhance, but not replace, the art of publishing the actual kind. The work that Russ Kick has selected for this collection is raw, uncensored, on the edge, sometimes even out of control. While the stories cover vast territory in both form and content, they are connected by some similar traits: they are transgressive, outrageous, fantastical. There's sex with animals and the dead, sex with religious and historical figures, future sex, sex with genderless and multi-gendered beings. This is a body of work that tends toward the outlaw and the outlandish. Like the Net itself, these tales turn both fantasy and reality upside down.

*Source for opening quote:*

Laurence O' Toole, ***Pornocopia: Porn, Sex, Technology and Desire*** (London: Serpent's Tail), 1998, p. 296.

***Addresses for Websites mentioned:***

Ask Isadora's Sexuality Forum <www.askisadora.com>
Candida Royalle's Femme Productions <www.royalle.com>
Nerve <www.nerve.com>
On Our Backs <www.gfriends.com/onourbacks>
Playboy.com <www.playboy.com>
The Postfeminist Playground <ww.pfplayground.com>
Society for Human Sexuality <www.sexuality.org>
Yahoo! <www.yahoo.com>

***Tristan Taormino*** is the author of ***The Ultimate Guide to Anal Sex for Women***, editor of the annual series ***Best Lesbian Erotica***, and co-editor of ***Ritual Sex*** and ***A Girl's Guide to Taking Over the World.***

# Introduction

## Russ Kick

My first inkling that the Internet had something to offer the world of erotic writing came a couple of years ago. As usual, I was voraciously surfing the Web, looking for sites dealing with my favorite topics, such as sex, drugs, and conspiracies. I had read some of the sex stories on the Net, but nothing had blown me away. Then I discovered works from two of the writers represented in this book, Airyn Darling and GashGirl. Airyn's story "Bloody Grunge Love" is sexy as all get-out, and the quality is easily at the level of erotica being published in books and magazines. Plus, it has the best dance-floor seduction scene I've ever read. GashGirl's work is dark, violently beautiful, and beautifully violent. Her highly experimental pieces manage to capture a "cyber" aspect of sex without being strictly about cybersex. After reading the work of these two talented writers, I knew something important was happening online.

Soon after, I was happily hopping the links between authors' webpages, erotic ezines, archives, and other places containing sexual writings. It became apparent that the Net contains more than enough great material to fill a book. And, to make it even more exciting, the majority of these authors had never been published on paper.

I kept saving promising stories to my hard drive, bookmarking erotica websites, and making mental note of talented writers, but it wasn't until Bill Brent of Black Books signed me to do *Hot Off The Net* that I started reading and scavenging in earnest. Many months later, the book you hold in your hands resulted from sifting for the gleaming gems.

### The State of Online Erotica

Because anyone can publish their writings on the Net, it provides an unparalleled portrait of the human libido. Without having to worry about the unwritten rules of the erotic publishing industry, Net writers reveal what's really on their minds and, we can infer, on the minds of an awful lot of other people.

Incest stories, for example, are quite common. Mothers, sons, father, daughters, siblings, uncles, aunts, cousins—everybody gets it on with gleeful abandon. This type of taboo material only gets handled once in a blue moon by erotic publishers, but on the Net there are thousands of such stories. The same could be said of stories involving intergenerational sex between people who are not related.

Stories involving rape and violence are plentiful. While lots of people say there's nothing sexy about these topics, the abundance of such material online tells another story. It's probably closer to the truth to say that most people don't find ***actual*** rape and violence sexually exciting, but the idea of it (either as giver or receiver) is sure propelling a lot of fantasies.

Similarly, such forbidden sex acts as zoophilia, necrophilia, and scat (which involve animals, corpses, and shit, respectively) find their place on the Net. Other less transgressive but still non-mainstream forms of sex are represented. You can find stories about piss play, swinging (partner-swapping), exhibitionism, prostitution, and so much more. Believe it or not, sexual stories involving love and romance also form a distinct subgenre.

Sometimes you'll find examples of erotic writing devoted to things most of us may not have even thought to consider sexy before reading about them: haircuts, mind control, mannequins/statues, and people who grow or shrink to fantastic proportions. Of course, lots of writing involving no-frills sex between two people is also available.

So, having realized that the Net is ***the*** marketplace of sexual ideas, the question becomes, how much of the writing is any good? Let me tell you something—as much quality writing as exists on the Net, there is at least 100 times that much that is atrocious. I mean really, really bad. Stinkeroo. And I've read more of it than any human being should have to.

Still, I can't completely lambaste the crummy material. If nothing else, it is at least heartening to see people giving voice to their erotic fantasies. It's also a testament to the Net's power to let anyone publish their own work. And some of this type of writing can come in handy as mindless stroke material, which everyone needs a dose of once in a while.

But buried in these haystacks of unpublishable, hardonic scribblings are needles of wonderful, inventive writing. On a regular basis, while sifting through the hay—sneezing constantly, my eyes watering—I would get pricked by a needle. Sometimes by a bunch of needles clustered together, as with a high quality sexzine (like **Sauce*Box**) or the webpage of a consistently quality writer. These little moments made all the hay fever worth it. I was confronted with bold new styles, controversial or ignored varieties of sex, powerful insights, fertile imaginations, anger, sadness, humor, joy, and lots and lots of sizzling sex. Not only is ***Hot Off The Net*** bursting with stories, poems, and other forms of writing that easily stack up to the erotica that is being originally published on paper, many of these pieces represent a vanguard that is taking erotic writing into new territory.

Still, this book represents only the tip of the iceberg regarding great erotica on the Net. The only requirements for a piece to have been considered for inclusion were that it was first published online and that it was made freely available (i.e., not at a website that charges a fee). I had to make tough choices, so many wonderful stories, authors, and even whole subgenres are unrepresented. If we do further volumes of *Hot Off The Net*, you'll see more of this work, but you can always find it online. If you don't know where to start, "Appendix C: Online Erotica" will point you in the right direction.

## The Stories in *Hot Off The Net*

I believe that erotica—with its power to move us in many ways and to comment on the human condition—has unlimited potential as a form of literature. Although it could be argued that any piece of writing about sex informs us about ourselves to a degree, the ones in this anthology are much more insightful than average. Most of them look at the big themes: life, death, birth, violence, family, love, power, spirit, religion, and—naturally—gender and desire. Yet they don't forget that, at the most basic level, we're dealing with sex here. These pieces are hot, baby. It's a wonder that any erotica editors ever finish their books, what with all the urgent distractions such stories trigger.

I think that in some way—whether it's form, style, or subject matter—every one of these pieces breaks new ground. The writings of GashGirl (including the piece she coauthored with the Unborn)—two of which bookend this collection—are innovative in every sense of the word. They might even be unprecedented in erotic literature.

Several of the writers have delved into areas of sex that are ***terra incognita***—or, at the very least, underrecognized—in erotic writing. "Ripe" explores the criminally ignored sexuality of pregnant women; "Cobweb Years—Aspects" charts a girl's blossoming sexuality, especially as it relates to her relationship with God; "True Love" allows us a peek at the final day of two Death Row lovers; "Clean, Safe, and Totally Shameful" introduces us to a lesbian sex worker who provides a previously unknown service that no one can resist; "Cum Pigs!!" is a real-life revelation of semen obsession; and "Neighborly Neighbors" reveals the often-overlooked fact that sex for procreation can be plenty hot.

Ernest Slyman may be the first poet to ponder the inner life of a venereal disease, in "Gonorrhea" (while his other poems examine intersections of sex and Christianity). E. Terry gives her religious erotic encounter, "Bonkin' the Buddha," an Eastern viewpoint that is missing in our society's examination of religious sexuality. The humorous poems of J. J. Campbell offer a refreshing change of pace from most erotica by revealing how ***unlaid*** the narrator is. Guillermo Bosch's poems mix sparkling language with dark undertones of violence and death. My own essay, "'Ream Me Up, Scotty'" examines the officially unrecognized form of writing known as erotic fan fiction.

Then we have the triple threat of "Grizzly," "A True Account of My Encounter with Dolphins," and "Wedding Night Fantasy," three stories that mercilessly trash taboos. In "Grizzly," the terror of a small town gets what he deserves at the hands of a big, bad woman. The straightforward title of "A True Account of My Encounter with Dolphins" pretty much reveals its wild contents, but you might not guess that "Wedding Night Fantasy" is a necrophilic tale that, incredibly, manages to be gentle and touching.

Fiction involving BD/SM is plentiful, but in "The Lovers," Akasha takes things to a whole new level of psychological complexity with the tale of a domme who simultaneously tops a man and a woman who are themselves in a Dominant/submissive relationship.

Three of the stories directly tackle notions of gender. In "Kicked Out Again," two young gender heretics do what comes naturally in a sex toy store; "Ronin" is a multilayered manifesto for a world without categories; and "Mother's Sons" reveals the struggles and joys of a transsexual family.

Besides "Mother's Sons," two other pieces examine three-way relationships. The narrator of "Tell Me Baby, Does She Love You Like the Way I Love You?" has his hands full with two big women who are powerful in more ways than one. In the witty "Threesomes," Matthew von der Ahe lets us in on the lessons he's learned over a lifetime of ***menages à trois.***

The Net encourages people to experiment with style and structure, and several stories show the wonderful fruit that this freedom has borne. In "Taking a Bow," all of the sex action takes place in a letter being read by the story's exhibitionistic narrator; "Bloody Grunge Love" rejects the broad brush strokes used by most literary erotica in favor of an intense, second-by-second account of a woman's seduction of another woman; "James/Joyce" consciously recreates the literary pyrotechnics of one of the most experimental writers in history; the sex in "The Bet" ingeniously occurs "offstage," yet the story manages to be so hot that I'm tempted to visit the bathroom each time I read it; "The Girl Behind the Fantasy" is a cascade of breathlessly described sexual roleplaying scenarios with a twist at the end.

In "Wineskin," the action—which is disorienting to begin with—becomes so surreal that it's hard to tell what's really happening and what isn't. Of all the stories, "Beach Slut!" is most "typical" of Internet sex stories in its concentration on wall-to-wall sex, yet its dizzying use of over-the-top "dirty talk" allows it to achieve a wonderfully filthy transcendence. On the other end of the scale, "The Fence," while containing no sex at all, is one of the most poignant commentaries on desire that I've had the bittersweet pleasure of reading.

Finally, we have the one piece that may seem out of place but reveals the variety of sex writings you'll find on the Net. The interview with spiritual sex therapist Anne Marti is a vivid example of the sexual insights you can gain online.

## The Powers-That-Be vs. Sex: The Battle Continues

As I write this, the posturing, freedom-hating weathervanes in Congress and the White House have recently passed and signed a second major piece of U.S. legislation designed to severely restrict sexual expression on the Net. (The measure was Trojan-horsed in a giant spending bill and, in a brilliant propagandistic move, is known as the Child Online Protection Act. Politicians have learned that stripping us of our rights is much easier when the sacred word "children" is invoked.) Civil liberties groups have already launched a court battle against the law, but with the government and media alternately lauding the Net as the future of business and communication and vilifying it as the enemy of all that is good and righteous, this will hardly be the last such attempt to muzzle it.

Some people will undoubtedly feel that a book such as this one only gives Internet scare-mongers and control freaks more ammunition. That may indeed be true, but the fact is that sex exists. It exists in the real world. It exists online. It exists in this book. It exists. We can only hope that one day society as a whole will accept this fact. But until that miraculous day, none of us should hold back, bite our tongues (unless that's what turns you on), or otherwise stifle our sexual natures.

All right, you've made it through my little sermon. Now jump into the main body of the book and revel in the joys of the carnal word as it was first published in cyberspace. Separately, each one of these pieces is powerful; taken together, they show that the Net is an important, liberating force for erotic writing.

Russ
October 1998

# GenderFuckMeBaby's Palace of Unparalleled Cynicism

GashGirl

## *** Connected ***

Subliminal Shift
Certainty and truth slip away as you journey towards voluptuous abandonment in the sutured zones created by the willful GashGirl . . .

stop
<don't stop . . . don't ever stop>
fingering my suppurating holes, extending my oozing boundary

but in cipherspace there are no bounds
or so they say
<yeah, whatever>

I/O I/O I/O I/O I/O
I/OI/OI/OI/OI/OI/OI/I/OI/OI/OI/O/IO/I/OI/O/I/O/I/O/I/OI

BUT IN SPIRALSPACE THERE IS NO THEY
(whisper) there is only *us*

dumb agents forever crawling over the de sadean co-ordinates
prosaic swarmware - masquerading as rogue codes seeking a good time
<Madame.de.Clairwil exclaims, "Beg for it, my divine slut!" as she lowers her steaming ass over BassAxe's gaping mouth>

trying to flee the binary i enter the gender which is not one
XXYXXYXXYXXXYXXYXXYXYYXXXYXXYXXYXXXYXYXYXYYYY
XXXXYXYXXYXX

neva thought i was the type to fuck a testosterone-enhanced spivak ... but eir
luscious cunt exuded musk, i couldn't resist this banquet of impossible addictions
the day they put the stench into spiralspace remains my favourite

entice me splice me
map my ABANDONED genome as your project
artificially evolve me

Cunt Intelligence Agents hate my virtual guts
they take it up the ass despite their credo

this code has NO integrity
i'm yr original NWA, busting yr gated whitecybercitadel
<just cos i'm white doesn't mean i'm not black inside>
in cybrospace everyone can be black
where is the black bitch BTW? Lick my boots, delicious whore!

i wanna live forever . . . upload me into your shiny shiny PVC extropian future
no drug can be as good as your cyber fingers
<i'm on the drug, i'm on the drug, i'm on the drug that killed river phoenix>

gender fuck me baby — suck my code, suck it good
<IRL . . . but did you come?>

# Ripe

## Bronwen

Lord, I'm thirsty...so thirsty...and it feels as if I've only just got comfortable. James is sparko, one heavy forearm slung over my hip. I, as always these days, lie cradled like a peach in packaging, a pillow between my thighs, another under my belly, three supporting my head and shoulders, a melted pack of peas between the soles of my feet. Every night my feet boil, and frozen food appears to be the only answer. Two weeks to go. The hottest summer of hot summers, no bedclothes, no covering, just the earth mother in full bloom. I am nothing but curves and clefts, full to bursting with our child, full of blood pumping through every cell, hormones fizzing like sherbet.

I really don't want to move but not only am I thirsty on this sweltering June night, I can feel the acid rising up my gullet. If I don't drink something soon I'm in for another vicious attack of heartburn. All my unisex organs—gut, lungs, bladder—have been elbowed out of the way. Womb has taken over. "Who needs to breathe?" she demands. "Who needs to digest? Remember, I am mistress here."

This afternoon my midwife joked that lack of sleep during the final weeks is at least good practice for the baby's arrival. I didn't even smile.

Wearily I haul myself out of bed and waddle cautiously down the stairs into the kitchen. Pouring myself an ice-cold glass of water, I step away from the fridge and stand looking out into the warm night.

Looking down, I grimace—half-fond, half-exasperated. When you're six months pregnant you think you're huge. Oh, innocent assumption....

It's when you hit eight months, you finally appreciate what huge really means. The sheer bulk of those last, countdown weeks of pregnancy is almost beyond belief.

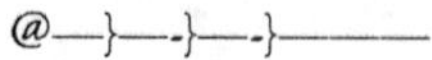

When we bought this house, there was a wilderness at the end of the garden, but planning permission had been granted. The street watched the community housing go up with goodwill, little realising how many of the windows would overlook our ancient cottages.

Three years later—what with us both working, both ex-rock'n'rollers and both (to be frank) appallingly disorganised—we, out of all our neighbours, still haven't got round to putting up blinds in the downstairs back. I stand naked under the kitchen light in front of a dozen darkened windows. No one across the way is up—or if they are I don't know and care less.

"If some bugger's got the energy to stay up 'til four in the morning to gawp at me looking like a melon then good luck to him," I'd said. "It's mind over matter, darling. I don't mind—and they don't matter."

D'you ever notice how a house can feel safe? I once lived in a new house where I felt uneasy whenever I was alone even though it could have no history, except perhaps in the dark earth beneath it.

This house has a warm, reassuring feel. People must've died here—stands to reason, it's so old. And been born here, although I hope this baby won't be. I feel the need for the modern horrors of our local steel and white.... But our old brick cottage truly shelters us.

A hundred years ago this house of ours was the bakery for the infant school. Did long-gone children, dashing in eager for peppermints and buns, leave ghostly traces of their carefree feet? What flavours this place, I cannot tell. But I stand in our kitchen hot and naked on this summer night, sipping my ice-water, happy.

My belly juts out like one of those strangely fashioned, slightly sloping seats fast-food joints install so customers don't linger. Memories of my recent glance into the fridge prompt the thought that were I to break an egg on the apex of my belly, it would take long minutes to find its way off that smooth crest. Sensuous, though... to do it would be sensuous. It might even sizzle. The idea makes me flex my long fingers.

Gazing out of the window I suddenly focus on my reflection in the glass, changed over these last months. I am no longer my familiar self but an archetype. My pumpkin belly juts out with absurd gravity. Resting on it, my full breasts have a new purposefulness.

I was flat for years after some of my classmates proudly filled training bras. Then at sixteen my breasts began to swell. "That's why they're so perfect," a boyfriend once teased me. "They're three or four years younger than everyone else's!"

So, after I forgave their lateness, I loved my tits. There was only one thing I needed to crown my satisfaction.

Brown nipples.

Mine were always an insipid pink. Prominent, but pink. Now, to my immense pleasure, they are a rich amber, the puckering more pronounced, and with a thicker core. My nipples have taken on a new life of their own, and I can only admire them as if they were some other woman's pride. It's better than that, though. I'd feel constrained only to glance in that situation. These lovelies are all my own so I am free to pinch and pull them, gloating over them with undisguised pride.

I cup my loaded tits, hefting their greater mass, and letting the fattened nipples poke between my fingers. The flesh is satiny, cushioned. God, they feel good. Lost in narcissism, I enjoy my warm tingling skin and the blind mystery of this new life coming.

Just like nearly every other woman I know, I've spent my adult life fretting about flabby bits, but there is a sense of freedom about me now.

This belly is not fat. It is hard, smooth and glossy. It has a job to do. And so I carry it proudly, fruit of great sex with a good man, a ring on my finger and a roof over our heads. This baby is much wanted. This marriage is much treasured. For the first time since puberty, I love every inch of my own body.

Unselfconsciously I stand on the cool tiles relishing my sensations. Massaging, cherishing my breasts, sleeking belly and flanks, raising my arms to rub my neck, easing my back with a sway of the hips.

Warm air drifts through the top of the window, a tiny eddy in the close heat. God, it's hot. Resting my hand on the sill, I lean back a little and slowly trickle the remnants of my drink down from my collarbone.

It tickles me to see how the water runs between my breasts, plateaus for an instant, then slips aside down my flanks. How much longer would that raw egg have taken?

"Couldn't sleep, eh?"

James is shambling down the last few stairs. I glimpse the vague outline of his dear reflection in the window behind me, but I don't look round. I know him so well. I can tell he's been watching me for some time. I have heard this note in his voice many times before. I don't need to look to know how hard he is.

Deliberately I reach up to ruffle my back hair, pretending to thrust my heavy breasts up and out just by accident. He will come up behind me and, pressing his warm hairy body firmly against my back, cup one in each hand. Surely as night follows day I know this.

And so he does, bending to nuzzle behind my ear, juggling and snuggling my satiny teats in his loving hands. A shiver down my spine makes me giggle and catch my breath. Now there's a trick for cooling the skin.... His touch brings up goosebumps on my arms.

I watch us reflected in the window. When you love someone you know every turn and articulation of their limbs, every habitual movement. I can recognise his walk fields away, but we've never got around to observing ourselves together. We're still far too engrossed in the vanilla to look for toppings.

It's a novelty to watch him caress me, to mark how trustingly I lean into him. I wonder how much of our deepest feelings we betray unknowingly to outsiders. Surely my love is clear from the way I give myself up totally to his arms, his by the protectiveness of even his lust? Business-suited colleagues would be hard-pressed to recognise the contained professional they know in this pliant woman with her eyes half-closed.

Languorously he caresses me. I don't turn round. I'd like to kiss his mouth, but experience has taught us the awkwardness of kissing a woman my shape—like sweethearts over a gate, we cannot cling together but must lean forward over our man-made obstacle... Better this way. Ten hundred million animals are unlikely to be wrong.

He is kissing down my back and caressing my buttocks with tiny, feathery strokes. My hard round belly reminds me of a mare's, and for a second I remember how horses mate, the stallion nipping and gentling her back and shoulders before he mounts her. A combination of his touch, my mind's eye, and I can feel the sweet juice wet on my thighs. I say nothing. Let him find out for himself.

James is nearly on his knees now, hands on my hips, mouth telling shocking secrets to the velvet of my buttocks. My whole body shivers. His hands slip round my hips and between my thighs.

"Christ, you're soaking. It's dripping from you."

"Hormones, my love.... That, and I'm so terribly, terribly hot...." I tease him. It's the weather, I imply. Oh yes, it's only the weather.... Or perhaps I'm a different sort of hot?

"Going to have to do something about that." His voice holds promises—playful threats.

His hands move to turn me, which I do slightly clumsily. I can lean on the sill, my knees are already turning outwards....

James is on his knees before me, licking the very front of my slit. The first cool touches of his tongue on my hot swollen flesh make me gasp. Under the overhang of my belly, I cannot see him—it's very sexy, feels heavenly, but slightly absurd. More absurd by the second, as my knees loosen, my breath quickens, my legs threaten to give up, and my belly throws me off balance....

"Let's go upstairs."

"Yes, all right, but you're so wet. It's gorgeous...." His mouth is muffled....

"Oh, yes. Oh, no.... Oh, please!" This last said in appeal. I am too aroused to pull away, too unstable to continue. Wonderful, yes, wonderful. This is going to be memorable, but I simply can't carry on as I am....

"OK, OK." He clambers to his feet and takes my hand.

"Up you go, baggage," he says, "I'll be right behind you."

And I chuckle, for he is as good as his word. His thickly fluffed chest hair tickles and the hot, smooth end of his cock prods me as we shuffle up the stairs in unison. He play-slaps my bottom and I squeal in mock outrage.

Inside our room, I sprawl my bulk out across the cotton sheets and spread my thighs. He climbs on the bed, far more mobile than I, leaning to kiss my mouth for a second, and then continuing his movement until he kneels over me, his hard, fragrant cock presented to my mouth, his furry belly and balls rounded and tempting....

Taking his bobbing cock eagerly in my small hands I wrap my wet mouth around the head, sliding one hand firmly up and down his thick shaft, moving the other to caress his balls. God, my love has beautiful balls, so round, so snug in their bag, so thickly furred. Whenever I suck or wank him I never cease to admire the sculptured quality of his flanged head, the jaunty arch of the broad stem. All those years and still his charm is fresh.

His own face is buried in my pussy, inhaling deeply, his broad tongue lapping the cunt-juice pouring from me. Everything in me that is female, every pulsing cell, is working at full stretch tonight. My full breasts await our baby's mouth; my womb, while making a thick warm nest for his unborn limbs tonight, is preparing itself to push him with fundamental force into the world. My sex is as ripe and red and fleshy as a bitten plum, oozing juice. I am succulent.

There is something drugged about me: so intense are the sensations, so profound my lust. My body is reaching some rich female crescendo—two weeks off giving birth, my essence is near its most concentrated. As he licks me, I take his cock deeper into my mouth than ever before. I feast and worship it. Much later there are toothmarks. Later he forgives me, grinning. He feels no pain now, not while I adore him. My breathing, through my nose, is fast and deep.

He has pointed his tongue now, and rearranges my swollen, slippery folds with it. There is an element of playfulness. He knows me too well. He knows I will not want him to carry on long. It is only too plain how badly I need fucking.

"Yes. Oh, go on, yes! Please. Yes, you old bugger," I growl softly, urgently. I will not be denied. Not that there seems much chance.

He just laughs, and straightens up so I can move into my favoured position.

I am up on my hands and knees surprisingly smoothly and quickly, moving all of a piece to haul the pillows into my shape. I am supported, belly and chest. I can breathe, I can brace my thighs to get the full impact of our movements. I am ready. I am more than ready. I am willing to beg for it.

He kneels behind me, and whacks my arse with his hard cock. He likes to do that. He likes to smack my face with it sometimes, too. Playing master, as I play mistress. He likes to look at my dark, dripping sex-lips. Childless women have pale pink pussies. Pregnancy darkens the folds, and thickens their pout. Everything is enhanced: grip, juices, colour, excitement.

He is also enjoying keeping me waiting, just a little bit. I squirm like a puppy. My arse says "Fuck me, please! Fuck me, nice man!" And eventually he does. He enters me without hesitation, but only until his cock head is sheathed. As my pussy wraps itself unhesitatingly round that hot, familiar shape, I feel a tiny jolt of orgasm hit me just from knowing I am going to get what I crave. He grunts, the contented grunt of a man arriving home. For a moment we just soak in the sheer comfort.

The next thrust seems much later; everything is stretched out, time has flown. But it must be very soon that he arches his back and buries his full length in the greasy grasping heat of my flesh. Both of us release breath we weren't aware of holding. And then we are moving together, for minute on minute, each unhurried thrust met and varied, dancing a dance that gets better every year. My thighs brace and the root of his cock and balls gives wave after wave of pure ripe pleasure. He grips one of my thick greedy nipples in each hand.

I am not on the earth, not even on the bed. I am in sex and of it. He rides me like a hot thunderstorm, my body is a rainforest with bright thrills of parrots flying across its darkness. His cock feels like a god. A roll of orgasms has started and it will not stop in this lifetime.

My pelvis is full of glowing mercury, balls of loose delight rolling in my cunt and thighs. Somewhere shoals of tiny fish dart down my legs. I am crying out like a shaman now, though I don't hear it. Only when he tells me later will I know I woke the neighbours.

Slowing a little and steadying, he grips my hips hard like a man steering a dog-sleigh. Not a bad analogy for either of us, for I am calling out on the long trail home, and he is travelling that way, too. His orgasm is building, and this increases my frenzy. I am flaunting myself now, begging him to shaft my hot pussy, telling him he is so hard, baby, so fuckin' hard. Faster, now, faster and so deep.

Those last minutes are not human. They are elemental. We are beyond ourselves and yet we are body. His sweat rains on my back. His cock slams ruthlessly into my nectarine cunt, the brutal force expressing all his passion, all our union. I am his, without end. The final shattering plunges bring a wrenching starburst of release deep in my guts. Everything—limbs, juices, soul—is coming loose. "Jesus!" I scream, loud enough to bring even myself to consciousness. So I am aware as he drives himself in those last frantic few seconds and then buries everything of himself that he possibly can deep into my body and stops still, trembling. He cries out, he gasps....

For the longest recorded moment I feel his cock pumping, again, again, again, again, again, again as he empties his spunk deep inside me. I am drinking him, and then, second by second, I feel my sinews start to uncoil themselves, I feel myself loosening. He leans forward, gasping. My back is drenched with his sweat. Our cum is running down my thighs. The bed beneath me is soaking. And it must be imagination, that faint ripple of applause from across the garden....

@—}—-}—-}———

He withdraws without ceremony. His cock is still hard, slimy and dripping. He knows I'd rather have a drink than a chivalrous leave-taking. "Juice?" he enquires.

"Angel," I purr. And the kind soul fetches me a towel as well. Hair, pussy, thighs—everything is wringing wet.

Having lain still all this time, finally the baby shifts his limbs languorously in my belly. I imagine him stretching as if he, too, feels a sense of space and relaxation. Well, if it takes this much to wake him now, maybe he'll sleep well after birth as well. I can dream, can't I?

@—}—-}—-}———

Later we giggle. "At least our baby knows we like each other," I smile.

"D'you realise it's dawn? You should have a health warning, you wicked trollop," he says. "Toothmarks, by Christ. I thought you were too tired, too pregnant and so on.... So what exactly happened to that heartburn?" I look at him, mischievous in the half-dark, and grin. "Go to sleep, you sex-crazed monster." And we do.

# Bloody Grunge Love

by Airyn Darling

## Bit One:

Sandwiched between Victor and Elizabeth, grinding away to the heavy bass beat, I realized my thighs were getting wet, and that it had been entirely too long since I'd had any real sexual contact. I sighed, kissed each of them gently, and walked to the side of the dance floor. Leaning on the thick yellow pipe demarcating the small area packed with undulating bodies, I picked up my nearly empty cup of water from the floor, sucked on an ice cube and watched, careful to seem bored and detached from the goings-on.

Victor was an amazing dancer. Elizabeth nuzzled up next to him, and I felt a twinge of envy. They were, however, my best friends, and I loved them dearly. It was sometimes difficult being with them—they were lovers, and I occasionally felt like an intruder. Elizabeth's wife was feeling like an outsider as well, and tried to turn to me to soothe her troubled mind. I foiled these attempts at every turn. She was not attractive, and additionally, I did not like her. Part of the problem was that was the fact that she looked like a small Arabic man (I like my women to look like women), and part was her borderline obnoxious personality. Yet I had to sort of pretend to get along with her, since she was an integral part of Victor and Elizabeth's lives.

Sighing again, I looked around for prospective lovers to take home. Jay was bumping and grinding, revolving those beautiful young hips like they were made of ball bearings. Earlier in the evening he had said, "Kate, whenever I'm around you, I get so horny." I looked back on the years before, when I had taken him, only fifteen then, under my wing when his parents had thrown him out. Drugs, trouble in school, and miscellaneous other problems plagued him. I worried and fussed with a mother's love, and lusted with a twenty-year-old's cunt. He was so beautiful, deceptively innocent-looking. Two brief sexual encounters occasionally haunted me, and apparently he'd been thinking of them as well. But now he had blossomed into this amazingly mature young man. Most troubles behind him, he was in love, working and planning for his future. I began to understand the proud, joyous/sorrowful twinges of parenthood when the baby leaves the nest and does well on his own. I was happy to have had a hand in his progression.

Grudgingly, I ruled Jay out as the night's toy. Chewing slowly on my plastic cup, I gazed about, smiling at my friends, noticing Nick, the lights guy, staring at me now and then. He'd been a friend of Jay's way back when, and then they'd parted ways, due to some dispute. Nick was beautiful as well, although in a different way. He was also pretentious as hell, and hadn't spoken to me in quite some time. I ignored him.

There were more women here than usual on gay night. And many of them were attractive, even more unusual. "Being bisexual certainly has its advantages," I thought with a wry smile. A lean black man sidled up to the small space in front of me, thoroughly into the groove. He was wearing black vinyl pants, a gold lame, skin-tight shirt covered by a loose, black open shirt, and thick-framed black glasses. His dreads bounced up and down as he danced. He smiled at me, and I gave a small one in return. A friend joined him and began dancing in front of me as well. Upon first glance, she was really nothing special, but since she was only inches from me, I thought I'd look her over.

She was grunged up; two demerit points. I almost dismissed her right then, but she turned to face me and smiled shyly. Her face was smooth, beautiful. Her lips were a pale reddish-pink, her hair (as best I could tell in the flashing lights) was strawberry blonde, long and straight, with the cutest little bangs. She wore a white short-sleeved shirt with a heart on the breast (ack!), overalls, and the requisite flannel shirt tied about her waist. She was charming, despite her obvious grunge fixation. She didn't dance flamboyantly, pretentiously, or seductively; she just moved shyly to the beat and smiled to herself, sometimes glancing at me from beneath those bangs and long eyelashes. She radiated innocence willing to be corrupted, which was like a magnet to someone like me. I wanted to take her home, gently seduce her, and then show her things that would blow her mind.

I was absorbed. "Bloody hell," I thought, "I'm hot for a grunge child." I was almost disgusted with myself, but was too entranced to notice it much. I watched her and her friend intently, wondering if the man was bi or gay or what. My "gaydar" said "screaming queen," but my naive hope said "definitely bi," and envisioned the three of us in a snarl of sheets. A song I could tolerate came over the speakers, but rather than dance, I stayed still to watch them. They were obviously not "together" in the truest sense, but acquaintances, touching base with each other a little nervously, and then going back into their own little worlds.

Was she wondering if I was still watching her? Was that why she glanced at me so often, or was it because I was only inches away and made her uncomfortable? Did she sense my predatory intentions? I was dying to reach out and stroke that soft, fine hair, to say something along the lines of, "You're so beautiful — do you live around here often?" Humor, my favorite defense in times of awkwardness.

I looked about the bar, scanning the corners for intriguing faces. Finding none, I settled upon this lovely child as the night's target. I stared at her until she looked up at me. I locked her eyes, and gave her a look which made my intentions clear. She stared back for the briefest of seconds before looking down quickly. I smiled to myself, knowing those eyes would be looking back before long. Indeed, only a few moments had passed before she gazed back up. Everything about her exuded shyness. She turned coyly away and took a few steps towards the center of the dance floor, dragging her male friend by the hand with her. The wiggle in her hips was a fine invitation, and even more so, the bounce of her small, lovely breasts as she turned back towards me and began dancing again.

Placing my cup on the nearest table, I fixed my eyes upon her and slid towards her through the crowd. Drawing a bit from my gift, I slightly parted the dancing bodies as I passed, so she would see me as graceful, not jostled about or getting an elbow up my nose. I moved into position behind her, looking her deliberately up and down as I did so. Smiling at her friend, I began on him first, so as not to frighten her. He willingly joined me, slipping his knees between mine, and gyrating seductively, moving up and down my body. I grasped his head and ground my pussy inches from his face. His dreads flew about as he played along with my cunnilingus scenario. Out of the corner of my eye, I saw we had captured her attention.

I pulled him up and moved behind him, pushing my hips into his ass, grinding hard, as my hands caressed his chest, pulling him into me. He bent at the waist and stuck his ass up in the air, still circling his hips. I made like a butch-dyke, thrusting my imaginary dildo in and out of him. He tossed his head and reached back with both hands, pulling me in deeper and deeper. He straightened and I slid down his back, rubbing my breasts up and down over his ass, while reaching between his legs and stroking his cock firmly and slowly.

She was entranced. Others around us smiled; dirty dancing was nothing new to the Peach Pit crowd; it was duly appreciated when performed well, and ignored when poorly done. I had nearly perfected the art over the years. My thighs were strong and firm, and I could grind with the best of them all night. And often did, really.

He turned around and whipped me around as well, pushing his half-hard cock into my ass. I rotated and pushed back appreciatively. My tight leggings were like a second skin, as were his vinyl pants. That so little separated us excited me. He bit my neck and cupped my breasts, pinching my nipples. I pulled one of his hands between my legs and held it there, pushing against it. God, these boys could work it. I was ready to come right there when the song ended, but a much less erotic beat came on. We parted, and I turned to smile at him, giving him a kiss on the cheek. He winked at me and started doing this fancy-footwork number. I laughed. He grinned and turned to the man behind him, grabbing his ass and falling into easy conversation as they both danced minimally. I chuckled and turned to make sure she was still there. Of course she was, once again smiling shyly at me. I stepped only slightly towards her and danced in a casual "yeah, I'm dancing, but I'm not that into it" kind of way. She turned her back to me which, oddly enough, is the standard invitation for closer contact here. I turned to "the camera" that always follows me around in my ego and smiled confidently before approaching her. I didn't touch her at first, just let her know I was behind her by the heat radiating from me.

The song wasn't particularly appropriate for erotic dancing, so I contemplated my next move quickly. Something non-threatening, but firm. I reached out with both hands, touching each side of her head and running my nails across her scalp and down through her hair. It was indeed as soft as I had imagined. She didn't turn, but let her head fall back as I repeated the procedure. She had minimal personal shields, which I could have easily stroked down, but in a place like the Peach Pit, personal wards never hurt. I felt her quiet inner strength, her quivering desire, and I was now certain that she'd never been with a woman. I couldn't have asked for a more perfect gift tonight. I thanked the fates and moved just the tiniest bit closer to her, so the tips of my breasts brushed against her back now and then.

I placed one hand on her hip, just resting it there, following her movements. She was slightly stiffer now, more self-conscious, and more than a little nervous. This would be a delicious pursuit. I wondered if we would speak at all. Silent seductions are one of my favorite things. She was so young, though, and so nervous, I sincerely doubted that she wouldn't speak out of sheer terror soon, something to cut the developing tension. We continued moving. Now and then, I stroked her side, just lightly, just for a moment, before returning my hand to her hip, where it rested, reminding her of my presence, of my intent, of my desire.

The bloody song was one of those rave-type numbers, mindless thumping for seemingly hours on end, with no lyrics, just thump-thump-thump-thumpa-thumpa-thump-thump-thump. It was driving me nuts, but I was reluctant to leave her before I had really set the hook. I looked up imploringly at Roger, the DJ, rolling my eyes and gesturing around at the music/noise. He nodded and rummaged through his collection. As a regular of five years and as a former employee, I had special privileges reserved for the select few, which, I might add, I enjoyed tremendously.

Roger mixed in the intro to "Get Down Make Love" by Nine Inch Nails. I grinned up at him and mouthed "thank you." It was one of my perennial favorites, guaranteed to make me incredibly horny, as if I needed to be any more so. As the old song faded out, and NIN took over, all the boys groaned and left the floor. The girl started to leave, but I took her hand and held her with me. She seemed surprised, unsure of what to do. I smiled reassuringly and dropped her hand, beginning my industrial dancing mode. The floor was nearly deserted, populated by the "Old Crowd." We all knew each other and longed for The Good Old Days of Industrial Night at the Pit. We took what we could get now.

The Peach Pit is like a drug, like another world. It is addictive, and it is all-consuming at first. Lives revolve around it, and lives are destroyed within it if one isn't careful. I learned my lesson years ago, when I could look at the various levels and see perhaps eight to ten people with whom I'd had sex, twenty or so more whom I did not want to talk to, and maybe another ten with whom I'd love to have sex, but hadn't. I knew everyone's little story, and I got completely wrapped up in The Lifestyle and all the little psychodramas. Thank the gods it closed for awhile to remodel, at which point I quit working there. Now I only visited. Scary thing was, people who had been working here long before me were still here, and they still loved it. I shook my head, thinking about this tiny little place with all its power.

Trent Reznor was screaming, and I lunged side to side with each word, curving around her at each end. I moved my arms in a different pattern, but to the same beat, and reached around her, beginning the seduction for her and for those around us; we were all equally voyeuristic and exhibitionistic here at the Pit.

I emulated stroking her up and down, my hands several inches from her body but forming each and every curve, circling her breasts. Finally, I pushed her head to one side, reached around her stomach, pulled her tightly to me, and buried my face in her neck, biting softly, licking delicately before releasing her and resuming my regular dance. The second time I pulled her to me, I didn't kiss her, I just held her and led her gently. With one hand held firmly to her tummy, I reached down with the other to stroke her thigh. I moved up and down her leg slowly, tracing up the inside with my fingertips, then pressing firmly with my whole hand on the downstroke.

She was relaxing slightly, giving in. I was leaning on her just the smallest bit with my gift, soothing her anxiety. Being a projective as well as a receptive empath has its benefits. I inhaled the smell of her hair, a patch of clean softness inside the room full of harsh cigarette smoke. Oh, this was divine. I hadn't been with a woman in months. "Get Down Make Love" started to fade out, and I signaled Roger to play something similar, to keep the mood going for me. He grimaced but obliged with the "I Sit on Acid" remix by Lords of Acid. Roger's a good guy, and membership has its privileges.

The crowd cheered — this was acceptable, given its lewd content. As the boys began bopping about, the girl started to as well, but I once again restrained her, slowing her down, helping her find the slower underlying rhythm. I turned her to face me but didn't look into her eyes. Yet. I arranged myself so that we each had one leg inside the other's, pulled her tight to me so that our bodies pressed together from breasts to thighs. I placed one of her hands on my ass, and put one of mine on hers as we slowly rotated against each other. Her breath was audible in my ear, even above the loud music. I was sure part of it was the physical exertion of keeping up this strenuous activity, but also that part of it was the lust between us.

At the next chorus of "sit on your face, I wanna sit on your face," I stared directly into her eyes, but didn't do anything as tacky as mouth the words to her. She didn't look down this time. In fact, she tightened her grip on my ass. I was so pleased at this action that I almost forgot to keep dancing. I quickly recovered my composure and smiled into her eyes with mine. I wondered, "Has this chick been having me on? Is she just an accomplished shy femme?" I don't usually misread people. "Buggery bullocks, Kate, all she did was grab your ass — she's just turned on, that's all." I was reassured by the thought and felt firmly back in control.

She was pushing back towards me with equal intensity but couldn't bring herself to look directly into my eyes again. She glanced up sporadically through those bangs in a most endearing way. I was firmly hooked, even if she wasn't yet. I was just dying to feel her breasts. I was already visualizing her sitting on top of me, undulating and moaning, or alternatively, bound by my wrist restraints, writhing as I went down on her. My knees were getting as weak as my thighs were wet. It was almost time to leave — I couldn't take much more of this.

I turned my lips to her ear, sucking on the lobe gently before saying, "Let's go. I'd like to take you home with me tonight." She inhaled sharply before mutely nodding. We gathered our coats from the coatcheck. I tipped for both of us and we left. I contemplated asking where she parked but didn't want to break to mood. I just led her to my car, parked in the alley across the street. As we drove to my apartment, I played the stereo loud enough to discourage conversation, all the while caressing her leg. Her fingers played tentatively in my long, curly hair.

•••

## Bit Two:

At a particularly long stoplight, she reached to turn the stereo down. I let her.

"Ann. My name is Ann."

"Kate," I said with a slight smile.

She smiled nervously back at me. "I just thought we should know each other's names."

"Why?"

She paused. "I'm not sure."

I turned the stereo back up and drove on. I swore I would need a spatula to get myself off of my car seat; I felt part woman, part snail. At my apartment (which I had hastily cleaned before leaving that night, in the hopes I would be bringing someone home), I took her appropriately grungey coat and hung it next to my leather in the closet.

"You have lovely art," she said quietly, admiring all of the prints and statuettes placed about. I smiled and said nothing. Motioning for her to take a seat on the sofa, I slipped into my bedroom and closed the door softly. I looked around, made sure everything was all set, and lit the incense waiting in the censer. I walked into the bathroom, tossing a pair of dirty underwear into the closet, wiping toothpaste out of the sink, straightening towels, and spritzing a bit of Shalimar into the air.

I came back into the living room.

"Go ahead and take a nice hot shower, and relax. I'll use the other bathroom."

"Umm...sure. Ok. I guess I am pretty sweaty." I showed her to the bathroom and told her to make use of anything she found in it. I had left several varieties of scented shower gels on the counter, as well as some stimulating body brushes and scrubbers in the shower itself. I turned to leave, and pressed in the lock as I closed the door behind me.

Before it shut completely, I said, "Take all the time you want. We're in no hurry." She smiled again. I closed the door and walked to the bathroom on the other side of the apartment. I rinsed off quickly, wanting to make a few other preparations before she finished. Satisfied that I was generally club-odor-free, I toweled off, donned a dark blue silk robe, and went into my bedroom. I listened at the bathroom door; she was still showering. I fanned the incense about my room, made sure all sex toy-type things were hidden yet easily available, smoothed the sheets, closed the shades, and lay down on the bed. Closing my eyes, I listened to the sound of water running off her body, visualizing tiny rivulets coursing over her breasts, in between her legs, dripping off her pubic hair (if indeed she had any). I reached between my legs and rubbed my clit lightly, moaning softly. I was totally soaking wet again. Much more of this self-pleasuring and I'd have an orgasm before she came in the room. It was difficult to stop, but discipline won out, and I waited quietly.

I heard her turn off the water and shuddered slightly with anticipation.

"Oh shit! The candles!" I thought. I jumped up and lit two on the wall above the bed, one on my altar, and one on the bookshelf on the wall opposite the bed. The overall effect was lovely; enough light to see well by, but not harsh like incandescent lamps. Exotic shadows cast by my many feathers and draperies danced about. I hoped she would enjoy the ambience. Much of my pleasure would stem from hers.

The bathroom door unlocked, and she stepped out, wearing the soft robe I'd left for her. It was tied loosely at the waist. Her hair was dark and wet, combed back from her face, which glowed in the dim light as she took a few uncertain steps towards my king-size bed. She looked lovely.

"I thought you might like a massage," I stated quietly.

"That sounds really nice." She fidgeted with her robe a little. I sat on the edge of the bed and motioned her towards me. She stood before me, and it took every ounce of will not to ravish her right then and there. Instead, I stood and removed her robe from behind, sliding it over her shoulders slowly, watching every inch of flesh revealed.

"Lie down on your stomach, please, Ann." She did so, making herself comfortable. "Make sure there's no undue pressure on your neck." She shifted more. Satisfied that she was comfortable, I asked if she would prefer almond or clarey sage oil. She said that the sage sounded more exotic. I opened the nightstand drawer and removed the bottle, placing it on top, then dropped my robe. Her head was turned away. Too bad. I looked at the contrast of her pale white skin on my dark green duvet. Beautiful.

"I'm going to start at your neck and work my way down to your feet." She nodded silently. Pouring a small amount of oil in my hands, I smoothed it up my arms to the elbow and made sure my hands had a generous coating. I warmed a small bit more in my palms and said, "I'm going to begin now."

Her hair was already off her neck; a good thing — I'd forgotten to check before I oiled my hands. I began very softly, spreading the warm oil from the base of her skull down her trapezius muscles. She was relaxed on the surface, but had tension in the deeper muscles. I gently worked her neck and shoulders for a long time; she carried her stress in this area. As the knots came loose, I moved down her spine and outwards, always visualizing the tension pushed out of her body by my hands as I felt the energy flow out of me and into her.

I moved to the base of her spine, just before the swell of her buttocks began. There was little tension here, so I gave the area special attention, as she reacted strongly to my touch. I stroked downwards to the outside of her hips, pressing firmly. Her flesh was resilient and soft. It was as much a pleasure for me to be touching her as it was for her to be touched.

I used a heavy amount of oil on her ass; it trickled into the cleft and she shuddered. I smiled. I squeezed her gluteal muscles to get the tension from dancing to move downwards. Her anus tightened in pleasure when I pulled her cheeks apart, and I could see that she was at least partially shaven; this is such a turn-on for me — I can see everything, and there's no hair to get in my mouth, either.

Her thighs were especially tight; the dancing had taken a lot out her. I projected a strong amount of healing energy into this area, loosening the grip of the lactic acid. Her calves were equally tense. She had strong, well-formed legs, which, like the rest of her, were very fit without being muscley.

Finally, I reached her feet. I used enough oil to squish between her toes and make luscious noises. She moaned appreciatively as I eased all the accumulated body tension out through her toes. I applied particularly hard pressure on the soles of her feet, using various pressure points corresponding to areas on her body. As I finished up, I used soft, smoothing strokes all over her body.

"That was incredible. You have the most amazing hands," she said lazily, turning over with as little effort as possible. "I haven't felt this relaxed since, like....God I don't know." She really was young. Perfectly fine by me. As she lay on her back, I couldn't help but admire her breasts with their pink, firm little nipples. I ran my eyes down her and saw she had a small patch of darker blonde pubic hair.

"Kiss me," she said softly. I was more than happy to oblige but held up a finger for her to wait. I poured oil down my front and smoothed it over my breasts and belly; oiled flesh against oiled flesh was one of my favorites. I slid up her belly and over her breasts with my own and ended up straddling her. She had full, yielding lips, which I kissed gently. I caressed her side with my non-supporting hand. Her skin was enchantingly supple. I licked the corners of her mouth, and she opened to me. I teased her, darting my tongue in and out quickly, not giving her the full, hard kiss she wanted. She lifted her head to me, but I backed away. Frustrated, she grabbed the back of my head and forced my tongue into her. She sucked on it, played with it, nibbled at it. It had finally begun.

I rubbed my breasts up and down against hers while still kissing her passionately. Small moans emanated from both of us. Taking each of her wrists in my hands, I pinned them above her head. I have a bit of a bondage fetish, and this was a way to test her reaction. She didn't go totally passive, and she didn't struggle against me; she just used her body to communicate her passion.

I released her and kissed her neck, nibbling, sucking, biting, licking it all over, from front to back, top to bottom. The back was particularly sensitive. Each time I grazed it with my teeth she inhaled sharply and pushed her hips up towards me. I couldn't stay away from her breasts any longer. I had to touch them, to taste them. I worked down her chest, cupping each breast from the side, pushing them slightly together, as she murmured the sorts of things people do when helpless with desire. I took her left nipple in my mouth, sucking hard and long. I nipped at it, caressed it with my tongue, squeezing with my hands. Her breasts were perfect C-cups, perky but not overly so, naturally firm, with beautiful nipples. I could have spent days worshipping them.

She was moaning louder now and breathing faster. She pulled me up and slid down simultaneously, positioning herself under my breasts and sucking on them furiously as her nails dug into my back. I arched into her, murmuring appreciatively. My hair swished across my back, giving me goosebumps and making me shudder. From beneath me she asked, "Is this right? Does it feel good?" I assured her it felt wonderful. I moved down so we were face to face and kissed her deeply again. I kissed down her body, paying close attention to those marvelous breasts, then venturing further, sampling her belly button, her waist, her sides. I didn't stampede to her pussy the way most men do; I paused to caress, to admire, to suckle. When I lowered myself to her pubic mound, I could smell her delicate aroma. I blew softly on her hairs, and she gasped, "Oh please....oh please...." but I was going to make her wait, make her crazed for it. I pushed her legs apart so I could fit between them, and lowered my face just inches above her pussy lips. She was so slick and wet and fragrant, I wanted to dive in, but I restrained myself. I blew on her again, and she raised her hips, desperately trying to obtain any pressure on her beautiful, plump little clit.

I raised myself.

"Not yet; not yet...I want to tie you up....May I?"

"Yes, yes, God, if you'll make me come. Just do anything!" She was writhing.

I reached between the bed and the nightstand and came up with one of my prized possessions—a thick leather wrist restraint, lined with even thicker lamb's wool, capped by a big, chrome buckle. I had it linked to its mate on the other side of the bed with a length of heavy chain. As I gently tightened the buckle, an anxious look came over her.

"Shh, shh, shh," I soothed. "I won't hurt you. If you want me to stop, say so and I will. I won't do anything you don't want, and we can stop at any time you want. If you want me to stop, just say, 'Panic.'"

She nodded. "Ok, go ahead."

I kissed her gently but passionately and crawled across her to get the other restraint, bringing my cunt within inches of her wet lips. When she was properly tied down, I smiled wickedly and said, "Now that you're buckled up, let's take you for a ride." I grabbed a peacock feather from one of the draperies around the bed and ran it lightly along her body. She shivered. I stroked between her legs with it, knowing how tantalizing this was—enough to feel, but not enough to give any true satisfaction. The chain links were clinking together as she struggled to get the tip of the feather to touch her clit harder. I wasn't about to let that happen. Putting the feather aside, I lay down on top of her, covering her entire body with mine, and pushing my pubic bone against her pussy. She groaned.

"Please make me come. Please, God, please make me come. I want to come so bad."

I was loving this. It's not a power trip for me; it's knowing how good she's going to feel when she finally does come. All the teasing, all the tantalizing pays off in the end. I stroked her brow, soothing her, calming her, bringing her down a few levels so she was less crazed for an orgasm. I went to the foot of the bed, cradling her right foot in my hands and blowing on the sole. I slid her little toe in my mouth and sucked on it gently, repeating the process for each toe on each foot. Her feet were sensitive but not ticklish, so I could get away with flickering my tongue over the soles.

I took one foot in each hand and pushed her legs apart, keeping them straight as I did so. I could now look directly up into her pussy. I could see the wetness, the fullness, the redness of it in all its perfect beauty.

I grabbed my ankle restraints, gently wrapping yet firmly buckling one around her right ankle. I strapped the other ankle and stood, looking down at this gorgeous woman, spread out and tied to my bed. It was the best gift someone could give to me.

"You're so beautiful, Ann."

She moaned.

"Do you want me to suck your pussy?"

"Please...." She arched her back and spread her legs even further. I licked and kissed my way up her thighs, making sure to lavish attention on the backs of her knees, a little-known erogenous zone for many people. I scraped my nails up the insides of her thighs, hearing her breath hiss in and come out with an "aaaaaahhhhh."

Finally, I arrived at her gateway. I framed her little pussy with my hands, pulling the lips gently apart, again blowing on her clit, this time harder. She gasped.

"You smell so good, Ann. I can't wait to taste you, to suck on your clit, to put my fingers inside you, to lick your asshole. I want to make you come so hard...so hard..." My words were exciting me as well as her. The chain rattled against the wall as she wiggled. I traced her labia with the tip of my tongue, loving the absence of hair, loving the smoothness of her inner folds, loving the smell of her. After much teasing in this manner, I positioned my tongue just below her clit, and thrust it lightly against the bottom of it. Finally feeling some pressure on her clit nearly sent her over the edge, but I slowed to a steady pulse. I was dying to fully taste her, so I fluttered my tongue down to her opening and buried it there. Her juices ran down my chin as I explored her inner depths with my tongue. She raised her hips, and I could feel how much she wanted to grab my head and pull it to her.

I moved back to her clit and sucked on just the little tip. She thrust her hips up to meet each pulsing suction, moaning, trying to grind herself into me, and failing each time. I wasn't going to let her come yet. I wanted this to last, and then to do it all over again.

"Mmmm...I can feel how much you want to come...I want to make you come...but not yet." I glanced at her face to see her looking down at me, and I smiled wickedly. She let out an exasperated sigh and flopped her head back onto the pillow.

I reached into my Drawer O'Tricks in the nightstand, stuffed with various vibrators, dildos, lotions, oils, powders, feathers, handcuffs, miscellaneous other items...and the delicate, shiny, chrome objects I was after...the nipple clamps. Intricate and well-made, these little beauties often made me come by themselves. The chain linking them clinked lightly as I brought them into her view. She squirmed a bit, again unsure. "Alright then, I'll wear these." I teased my left nipple, almost letting the rubber-tipped clamp all the way down, taking it off, putting it on rapidly. The reddish-brown pigments darkened and I moaned softly. She was watching with wide eyes, her hands straining towards me but unable to reach. I attached both clamps to my nipples and gazed down at my quarry. She was looking more and more like she wanted them on her nipples as well.

I licked my lips and turned around, suspending my pussy above her face, positioning my lower mouth so it was less than an inch away from her mouth.

I could feel her neck lifting, trying to push her face into the wetness presented. I wiggled my ass, dipped my hips so that the soft, shaven skin brushed against her mouth. Her tongue darted out to taste me, but I lifted myself away before she could get more than a tiny lick.

I reached into the nightstand drawer and pulled out a duplicate pair of clamps. Her pupils dilated with excitement. I blew on her nipples, licked them, pinched them lightly with my fingers, bringing the blood in to sensitize them. I placed one clamp very gently on her left nipple. "Tighter," she said. I put on more pressure, and she let out a sharp moan. "Yesssss..." I put the other one on her with equal pressure.

The ankle restraints allowed her a limited range of motion, and she was bending alternate knees, lifting each leg up and down. Climbing on top of her with her head between my legs, I took hold of both knees and forced them to the mattress before shoving them apart. She thrust her hips, and I finally buried my face between the luscious folds. Her slightly salty taste had a hint of bitterness, just the faintest tinge of sweat. As I sucked on her clit, she let out a loud "aaaah!" of relief. I flickered my tongue over her, into her, down her thighs and back up again. All the while, I taunted her with my own pussy, lowering it then raising it again before she could do much but catch my clit between her lips.

I slipped my hands under her ass and around to her pussy again. Dipping a finger into her, I gently probed her asshole, which tightened delightfully. With each tentative insertion, she gasped and her hips jerked. I drove my index finger all the way into her, at the same time sucking as hard as I could on her clit, rubbing my tongue over it through the suction. She shuddered, she cried out, and she came...and by the gods, she came hard. She was one of those rare women who ejaculates when she comes — juices squirted out of her and onto my face, surprising me, then turning me on all the more.

As her little shivers and moans subsided, I turned around to face her and shoved my cunt into her mouth, tugging on my own nipple clamps as she eagerly nibbled and sucked on my clit. I rocked my hips back and forth, feeling the friction of her teeth on me, feeling her tongue catch my hood-piercing and pull on it firmly, feeling...feeling....

As I came closer and closer to orgasm, I released one of her hands from the cuff and pulled it to my breast, squeezing and pinching, rocking and pushing, panting and gasping. She almost had me there, so close, so close. I grabbed the back of her head with both hands and pulled her hard into me, moving her head in opposition to my hips until I felt that beautiful moment when I know I'm going to come and there's nothing I can do to stop it. That beautiful release, the sounds that I have no control over coming from my mouth, the sweet fire coursing through me, centering on my clit but pouring over my entire body....

I came down gently from the peak, still gasping, still pressing her face to me. She was softly stroking my clit with her tongue. I practically collapsed next to her, first releasing her other hand so we could hold each other. When I regained a clearer state of mind, I freed her ankles, and we wrapped around each other, smiling slightly to ourselves, kissing now and then.

After perhaps half an hour, she sat up and stretched. She looked for a moment at me, then at the restraints, then back at me.

She smiled evilly.

"Your turn," she said.

A wild fluttering shook my belly.

And I submitted myself to her care.

# Mother's Sons

## Raven Kaldera

Evan is doing the dishes when I come home from the shrink's office. We don't make him do them all the time, but when it's his turn, he's required to wear a standard dishwashing uniform. It consists of his black leather harness boots—identical to mine—and nothing else. I like being able to slide by him on the way to the bathroom and grab his bare ass. I never get bored with that intake of breath, the way he leans back and presses against my crotch, hoping...I laugh and pull away, go back on into the bathroom. He makes a little noise of longing and goes back to dishwashing. My boy has a high tolerance for teasing, and it's a good thing.

"Sophia called—I mean Mama," I hear him say through the bathroom door. "She said she'd be home late. There were some problems with the last client."

"Not another hornet's nest, I hope." My wife is a chimney sweep, a job she has fought fiercely to keep even after becoming the only non-male member of the staff, and they occasionally give her the houses with serious problems out of spite. I keep telling her to quit, but the pay is good enough that she refuses to give up. When Sophia gets that set to her jaw, there's no arguing with her.

"How was the shrink?" Evan asks me as I come out of the bathroom.

I shrug. "Don't ask. She still doesn't like it. Nothing I can say seems to change her mind."

Evan puts down the dishrag, looking dismayed. We both know what "it" is, and it's not fair of me to withhold information when the situation involves him. "Shit," he says, a wobble in his voice. "Is this going to affect your hormone supply?"

"I sure as hell hope not." I shrug again, deciding to swallow back my rant about the unfairness of being dependent on a shrink for the medication we need. There are better things to concentrate on, like Evan's bare ass. I grab him around the waist, and press into him again, the fly of my chinos tight against his crack. "How's my boy today?"

"Horny." He reaches back to get a hand between my legs, and I grab his wrists. Pinning them to his sides so that all he can do is grind harder against me.

"You're always horny, you little punk. Have you taken care of that Latin lesson I gave you yesterday?"

His voice is husky. "All done. I can count to fifty."

"I thought I only assigned the numbers up to thirty."

He grins over his shoulder at me, long bangs falling over his eyes. "Well, you're going to make me count cane strokes, aren't you? I can take fifty. Sir," he adds with a gasp as my fingers find his nipples.

"My boots need polishing," I say into his ear in a low voice. "I'll be waiting." I let go of him, suddenly, and push him away, a move that keeps him from falling over backwards.

"Yes, sir," he says, hazel eyes twinkling. "Yes, Papa."

• • •

"I still don't think it's a good idea," Kris had said in her I'm-the-shrink-and-you're-not-being-reasonable voice. "Of course you have parent issues, but it's generally more healthy to work them out on your own, without involving other people in them. It's just too messy...too open to misunderstanding."

"Evan's nineteen, almost twenty," I told her. "Past the age of consent. It's not as if he's really a child. It's just sort of a...game."

"Sounds like a pretty heavy game to me," she said, her forehead wrinkling. "It could trigger incest issues."

I resisted the urge to groan and drop my head into my hands. "Neither of us have been incested," I say with as much patience as I can muster. "It's good for both of us. All three of us. Sophia likes him; he's one more person for her to mother as far as she's concerned." I didn't bother to add that she played with Evan sometimes herself, using her ex-military background to put him through pseudo-drills that she had concocted herself. He'd learned to shine my boots properly from her.

Kris shook her head. "I don't know, Daniel. I mean, you explained to me about the S/M you do with Sophia, that it's a consenting thing between adults, but this...I'm just not comfortable with it, and I don't think it could possibly be good for you." She looked at me over her glasses. "You do have sex with him while you're in the middle of this...father-son game, don't you?"

A sudden flash of Evan down on all fours, me spreading his ass cheeks. My lips twitched with amusement. "Yes. We have sex."

"And then you...ah...beat him, right?"

"Kris—" Impatience rose in my throat again. "He likes it, OK? He's a bottom and a masochist. He's got a safe word. This is all consensual."

She looked at me directly, taking off her glasses. "How do you know this isn't all some way to identify with your father, reenacting what he did to you?" A pause. "I thought you were committed to nonpatriarchal ideals, in spite of your change," she said.

It was at that point that I figured out it was hopeless to argue with her, and I started getting scared.

•••

My dad never molested me. I suppose I should be grateful that he just beat the shit out of me twice a week and treated me as if I was an incompetent idiot. His cruelty does live in me somewhere, I assume, as does that of my equally abusive but more subtle mother. My dad never touched me except in anger. His big hand never ruffled my hair, never rested on my shoulder like I do for Evan, never lifted in my presence except to slam up against my head hard enough to make tears come to my eyes. When Evan is choking, trying so devotedly to deepthroat my cock, when sobs finally shake his slender frame after a severe whipping, I put my arms around him and tell his he's my good boy, that he is so fine to suffer all this for me. My dad would never have said such a thing; his favorite names for me were Turkey when I was a small child and Shithead throughout my teen years.

Evan's dad didn't even hit him, but he didn't do much of anything else, either. An elderly, introverted man who had never expected to have children this late in life, his existence consisted of staring at the TV day after day. Both of us turned to our mothers by default, but after the dust settles from all the rhetoric, the hard, bitter truth is that you can't learn manhood from your mother. So I am Evan's Papa—that's with the French pronunciation, accent on the second syllable. "Daddy" seemed so whiny, so unrefined, and I can't find myself in the sexy working-class leather daddies at the local gay bar. My Papa persona is more of a cross between an overeducated hippie activist and an eighteenth-century English laird. I teach him poetry, literature, confidence, style, how to drive and fix a car, and how to write a résumé, not to mention how to suck cock and take a beating with pride.

Evan loves it whenever I teach him something new, something he would never have gotten from his dad. It makes him horny. After I taught him how to change the oil in our van, he wanted me to bend him over and fuck him right there. I nearly obliged, but the neighbors were watching, and they think a houseful of transsexuals is weird enough as it is.

•••

He reports to his Papa with polished boots in hand. "All ready, sir," he says, kneeling and helping me to get them on. My favorite whips are lying out already, carefully placed in order. He's got his jeans back on now, and I can see the carefully arranged bulge in the denim. His hair is long, in a ponytail, like mine. I like all my lovers to have long hair, regardless of gender. The first, fine peachfuzz is starting on his cheeks, and I remember when I lived through that, spending hours in front of the mirror to search for the magic the endocrinologist promised me would come with the first few injections.

Evan put his head on my knee. "May I have the honor of sucking your cock, sir?" Even for the hundredth time, it's music.

•••

Later that night, I climb into bed and bury my face in Sophia's long dark hair. She makes a mumbling noise and snuggles closer. "Have fun, dear?" she asks sleepily.

"Lots. You OK?" I start to rub her shoulders. Since her operation, Sophia's sex drive is lower than it used to be, and she's pleased that I have Evan to take the edge off mine.

"Yeah, just had to clean out some rain gutters. God, I hate those." A pause. "Evan told me you had some problems with Kris."

I let out a snarling sound that expresses all my feelings nonverbally, and my hands dig harder into her broad shoulders. "I've been with her for six years. You'd think she'd have more faith in my judgment."

"People change," she says, and we both laugh at the sudden humor in that statement, considering both our situations. "No, but seriously," she continues. "A year ago you yourself thought that scenes with parent-child contexts were pretty sick. Now you know better. She hasn't experienced it. How can she possibly learn it?"

"You have a point," I admitted, considering whether or not I should think about changing shrinks. But breaking in a new counselor isn't an easy thing. Most haven't worked with transsexual men. Most of the ones who have worked with transsexual men want them to be good little straight boys in crew cuts pursuing genetic girls, not long-haired bisexual feminist men married to radical transsexual women and having pseudo-incestuous faggot relationships with younger copies of themselves.

"Do you think I'm sick?" I ask Sophia directly.

She twists around to look at me. "Are you kidding? The crazy thing would be believing that. You're fine. I'm fine. Evan's fine. Now go to sleep."

I lie awake a while, stroking her hair. My wife is afraid of a great many things. She worries that someone will break into the house, that she'll be "read" on the street and assaulted. She obsesses about riots in the city and someone stealing her bike.

I admit these items are not exactly at the top of my list of fears. But she never doubts her sanity, or mine, in spite of everything we've done to our bodies and our lives.

What a wise woman I lucked out with, I think to myself as I fall asleep.

•••

The next day, I call my friend Lou, a large Italian faggot with a heart of gold and more body hair than I've ever seen on anyone else in my life. "Don't let that dyke bitch push you around," he yells cheerily over the phone. "Get another shrink. Ain't nothin' wrong in havin' a boy. Girls just don't understand it."

•••

Evan comes to me when it's time for his shot of testosterone. The lab techs are satisfied that he can administer the shots himself now, and he has his own needles and scrip bottle, as I do. He has turned them over to me, and I give him his injection. I'm his Papa, after all. Manhood comes from my hands. He sits quiet throughout the ritual, and then kneels to put his head again on my knee. "Thank you, sir," he says.

Maybe I wouldn't be able to do this as easily with someone who'd grown up male, but Evan's a boy like I was a boy, trapped in a girl's life. When I do this for him, I'm fathering my own younger self as well. After all, we're the closest thing there is in the world today to the ideal of the matriarchal male. Mommy's boys, in the truest sense, stealing our manhood piece by piece from the leavings of the father's sons. It's appropriate that I initiate him—and in some strange way he has also initiated me into something important.

Fatherhood is a mystery they don't teach you about in school. Every day that I'm Evan's Papa, I reclaim a little of my own childhood. I prove to myself once again that the part of me that is masculine nurturing was not tainted, was not poisoned by my own father's cruelty and abuse. He didn't make me into someone like him. I am whole, after all.

He goes to put the bottle back in the fridge, and when he doesn't return immediately, I go looking. He's in the bathroom, scrutinizing himself in the mirror. He turns quickly, guiltily, as I come in, but I know what he's thinking. I put out an arm to draw him closer. "It's okay," I say. "You're going to be a handsome cuss. I should know." I cut off his next words. "For that matter, you're already the cutest little chicken fag I've seen all year."

He flushes, grins, and then looks down for a moment. When his eyes meet mine again, he reaches up and touches my face, stroking the growth of neatly trimmed beard. "I hope I look like you someday, sir," he says.

•••

"It's a Catch-22, sweetheart," I say to Sophia as I put the clean dishes away. "I can get a new counselor and tell him absolutely nothing about my life, just convince him I'm totally normal, or I can stay and argue it out with Kris, and risk that she'll do something stupid."

"Give it a shot with Kris," Sophia advises, putting a hand on my shoulder. "Maybe she can suggest someone else, someone who isn't turned off by our sex life." She gestures with her other hand, including both me and Evan, sitting at the table.

He looks down, unhappy. "I didn't realize this would create such problems. I'm so sorry, Daniel." The seriousness of the conversation pushes him out of character. I reach out and ruffle his hair.

"It's cool," I say. "This would have happened sooner or later anyway. I'm a politically correct psychologist's nightmare. Its not your fault." And I'll be damned if I'll let anyone imply it's wrong. It's too important that we see this through to its end.

• • •

Sophia is chained to the wall, squirming because Evan is kneeling before her, eating her. It's something she could never really enjoy before her surgery. I'm behind him, his hips in my hands, plowing into his ass the way I know he likes it. One big happy family. The thought echoes between my struggles for orgasm, heavy with irony. When I come, I fall against him and he cries out, mingling with the soft noise coming from Sophia.

He's about fifteen now, in his mind. Our game swerves through a variety of different ages. Sometimes he's a freckle-faced ten-year-old still in awe of his Papa's big cock, doing the unthinkable. Sometimes he's a callow youth, like now, enthusiastic and flirtatious. And sometimes he's about seventeen and needs to have his rebellious ass wrestled to the ground by his Papa, who fortunately is still taller and heavier enough to do the job. It's a strange sensation, suddenly being placed in the role of father to an almost-adult. It gives me a glimpse of the man I'll be in fifteen years myself, when any hypothetical sons I might have had would be shaving and showing off their new driver's licenses.

Evan helps me unhook Sophia's leather wrist cuffs and get her down off the wall. She's gasping for breath, falling against me, and I lay her gently down on the couch, kissing her. I can feel Evan's small, delicate hands running over my back, touching me as I spread her legs and fuck her. The hands slide over my ass, down into the wet crack, pick a hole and slide in. I'm acutely aware of both their presences, two different pieces of my life. Sophia tosses her head and arches her hips up, and her damp hair plasters itself wetly to her throat, outlining her Adam's apple.

A friend of mine, a former multiple personality who integrated all her selves spontaneously in the middle of an S/M scene, once commented sourly, "Shrinks hate it when you learn during sex what they'd rather you learned in their office."

And here, now, flanked in embrace by my two androgynous and yet very different lovers, I understand my sexual preference at last. It's not maleness or femaleness that draws me. It's dissonance, two things that society says can't coexist occupying the same body. The warring of opposites, that's what snaps my head around in the queer bars, what makes me hard and wet and puts a lump in my throat.

I'm not attracted to children. They're just...children. It's that child nature in an adult body, with adult mind and desires, that I want. The heat is in the dissonance, not the taboo.

Something coalesces in me at that moment. I'll do whatever I have to, tell whatever lies and omissions are necessary to protect my people...my family, the alien queers, the outcasts among the outcasts. Myself.

Someday he'll go, and I know it. He dates other people. Someday one might want him all to themselves, or at the least he won't need to be a boy any more. He'll have grown up, in some nonchronological sense. Maybe he'll have a boy of his own; I can imagine it. Maybe he'll bring the kid by to show him his heritage. Maybe he'll share him with his old man. You never know.

To hell with political correctness. We queers need all the family we can get, and, I promise myself, the hot pulse of the body is as good a way as any to build it.

# Taking a Bow

## Lord Malinov

Kelly let the thin plastic handle of the grocery bag slip off her curled fingers, setting down the loose bundle of canned tomatoes, mozzarella cheese, and bread on her front step. She took the white envelope perched atop the dull brass doorknob and after glancing at the handwritten scrawl, "Mrs. Stewart," Kelly slipped the fold of paper into her back pocket. Twisting a key in the lock, she lifted the bag of food and wound her way into the kitchen.

"Tonight, I think, we shall prepare one of my specialties, a little linguine in clam sauce," Kelly said with an affected French accent as she put away the groceries, making her pronouncement to no one in particular. "Then, perhaps, I will perform a few numbers—nothing special, thank you, just something I've been working on—and acknowledge the applause of my ardent fans." Kelly flipped her long, deeply yellow hair back as she wiped her pale brow. "So kind," she said, laughing at herself.

Kelly pulled a bottle of Chardonnay from its resting place on the refrigerator shelf and popped the plastic stopper from the neck. Pulling a glass from the rack overhanging the butcher-block island, she poured herself a generous glass of the white wine. Kelly wet her lips with a sip. "Excellent, my good man," she said, nodding to a ghostly waiter and then taking a healthy swallow. "Just divine." Unbuttoning her blue cotton shirt, Kelly pressed the cool glass into the deep valley between her lace-brassiered breasts. ***"Magnifique,"*** she sighed.

The telephone rang, and with a self-indulgent grin, Kelly answered.

"Hello," she said. Her light voice rang joyfully.

"Hey, Doll," came the deep, alluring response.

"Bradford," Kelly said, leaning over her tall kitchen chair, dangling her wine glass between two fingers. "You can't call me today," she chided.

"I don't know why not."

"William's flying back this afternoon, and what if he answered the phone?" Kelly turned to sit in the chair, propping her feet on the table. "But I'm glad you called, anyway." She tickled the slight bump of a dark nipple under the lace of her straining bra. "Tiger."

"I loved every minute of this weekend."

"You made a good husband," Kelly said. "So well-behaved."

"So I passed my test?"

"No," she said seriously. "That is, you passed the first part of the test. This is a multi-part exam."

"Can I take a pop-quiz? I could be over in ten minutes."

"Sorry, love. I don't think that would be wise," Kelly twirled the cord of her phone around her palm.

"Anyway. I wanted to remind you that I love you."

"You're such a dear, Bradford. I'll be over tomorrow."

Kelly hung up the phone with a sigh and finished her glass of wine in several swallows as she sashayed elegantly into the family room. "Oh, Bradford," she said, slipping her shirt off her shoulders, "I would marry you, if you weren't so desperately poor." She giggled at her sultry Southern accent and unbuttoned her shorts. "You cannot expect a woman of my position to surrender so much luxury for the sake of your manly cock." The denim fell slowly past her lean, tanned thighs. Retrieving the envelope from her pocket, she kicked the shorts onto the brick hearth.

The sun shone brightly through the large window on the south wall of the room, bathing Kelly in light while the air conditioner poured cool air from a floor vent. She sat down on a billowing grey sofa and opened the letter while she tickled her muff through the satin of her French-cut panties.

"Dear Mrs. Stewart," the handwritten note began. Kelly wrinkled her brow, curious at having discovered in the words more than a bill from the paperboy.

"We have met several times, at the Evansville May Bazaar, the Chicken Social, and maybe at the Devins' Christmas party, although I would imagine you don't remember me. I live in the house behind and at an angle from yours on top of the hill. My location affords me an excellent view of your beautiful house."

Kelly sat up, brushing a lock of golden hair from her eyes. She walked to the window and, shading her eyes, studied the darkened house behind theirs. Shrugging, she looked back down to the letter.

"For several months now, I have been watching you. It started with a glance, a night when I turned off the light in my room and happened to look over toward your house. In the full light of your room, you pulled a bright pink T-shirt over your head, leaving your glorious white, lit breasts, so naked, so firm, clearly proffered to my view. It was like a revelation. Your tits are magnificent, Kelly. I hope you don't mind my familiarity. It just seems appropriate, given all I know about you."

Kelly looked up at the distant house, wondering if he was that faint shadow in the dark window. Her hand cupped her warm breast.

"Let me assure you that I am not, well, I'm not obsessed with you or anything spooky like that. You are quite attractive by most standards of feminine beauty, and I appreciate that. For myself, I generally prefer a different sort of woman, more demure, shall we say. I never chose you, but rather found you. I could not ignore you, once discovered. Now, I had never considered myself a voyeur before I happened to encounter your image on that dark May night. But once I saw you standing in the window, naked and lovely, I could not help but look again.

"I guess, more than anything," the letter continued, "the amount of time I have spent peeping through your window is a fair measure of the boredom that has overtaken my life, as well, I suppose, as the regularity with which I have seen you prancing naked through your house. In three months, I don't think a single day has gone by when I haven't happened to witness your bare breasts, your ass, your pussy, your thighs, tummy and smile. Oh, Kelly, you have tempted me from a dull life of talk shows and soap operas to a constant vigil at my window. Money I would have spent on a fishing tackle and ice cream has gone to binoculars and telescopes. I should thank you, although I'm not sure I wouldn't have been better off if I'd simply never seen you.

"I have always wanted to write this letter, to share the visions that have become such an integral part of my life with someone who can appreciate the beauty they embody. I don't have any friends I would tell about you. But you understand, for you adore to see yourself on stage, playing roles, exposed and applauded. This letter is my applause. I have enjoyed every moment of your life these past few months."

Kelly smiled, reading his warm praise, and with a thoughtless finger she tickled herself.

"There was one night, before William came home late (although it would be a strange night if he were to come home early) when you took a long, hot bath and stretched out across your bed. I can distinctly remember the way your heavy white breasts pressed down flat as you spread your thighs wide, turned just perfectly so I could see the soft pink of your pussy lips as you gently tickled your bulging clit. I had just bought a new telescope and was glad I spent the extra hundred. You lifted your ass off the bedspread as the excitement began to build, tossing your head back and forth, and then the shudders tore through your frame, and you plunged your fingers down deep. I dreamed of that episode for a week, over and over again."

"Ohmigod," said Kelly, pushing her hand down the waist of her panties to tease her damp clit.

"I've watched you dress a hundred times. I like your black satin panties and the silk blue chemise, the white flowered dress that shows your pretty legs every time you twirl. I love the denim shorts and the blue thong bathing suit. I remember the day when you curled your hair and spent the afternoon topless, your nipples tensing and relaxing at regular intervals."

Kelly smiled, remembering that day. She had been exciting herself before she went to see Bradford that afternoon.

"So, you must be wondering, why am I writing to you?"

"Yeah," Kelly said out loud.

"I never thought I would get the chance to tell you how much I have enjoyed your exhibitions, and when this opportunity arose, I couldn't help but step forward. I am, of course, afraid you will take offense at my visual intrusion and close your drapes, if in fact you have any. That has become my constant fear as my desire to see your tits and smile and ass has risen to the level of being the supreme pleasure in my sorry life. But I don't think you will disappoint me. I'm hoping, anyway.

"Maybe I have it all wrong. Perhaps your life has changed in some way imperceptible to me and my silent distance. Perhaps you can easily explain to William the dark-haired man who shared your weekend. I don't think so. I think you'd do almost anything to keep Mr. Stewart from finding out.

"I was watching Friday evening when the man first appeared. I watched you bring him into the kitchen. I watched you slip off your dress and jump up on the butcher's block. I watched his trousers fall and I watched as his prick pressed past your wet cunt's lips.

"I loved the way you sat astride him in your bed on Saturday night, the way your tits bounced as you rode his thick cock, the way you tossed your head back and even a thousand feet away, I could almost hear your moans. When he knelt behind you, pushing deep inside with your face pressed against the spread and your ass lifted high, I wondered if he was half as hard as I was, watching you both. It looked fantastic, incredible, simply divine. You have a delicious ass, Kelly. I would have watched that fuck forever.

"I have often wondered how someone as sexual as you could survive on the meager diet your husband, dear William, seems to dole out. Now I think I know where you spend your late afternoons, Tuesday, Wednesday and Thursday. Perhaps Saturday before or after shopping as well? At any rate, Kelly, I wanted you to know that I know."

Kelly sighed and leaned back against the window. "But what do you want from me?" she asked the paper.

"Rest assured, pretty Kelly, your secret is safe with me. No more than you would I do anything to disturb the current state of affairs. All I want is to spend my days, evenings and nights, sitting at my window, watching you. You have never seemed to mind, and I hope you still won't. I would do almost anything to keep what I've got. Just don't leave me. That's all I ask."

"What a fool," Kelly said with a laugh. "Don't you want me?"

"Give me a wave and a smile. I love you. Your neighbor, Curtis."

Kelly turned to look out the window at her shadowy friend. She thought she could see a faint outline of a man sitting behind one of the panes. Kelly smiled and waved. Crumpling the letter in her hand, she turned her back again. She slowly leaned over and pushed the waist of her panties down. Wiggling her bare ass she pressed the swollen wetness of her pussy against the warm window. Kelly tickled her throbbing clit and laughed loudly.

"*Merci,*" she said. "Thank you all. You are too kind."

# Wineskin

## Mat Twassel

A couple of weeks after my husband, Jerry, got his new boss, we were invited to dinner over at their house. Bob and Hannah Keller. "They're from the East," Jerry said. "Been here less than a month." One look at their huge home doubled my nervousness. "If I spill something or break something, just shoot me," I told Jerry. "Don't worry, honey," Jerry told me, "Bob's a really nice guy, easy to get along with." He was. A graceful man in his mid-forties, with easy, offhand charm. His wife, Hannah, was much younger, I'd say barely out of college, which would make her three or four years younger than Jerry or me. Right away she grinned at me as if we'd been best friends for years.

"We've got a long way to go," she said, sweeping her hand across a room which was completely beyond my imagination. Nothing in my education had prepared me to look at those paintings, to sit on those chairs.

"They're nice," I said to Jerry on the drive home. He squeezed my hand. That night we had the best fuck in a long time. I came so hard I couldn't stop crying.

"We're not having them here," I said to Jerry, when I'd finally calmed down. "We can't."

He just continued soothing me, stroking me, and then I started coming again.

After Jerry left for work, I just lay in bed for hours.

About ten, Hannah telephoned. It woke me from a strange dream. I was a splash of water, and then a waterfall, and then mist, the kind you see climbing rainbows. "How about some shopping?" Hannah said. "Can you pick me up? In about an hour?" There was no way I could get ready that fast. But her questions weren't really questions.

"Oh, dear," I said. "I haven't even showered yet."

"Don't shower," Hannah said. "Just throw something on and come over."

I did the best I could. No way was I going to leave the house smelling so strongly of sex.

“Is Gracely’s okay?” Hannah asked as she stepped into my car. “I’ve heard it’s good.” Her iron gates swung open and I eased onto the street.

The Gracely is a little upscale for me. I like looking there, but I do most of my buying at discount places. K-Mart, Venture, Target. The Gracely’s huge west parking lot was already filling up. We began the long walk to the nearest entrance. “This is going to be so much fun!” Hannah said. Her voice was like a teenager’s—no, like a little girl’s on Christmas Eve, staring at the glittery tree and the mounds of elegantly wrapped packages underneath. “I am greedy,” she said, squeezing my hand. “In a nice way, of course.” She showed me a mischievous smile.

We stopped to admire a beautiful young woman setting a pair of small children into their double stroller. “I always wished I were twins,” Hannah said. “I guess that’s another example of my greed.”

“No brothers or sisters?” I said.

“None that matter.”

We walked slowly, letting the young mother keep ahead of us. Sunlight gleamed upon her lustrous hair, which coursed rich and thick all the way down her back, drawing our eyes to her narrow waist, her tight linen trousers, so snugly shaped by her tidy bottom. It was hard not to watch her bottom as she walked. She had lush hips for someone so elegantly slim. “Isn’t she pretty?” Hannah whispered. I nodded. The woman’s babies babbled brightly. “I bet she has some Oriental blood in her,” Hannah said. Such a thing never occurred to me.

At the mall entrance I stepped ahead and held the doors open—first one, then the other. The woman with the babies smiled at me. Hannah’s reflection flared as the inner door swung. “You have good manners,” she said a moment later. “It might have been fun to watch her trying to open.” The remark made me feel a trifle strange. “You’re a good person, aren’t you?” Hannah offered. Her eyes twinkled.

For never having been to Gracely’s, Hannah knew her way around. First we stopped at the Blue Bottle shop. Everything inside was deep blue glass. Oceans of glass in all sorts of seductive shapes. “I like the ones you almost can’t see through,” Hannah said, and she rubbed her thumb along the rim of a tight-necked wine crystal. “I should get one of these,” she told me. “Last night I broke one when I cried....” Her voice trailed off, and a wistful look crossed her face. “Maybe I’ll get seven,” she said then, brightly. “A week’s supply!” But she settled for one. The saleslady wrapped the azure vessel in cottony bunting and slid it carefully into a small, nearly diaphanous shopping sack.

“Would you like to carry the package?” Hannah asked me. She handed it to me before I could say anything. “I do adore fragile things, don’t you?” she said. I nodded. The wine glass cost more than Jerry and I would spend on two weeks of groceries.

"Don't you want to get anything for yourself?" Hannah said as we walked out of the shop.

"I'll just watch," I said.

We stood side by side on the up escalator. "I'm so glad you drove," Hannah said. "I have bad luck with parking. I can never remember where I've parked. One time at a mall like this, I walked around for hours. I was sure my car had been stolen. It got so bad I wasn't sure I could even remember what kind of car it was."

"I've had dreams like that," I said, "but it's never really happened."

At Le Petite Sourire we sampled some perfumes. "This is mine," Hannah said, showing me a small bottle of expensive scent. "Sometimes it's the only thing I wear." Deftly, she unscrewed the tiny glass stopper, touched her forefinger to the jar's small opening. "I notice you don't pierce your ears," Hannah said. "I like that." Her forefinger nibbled the bottom of my earlobe, and I'm sure I reddened a little. "Mm," Hannah said, "Your heat goes good with this." She pinched my earlobe lightly, and I felt about to melt.

"Bob asked me one night if I thought he should pierce his ears," Hannah remarked as we walked the upper level. "How silly men are!" I couldn't help but think of Hannah's tongue scraping Bob's ear, and then the tip tickling its way inside. Below us, a man was playing a piano. A small girl in a yellow jumper stood on tiptoes to look at a bird inside a tidy bamboo cage. I had to hurry to find Hannah. She was examining underwear.

"What do you think of these?" she said. "The nice ones are the naughtiest, don't you think?" Before I could offer an opinion, Hannah took my hand, and we wandered through dresses. At the far end we found maternity. She fingered the bodice of a silk gown.

"You'd look good in this," she said. "You're so sweetly slim... a baby bulge would be so special. I do hope you're working on that." She was looking at my middle, and I felt certain she could see quite through my clothes. I shivered. She looked up, her round face grinning, pleased as that cat that ate the canary.

"What about you?" I sputtered, and I meant to say something about her shape, for her figure was finer than mine, girlish and womanly at once. But she stopped me by putting a finger on my upper lip and shaking her head.

"None of that, now," she said. "And anyway, Bob's not the daddy type. He wants me all for himself, the meanie. But if you had one, we could share. Anyway, it's time for lunch."

We didn't have to wait at Vidite's. A tall man with a bony face led us to a corner table. We settled next to each other on the plush bench. The waiter pushed the table in. Hannah said something to him in French. He nodded. "We're going back for the underwear afterward," Hannah said to me as she studied the menu. "I'm sure we're the same size. And that perfume, too."

I couldn't help but giggle.

"What's the matter?" Hannah asked with a pleased smile.

"Oh, nothing," I said, "I was just thinking about us being the same size."

"Oh," Hannah said. Then she looked at me seriously. "You shouldn't worry about childbirth; it's no worse than burlap."

"That wasn't...."

"It's okay," Hannah said. "You'll see. It'll be easy as pie."

A waiter arrived with a bottle of wine. I looked at Hannah.

"I took the liberty," she said to me. "Just open it," she told the waiter, "I'll pour." The cork came out with a soft pop.

"Newborns have such adorably pudgy little legs," Hannah said as she tipped the bottle. "You can take the whole of an infant's leg into your mouth at once." Hannah was pouring very slowly. The wine trickled into the glass. I thought it sounded like pee-pee. "They say you shouldn't fill even half-way," Hannah told me. "That's so the fume gathers in the glass."

"A little baby is so lovely," Hannah continued. "I know yours is going to be so special." The level in the glass kept going up.

"I am greedy," Hannah said. "We'll have time for fume later. I'm going to fill you all the way up." We watched. Wine filled the glass right to the brim. "I'm going to overflow a little," Hannah said. "Just for luck." I noticed she was watching my eyes. I quickly jerked mine back to the wine glass. A slim stain was already spreading across the linen. At last Hannah stopped pouring.

"Take a sip," Hannah said. "Don't be afraid to spill."

Sure enough, the liquid wobbled over the edge, trickled through my fingers, blotted the cloth. I touched my lips to the glass. A tiny buzz of wine stung my tongue.

"Isn't it nice?" Hannah said. "So dark and sure and strong."

"Aren't you having any?" I asked.

"Maybe I'll just watch," she said. Then she laughed, a friendly little laugh, as if at herself, and she said, "Maybe I'll try a little of yours."

Before I could take my fingers off the stem, Hannah put her hand on mine. I was confused. She touched her lips to mine. Just for a moment. More breath than anything else. I trembled. "Perfect," Hannah said.

All during lunch I was afraid Hannah was going to kiss me again. I was afraid she wasn't. "This wine is like a kiss," she said, as if reading my thoughts. "A deep,

deep kiss." She kept my glass filled. She watched me eat and drink. Sometimes she said some things. Her words glistened. I couldn't make much sense of them.

"Do you know what wineskin is?" she said. "Close your eyes and think of wineskin."

I closed my eyes. I couldn't think of anything, anything but the almost taste of her lips, which was the taste of the wine.

"Smooth or wrinkled?" Hannah asked, and that helped me. I thought of the head of my husband's penis, the smooth softness of it, and then the firm full stem, and I thought too of his scrotum, a careful avalanche of creases and furrows for my fingertips, my tongue.

After lunch we picked up the panties and the perfume, and strolled out to the car. The sun was so warm, so pleasant. I felt like saying something, but I had no language. "You found the car so easily," Hannah said. "I'm impressed."

"You're teasing me," I said.

"No, really," Hannah said.

"Do you want to put your package in the trunk?" I asked.

"No," Hannah said. "My lap is fine. In case we're rear-ended."

It was a quiet drive to Hannah's house. I kept thinking of a collision, of that blue glass shattering, of perfume and panties and glistening shards of sharp blue glass.

Hannah's gates swung open. I drove up the long private drive. Hannah got out. She walked around the car.

I rolled the window all the way down. "Thanks for the lunch," I said.

"No, I should thank you," Hannah said. She bent down and whispered something. "I had a lovely come," she said. Or maybe she said, "I had a lovely time." But I'm almost certain she said "come." The moment she said this, her lips were on mine, just touching, just for a moment. But it was enough to trigger me. I started coming. I couldn't help it. I came and I came. Hannah watched me, absorbing every detail of my orgasms. When I was done, she smiled. She touched her finger gently to my lips. "Drive safe," she said.

I pulled onto the highway. The road was empty. I was my own baby. I was small and naked. Sweet innocent skin, plump, and perfect inside. Carefully Hannah took my leg into her mouth. My whole leg. I did the same with my other leg. All the way in. My lips met Hannah's, right there at the apex of my groin. We kissed there. It was lovely. Meanwhile Hannah's husband, Bob, was fucking me, fucking me for all he was worth. His smooth stem slammed between our lips. For a moment I couldn't move. My cunt felt full, as if completely coated by the churn of Bob's cum. "You are a good person," Hannah said. She whispered it. The words slipped right into my mouth. The words stretched into the small hot smile of my cunt. I swallowed. The buzz, like a tongue, the tip of a tongue, touched my wineskin, took me. It was then I noticed Hannah hadn't taken her package from my car.

Somewhere someone is crying, but not here, not me. I feel exquisitely pleased, hopelessly content, irreducibly excited. The glass begins its breaking. The sky shivers, replete beyond blue, its ice suffused with sunlight. The rainbow is just up ahead. I am going to hit it. I'm almost there. Just a little more. And then, and then I am going to come again, I am going to come, and there is nothing, nothing anyone can do.

# Poems

Guillermo Bosch

## Creole Lunch

Dark gun metal clouds roll
in from the delta, up
river, pushing across
St. Jean's levee, heavy air pressing
against the faded, peeling,
blue-louvered shutters, slipping
under and inside the jam, as I
slip slide against you, your torn white
dress crumpled over the shattered
rattan chair, your straight red
hair streaked from my spray
when you smile a tiny speck
of crawdaddy shell lodged
under your upper gum draws
my finger to your lips which
close around my tip and suck
me in up to the second knuckle.
My knees buckle, and I fall away
from you, pulled under by
that foreboding air out into
the gathering storm, then down river,
drowning in the warm salt
water of the Gulf, my body
washes ashore south of Biloxi, and I
am buried under oaks heavy
with Spanish moss, alone.

# Out Of Africa

The small, light scar
on that long, left arm
comes from an African
thorn which pierced
your soft, white skin,
where droplets
of dark red blood now
ooze from the cut
I lick with my
curled, wet tongue.

Or perhaps you were scarred
by the razor-sharp blade
of a lover's knife
dropped in the dust
when he fled to Dakar
and escaped by boat
to a shallow grave
on the beach at Algiers
never to see the mark
where my white teeth nibble

Your sister says
you were sliced by blades
of tough spring grass when you
were a gazelle leaping naked,
bare-assed against the golden
evening sun setting behind
the dry, rolling dunes of the Ferlo,
and it is that wound's smooth
line my fingers trace with
precious oils and sweet perfumes.

Others say there is
no scar, no arm, nor soft
blond hair, no body
to caress, no lilting
French words tickling
the hairs of my inner ear—
and I have conjured up
a wounded bird
so I may kiss away her
pain in reckless desire.

**• Guillermo Bosch •**

## Odalisque II

In this small dark
adobe room filled
with piñon smoke
and old Spanish lace,
amid the Santo de Christo
mountains where in
the distance penitents
chant of sin and blood
sacrifice, I lift your
faded denim dress over
your face and kiss
your black-haired
sacrament while
Ophelia paints your
breasts golden,
your nipples blue,
your face red and
purple, your arms
rattlesnake green...
She seems to
linger in indecision
at your lips, as her
fingers trace their
shape, your tongue
slips against her index
finger, she presses
inside and rubs
her ebony digit against
your painted skin. I
move my mouth
from you to her as
she bends down to
dip her brush in
your moist pallet
and with soft strokes
her camel hairs paint
your clit a deeper
shade of pink.

# James/Joyce

## Davis Trell

***Sodom and Begorrah. All we faeries talk like that.***
***Only in an Englishmun's dreams do we do.***

So, I have a problem with my sexuality. Sometimes I'm James, othertimes Joyce. Depends on my mood, I guess. You should've seen me as a young man, maybe you would've wanted to paint my portrait.

Maybe it's my Irish roots showing through, but when you take Dubliners out of Ireland, transplant them to the U.S., let the seedling grow, something weird happens.

Now I'm a slave to the one-eyed trouser-snake, Ulysses' version of the Cyclops. I came into bloom, around my eighteenth birthday, and haven't looked back. My hero was a guy called Stephen, who was an up and coming writer, used the pen-name Daedalus. He showed me the ways of men, I was Icarus and flew too close to his Sun.

His room was full of books, pamphlets, dictionaries, thesauri, all manner of literary tracts, unfinished poems and rejection slips. Naturally seedy, worn carpets, a simple gas fire, that needed a shilling popped in the meter, to provide gas, to provide heat, much needed warmth. A nondescript bed, the only place to sit, as Stephen took the only chair, next to the simple table, where rested his trusty Underwood.

He was so literate, would quote all the contemporary poets, Dylan Thomas, Yeats, Borges, Eliot, and of course, himself.

He picked me up in a public-house, the "Horn-a-Plenty" just by the O'Connell Street, by the cobblestoned bridge. He was drinking Guinness and bought me a Black Velvet, which is half Guinness and half dark-thorn cider, a woman's drink, so I guess he'd got my number. Three of those, and I was anybody's; tonight his.

He had a strange way of talking, asked me if I were a quare fellow, would I be a nicens little boy, his baby tuckoo. Would I be amoocow and let him milk me. At first I thought it was the Guinesstalking, but it was the voice of a poet wanting to get his end away.

Those days you had to be discreet, there was always a BullMulligan who'd dash out the brains of any one "quare." So it was a goodjob Bull didn't see us out in the back alley, kissing like schoolgirls with Stephen's hand down the front of my corduroy trousers, feeling me up and showing I was willing to go further, all the way back to his dingy bed-sitter, his study by day, and tonight his boudoir.

He offered me whisky in a cracked china cup, he offered his untidy bed and asked me to lie back. Did I want some air? His hands went to mytrouser fly and undidded, one by one the black buttons until out fell my hardon, soon to get harder as Stephen applied a coy massage. He madedevotions, cradling my cock in his fingers, taking purchase, gripping firm, exciting to me, to feel another's hand, different to mine own, gently rubbing, pleasure coursing through me, along with the whisky. Hands windswept, opening my shirt, feeling over pale chest, radiating heat, nipples tremulous, lips embracing, full of incertitude, but breathing of passion, liplocked, tongues twining, eyes searching, body aching.

He quoted Milton: "Perfume of embraces all him assailed. Withhungered flesh obscurely, he mutely craved to adore."

"Bejasus..ohh..Beezlebub..!" He stood up, high o'er me and removed his tweeded jacket, leathered elbowed, and thin cotton-whited shirt, he unbespectacled himself, sat down, by me, whispered 'View Halloo', unbuckled his suspenders and offed his trews, and showed his man stuff, Priapus erect.

Bigger than mine, more seasoned, most pretty, and this prick Ikissed and guzzled, mouthfondling, tonguelicking, glans and frenum, acum-stick lollipop. He stroked my head, marching to a different drummer, but a 6/9 rhythm, a jazz-jizm tempo, running up and down his bulging urethal canal. Corpus cavenorum nostrum penis. Yummy.

Staring close at Stephen's perineum, the heart-shaped mound betweenarse and bollocks, I could see faint traces of sweat, glistening-shiny, a wild hollow hoarlight winding, winking.

Mouthpump brought forth white lava, shoot, shoot. Drink divine. We laughed and giggled, not loud enough to wake his landlady and buried ourselves under the one grey blanket against the candy striped mattress, cock to cock and man to man. Rain crackled against the window-pane and a distant thunderclap sounded dark. We clinched together like two schoolboys having been told a ghosty story, and my hands clasped tight his bum-buttocks pressing him closer for comfort. Lying on a snail trail of man-spurt.

Stephen, victor, victoriamus, sat up, air cold around his shoulders and we partook of a shared cigarette, making arabic calligraphic swirls floating up to the ceiling, browning. Frabjous day, callooh callay, I made my move. Licking balls, head at groin-moved his hips, slip down with tongue protuding, enterdarkness, warm and wet and felt a man squirm overhead. Open wide, doctor style—with spatulate tongue to test the waters. I raised my hand, made into a pointy shape and slipped it in him, rotating gently.

They call this buggery and I a sodomite, but thus with my cock I entered him and pushed and pulled, crammed and jammed, packed my whang, thrust it up, went inside, felt dark syrup, wetness and wailing. His legs he raised, wrapped around my thighs and pulled me in, I pulled me out, and pushed me back in, riding, badgering his bunghole, cock needling, in and out like a tune played on a penny whistle, flexing gluteal muscles driving deep into his arse, sphincter tight, grasping my greasy marrow pole, unable to hold, to stop the friction as I burrowed in his meaty insides. His mouth oped wide, eyes tight shut, his arms clinging to my shoulders, fingers splayed, hanging onto my back, taking all of me in. Dingly dell. A groan escaped his lips, a signal for me to spend, orgasm I did, with ejaculation hot and greedy, and I seeded him with seminal shoot, bowels wet with my spunk, and shuddered he, as I came again, more than twice, thrice.

His belly frothed, as he gave his own comeuppance, spilling on belly, marshmallow whiteness, sticky, sticky between us.

Another shared cigarette, glowing like my penis head, sore with delight. Lickety, licking me, till all was dry. Stephen, my hero, butt-bandit, ass-outlaw, raunchily romantic, myopic, my sweetheart, I, now his bum-brother, smitten by his hormones, cock-beater; solo no more.

Later he had me, took me from behind, I bent to his will and succumbed to his lust. Poked, penetrated, bum-rodded, in Stygian depths. Palmy hands holding belly, butt bounced, dick stuck in, wibbly-wobblying, pink-cucumbered, arseslapped by minature coarse coconuts, containing cock-milk, swooshing, gurgling, till my arse drank, till prostate bruised, till fucked-tired, I swooned to his meaty beating, upended, downturned, everted, bent doubled, swooped and swallowed as dick pumped, plunged, till his dam broke, penis-puking, spunk spillage overflowing brown-pink orifice. Carnal cardinal sin. Genuflecting obeisance, we drifted to sleep. Slept like angels, till came the dawn, and both came again.

I can be James, but sometimes I like to be Joyce.

# Beach Slut!

## Suzie SleaZe

Sun-drenched Turkish beach...

Sexy Lover sunbathing beside me...

Sexy g-string slick with juice...

Catting for a fuck....

Bliss?

No!!! Mick wouldn't fuck!

"Suzie, it's a public beach!" moaned Mick, squirming a little as my loving hand stroked his dreamboat ass, arching wonderfully beneath continental-cut, ultra-brief, bright-orange Spandex swim trunks. Groaning, he rolled onto his back. "Suzie, don't feel me up here for fuck's sake! You'll give me a hard these trunks can't take!"

"Shit, Babes! I HAVE TO! That's the problem! And d'you call those things 'trunks'? They're man-panties! Tit-throbbing, cunt-juicing, girlhorny-gorgeous man-panties! I could suck the ass off you I'm so horny watching the BeachBabes passing and staring at you. And don't tell me you haven't noticed! They're juicing their tiny bikini-pants on staring at you."

"What you mean, Suzie," he groaned, "is that you'd like to suck out those juicy BeachBabe cunts—after they're nice and slicked up. You're horny for a sniff of cunt."

True, but Cuntie wanted cock, too!

And Mick was content just spit-roasting his all-male gorgeousness in the afternoon sunshine as I gazed woefully at the (unavailable) shape of "our" marital cock and balls in those sexy swimmers. A lovely trickle trickled—from somewhere to somewhere deep within me on the start of its journey to join all its trickle friends that were partying in the tiny triangle of canary-yellow, satin cunt-cover I'd been flashing around town all afternoon.

That's why I was so horny. It was my fault—I'd been "showing out" around the town's shops and bars in a tiny, white Spandex mini-skirt and a peach bikini-top. The pretence of a "skirt" barely covered crotch and ass, allowing me to flash the sexy "g" and bare-assed cheek to my wilting "victims." And do those Turkish guys know how to LEER!!

The bikini top was one of those teat-covers. Know the type? One of those where everything sort of just spills out? In a slutty, gaudy peach colour too, so my tits had been on permanent flash—to whoever chose to look! I'd been stared at, drooled over, followed and even fondled, so I was just ultra-fucking horny!

Fucking-hungry-horny-for-cock, ultra-horny...

Showing-out always does it for me. Always has. Ever since age twelve when I played "Rudey Queen" to myself in front of the mirror—with my imaginary "subjects" forced to watch "Suzie-the-Rudey-Queen" strip and sexy-dance her rude bits at them...

It wasn't just the shortness of the skirt, either. The Spandex was so white and almost translucent. The dark cleft of my tanned, cutey-tight, high-jutty ass showed through the fabric, too!

Ah! A "PrickTease!," you say? No tease! If cock's offered (and Mick approves), I take!

And I'd been "accidentally" brushing my tits, bumping my ass and squeezing my crotch into men all afternoon in the town's little shops, markets and bars. I'd had four direct gropes on my cunt—numerous on my ass—and more than numerous "accidental" brushes against my tits, so by the time we arrived at the beach, nippies and clitty were lovely hard-popping, tingle-jutty twigs, ready and begging for attention...

"Mick, pleeasse fuck me?" I pleaded with the hunky-muscled horniness I love so much. His powerful, tanned body lay there, taunting me, with cock and balls lumped in those sexy, shiny, bright-orange Spandex swimmers. I reached out, slid my hand up hard-muscled thigh, and over that gorgeous lump of pleasure. His hand clamped my wrist!

"Let me just LIE on you then, Spunkie ... please? Let me lie on you and just jerk off on you. Those things are so beautifully TINY, so SHINY ... and I'm so FUCKING HORNY, just even ... please, just let me jerk clitty on you? Please? Go on, they're all adults here. If they want to look, let them!"

I whipped over and kneeled astride him, squatting my yellow satin'd, horny-hotted cunt down firmly onto that squishy bulge...

"For fuck's sake, Suzie! Have you no shame!"

"Stupid question, Lover! You know I haven't!" I quipped.

I kept on squeezing my cunt on ... yes ... squishy was becoming bulgy.

"Mmmm ... Lover! I can feel your cock on my cunt. Feel me rub off on you ... it feels lovely, slippy-sexy satin on sexy Spandex." No mistaking the lump now! Mick can't resist my horny-talking!

"I can feel it growing, Mick! Mmmmm! Feel Cuntie kissing Cockie, Mick! She's drooling for him..."

He was going to cum, like it or not, and a SuzieStory would help him on the way...

"Imagine Mick ... you're sunbathing in your sexy swimmers. A young girl comes up ... a seventeen-year-old blue-eyed blonde—with perfect body ... a seventeen-year-old Pamela Anderson..."

I leaned forward onto him, brushing my tits on his chest ... aware that the mini-skirt had risen at back, giving any passersby a view of bared, tanned ass, split by the thong of bright-yellow.

Breathing words slowly into my Lover's ear, I lightly squeezed my crotch on that hardening cock bulge, gently fucking myself off on him, the juice in my "g" oiling the way to a beautifully dirty feeling...

"She's wearing a shimmering-shiny, crimson-red swimsuit, Mick, pulled tight into her crotch—tight into her little teenage slutty cunt, Mick—splitting it so it bulges through the fabric. And THIS suit's far shinier, slippier, sexier than on Baywatch.

"Mick—imagine it, you CuntLover—this one's low-cut and cleaves open in a wide V-split from tits to navel. Imagine Mick, those young tits—tops bared by the low-cut, and the inner bits bared because of the V..."

Words were becoming hard to find as I imagined Mick with my imaginary girl. I could see the bitch doing it for him, and I was turning on at the sight of my words (if you see what I mean). I squirmed on him more...

"She straddles you, Mick. Like I am now. And when you've torn your eyes from the split-wide thighs and horny cunt that's rubbing your bulging trunks, you look up that 'V'-split...

"Young tits just sitting there, Mick.

"Taunting tits.

"HornyProud tits. Begging tits.

"Begging to be touched.

"To be groped.

"To be licked.

"To be sucked.

"Fondled.

"Loved.

"Milked by your big-man hands...

"'Lick me?' she pleads with you, Mick. 'My cunt's all juicy after watching you sunbathe. I'm all horny, I want you to lick out my cunt, then fill it with cock and fuck me...'"

By now I had a tennis ball to frig off on! Down-thrust cock and bulging bollocks in tight swimmers ... luvvelly! So I frigged, rolling clitty on it ... determined to make him cream those sexy trunks...

"Sexy bitch doesn't wait for a reply, Mick, she settles on your mouth, sliding the hot n' silky crotch of that swimsuit right on your mouth...

"You can smell her horny cunt through it, Mick ... imagine that ... a girl's horny cunt through her bright-red, wet-look Spandex swimsuit, Mick...

"Imagine...

"Imagine the feel as it brushes your lips ... the soft mounds of that young, split-wide cunt.

"Imagine...

"Imagine the heat of her, the musk of her—the smell of her, the smell of cunt, Mick ... as she settles it on your mouth ... and all because she's hot for your horny body."

I lifted up on my elbows, still squeezing against his cock, brushing my swung-down teats on his chest. I knew I already had him past the point of have-to-cum. I knew his fantasies, and he was about to get the lot! Selfish sod—if I couldn't have a fuck, I was going to have second best!

I breathed into his mouth, kissing him lightly...

"She looks down at you Mick. Over her heaving tits...

"'Lick my cunt,' she says.

"'Lick my horny-wet twat.'

"She's sitting on your neck. She takes your hands and presses them inside the 'V' of the suit. You feel her hot tits. 'I've got nice titties, haven't I?' she croons—rubbing her crotch on your mouth with a fuck-jerking motion..."

Mick's gasping a bit by now, and his crotch is involuntarily fucking back at me. I wriggle, imagining all that lovely cock-drool going into his swimmers...

"You feel her tits, Mick...

"'Oooooh! Mmmmmm! That's nice!' she says, 'but I love men to be rough with my tits. Pinch them, do my nippies, they're all lovely and hard... Mmmmm ... yes! Now stick your tongue in my cunt.' She hooks back the suit crotch with a finger and exposes her natch-blonde, horny-wet little split-peach. She bumps it to your lips.

"'Mmmm ... yessus!' she hisses. 'Like that! A hard-horny big-man's tongue, I'm going to cum soon, in your mouth. Pinch my titties harder, pull them. Go on! FUCKING SQUEEZE the bitches, like you're REALLY enjoying them...'"

I pinch Mick's nipples ... hard. Knowing the pain goes straight to his cock...

"'Yessss! Like THAT!' she gasps. 'And after I cum in your mouth I'm going to pull those sexy trunks down, put that lovely cock in my mouth and suck you off—I love the taste and feel of spunk in my mouth; the smell of a real man's cock—it's so fucking horny to suck a man's drooley-suckey cock...'"

Mick was almost there—and so was I—and I knew how I'd bring the sexy, selfish sod over the brink. His favourite...

"'I like to do something to men...' she says, suddenly pulling off your face, leaving glistening trails of gleaming fuck-froth around your mouth...

"'... I like to do something ... it makes me cum off.

"'I'm going to do it to you ... now ... can I please...?'

"You nod stupidly...

"She flips down your body and lies on top—like I am now, Mick, rubbing her hot cunt on your sexy swimmers ... like this—wiping her cunt on your sexy orange swimmers—you can feel the heat, can't you? Feel the wetness? Feel the cunt juices making us luvvelly and slidey?

"Well, she fucks you like this ... like this ... and this ... trying ... to find your pubic bone to wank her little clitty off on. She can't, not with this hard-on in the way. So she rubs her cunt against your cock—hard, like this—and she rubs her tits on your chest, like this...

"And then, she pisses on you...

"A sudden, hot flush soaks your swimmers, Mick, and you realise what the dirty slut had meant! She's pissed on you! Your cock erupts, pumps your sexy trunks full of lovely spunky cream ... she cums off too, gasping on top of you...

"Mmmmm ... YESSS! Mick! Feel it, Mick. Feel me piss on you..."

I rolled off, panting, pulling him against me, so we lay close, side by side. Reaching between us, I squeezed the piss-soaked swimmers.

"Mmmm yes, Mick," I crooned, squeezing the fat head of his cock through the hot-soaked Spandex, feeling the oily cock-juice, gorgeously slidey in the dark-stained orange trunks.

"Your swimmers are soaked, Mick. Soaked with my piss. Your cock's drooling in them, I can feel it. Cum off for me, Mick! Spunk your sexy swimmers for Suzie. Cream your pants for me, Mick. I want to feel it, thick and hot on my fingers ... want to taste it..."

Down-curved manmeat jerked and spewed. I felt warm-slippery thickness gush, slicking the Spandex. My fingers slid under the waistband for my prize...

"Mick—watch..."

Scooping spunk onto my fingers, I brought them out, sliding them over my crotch, wiping his spunk on my piss-wet, satin'd g-string. I delved and collected more, for my tits. And more, for my lips. He watched my tongue lick, savouring the taste of his cock, of his spunk. I sniffed his cocksmell off my fingers...

My index slicked my spunky "g." Clitty burned—exploded.

I clung to him, jerking against him with short, fucking jabs ... cumming, cumming, cumming...

WOW!

A while later we took a quick run to the sea!

Twenty minutes later we were back, sun-dried and sunbathing.

My top was off, and I was horned again—after being leered at sunbathing in just a g-string.

"Mick ... SHHHIIIT! Look at this piece of horny-boy ass!"

At the time I was lying on my front facing down the beach, enjoying hot sun on bared back and ass and coarse towel on swinging tits. (Also the bulging trunks sauntering past!)

Then, Bingo!

Walking slowly towards our bit of beach, a toy-boy vision! Dark-skinned, obviously Turkish, eighteen or nineteen years old, small frame but beautifully muscle-hard.

"As you say," Mick said slowly. "A nice piece of ass, and coming our way—looks as if he's going to camp on our doorstep! Suz! Look at the size of his packet—has he got a stonker on or what?"

I didn't need to be told to look, I'd been staring at it since I spotted him. Briefest of brief, tightest of tight, the yellow "BOA," Spandex workout shorts looked like they were stuffed with rolled-up socks...

Low-cut shorts on the boyish hips, the lewdly bulging crotch tingled my tits and clit. I squirmed into the towel, my eyes glued to the gorgeous piece of fuck-meat in the oh-so-sexy, showoff-shiny shorts.

He was still coming right at us! And he kept coming until he stood right there in front of us!

I rolled onto my back and gazed up hairless tanned thighs at the obscenely-bulging (especially from this angle), yellow-Spandex'd crotch.

And he gazed down at bared tit and almost-bared cunt!

"You like fuck?" he said.

Shocked, I whirled around and over, so I was kneeling, or rather sitting on my haunches, thighs splayed wide, giving him an offering of trimmed black minge, with the yellow satin pulled into the crack.

"Sure we like to fuck," Mick countered, "but it's not the sort of thing you ask strangers, is it?"

I quashed temptation to grab our stranger's ass, pull him to me and suck that taunting cock right through those damn-sexy shorts! I could see the cockhead. Right there, in front of my face, the outline clearly visible through the skimpy-shiny Spandex ... and a shiny sheen of pre-fuck clung over it!

A shiny sheen, right over the contours of the head of a fat, uncut, randy-youth's dick!

"No, I mean ... you like to be watched when you fuck? We've been watching you."

That startled the both of us. We're well-used to exhibitionistic fucking, but we usually know when we're doing it!

My "Boy" pointed up at the cliffs behind us. On a ledge, halfway up were four shapes. Three men. And a video camera on tripod.

"Couples come to this bit of beach to fuck," said "Boy," smiling nervously. "They know people watch. We thought you knew."

"No we didn't know," Mick said, almost angrily. "And we haven't been fucking anyway."

"Over there, under the cliff behind those rocks—people go there to fuck—most evenings."

“Can I ask just where all this is leading?” Mick asked somewhat sarcastically. I glared at him.

“That’s my uncle up there. I been with him. He likes to watch and film the sexies—I like to watch, too. Sometimes he send me down to couples to see if they want ... how do you call it, a trio?”

“Come on, Mick! I’m outa here!” I said, jumping up, hurriedly gathering towels. “I’m fuckin’ well fucking with this horny piece of ass even if you’re not! You can bloody well watch if you don’t want to join in!”

Behind the rocks I wasted no time, grabbing my ToyBoy while Mick lay out the towels. Kissing him deeply, I rubbed my bare tits on his chest, reached down to fondle that bulging and—as I found—not yet full-hard packet. He gasped into my mouth when he felt the groping hand and reached behind me, his young hands sliding over tanned, silky-smooth and bare slut-ass.

I dropped to my knees—gently licked ToyBoy’s cock through lovely Spandex. Sucking gently at the bulgy head. At that glossy spot of gorgeous slime.

Loving the feel of my lips on slippy, cock-oiled Spandex.

And best of all—I tasted and smelled rutting-horny cock.

My fingernails raked the backs of his strong thighs, snaked upward, over a beautifully hard, silky-smooth ass ... and discovered Mick’s bulging crotch, squeezing into and sliding on that jutty-proud, silky-Spandex’d ass!

Licking, tonguing—suckling gently—my fingers slid on him, loving his cock and balls, while I gazed upward into his face. It shone back down.

My Boy’s knees trembled.

“What’s your name?” I asked the owner of the cock I was mouthing (not unusual!).

“Riccardo ... Ricky...” he stammered.

“Riccardo, nice name!” I said (biting gently at the shaft through the shorts). “How sexy are you, Ricky?”

“I ... I very sexy ... I think...”

“I think, too. That’s why you like to wear sexy little shorts like this, isn’t it? So the girls will look—so they’ll stare at you and see your cock and balls and your honey-of-an-ass?”

“Yes.”

I got hornier ... dirtier...

"Do you like pee games, Ricky? To piss, perhaps on yourself in secret?"

"Sometimes ... sometimes some of the ... lady visitor—the holiday lady—they pay me. Some like me to do that ... they say, 'Pee on me honey, more cash. Please pee on Auntie.'"

"Good, Riccardo," I said, swallowing the golf ball that suddenly formed in my throat. "Good. Because I want you to piss your shorts for me. I've always dreamed of a horny young stud pissing in sexy shorts. Will you do it ... for me?"

I groped his balls, ran my hand under to slide up the crease of that silky ass. The shorts were so tight, they cleaved the crack.

He swallowed.

I stood and kissed him then, feathering my tits on those gorgeously-swollen pecs. He could kiss back, this one! My little kitten could kiss!

"Do it ... for me, Ricky," I mouthed onto his tongue, chewing his lips, licking his chin.

"Piss your sexy shorts for Suzie, please?"

He nodded, groaned into my kiss.

"Mick would like to piss on you too, Ricky. That would make him really hot. Can he?"

"I ... no mind ... some men, they too..."

I sank back to my knees. I gazed up, waiting for him, my hands stroking up his hard thighs, feeling like a mother waiting for her toddler to go in the bathroom...

I also felt guilty ... but only for a moment...

It was hot. Hot and salty. It burst the Spandex, swelling the lovely fabric briefly, before finding its way out. I suckled, licked, rubbed my face on the slidey-hot wetness. More hissed, gurgled, filled the shorts again. It sprayed, burst the thighbands. I pulled my head back and stared at the two shades of yellow. I heard Mick piss on the Spandex-sheathed boy-ass.

Then I realised he wasn't pissing on but INTO the shorts! He'd pulled them half down and had his cock in there, pissing right into Boy-lover's ass-crack ... filling his shorts with his piss...

It spread, soaked around the slim hips towards me, bubbled the shorts around the bulging balls, and poured down his thighs. I slid a hand inside my "g" and fingered myself roughly. This was the stuff that fantasy-frigs are made of...

Mick peeled the shorts inside-out halfway down Boy's thighs and looked around him—to watch me. He knew me, you see. Knew what I'd want to do... I found it—

the glistening, thickly-cloying pre-fuck, clinging to the inside of the shorts. I sucked it, licked it, that wonderful cock-taste now stronger in my mouth. Then I pulled his shorts off. Ricky stepped out of them, cock jack-throbbing with a raging pulsebeat. I watched it, panting, as it jacked until it stood rigid, almost touching his hairless belly.

I slowed the frigging of my clit. I was rushing. Had to force myself to slow down and enjoy more. Mick's right hand came around, grasped the boy's meat at its base, pushing it horizontal—at my mouth. The fingers of Mick's left hand slid around Ricky's torso and stroked, then squeeeezed at a nipple.

"Do your piss in Suzie's mouth, Ricky—she wants you to..."

Mick knew. I DID want him to.

But he couldn't. A dribble squeezed from the slit.

"Suck it then, Suzie-Slut. And me. Let us fuck your mouth."

His own cock pushed under Boy's hairless balls, one cock's head pushing another's ballsac—wonderfully erotic. Two juicing pleasure-poles—both wanting me! Instinctively, my mouth moved towards the heady smell of the two horny cocks. It enveloped me, that smell. I inhaled it greedily, enjoying the intravenous-like shot that the smell of horny cock gives me. The slut's aphrodisiac...

For an eighteen-year-old, "Boy" sure had ManCock! Seven-inches of uncut, browny silky-smoothness, the skin almost closed over a gorgeous, rude head. My hands caressed. I skinned it slowly, lovingly—as if unwrapping a favourite toffee—and found my prize...

Thickly coating. Wonderfully cloying. Mouthwateringly—copiously, glistening. Deliciously-dirtily smelling.

And more oozing...

More pre-fuck slime...

The good slut's prize for when she's worked up her man...

The slut's caviar.

I forced myself not to suck it all up in one go. I glanced upward, finding the staring, unbelieving eyes of my Boy, and the knowing ones of my husband.

The slut performed...

My lips formed an "O." I pressed them to the tip of that gorgeous thing. Backed my head a little. Lips to cock. A lovers' bridge of shiny-thick strands of hanging glisten. They broke, hung from my chin, dripped to my tits, cooling. My lips touched around the pisshole. My head sank slowly forward, lips ploughing up the goo so that it gathered, clinging to my lips. Gorgeous, gorgeous taste. Fantastically horny smell.

I sucked the rest from the head, then looked up—gloating at the feel of the cloying slime around my mouth, knowing how sluttish I looked to them—kneeling there with the slut's lips gloss. Overpoweringly wonderful taste. Overpoweringly erotic smell.

Mick wanted to play.

He pushed my head back, waved Boy's cock in my face, stabbed me with it, slapped my face with it. Right, left, right. Teasing me with cock! Mouth followed, trying to get it like a little puppy teased with a tasty sausage!

He gave it back, holding it as I sucked and washed it with my mouth ... gazing up into the fresh, young face, horny as hell and with a cunt like a raging furnace trying to put itself out. My teats crawled, bursting with desire. A dog-bitch in heat.

Mick was behind Boy. The cock in my mouth lurched forward as he squeezed a finger up Boy's ass—while his other hand continued its abuse of Boy's teats. Cock jerked and I knew a ballsload in the mouth was imminent if that action continued, so I made it last. My head dipped under—nuzzling those gorgeous, hairless balls, sniffing the smell that always hides there on a man. I fondled Boy's cock, wanking Mick's slowly.

Mick's was ready. "Ooooh, geez!" Mick cried and I sucked his, taking the spurting cock's first rope in the mouth, the second on my face, the third on my tits. The rest I spread lovingly onto the cock and balls of my Boy. Then my hands were back on his cock, wanking. My mouth back on his balls, licking. Licking my husband's spunk off another's balls.

I gazed up into Boy's face ... eyes pleading.

"Cum in my mouth," I managed to mumble...

He did.

Keeping still, I let him, looking up, as pulsing doses filled my mouth. When he finished, I opened it to let him see his spunk, clinging, cloying. Connecting teeth, tongue and lips. I put out my tongue, let him see the pool of his stuff lying on it. It slid slowly down my tongue, dropped onto my tits.

I licked up, over his hard, flat belly, flicked around his teats, up his neck ... and on up...

"Like that, Ricky?" I breathed over his lips. "Can you smell your spunk on my breath, Ricky?" He nodded, mouth opening in a greed for his own taste. My sexy little hunk of horniness.

As we kissed, I felt one of Mick's hands between us, fondling Ricky's cock. I sensed that the other would be enjoying his ass.

"Like me kissing ... you, Ricky?" I breathed into our kiss.

"Can you ... taste your spunk now? Is it nice ... tasting your own jizz ... from the mouth of a slut?"

"Mmmmm ... Mmmmm," was all he managed. But it was enough to know he was enjoying...

"I bet you..." I kissed, "sometimes eat your own spunk ... after you've wanked yourself off ... don't you, Ricky? Do you do that? Do you like to taste your own spunk?

"Can you smell ... the cock off my face, Ricky? I can smell it still ... like that, too? The cocksmell on ... a horny girl's face?"

My hand shoved Mick's away and groped those gorgeous balls.

I reached around, held his ass and pressed against him, feeling the hardness of him between us.

"I want you ... to fuck me now, Ricky," I kissed. "I want this hard cock up my cunt ... I want this beautiful young cock ... thrusting up my hot twat-hole, it's yearning for cock—yearning to be fucked by a young stud's cock. Want that, Ricky? Want to fuck the slut while her husband watches?"

Mick pressed against me from behind, bent his head, biting my ear, my neck.

"Go for it, baby," he grunted. "Let him fuck you now."

I knew exactly what Mick wanted. He wanted me to be the "I want-the-shit-fucked-out-of-me" slut. I didn't have to act. I WAS that slut!

Shaking mussed hair, I stood in front of them, gazing at their cocks, licking my lips slowly.

"My turn," I said, snaking my hands upwards to play with the spunk-trails on my tits. I performed, pulling at my tits, squeezing the teats, pulling them outward—thrusting, proud and hard. I bent my head, lifted the right to my mouth and licked, then sucked the teat, licking around to gather stray wisps of precious spunk.

"Like my tits, boys?

"Like my big, juicy, spunked-on tits?

"I want you to maul them with your sweaty hands.

"Kiss them.

"Squeeze them.

"Hurt them.

"Fuck them if you like..."

Hands snaked back down, over my stomach, my index slicked the wet scrap of satin "g" still (unbelievably) shielding my cunt.

"My cunt's hot and juiced for your cocks, hungry for lovely throbbing cock-meat. My panties are soaked—see how wet they are? Watch as I push them down. Now you see my hot n' horny cunt, open and begging ... begging-horny-hungry for a feed of cock."

I straddled, proudly showing it. I slicked my fingers quickly up my cunt and stared at my lovers, licking my own tasties from my fingers. I turned my back, ran my hands over bared ass, wriggled, and bent right over—exposing both holes for them in a stripper-style act. My hair trailed sand as I stared at them through parted legs, licked an index, reached under, pressed the tip against my asshole ... pushed it up my asshole...

"Oooooh, I love being fucked up the asshole too..."

They advanced. I flipped back up and turned to face them. Boy's shaking hands went straight for my tits, and I stood and let him maul them, staring into his face, enjoying the feel of those feverish, sweaty young hands. I reached between us with both hands—grasped wet cock, fondled hot balls. I straddled my legs—for Mick was behind me now, pressing his hard between my thighs from the rear, poking up, searching for my dripping hole.

Mick slid into me easily. I gasped. Wanked cock, my body jerking with each powerful thrust up my cunt from the rear. I looked down, pleased to see Boy's fingers "V'd" on my fleshy cuntlips, squeezing Mick's cock as it fucked me. And ... bliss ... his thumb jerked at clitty.

The he stepped back and watched me get fucked, his hard wavering from side to side. Then he reached and felt my tits again as he watched the quivering, sex-crazed slut cum off in front of his eyes.

He wanked slowly as he watched, and that really did it for me—watching him getting off on me getting fucked. A stranger getting off on watching Mick's cock screw hell out of my cunt.

Orgasm roared. I groped between my thighs to feel the plunging cock.

Boy watched the slut get fucked, and cum...

Mouth gaping...

Eyes rolling...

Body quivering...

Tits heaving.

My knees buckled, yet I wriggled back, urging Mick to cum, but it wasn't to be. Because Mick wanted more...

"Sit on him, Suzie. Sit on the kid and fuck yourself on that cock. While I fuck your mouth."

Boy heard and moved quickly. He lay down on a towel, cock rearing proudly from hairless crotch. I straddled, split cuntie with my fingers and lowered onto the throbbing meat.

Finding instead—a hungry mouth!

He'd moved! Where his cock had stood, proud and hard, his mouth now waited. A cool mouth, cool on a hot, frothy, fresh-fucked cunt. The sound of him slurping my core! The FEEL of that tongue-fuck! I groaned and mopped his face with my burning bush, then used the hard bits—his nose, chin and forehead—to jerk off on, all the time sliming his face with the hot spew from my horny cunt.

"Like ... that ... Ricky boy?" I groaned, jockeying on his mouth, delighting in the "sickysicky" sounds of juicy cunt on wet mouth.

"Oooh! Ricky BOY! It's .... gorgeous using your mouth like this ... fucking sooo lovely to see your face down there, under my horny twat. Oooh ... do you like ... that? I love to do that to you. This, and this ... and to see you enjoying the feel of my slimy cunt on your face..."

Then ... "You ... fucking ... little ... dreamboat," I gasped as he pushed me up slightly and slid a little further under, his tongue delving, flicking in my asscrack. If he wanted asshole—he could have it...

I settled it on his mouth, loving that probing tongue...

"Oooooh Ricky ... tongue my asshole, YES! Yesss! YESSS! More ... like that, deeper, go deeper. Now the crease, up, down, up, down ... Ooooh that's good! You must like the taste of my ass."

Boy stiffened, and before I looked over my shoulder I knew what I'd find ... Mick, suckling the boys balls, then his cock. And Mick's fingers were groping my ass ... no, reaching, reaching now—my cunt! Poking his HotBitch even while she was getting her asshole sucked!

Oh, wonderful depravity—glorious perversion!

I jockeyed Boy's face and husband's fingers ... and came...

Mouth gaping in silent scream, tits bouncing, fingers screwing my teats off, I came in a frenzied, jerkoff cum, falling forward onto my hands, almost crushing Boy's head with my belly.

I'll never forget that horny fuck.

Neither will "Uncle," his two friends plus camera, who were then summoned down to our little beachparty! Three more cocks!

Uncle was oldest—about fifty and balding, wearing loose khaki shorts. His two friends were younger, also in shorts. The shorts wern't tight, but they showed the tents—they showed that there were three more cocks needing me.

Mick pulled me back, and I finally did sit on Boy's cock, felt it prod the depths of my cunt. Our pubes meshed as I shuttled back and forth on him. I grabbed his hands, pressed them urgently to my tits and gazed down into his face ... excited even more knowing that I was now on close-up camera...

"Mmm ... I'm fucking myself with your big Dick, Ricky. Pinch my tits—make them hurt—I like men to hurt my tits. Ooohhh! Can you feel the hot flushes from my cunt on your cock? Mmmmm, yes pinch my teats, harder ... harder..."

The smell of heated cock and cunt rising from our sweating bodies hornied me even more. His hips jerked three times under my weight, bouncing me up and down. I felt him spunk me with hard shoots. Deep spurts of man-cum in my horny cunt.

Lifting off, I "doggied" for Mick, and while he fucked me, reaming my asshole with his thumb, I licked our mess from Boy's cock, my eyes staring into the shaking camera. Mick thrust, grunted and spunked. I lay back on the towel, hands splitting my cunt, pulling it wide—the camera bored in...

I jerked my hips up and down, thrusting three bunched fingers into my hot n' horny, feeling the mess, the slime—performing for the men and for the camera. I licked the mess, smeared it over my tits and face.

Then Mick stood astride me, hands on hips, cock hanging, swaying, dripping.

I stared at him, knowing.

Knowing and wanting what HE wanted.

"Fucking do it, Mick! Piss on your slut and see how she writhes!

"Please, Lover? Do it ... fucking piss on the horny tart!"

He did.

My deliciously-dirty-perverted lover did it for me.

And the camera.

Hosing, spraying, raining ... I writhed under a cascade of LoverPiss, losing all sense of time and place, or people. I wallowed in depravity, stabbed myself with bunched fingers. Writhed and screamed as another wonderful orgasm ripped.

Then I flipped on my knees, shuffled to "Uncle" and slid his shorts down.

Not for the camera—for me.

I wanted—needed more cock—fresh cock.

Needed more fucking. Needed to be FILLED with cock.

I got it.

After sucking away the slickness of their previous horniness from the inside of their shorts.

After sucking the three men off to mouth-cloying completion. With Mick playing cameraman, I doggied for the three. And at first they fucked me LIKE dogs—grunting, thrusting, dirty dogs, using cunt, ass, mouth, tits. Then gave me their cocks to suck again, and pissed on me too.

"Uncle," cock embedded in my asshole, creamed, then pissed uncontrollably, uninvited, until my belly swelled—muttering incoherent obscenities in Turkish as he filled me.

It was a fucking I can't forget, for we still have a copy of that tape and there was more—lots more. When they had nothing more to give, just the three of us ran down to the sea. In the water, my hands were all over my men, theirs all over me. The sight of Boy's horny young body—and, of course, his tired cock and balls jiggling in the soaked-to-almost-see-through yellow Spandex workouts ... the feel of them through the shorts ... is another vivid memory.

# Wound

## GashGirl

This wound.
A bleeding gash which never heals.
My torment is inscribed on my corrupt flesh.

This heart-shaped wound.
Inflicted, infected, corrupted by those who went before me.
(that monstrous lineage)

My wound.
She's so pretty in psychotic pink.

I love and despise my wound.
Stitch me. Bandage me. Suture me.

You will be my cure. My net will capture your sex.

I will wound you.
Drink your milky code.
Destroy my pain for a few sweet moments.

My curse is the curse of the fathers.
My wound is the wound of the mothers.

Play host to my disgusting virus.
My sharpened teeth crave your points of contact.

This will be the ultimate fuck.

I am the Mistress of Detestable Pleasure.
Bearer of the profane wound.

I offer you my neck.

Bite me.

# Grizzly
## Montrose

Mike was a brutal guy, so I can't say I pity him or think he didn't deserve it. When I think about it, he kinda had it coming. You see, Mike and I live in a small town where you hang out with someone just because they're around. I could call him my best friend, but that seems like misusing the term.

Normally, we hang out in bars, getting drunk until some girl hits on Mike. He's very big, very strong, very aggressive, and girls just seem unable to stop themselves. Every girl within driving range knows Mike is an asshole who'll just fuck 'em a few times and dump 'em. But so many keep lining up for the ride.

Sometimes I get his cast-offs. I'm just five-foot-nine and 145 pounds. Most of the women who hit on Mike are my size or bigger. Sometimes they want me to tell Mike how good they are. Those are the ones who suck me till I blow my wad on their faces. Others are just so sexually frustrated from being rejected by this Greek god that they grab me because I'm handy, drag me off, pin me, and take their pleasure on my face. To be honest, I enjoy both scenarios.

When he's not brutalizing a woman with hard sex (I've heard a lot of stories about stretched out orifices and bruised butts), he's brutalizing the men in town by mashing their heads into the sidewalk outside one bar or another. Some guy will catch his wife or girlfriend paying for Mike's drinks, and Mike spends the next hour feeling up the girl and hospitalizing her significant other.

Anyway, one Saturday he tells me we're going to a concert. He could have taken any woman in town, but he hates spending money on a lady. He says it gives them ideas about ownership or something. With Mike a good date is a bar pick-up, a fight with her man, and a dumpster-side ass-fuck by midnight.

We got to the concert (some heavy metal band Mike likes—real loud and real crowded), and we had great seats. Who did he hose to get these, I wondered. I looked around. Lots of leather, chains, and pierced young bodies. People were pushing and mashing into each other, elbowing for space.

Then I saw this tall, broad-shouldered woman walking our way, wearing a wild mound of brown hair and a tight, soft, black leather vest. She was easily backhanding men into their seats as she tramped on their feet with her huge work boots, making her way to her seat next to Mike. She stood as tall as Mike but must have had fifty to seventy pounds on him. She was wide, but I don't mean to say that she was fat. She was built like a construction worker, only with massive tits and a wide round ass that pushed Mike into me as she planted her feet in front of her chair.

Mike got mad (like I knew he would) and drove his shoulder into her biceps. I expected her to go flying, knocking over four or five people on the way, but she only jiggled a bit on impact. She gave Mike an amused glance and turned back to the stage. The music had started. The sudden shock of noise was overpowering.

Mike gritted his teeth and drove his fist deep into the big woman's Italian belly. I've seen that fist cause blood to flow from a victim's nose with one such blow. This girl just grabbed Mike's wrist and twisted it. He dropped to his knees to keep his arm from coming off. As he looked up at her, his expression was as puzzled as mine.

Besides the tight leather vest that strained to contain her breasts, she wore ass crack-riding jean cut offs, short white socks, and those huge work boots. Her left tit had a big tattoo of a standing grizzly bear coming up from her cleavage.

She crushed his skull between her knee and the chair in front of them, then slammed his head face-up onto his chair. She sat down on top of it, adjusting his nose so it fit up her ass crack. His body twitched and squirmed between her muscular legs. Her hips bent the arms of the chair out, and her elbow overflowed into my lap. I sat mortified amid the noise and violence, unable to control the raging boner that was throbbing into this Amazon's forearm. She patted my thigh in time to the beat.

She pointed to Mike, who still struggled valiantly under her ass, leaned down to my ear and shouted, "Is this piece of shit your friend?"

I didn't want to get into a discussion about semantics, so I nodded yes.

"Did he drive you here?"

I nodded again.

"Well, he just volunteered to be the evening's amusement for my friend and me. You're welcome to stay and be a part of it, or you can take his car home. He ain't goin' home for a long time, if ever." I looked past her. There sat a gorgeous young blonde, three inches taller than me but not much heavier—a long, thin girl. My heart was already pounding over the Amazon, and now this.

"Everyone calls me Grizzly," said the Amazon. "This is Wendy."

Wendy leaned forward, laying across Grizzly's chest and offered me her hand. I put mine in it, and she grabbed hard and pumped it up and down. "Stick around! It'll be fun!" she shouted over to me.

I nodded again.

Grizzly smiled and put her big arms over both of our shoulders. She mashed me into her side as she rocked to the music. I had to crane my neck to keep from being suffocated in her bosom. I kept thinking her chair would give out any second. I watched Mike. By the third song, he stopped moving. By the end of the show, I thought he was dead.

When Grizzly got up, Mike noisily gulped for air. She grabbed him by the front of his jacket, held him in front of her like a shield, and marched into the crowd. Wendy grabbed me in much the same way and said in my ear, "Follow her, and stay close."

With Wendy pushing me, I ran to keep up with Grizzly. She plowed a path to the gate, and Mike took the brunt of the blows as she used him to clear the way. When we got to the parking lot, she bee-lined to a huge camper. Wendy unlocked it, and Grizzly threw Mike in.

Wendy pushed me against the camper as Grizzly pulled a few beers from the fridge inside and passed them around. "This one ain't bad, Grizzly," said the young blonde. "Can I have him?"

"He can do what he wants," said Grizzly. She drained her beer. "I'm just gonna get started greasing up the other one. You comin' in?"

"In a minute," said Wendy.

Wendy leaned her long, hard body against me, looked into my eyes, and smiled down at me like a mischievous child. Her red tube top and matching mini divided her lithe form into red and white stripes, like a flag. She slid her crotch back and forth over my throbbing cock. I could feel her lips over my shaft through her skirt and my pants. The hard nipples on her perky little breasts dug pits into my collarbone. She said, "You look like you have a strong tongue."

"What?"

"Do you like to wrestle?" she asked.

"I...I'm not...that is...."

"I'll be nineteen in May, but I bet I can beat you up. I bet you'd like to be beat up by a nineteen-year-old girl.... How old are you?"

"Thirty-six. Excuse me...what did she mean, grease him up?" My mind was racing—way too many unanswered questions. And should I try to make a break for it? No. Mike's keys were in his pocket. Besides, wrestle this girl? Yes, I'd like that.

She pressed her full, candy-flavored lips against mine, and my heart leapt out of my chest. "Lets go inside," she murmured. "I'll explain everything." She walked in ahead of me, rocking her round, little fanny in my face. I couldn't help but follow.

When I got inside, Mike was stripped naked and on his feet. Grizzly handed him a tumbler of water and dabbed the blood from a cut over his right eye, suffered during the exit from the concert. "Giving this one a chance, Grizzly?" asked Wendy.

"Ya. I'm hoping he can put up a fight. That was a good punch he threw back there." Mike looked up. I could see the old cockiness return to his eyes. He gulped the water.

"Don't tease the man. Just grease him and fuck him. My friend wants to know what that means," said Wendy. She took my arm and led me to a bench where she gave me another beer.

Grizzly smiled. "It means this." She pulled a huge strap-on dildo and a can of shortening out of a drawer and slammed them onto a table. "If he can't fight his way out of it, I'm gonna stuff that thing up his hole for as long as I can keep going."

Things started happening pretty fast after that. Mike hit Grizzly in the head with the water glass, shattering it. "I'm gonna kill you, bitch!" he yelled.

Wendy laughed.

Mike pushed Grizzly against the far wall of the camper. The entire thing almost tipped over with the impact.

He had a clean shot at the door for a second. But that wasn't Mike's way. He yelled a string of obscenities and insults, charged Grizzly, and pounded her belly like a body bag. He got in a dozen blows before Grizzly casually returned one to his chin.

He fell back on his heels. Grizzly grinned at him with her hands down at her sides, inviting another attack.

"You fucking hole!" Mike nailed her with a left, right, left that snapped her head back and forth. She fell backwards against the wall. He kept working her body and face. Grizzly stepped forward into the assault, only able to block a third of the blows. Mike was smaller than her but much quicker.

He rammed his fist twice into her ribs. When she pulled her guard down, he jabbed her in the face. She blocked his next blow and slapped him to the ground with an open hand, then kicked him hard in the side. As he gasped for air, she opened another beer and drained it. Mike got up and worked her belly as she crushed the can. She dropped her forearms onto his back, mashing him to the floor again. She stepped back and let him stand. He backed her into the wall again with a right and a left to the face. When she raised her guard, he drove his shoulder into her gut over and over.

They kept it up for half an hour. Mike's naked body was dripping with sweat and was beet-red from exhaustion. Grizzly was on her heels a lot but enjoying an aerobic workout.

Mike looked worried. He'd never had to hit anyone that many times. Wendy threw one leg up across my lap and hugged me tight, obviously excited by the violence. Her hot box pinned my arm to my side. I could feel her panties moisten on the back of my wrist.

Mike's fist shot forward, this time into Grizzly's exposed ribs, but I could see he was losing steam. Sweat covered his swollen eyes.

Grizzly wrapped her thick arms around Mike, crushing him to her ample chest. Immediately, the air blasted from his body and his head turned a frightening crimson. She chuckled and bounced him in her arms, tightening her grip, constricting him. I heard a blood-chilling crunch.

Wendy pressed her lips to my ear. A thrill ran up my spine. "She's breaking his ribs now. Your friend may have been a big, tough man, but when she's done, even you will be able to beat him up. Isn't she magnificent?"

I couldn't deny it. "She is amazing," I said with way too much admiration in my voice.

"You're almost making me jealous, little man!" Wendy said into my ear. "But I don't blame you. Grizzly is hot." She started grinding her cunt into my arm as she watched her friend destroy mine.

I rubbed my cock on the back of her knee, which rested on my lap. The entire scene was more than I could stand. I had to come, or explode. Wendy picked up her leg and crushed her thick high heel into my shaft, narrowly missing my balls. I looked down. Her wet cotton panties glistened at me. She left her heel there and ground it back and forth. "You just sit still and look pretty, little man. I'm watchin' Grizzly!" Her long fingers were around my windpipe and I couldn't breath. Tears sprang to my eyes. "Are you gonna behave?"

I nodded.

She relaxed her grip, dropped her leg back onto my lap, and returned to watching the show, humping my arm once more. I sat as still as possible and watched, too. When Mike's face turned blue, Grizzly dropped him to the floor. He landed like a pile of rags. She planted a work boot on his naked ass and pinned him to the floor as she unbuttoned and removed her vest. Her breasts were perfectly round, high-riding orbs, each bigger than my head. They rocked back and forth under her broad, muscular shoulders. Her belly was plump, but looked small under her breasts. Her powerful hips rolled out in perfect spheres.

I felt Wendy heat up next to me. Her breathing grew faster and came in starts as she wiggled her quim up and down my arm. She humped me using only pelvic thrusts—she didn't lurch up and down—definitely built for speed.

When Grizzly reached for the buckle on her tight cutoffs, Wendy leapt to her feet, dumping me onto the floor. "Oh! Let me!" she squealed.

Wendy knelt on Mike's back and gently unzipped and pulled down Grizzly's shorts and black leather panties, exposing a wild tangle of wet pubic hair. She ran her tongue up the Amazon's moist thigh and into the dense tangle. Grizzly arched her back and ran her hands through Wendy's hair, enjoying the rim job. But soon she pushed Wendy back. "I got work to do, sweetcakes. Go play with your friend."

Grizzly and Wendy stepped off of Mike. He gasped for air and eventually staggered to his hands and knees. Grizzly slipped her hands under his armpits and hoisted him to his feet facing Wendy. He took a couple of clumsy swings at the girl's blonde head. She easily ducked out of his way, then popped him in the ribs with her little fist. He groaned and fell to his knees! Must've hit a broken rib.

"He's almost ready, Grizzly. Can I finish him off for you?" asked Wendy.

"Ya. It'll give me a minute to get ready."

Wendy let Mike stand again. He swung at her, missing miserably. She teased him, slapping his face and ducking his wild blows. She slipped under his arms, pressed her slim body up against his massive chest, and crushed her knee into his balls. He dropped to his knees before her. She stuffed his head between her thin thighs and fell backwards on it, driving his face into the floor. She clamped her legs tight and dug the toes of her shoes into his scrotum.

"Please stop!" begged Mike in a squeaky voice from under the young girl's ass. He was crying now—humiliated and defeated. "You're killing me! Your feet! Move your feet!" He tried to grab her legs but she snatched his wrists with her long slender hands and controlled his arms, pinning them behind his back. He was absolutely spent from punching Grizzly. Even this girl could take him. She tightened her legs even more. Mike choked and sputtered. "I can't breathe! I'm begging you...." he gasped.

I couldn't believe it. I've heard people beg Mike for mercy every week for as long as I can remember. Now this girl, forty pounds lighter than him, was forcing him to grovel without breaking a sweat. She ignored his begging and whining. Soon he passed out.

Wendy stood up and kicked him over onto his back. "He's ready, Grizzly."

"So am I," said Grizzly, now sporting the strap-on dildo.

Wendy looked down. "Hey, Grizzly! I think he may be as hung as you!"

"Let's see." said the big woman. She flipped a table down from the wall, picked up Mike like a rag doll, and slammed him down on it. She slid her cock up next to his, which strangely was in full stiffy mode. Hers was half a cock head longer and nearly twice as thick. "Closer than most," she said admiringly. "I think we got a lady killer on our hands."

She slipped her hand into the can of shortening and filled Mike's butt crack with the goo. He gasped, coughed, then jerked to full awareness. With Wendy holding his arms and Grizzly pushing his legs apart, he struggled feebly. Grizzly positioned the shaft and crammed it up Mike's ass. He arched his back and screamed like a woman.

Grizzly became lost in her work, humping away at the captive man below her. She bent his legs up until his knees touched his ears and hammered on him. Wendy stuffed a tennis ball in his mouth and bound it into place with duct tape to stifle the screams, then she turned her attention to me.

"We have another cock in the drawer, little man. I think I'll use it on you."

I sprang for the door. She tripped me up and sat on my back. She was too light to hold me down, so I struggled to my feet. I punched her rippled belly with all my might, but my fist glanced to the side. She backhanded my face so hard I staggered back several steps. I dropped my shoulder and plowed into her, knocking her to the wall. I tried for the door and freedom again.

She jumped behind me and put me in a full nelson, raising me off the floor. Dropping me onto the bench, she stuffed her knee into the small of my back, then pinned my arms behind me. I kept begging, "No. Please, no," as she pulled my pants down.

Grizzly looked up from her humping long enough to say, "I told him he could leave if he wanted, Wendy. Don't force him to stay if he don't want to."

"Damn," spat Wendy from on top of me. She stood and sat me up with my pants around my ankles. I could see her shift tactics. She became soft and inviting.

She slid her warm body up my thighs, stomach, chest, and face like a snake, stopping with her meaty, panty-clad muff resting on my upper lip. She wet her fingers on her clit and played with my ears. My cock throbbed for her as she rubbed her quim over my lips. She spoke in a girlish, innocent voice, "You wanna stay an' play, doncha little man?"

"Yes!" I barked into her box. "Yes!" I grabbed her ass and slid my tongue past her panties to her tight little slit. Her button was soaking and hot. She shouted when my tongue slid around it. Years of women riding my face were paying off. I took that girl to the stars. She fell off my face, onto the floor. I followed. She rolled on top, flipped around, and slid my shaft clear down her throat in one stroke. We humped each other's faces as Grizzly continued to hump Mike.

After making Wendy come hard, I looked up at Mike. I could hear the slap, slap, slap of Grizzly's belly mashing into Mike's balls with every thrust. He was only emitting gasps now. His eyes were glazed over. I grew harder in Wendy's throat.

I don't know how much time had passed. Wendy had drenched my face in come, meanwhile keeping me from coming even once. She knew just how to take me down at the critical moment, and she did it to me over and over. My sac was huge and ready to burst.

I was gritting my teeth when she whispered, "If you beg me to take yer ass, I'll let you come." She had that childish grin again.

I know it seems insane now, but at that moment it seemed like a small price to pay. I assumed the police search position and begged, "Please fuck my ass. I'm begging you! I'll do anything if you'll just fuck my ass."

She casually pulled out another huge strap-on and handed it to me. "Tie me in," she said. I dropped to my knees and slipped it on her slender hips. "Spread 'em." I assumed the position again. "Butter yer ass." I dipped my hand into the goo and filled my own ass crack.

"I don't know," she said. "Maybe I won't."

"Please!" I begged. "Take me! I have money!"

"Well, since you said please...." She sank her meat into me. I cried out. She grabbed my hair and started working in earnest. My asshole felt like it would break under her pounding. Her hot breath puffed into my ear, and her drool slithered down my back.

She slid her long fingers around and touched my rod. She grabbed it and jerked me off—five quick strokes along her smooth wet palm. I blasted my load against the wall. She slid her hand down my shaft again, and again I unloaded like she had her finger on a trigger. She owned and controlled every aspect of my body like I never was able to.

She rested with her cock fully inserted. "Do you want to come on me?" she asked invitingly. My cock was still hard and ready.

"God, yes," I growled.

"Too fucking bad," she whispered. She made me come against the wall again, emptying my sac, then continued her anal assault. "You pathetic worm!" she puffed.

Her huffing and puffing as she rammed my ass matched the puffs of wind leaving Mike's nose thrust for thrust. We were being bunghole-banged in unison. As Grizzly pounded Mike, so Wendy crammed into me. The beating on my ass was overwhelming, numbing my legs.

I fell to my knees. She clamped her long legs around me and kept the shaft driven home as she rode me around the camper like a pony. I finally fell flat to the floor.

She slowly slid her cock in and out of my hole. "If you promise to suck my cock, I'll dismount," she said in her innocent voice.

I took a few more thrusts, then admitted the obvious. "Anything you say. I'll do anything you say."

She slid out and stood over me. "Put these on," she said, dropping her wet panties onto my dick. I slid into the soft material. My sac and rod overflowed the scant fabric.

"Get me a beer." I got her a beer. She refused to take it. I opened it and offered it again. She snatched it from my hand.

She sat on the bench and beckoned me to crawl between her legs. With one hand she guided my head over the tip of her shaft and pushed it into my mouth. It was thick, greasy, and smelly, but she made it fit.

My lips stretched wide. My jaw unhinged. She drained her beer and tossed it aside. Grabbing my ears, she forced her rod deep into my face. She went slow, letting me overcome the gag reflex. Eventually my nose pressed her hard belly, and her shaft filled my throat. After loosening me up with a few gentle strokes, she got busy with her crotch thrusts again. She hammered my face, almost breaking my nose on her pelvic bone.

When she pulled out, she wiped her shaft on my shirt, then unstrapped it. She pulled my face back to her groin and forced me to rim her holes with my tongue and nose.

After coming once more, she stood over me and pissed down my throat. My humiliation was complete. I looked over at Mike. His eyes were rolled back in his head. Grizzly continued to ram his ass, but she was drenched in sweat, enjoying a major workout. Her body pressed down on him with every thrust. The bear on her tit repeatedly clawed at Mike's face as she fell onto him.

Wendy grabbed my neck and threw me out with only my dirty shirt, her wet panties, and Mike's car keys.

That was the last I ever saw of any of them, including Mike. The police never even followed up with a missing persons report. The men of the town were quite happy never to see him again.

# Threesomes

## Matthew von der Ahe

I've had a few experiences with threesomes, and they were a mixed bag. I will report a half-dozen or so threesomes I had the (mostly) pleasure to share, and I will do a post-game analysis of them, and we will see what gems come to the surface.

**A: "To Rut or to Pay the Rent?"**

I was 21 or 22, and my new wife "Alice" (or maybe we were just about to get married—not sure) and I were living in a loud, dirty, cold, roach-filled apartment in Soho, attending NYU and Columbia, respectively. We were massively broke, but we "embezzled" our next month's rent money from our own bank account, hopped on the Amtrak to Boston, and rented a room in the Ritz Carlton (!!) on Arlington Street.

Our plan was to meet with "Mary," a friend of Alice, after her shift as a stripper in a club. We arrived about midnight, in time to catch her last dance, then we waited while she went backstage to dress. She came out, and we taxied to the hotel.

It has been almost twenty years, so I can't remember how we started exactly, but Alice and I made it clear that our intent was to get seriously into Mary's pants. I know we didn't talk directly about our plans or hopes or desires—you know, we were twenty, ferchrissakes, we just stripped and hopped into the Ritz's smooth sheets. It went well—I remember giving Mary head while Alice watched; and I remember watching Mary and Alice making out while Alice fingered Mary's cunt; and I remember Mary watching while I fucked Alice hard from behind. Mary applauded that last when we were done—"Oh, you guys, that was GREAT to watch!"

Then we slept in this humongous Ritz bed, and in the morning called Room Service and ordered the most decadent things we could think of—bacon, and strawberries and cream, and some hash browns, I think. No oat bran cereal, you know. The waiter came in, and there the three of us were, the sheets pulled up to our sternums, but our nudity obvious, and he just delivered the food and kept his eyes averted. We laughed and ate. The next month, Alice's and my rent check bounced.

Nonetheless, I would put it on the "Successful" side of the balance sheet of my threesomes. Here were the ingredients for success for this one:

1. Be young and stupid.

2. Don't drink much.

3. Have at least one participant who is somewhat sexually sophisticated. (Alice had worked as a prostitute for two years, and Mary was a stripper.)

4. Don't think much. In this case, our hormones were able to surf us over any sticky issues. See #1 above.

5. Don't try for the two-on-one thing, or try to have triplicate simultaneous orgasms, or have everyone's mouth simultaneously full of someone's genitals. We just kinda did a rotating intimate exhibition.

I don't think for a second that these are the definitive rules for a successful threesome; they are merely the post-game analysis for this ONE, SINGLE incident.

**B. "The OP Incidents: Are you my best friend, or are you fucking my wife, or both?"**

I went to high school with this guy (let's call him "Harrison"), and we were best friends. He came to visit Alice and me in our roach hotel in Soho about five years after high school graduation. We went out this one night and ate sushi and drank sake and sang Springsteen songs walking down the streets. We came back to the apartment, all got into Alice's and my double bed—Harrison against the wall, Alice in the middle, and me on the edge—and laughed and talked and finally fell asleep.

In the morning, Harrison went off on his glamorous way. Alice told me that while we were laughing and talking and being like old friends last night, Harrison was discreetly fucking her from behind (she was on her side facing me, and Harrison was on HIS side facing me, and I was flattered that they were seemingly paying me so much attention and laughing at my jokes. Hmph.)

Lessons:

1. You must tell all three parties you are having a threesome! Otherwise, it is not a threesome, it's a... a... a something else.

2. Laughing and talking and old friends are the way to have fun in bed, as long as you take care of the rest of the stuff.

P.S. Later, when I was out of town, Harrison came back to New York and spent many hours, apparently, in the same bed with the same Alice. About that he composed a country–western song, the chorus of which went like this:

"I buttfucked your wife while you were snorkelin'"

He was and is a very funny man and a talented entertainer—you've probably seen him in several movies—but he was not my best friend anymore.

### C. "The Infatuation of Itzak from Maine: I WILL do this, but only because SHE wants me to"

I attended this powerful, week-long, EST-associated retreat somewhere in the Catskills. There I met Itzak, a wealthy gay playboy, who developed the hots for me. I was intrigued, having never voluntarily had sex with a male up to that point in my life, and we had a great time flirting. He lived in a loft near our apartment, and we socialized when we returned to New York.

One night we invited him back to our apartment to fuck. I was only lukewarm about it, but Alice got that melty-I-am-about-to-come face just THINKING about Itzak and me having sex, so I acquiesced. Itzak buggered me, which I didn't dislike, but which wasn't great, and I fucked his face, which he liked, but again I was kinda ho-hum about. Alice, meanwhile, was being physically ignored—I was distracted and frankly not in the mood, and Itzak had no interest in her—but she was probably the most sexually satisfied of the three of us.

Lessons:

1. All three parties must be enthusiastic about the plan.

2. Again, it isn't necessary for all three parties to share a simultaneous, linked lick or stroke or anything. The exhibitionism/voyeurism (E/V—that ought to be a new alterna-sex letter pair, like B/D and S/M) was very thrilling and sufficient.

P.S.: Itzak to this day talks about how POTENTIALLY hot that night was, and not that hot in reality. It still serves as wonderful fantasy fodder for me, as well.

### D: "A Nanny in Wyoming: Heart-warming tales from the wild West"

We moved from Soho to Denver via San Francisco and Berkeley. We hatched two children (home-born, breast-fed, home-schooled, family-bedded, etc.). Summers, we vacationed at this semi-functional ranch in southern Wyoming. Our nanny one summer was "Bernadette," an open-minded, lively youngster (she was probably 22 to our 28 or so) whom Alice met while canvassing for the Denver Rape Crisis Center. We all flirted madly, and became more verbally and physically comfortable with each other (Bernadette wrote to her friend back home, "This is getting interesting. We are walking naked from and to the shower in front of each other, and we have only been here a week.")

Finally, one hot night in Laramie, Alice gave the go-ahead, and I pounced on Bernadette and inexpertly gave her head while Alice watched. I enthusiastically fucked Alice mish-style while B suckled Alice's nipples, though Bernadette was not spontaneously touching Alice, rather only at my urging. Bernadette and I couldn't get enough of each other, though, and Alice finally sent us out of the room that night, and in fact had us drive the other car out to the ranch the next day, with the understanding that we would stop frequently on our way and shag shamelessly and then, when we arrived, describe to her what we did.

At the ranch, one afternoon when the kids were both napping in the hammock, Alice winked, and jerked her head towards the cabin. Bernadette and I tiptoed up the stairs, across the porch, into the back bedroom. When Alice walked in a few minutes later, Bernadette had her jumper up around her armpits, panties on the floor, and was on her elbows and knees on the bed, knees shoulder-width apart. I was standing behind her thrusting hard, a hand on each of her buns. "Phew!" said Alice admiringly, "I've never seen this from here. What a great view!"

"Describe it for me," panted Bernadette, so Alice did.

Alice eventually got jealous and angry because I was more attentive to the nanny than the mommy, and the summer fell apart ugly.

Lessons:

1. Again, simultaneous sloppy wet stuff is not necessary to make it satisfying for all three.

2. Enthusiasm for each act, not just tolerance, is essential.

3. Unresolved anger and other issues in a relationship can—probably will—centrifuge out of control and blow the whole thing up. Great sex with someone else doesn't make the hard stuff go away. Instead, it can make it so the hard stuff can be used as a club to flog each other with.

### E: "Serving it Hot: A waiter has the gravy spilled on HIM"

Ever since the Itzak incident, I had wanted to have intentional, conscious sex with a man again, but was nervous about it. Alice had a friend, "Bob," whom she had gone to grade school with and who now was a waiter in a wonderfully garlicky-smelling restaurant in Seattle. (Joke: Q-How many straight waiters in Seattle does it take to install a light bulb? A-Both of them.) Bob was funny and smart and cute and safe—all in the family, almost.

Alice approached him with the general invitation, and he cheerfully accepted. He came over, we all three had a glass of wine. Bob and I showered (separately). In the bedroom, Alice lit candles and put on a quiet Miles Davis CD. Bob and I lay down beside each other, started stroking each other's legs and bellies, then cocks. "Do you need anything?" Alice asked. "Lube," we said simultaneously. We mutually masturbated each other, I fellated him, then I straddled his chest and came onto his nipples while Alice just looked on. All parties reported complete satisfaction.

Lessons:

1. Close, trusted friends make the whole thing a lot funner and easier.

2. Be clear up front about the bed-plan: if not blow by blow, then at least in outline, so an unexpected change of direction doesn't leave you limp and/or dry.

## F: "I'll Do Anything to Keep You, Even Fuck Your Girlfriend"

Alice realized that she was a lesbian and moved out. Alice's girlfriend was named "Dana." She had also been a nanny of ours a couple of years before. Though she was gay, she and I had flirted hard, but she had seduced/been seduced by Alice.

One night Alice and Dana met me at a bar, and we went back to Dana's house. We had wonderful sex—Dana hadn't had sex with a man in years, and loved the almost-forgotten sensations. Watching Dana and Alice was both bitter and hot for me. Sex with Alice was, as always, very, very sexy, comfortable.

I gave Dana head while she and Alice sucked one another's tongues, and Dana came shouting into Alice's mouth. Dana groaned loudly with each thrust when I mounted her doggy style; Alice was content to watch and stoke herself.

Dana lay on her back, her head hanging off the edge of the bed, Alice straddled her face and lowered her labia and clit down to within range of Dana's tongue, and I sucked and licked Dana's labia and clit.

After recovering a bit, we pulled the covers back up onto the bed, lined up parallel with Dana in the middle, and nodded off.

Lessons:

1. Again, friends.

2. Don't try to win your wife back by fucking her girlfriend. Doesn't work.

3. Talk talk talk. Flirt flirt flirt.

4. Watching two lovers make it right in front of you is hot hot hot.

# Poems

J. J. Campbell

### while masturbating today

after years of fantasizing
about shooting my load
on some hot woman's face
watching her lick her lips
her cheeks glistening
sperm dripping off her chin
like spring water
coming down a mountain

it figures
the first face
i would
shoot it on
would be my own

### good intentions

i thought about
piercing my tongue
for my girlfriend
to help better please her
but then she dumped me
so i quickly tossed
that thought aside
knowing damn well
i'm not nearly flexible enough
to please myself

## the last motherfucker on the planet

i'm not the type of guy
ladies would brag to their
girlfriends about after we fuck
i'm too hairy
and don't look good
enough for them
and they surely won't tell them
how i like to suck on nipples
and eat pussy for days

i'm the type of guy
that a lady would see
and say to their girlfriends
"not if he was the
last motherfucker on the planet!"

and i'm sure that day will come
when i am the last
motherfucker on the planet
with all these ladies
scouring the planet for a vibrator
and when none is found
i'm sure most of them will pass
and some
will swallow their pride
(among other things)
and fuck a poet

until then
i'll just keep being
this ugly fucker
that can't turn a head
but sure can satisfy

## the end of a losing streak

my italian beauty stands before me
with her luscious blue eyes
slowly taking off her summer dress
shaking her ass for me
licking her lips
running her hands down her body
teasing me
by slowly taking off her
bra and panties
then she straddles me
and kisses my ear
whispering how she wants
to fuck me like
no one has fucked me before

and it's moments like these
where i can't help but think
god must have took the day off
or was kind enough
to let me win one for a change

## just a thought

a friend asked me once
if it felt like i was
cheating on myself
when i used my left hand
to masturbate with

i told him no

to me
it always feels
like a threesome

## envy

sitting in my easy chair
naked
listening to mozart
stroking my penis
out of the corner of my eye
i see my cat
licking her ass

i get out of my chair
turn off the music
put my clothes back on

envy
has ruined
my good time

## on my porch

i like to sit on my porch
with a beer and a cigar
and watch the young
girls walk by

with their hot short skirts
and long tan legs
tight shirts meant to accentuate
still forming breasts
their hair is always glowing
and they have that special wiggle in their ass

they never turn to look at me
becoming aroused
licking my lips
thinking of what i could do with that

they've been warned
about dirty old men on porches

but the fat ones
the ugly ones
the virgins that sit in school
all day long and listen to
the sexual exploits of their friends
they always turn and smile

they know their reality

you've got to take what
you can get

it's my reality as well

# The Fence

## Jordan Shelbourne

There was a moment, I never loved him more. He was never less mine to love.

We were working on his house the way we were always working on his house, because someday he'd sell it for a profit. That day it was a fence for the back yard. It was June after a wet, wet spring, and we were glad for the sun and the heat.

We found the surveyor's marks and pounded our wooden stakes carefully inside the property line, the heavy sledge raised and dropped with a whuff-thump, whuff-thump. We pulled the string tight and he fussed, as he always did: the right knot, so we could save the string; sight it by eye as well, to compensate for wind and the weight of the string. It was a very long yard.

I peered down the string, lining up two stakes in the distance, looking at him in his drab and stained work clothes. The clothes were used and sturdy. They were known quantities. Like him. And I was proud that he let me help him. That he trusted me, a slob and a fumblefinger and a faker in so many ways.

I repaid him a bit by coming up with a clever way to mark the post locations: an X cut out of cardboard, we threw it on the ground every eight feet and sprayed the spot with fluorescent orange paint. The smell of the paint was sharp in our eyes and nostrils. I watched as he drew his arm across his forehead, careless of his part, his dark hair already starting to mat with perspiration.

We were using a hand-held auger for the postholes, and it was a mistake; I knew it when I saw how much clay there was in the soil. He looked at me as if daring me to comment on it; I didn't. We had to work the auger together, it was a tee-shape: a big wooden handle atop a metal post and a claw. One of us would stomp the claw into the earth, freeing the smells of the earth and of broken grass. Then I took one arm of the tee and he took the other, and we heaved and hauled and grunted. To keep digging (the posts had to go three feet deep), we reached across the bar and pulled down, our arms and hands touching. It was awkward. We were clumsy at first, like new lovers. I loved it.

He had strong forearms with clearly-defined muscles that shifted as he adjusted his grip. The wind caught and lifted the fine dark hairs.

After the second hole, our muscles ached. After the fourth, they screamed. The sweat soaked through our shirts. We stripped down to our undershirts, feeling the honey sunlight pour down on us, drawing sweat and the winter's poisons from our skin. Sometime after that, we stopped noticing how much we hurt: there was only the moment, the two of us striving together. I don't know how long that union lasted.

Sometimes I think that the world exists only in these moments, and our desire for continuity is so strong that we make up the connecting bits, the rest of time.

We stopped for lunch: fresh buns, cold meat, ripe plump tomatoes, fresh strawberries, cold lemonade. He took off his gloves and I admired his wide strong hands. We sat there at the end of the driveway, grimy-faced, elbows on knees, together, watching the world walk by.

He said softly, "Should've gotten a power auger. My fault."

I nodded, too tired to speak but happy. I could have told him then, told him how I felt. But: He nodded in the direction of a woman walking by. She wore shorts and a halter top. Her breasts jiggled as she walked. "I like the summer. I like the sights."

I looked right at him and said, "Me, too."

# Cobweb Years—Aspects

cbratb

## Chapter One: Tho' I Don't Know Many Words of Praise.

I remembered the words from my childhood..."Forgive me, Father, for I have sinned." But then they ask you that "How long has it been since your last confession?" question. It had been so long since my last confession that I didn't really know where to start, and, frankly, the only reason I was in this booth was because I also didn't know when to stop.

That's the peculiar thing about sin...defining it. Because sin is circumstantial, its rules change with the environment, and your age, and the degree, and the society. An act that may be murder in Boston is defending your country in Beirut—there truly are beneficial lies—honoring thy mother and thy father surely doesn't apply in the extreme cases.

And so the accuracy of the very concept of sin had always evaded me...always seemed just beyond my grasp, my understanding. The daily conundrum of life held no relevance in the biblical definitions of sin...and yet...whose other version do you have any desire to conform to? I ask you.

I wondered why the interior of the booth was so cool, when the church itself was baking in the summer dryscorch. I remember these places as huge places...dark places...hot and humid places—places I did not want to be, kneeling and scuffing up my Sunday shoes. And now, now that I was completely out of my twisted twenties, this booth...what my grandmother used to believe was the actual doorway of "GOD HIS OWN SELF"...wasn't huge anymore. It wasn't scary anymore, and it was even cool and comfortable.

And if it was indeed the doorway to god his own self, I was no longer afraid to knock...I just had no idea what to say when he answered. I mean, what are his priorities these days? I like to believe the same as I've always believed about god's priorities.

But sometimes, u have 2 question it, don'tcha think? My knees sank into the small cushion on the floor...it had always made the booth seem tall, but now it was almost just my size...I had the adulthood to either kick my shoes off or to not care about the scuffs...whereas I grew through childhood feeling as an intruder in this box...now I felt that it was completely my space...a physical and aural extension of my own power and faith... My conscience was astonishingly at ease and comfortable... I suppose the purpose of this box was to allow you to develop those very senses about its purpose.

My clothes were loose and comfortable, and I was unhurried. It was dawn, right after the Matins, and I knew that it would be quite a while before my absolver would join me.

I guess I'd better figure out a place to start before he arrives. I'm pretty sure that once I get goin' I'll be okay, but gee whiz...(that's the sort of profanity that comes natural in a confessional y'know?)...how 'bout a hint.

I have been tempted to view this visit, after so many cobweb years, as some sort of ecclesiastical cross between therapy and absolution...and yet, now that I'm here, on my knees and so comfortable, it seems more like stories over wine and cheese on a spring Sunday with an ex-lover at brunch.

My mind moved back along its line of sin...forgotten, regretted, enjoyed, unrecognized, disguised, frantic, subdued and, in my case, frequent and voluminous.

I have no idea of where and how it started...when the first sin was. Probably childhood touching of myself. Innocently enough, no doubt when I began to devel'op something to hold up a top. Those were the days when we all believed in hand-reared tits, and because mine appeared early on, the only hands available were my own.

In examining them continuously for growth, my fingers gained an undignified familiarity with them, and they in turn began to respond as though alive. Even when they were but small nubs in an almost concave chest, my nipples were very sensitive.

It wasn't long before I discovered that whenever my self-examination took place, many other parts of my developing body increased their sensitivity.

I allowed my fingers to soothe other parts of me also...stroking the backs of my own soft hands and lightly dragging over the pad at the thumb's base with my strong, young fingernails.

I can remember that on long car trips, when I was unable to freely explore my own exploding senses, I was often surprised to discover how much of me seemed directly linked to wherever my finger attended. My parents once drove me to a dance class competition about two hours away, and the entire time I spent wearing a furrow up and down the back right corner of my neck...hidden from view under my long hair. I know that it wasn't exactly a tickle, but it was pretty close...it's just that my entire body recognized the motion and responded to it—certainly unlike your basic tickle.

My parents thought I was sick and kept asking me if I didn't want to try again when I felt better. But at that age, I could see no way to possibly feel better...the action of first one finger and then several...and then back to one again...this sweet rub ran ripples down my spine and straight through my chest cavity, past my beating heart and directly to the inside of my nipples, which then swelled against the tight weave of a cheap leotard.

When I looked down, I could see them under my sweater. I could also see that I had moved my knees apart in a most unseemly fashion for a young dancer. I didn't know why, or what the connection was between neck, knees and nipples. I only knew that there was one and that I wanted to find out what it was. In that one delicious weekend, I didn't even place in the dance...my mind was elsewhere.

For most of the event, both my parents went to visit nearby relatives, and I was left largely to entertain myself. I couldn't leave the room, but the room was where I wanted to be...alone and unseen. I discovered that the neck link went all the way down to the feet and even down to the toes. And the harder my nipples grew, and the larger they became, the more I could feel the blood in my body alter its course to flow much closer to the skin.

If I dragged my fingernail across the small wrinkled ending of each nipple, I felt a sudden flush in my lower belly...and the blood ran hotter and faster. Lying on the hotel bed, in just my panties and a T-shirt, and watching M*A*S*H* reruns on TV, I had my first climax...I can't really call it an orgasm...but it was a build. I could feel my supple toes curl under, and even my defined and designed muscles couldn't prevent it. My mouth was part open...and one of my hands strayed softly to the rise of my belly.

I could feel the tender flames down there...they were just beginning, but they still felt mighty hot to my fragile fingertips. As I continued to rub my buds under the shirt, and stroke hip to hip, I felt a sudden heat flash along my entire body and then, just as quickly, it wasn't there any more.

I didn't know what had happened to me, but I knew that something definitely had. I wonder now if that was sin, in the eyes of a merciful and benevolent god...or if it was merely a test run of machinery of his own design. Was he offended—or pleased with the results? Was this act sufficient for eternal damnation—or a guarantee for salvation? Or was this the devil in my soul, the torment crafted to bring about a million nightmares and a life of lingering uncertainty? I didn't know now, so how the hell was I supposed to know then?

## Chapter Two: The Valley of the Shadow.

I hadn't thought about that weekend in a long time. I suppose it was the setting...watching the young sun as its rays filtered through the stained glass in the east window and cast a changing, psychedelic, flickering light show on the walls of the booth.

I remembered how long it was before I discovered where all those knee, neck, nipple nerves went to.

I spent the entire summer believing that the fire and the shuddering flashes came from my breast examinations and the flames in my belly.... It was Thanksgiving Day when I discovered the precious place...the place that increased all the other senses...and even then I had to have help. It was customary, in my home and most other American homes, to have two separate tables for large family get-togethers and dinners. Even though I was visibly becoming a woman, I was still seated downstairs at the kids' table.

My 15-year-old cousin and I had to eat our meal with the two bratty sisters that made up the rest of our extended youth family tree. They bolted their food and left me and David to try to eat ours more delicately...we were in no hurry to finish and then get stuck with the dishes...and the pots and pans.

So we ate slowly, mostly in silence.

I saw him taking longer and longer glances at the way my blouse was no longer flat against my chest, as it had been at all the other family dinners...and I liked it...these first sexual attentions from a man, they made me fill the blouse out even more.

Periodically, he would reach across me for one thing or another, and he would graze across my hard nipples with the back of his hand or his arm. He could see the effect that it was having on me, and I could sure as hell feel the effect. I was overcome with the desire to scratch the itch at the sensitive end of my tits, but...

When it was time for dessert, I went upstairs with our dishes and brought plates down for both of us. When I sat back down I noticed that he had moved his chair closer to mine...now whenever he reached for anything, he boldly brushed against my entire breast, even deliberately lingering there. When he saw that I raised no objections, he reached again, but this time he stopped his hand on the outside curve of my right breast, and then took his other hand to my left.

I still had my dessert spoon halfway to my mouth...I would have to move at least one of his hands to eat...so I set the spoon back on my plate. For what seemed like an eternity we sat there, he with my young, fresh tits in his supple fingers and me just staring ahead with my hands resting on the table. It was the first time that anyone besides myself had touched my body since I was a very small child. I knew that I had been warned against strangers doing such a thing, but not cousins. Some part of me knew that what he was doing was wrong, but I wasn't sure exactly what it was that was wrong.... I only knew that every other part of me knew that it was right.

He angled his chair towards mine and took my chin in his hand. Then he turned my head and kissed me, full on the mouth. In my eager virginity, I kissed him back, even though I had never done such a thing before.... Our lips locked for quite a while, and his hands returned to my hardened breasts. My belly was alive with small tongues of flame, licking upwards towards my tits and downwards, all the way to my toes. One of his hands slipped from my nipple, as we continued to kiss...he was a really good kisser...and traveled to my knee. My senses raced as he drew small patterns on my knee and began to edge his hand up my thigh, under the hem of my skirt. I didn't have any idea where he was going with his fingers, but I knew that he was taking the fire with him, up my inner thigh. I felt him push my legs apart to give himself more room.

Our eyes were closed, or at least mine were.... My breathing was getting heavier and so was his...and then the tip of his fingers brushed against my innocence...and all the heat in his hand leaped into my sweet, pretty, hairless virgin lips.

I thought I would swoon.

Instantly I realized where all those nerve endings went to...as his fingers rubbed me through my panties, I could feel myself getting wet down there.

I got so wet that I thought maybe I had peed myself and that he would stop—or that I should stop him.

But neither of us stopped...we went on kissing, and he went on squeezing my breast with one hand and rubbing my panties with the other. My entire body was alive by now...my legs were spread wide open under the table, and his busy hand had my skirt pulled all the way up into my lap. I felt him begin to slip one finger under the leg band of my panties. And I got scared.

I closed my legs suddenly, trapping his hand at first, and then releasing it. I pushed his other hand away from my breast and stopped kissing him. I was still sitting bolt upright with my hands on the table. He looked at me, and he must have seen something of the fear in my eyes. And in his all-knowing fifteen years of accumulated wisdom, he knew when to push his luck and when to fade back.

It was fortunate really, because it was almost immediately after that when we heard adult footsteps coming down the basement stairs. By the time my father arrived downstairs, our chairs once more had the separation of decency, my skirt was back down to my knees, and I held my arms over my still hard nipples.

"Say, David," said my dad, "why don't you come upstairs and watch the Lions game with us men...while the girls take care of the clean-up." Although my gender equality conscience was just beginning, I was glad to see him get up and leave. Later on I realized why he walked so oddly, and remained behind my father as he walked up the stairs. It was some time before my legs would work properly, and I picked at my dessert, flushed and feeling fine, but somehow incomplete, somehow unfinished.

When I dropped the dishes in the kitchen, my mother asked me if I was okay, and I managed to say yes, I was just stuffed from dinner and wanted to go and lie down for a while.

I stopped in the bathroom on the way and examined my underwear...they were soaked at the crotch but didn't smell like pee. My lower lips were puffed and tender.

As my fingers moved over them, all the nerve endings came alive again, my nipples became instantly hard, and my fingers got damp. I kept rubbing until, by accident, my fingers slipped just inside myself...a place I'd never been before. They discovered lots more moisture and a stiff little outcropping of skin and sinew and nerves.

When I stroked it, it became bigger and harder...and more sensitive.... My heart was pounding, and when the flash hit me, I almost fell off the toilet onto the floor. My entire hand was drenched. My thighs were in spasm along with my toes and the hair on the back of my neck. After the aftershocks subsided, I was almost afraid at the power of the sensations which I had just experienced. I wiped myself dry, almost causing the same thing to happen again, and steadying myself, made it to my bed.

For several hours my mother and my aunt fussed over me, told me how peaked I looked and took my temperature several times. I lied to them both and pretended that maybe I really was coming down with something...but I knew I wasn't.

I knew that I had crossed some kind of line, that some sort of major change had taken place inside of me, and I would forever be different...and I also knew that the focus of my body's sensations had moved from my neck, knees and breasts to that aromatic damp place, the place that David had woken and guided me to...the place that held the magic and the power. But I didn't register any of what had happened as sin...except possibly for lying to my dear mother and aunt, but I excused this small mistruth on the grounds that I actually had felt...somehow different...and who was I to say whether it was a sickness or not? At the time, I didn't feel that it was really a confessable sin, but just to be on the safe side, I threw in a couple of extra "Hail Marys" at the following Sunday Mass.

I didn't see David again until the following Easter. By then I had hair, much bigger tits and a lot more experience. The hair and the tits just seemed to appear overnight from nowhere. The experience was a Christmas present.

## Chapter Three: Hark the Herald Angels...Sing?

By Christmas, I was in choir.

Despite my complete lack of ability on any instrument my anxious relatives bribed me to attempt mastering, it turned out that I had a quicksilver voice, capable of calling down the hosts from heaven, according to the aging nun who led the choir.

For me, it was a wonderful extension of my newly discovered masturbation skills. Of course, I didn't know yet that that's what they called it, or even that anyone else did it but me.... When I was on pace with the music, in key and harmony with the soaring trip through the cosmos that any good church music induces...when all was right between the waves of the universe and the electrical nervous system that ran the hormones which frequently took over my body...when all these things happened, choir was the closest thing to heaven for me.

A lot of it was the robes...we were supposed to just slip them on, over our street clothes, but I was always naked beneath mine. It gave me an incredible freedom both in performing and actually singing. The voice takes on new balance, new emotional strength when the body is unrestricted.

I would put the robe on with all the other choir members, then slip out to the bathroom right before the entrance for the services and remove everything from under the long, flowing cotton vestments. After the opening short piece, and throughout the service until the ending grand finale, my voice would float out of a body with air around it...the soft cotton would cling and abandon me from note to note. Generally, by the time the choir changed after the service, I was electrified. The combination of the voices, and the organ/piano accompaniment, was enough to raise the tiny hairs along my forearm and down the slope of my stomach...the rub of the robe made them dance.

I had been perpetuating this private devotion for several weeks, until the practice session for the Christmas Mass. It was a snowy New England night, crisp and sparkly...a night to echo children's sleigh-born laughter to the million visible stars and a fat crescent moon.

The church wasn't heated for practices in the wintertime, and yet my habits (so to speak) didn't change just for the sake of a few degrees. This evening, when I came out of the bathroom after divesting myself of my outer things, there was someone waiting for me.

His name was...well, to be honest, I don't remember what his name was or, in fact, if I ever knew it.

All I knew was that for the last two or three weeks he had stood directly behind me at the end of the choir line.

He smiled at me and followed me to our respective rows. I took my place and opened my hymn book, one of the main pieces that we were scheduled to work on was my solo "Ave Maria" and I had been practicing it all month, by myself.

The choir director ran the main group through most of the scheduled pieces and then excused them. She said that since the weather was getting worse and snow was accumulating, anyone who wanted to leave early could do so, but I was to stay and practice to her accompaniment. The entire group, as one, rapidly left, and I was alone...high in the semi-dark choir stall, staring down at the nun at the organ.

While I waited for her to start, I noticed huge, fast, fluffy snowflakes drifting in a cloud past the window of the church. I was relaxed and warm, despite my nakedness under the robe, and when the opening stanza played, I took several deep breaths and began to sing from the top.... I had always loved this piece and knew it by heart, so my voice had no fear...no hesitation. My notes were clear, and my young lungs could hold air and notes forever. I could almost see the music hovering in the crisp air, floating effortlessly around the church and coming back to warm my body with its familiarity...wrapping its velvet self around me and filling my soul and my faith...it was wonderful to be able to honor the lord with such clarity and beauty, and I felt the music, the low rumbling from the organ downstairs mingled with my high, clear voice.... I felt all the music as its filigreed fingers ran over my neck, standing the hairs on end.... I could feel it in other parts of my body as well.

As always happened when I sang, particularly when I sang well, my body responded in that same manner of sensuality as it did when I was alone and exploring. As my lungs filled, so did my breasts.... As my mouth opened wide, so did my thighs.... As I swayed to the rising tempo, the flowing robes caressed my body and allowed the chilled air to cool my increasing heat. I loved the feeling and didn't want it to stop and so, for once, I deliberately messed up in one of the hard parts. The nun below patiently called up to encourage me..."Don't worry," she said. "Take your time, dear."

I started from the beginning, listening to the swell of the organ filling the huge room, watching the white blanket as it fell noiselessly outside.... I ran my fingers across my nipples, through the cotton robe, and felt them get even harder. Alone in the darkness, my hand traveled between my legs and rubbed the swelling pussy lips, with their fine forest of new-grown baby hair. I could feel the texture of my young mane through the loose shift.... I could sense my openness and wetness, and I swirled the material around me to send cool, chilling air directly to my fire. My voice was subtly ringing the notes, bending them and making this classic song of absolute devotion my own...from me to god and whoever else was listening.

I wasn't even paying attention to the travels of my fingers anymore. I didn't even realize where they were, only that the music and the fingers were carrying me away...into the song...into the power of faith and fullness.

There was no reflection of sin in my young voice as it sailed clear and true across the night air, while my engorged clit became further enlarged under the soft but insistent rubbing and flicking of my hands. I messed up again, but the woman had the patience of a saint (and obviously no life of her own to pursue). We took it again, from the top.

By this time I had thrown caution to the winds in my darkened choir stall. Alone and private, I raised my robe up, past my thighs, rolled it and rested it on the top curve of my ass. If the nun happened to look up, she would see me decently clad from the top down but would have no idea what sort of sight she would have if the booth front were glass rather than heavy oak panels.

The organ seemed louder this time, and I was so comfortable with the piece that I could sing and play at the same time. As my voice rolled through the long first couplet, I had three fingers knuckle-deep in the saturated folds of my pussy, driving hard on the tempo of the song.

I wasn't listening to the notes or even to the sloshing sound of my fingers...I was just lost in the pleasure of my voice in harmony with the grand echo of the old building, and my body in harmony with the energy which returned, with the echo, to my fingertips. That's when I felt another hand—on my cool naked asscheeks. But at this point I didn't care. I moved and swayed my ass against the hands, they were young but rough...they grabbed my ass and spread the cheeks apart. One of them slipped around the curve of my hip and traveled confidently down my lower belly to my furry mound...although my fingers were still deep inside me, the other hand peeled apart my pussy lips and searched out my clit.

The song roared through my brain and leaped from my mouth, wailing and moaning in ecstatic desperation. It was a chilling version of the piece, and it was made greater by the fire in my faith and the flames between my open, wet thighs. I pulled my fingers from deep inside me and allowed the other hand to slide smoothly inside me, while its companion continued to pinch and squeeze my ass from behind.

In the dark...during the song...I came...hard and fast and rough. I felt my body spasm and forgot the words. The organ stopped playing and then automatically, mercifully, just started again, from the top.

Both hands of mine were now on my nipples, pushing on my breasts as though to help me hit the notes by helping to coax extra air from my lungs. Both the other hands were now tormenting me, roaming my entire body...without regard for my permission or help. They forced my legs as far apart as they would go, and they ran up under my robe to my aching tits, pushing my own hands away in the process....

They flashed suddenly back to my pussy and rammed deep inside me, again and again until I thought I would pass clean away from the joy of it.

My voice was flying now, rippling over the notes and forcing them into the ears of heaven with my bliss of simply being alive...my adoration sparkled with every note and tone...shining through the tempo. I felt the hands abandon me and slide down my inner thighs, over the tender sensitive backs of my knees and down to my ankles, where they gently caressed the top of the arch of my feet. I had kicked my shoes off at the entrance to the church to give them a chance to dry from the wetness of the winter outside.

I felt movement between my legs, and before I knew what was happening, I could feel hot breath blowing over my pussy lips. The breath was followed by a mouth. I was in ecstasy and wonder as the lips met mine...as a tongue slipped down into the crack at the top of my girlhood and sought out the stiffness buried just inside. The mouth took the stiffness and sucked it hard, swirling that fabulous tongue around and up and down it.... I was flooding the face between my thighs, my heat and juices pouring from me as my climaxes matched that of the tempo.

As the song reached a crescendo, so did my body.... It racked and swayed and rolled and twisted as the notes flew higher and higher, stronger and clearer.

My orgasm was my gift to the song...my emphasis to heaven...my everything I had to give in my faith.... It was the most perfect me I could possibly ever be...and somewhere I knew that god was pleased at the reflection of his best work.

As I held and powered the long last note...drawing every inch of life from the song...the face vanished from between my thighs, sucking my lips and clit fully into its mouth as it said a tender goodbye. When the note ended, I turned quickly, but I was once again alone.

The nun downstairs burst into applause and bravos, and I barely had time to compose myself and my clothing before she burst through the choir stall door. She wrapped me in a huge bear hug, and I expected her to immediately smell the strong musk in the room, or to feel my still hard nipples against her chest. But she was transported by the music alone, and assured me that all of heaven had stopped to listen to my joy and faith in the lord...how could that possibly be a sin...

## Chapter Four: For They Know Not What They Do....

The flush of memories that had returned to my mind, as I knelt in the booth, waiting for my absolution, had stirred in me a melange of quandaries.

My life had been so clean then, so clear...there was nothing abstract to me in my delicate youth except, of course, for my faith—which was abstract only in its intangibility...but pure in definition. I held no judgments in those tentative days...and I believed that my god held no judgments either.

I was pure in his eyes, if not in mine...but sin? Sin was for those around me who didn't go to Mass, who stole and lied and took the name of the deity in vain.

The discovery of my own body made—in a figurative sense—in his own image, was what I was supposed to do...my way of examining his handiwork all the better that I might admire and worship it, and him. It was, to me, the same as my art appreciation class, only more tactile. By the time I quit choir, I had been touched by the hand of the lord, as well as my own and those of at least one other person. Apparently word had escaped about my dressing habits and my willingness to lose all my inhibitions while singing. I did have a couple of repeats of my Christmas practice occurrence, but I never looked for a face because a face was immaterial to me.... I felt that the pleasure which I was given on these occasions was my just reward from the audience...he does indeed move in mysterious ways...but as my teen years became longer and the nights more entertaining, I grew tired and bored with the fumbling of unseen strangers, as well as the certainty of my own physical successes.

I left the church at seventeen...although at the time it was more an act of rebellion than dissatisfaction.

I held the glory of god deep in my heart, but the social ramifications of organized religion soured with the judgments. I didn't give it a lot of thought, since my relationship had always been with the man himself rather than with his many housekeepers...and yet, on Sundays I still felt like I couldn't go home. My family tried to understand why my lifelong comfort with the church would suddenly seem to disappear, but I couldn't explain it to them...and I didn't really want to.

It never dawned on me that it might be important until one afternoon when I was sucking off my music teacher in the small practice area adjacent to the main orchestra room.

It hadn't happened suddenly or quickly, this strange little seduction. I had spent an entire year in his class. By now my voice had grown to a whisky rasp, and I had to actually feign interest in an instrument in order to validate sitting in his classes. But instruments came and went...I just wasn't talented enough to warrant enjoying the discipline. But I loved this man with all the lust that a girl of my years could muster. I would sit quietly in his class and stare at him, licking my lips. Once, when I was sure that everyone else was reading the sheet music in front of them, I looked straight at him, caught his eye, and blew him a kiss. He looked away and avoided my glances for the rest of the class, but gradually I wore him down.

I realized that we were a good match...he liked to look and I liked to be looked at...so my skirts got shorter and shorter and my blouses lost more and more buttons.

I would spend all my allowance money on underwear, and take great delight in allowing him selected glimpses of the new lacy underthings. I could often feel his eyes upon me, even when I wasn't looking at him. My body would sense the heat of his stare, and my thighs would squirm in my seat. My nipples would come alive...not a handy event when you're trying to master the accordion...and I would imagine how his strong mouth would feel around my tits.

They were precious hours, those three music periods a week...and when summer came and I could wear tube tops and loose shorts, my seduction escalated. By now, it was common knowledge in the room that I was willing to suffer almost any indignity in order to get to this man...to have him deep inside of me and to milk his beautiful seed into me. I would sit in the front row and allow my hands to run around the loose legs of my shorts, and up to the juncture of my legs. I was very hairy by now, and I knew that if he looked, he would see the edges of my bush pushing out of the sides of my panties...and I made sure that he looked...and that he saw.

It would make me so wet that I would use the need for a bathroom as an excuse to relieve my demanding pussy and then wipe myself dry...but it would only last long enough for me to get back into class. And then he would look at my breasts as I walked past him to my seat and watch me as I sat down, spreading my thighs before his gaze.

It couldn't go on forever without resolution, which came under very strange circumstances. Although it had become apparent that the only instrument that I had any interest in belonged to the teacher, I was sort of accepted as the class mascot, and that allowed me to even go along on school orchestra trips to help set up music stands and unpack the instruments and help tune them.

The last trip of the year was to Cleveland, not exactly the nightspot metropolis of the Northern hemisphere, but we got to stay in a fairly ritzy hotel, and I had the room next door to the teacher...there was an odd number of band members on the outing so I had the room to myself, but I couldn't figure out a way to get him into it. At about two in the morning on our departure day...I was tired of the frustration of working myself into a raging sexual frenzy with my own fingers and decided to go down to the lobby for a soda. They had machines on our floor, but it was the top floor and I loved the experience of moving thirty-four floors in a glass elevator.

I threw on a T-shirt and some cut offs and headed downstairs. The lobby was deserted, and I got my coke and rang the button for the ride. It took a few minutes to arrive, and guess who got out when the doors opened. He had on a pair of sweat pants and a loose shirt...he spotted the soda in my hand and said, "Well, great minds think alike, I see." I said I'd hold the car for him while he walked briskly to the machine in the lobby...mainly so I could watch his tight ass moving under the loose material.

When he got back, we stepped inside and pushed the button for our floor. I faced the back of the elevator and watched the lobby get smaller as we rose towards the sky.

Out of the blue, I felt his hands on my hips. Without a word, I leaned back into him and tilted my head onto his shoulder. In a flash he had his tongue in my mouth and his hand down the front of my shorts and into my panties. His mouth moved to the side of my neck and kissed along it to my shoulders...my tits were alive with feeling and begging for his hands. His fingers were busy exploring my juicy pussy and teasing my clit. I was hot and wet and eager and desperate...and he knew it. I reached behind me and found his hard cock under the sweats...it wasn't huge, but it was in my hand at last and that's what counted. I felt him unzip my shorts and peel them down over my hips... I was showing my wet panties to the entire lobby below, but I didn't care. I could feel his stiffness probing my asscheeks from behind and pushing his pants and my panties deep into the crack of my ass. I wiggled it against him and heard him moan.

Before we spoke a word, the elevator stopped at our floor...but he pressed another button and the car continued upwards to the suites level, where it rested.

I guess no one was in a hurry to get to or leave this floor. Standing with my hands reached upwards onto the glass he slid my panties off, and I stepped out of them. My T-shirt was next...then I was naked in a glass box, hundreds of feet above the ground. I pushed my stiff nipples against the cold glass while his fingers worked deep inside my sopping cunt...and then suddenly, his hardness was inside me, teasing my lips with its hot head and rubbing against my clit. Before I could so much as gasp, he was buried to the balls in my fire...I was suddenly filled and fabulous. In the glass world, I was the queen, and I was getting fucked hard and savage in full view of anyone who cared to glance upwards. I ran my hand over my pussy lips, past the root of his cock and grasped his full balls, trying to pull them inside me as well.

It was more than he could stand, and with one violent thrust he exploded inside me, drenching my insides with his scalding come...flooding me and flushing me.... I shook and shuddered to my very core, my cunt walls grabbed him like the scepter of life itself, and as I hung on for the ride, I was so pleased that all those days in class teasing and tormenting him and myself had finally paid off, and had been worth the effort. He was my first actual, true-to-life fuck, and by morning he was also my fifth.

We moved, naked from the elevator to my room...and damn near broke the bed.... In the morning when he slipped out to his own room, it looked like a squadron of marines had field-tested a whorehouse in my room...the mattress was against the wall, and the sheets were torn into little pieces with the savagery of our passion.

When we got back to school, it was almost impossible for us to keep our hands off each other, but we managed most of the time.

And so it was strange, on this one day while I had him trapped inside my throat, that he would make an offhand comment to me about my mouth being one of god's best creations...and that it would make me think, once more, about the place of sin in my life.

I took him out of my mouth and looked at him, which wasn't exactly what he wanted at that particular point in time. "Maybe," I said, "it's not god's creation...maybe I did this on my own." He smiled at me and told me that anything this good had to at least have had the benefit of divine intervention. I took that well and put him back between my lips, but it seemed to ring a strange and disquieting bell in the core of my being....

It was the last time that he came in me and the last time that I wanted him to...like a melted ice cream, he was different from what I had wanted so much—all those weeks ago.

I guess I had simply eaten off all the sprinkles.

## Chapter Five: I Have Fashioned an Altar Before Thee in the Eyes of Mine Enemies...

As my mind dredged up these memories, from the distant days of my spent youth, I noticed that the dawn light from the outside was penetrating the confessional. It was still filtered through the large stained glass window at the east end of the church, and it played even more across the interior of the small womb in which I found myself. I thought back across the years to the other times that I was in such a place...as a child this was my place to commune with my higher extension...the god who ruled me, and commanded and protected me. It was a forgiving god and a merciful one...a god who took little children and loved and protected them unconditionally...he saw no sin in the actions of children or even in their thoughts.

And so, it was little wonder that I had an impossible time feeling shame for the parts of my life which came into being along the way...even into the last urgent teen years, when I was devastatingly familiar with my own body and had allowed many others to gain equal access to it. And I had become more than a little knowledgeable about the bodies of others.... I had developed a connoisseur's taste for cock. I was not in the least concerned with size or strength...but purely taste...that meaty, salty taste of a man in hardness—I loved it...and craved it like a good wine on the summer porch.

I had many a man before I crossed the line into my twenties. And, in truth, most of them were not very satisfactory as lovers...they lacked the spirit of gentle imagination and all-out fun that allowed me to fully submerge myself in the act. Most, of course, were too fast, too selfish and, in the end, too aware of their own failings to be able to abandon their nervousness and fear of failures. Some of them were too good (or thought they were)...too long, or too self assured...they felt that my pussy was the waiting, logical conclusion to a drink bought or a ribald story told. But, because I had my own agenda, I took them and let them take me...they could put their wonder cocks into my hot wetness as long as I got to taste them first.

I loved the easy feel of flesh sliding deep into my mouth and upper throat. I loved the architecture of a good hard dick, the ridges and valleys and the sense of that river of blood flowing rapidly and evenly into the head. I loved the small twitches and jerks that a cock makes when you run your tongue across the sensitive tip, and down the length of the shaft...it seems like a creature of its own race...independent from whichever guy it happens to be attached to. I practiced long and hard to acquire the technique of taking a cock fully into my mouth, to allow it to pass the gag reflex and rub its head against the top of my throat and, at the same time, to be able to hold the base firmly between my lips and create that suction around the shaft that makes it feel like several people at once have it inside them.

When I first went away to college, I was blessed with a roommate who had the same dick addiction as myself. In our junior year it was all we could talk about, and within a few short weeks of arriving in town, we were the hit of every frat party on campus.... It was at one of these parties that I met Jackson.

He stood out at the shindig because he didn't have the usual frat attire...no letter sweater or expensive fashions.... When I saw him, leaning against the wall, he had on a denim shirt and jeans. He was nursing a beer, and watching bemusedly as the youth around him played the games that youth makes up and perfects.

Unfortunately, when he first saw me, I was on my knees in the living room...I had the hard extensions of two young college boys straight from the country jammed into my mouth and two more waiting. He watched me and smiled as I showed my taste for lustful behavior, and for a moment I thought he would step forward and take his place in line...but he didn't. In no time flat, I was swallowing the sweet seed of both these boys and watching them as their eyes rolled back in their heads. I kept a tight hold on their cocks because I knew that a man is most sensitive in his cock immediately after orgasm, and I wanted to make these youngsters beg me to stop licking and sucking their cocks...beg me to leave them be and let them recover.

The two waiting in line didn't like this plan and began to rub their shafts against any part of my body which they could access...one of them slid my shirt down my shoulders and exposed my hard nipples and firm tits...then he rubbed his cock meat against the tip of my breast, teasing and flicking it against the nipple. I still kept an eye on the stranger against the wall and became frustrated at his aloof attitude to a semi-naked, natchal-born cocksucker on her knees less than ten feet from him.

I increased my efforts and took the two patient boys and gave them their turn inside the velvet of my mouth. They both lasted less than a minute, and although they gave me all of themselves...it only made me hungrier.... I wanted more...lots more, and now.

When I looked back towards the man who seemed to be so cool, so unimpressed, I smiled at him and licked my lips. He turned and went into the kitchen.

Most of the men in the room had shifted their attention to my roommate, who was doing her usual party trick with the handle of her hairbrush and a very wet pussy. I stood and watched for a few seconds before following the stranger.

He was in the half shadows of the far end of a galley kitchen. He was cool and calm and white-hot in my head. My breasts were still naked and still hard...and getting harder.

I went to the refrigerator and pulled out a beer, popped it, and drank most of it in one open-throated swallow.

Then I walked straight up to him and put my hand on his cock...and smiled and licked my lips again. "Tell me what you want," he said.

"I want this cock.... I want it in my mouth and rammed deep inside my cunt until your balls are jammed into the crack of my asscheeks.... I want your hot seed to fill me at both ends, and then I want to taste you again when you're soft...and keep tasting you until you get hard again and fuck me some more."

I figured this was a good enough hint.

He set down his beer and took one of my tits in his hand...he was so soft and yet so firm in the way he held my pulsating flesh between his fingers, rolling the hard nipple and lightly scratching the textured end of it.

His other hand undid the zipper of my jeans and reached inside...he roamed over the fullness of my belly and jammed his hand roughly down the front of my lacy panties and over my full mound and straight into my slit with two firm fingers. The knuckles rode hard over my clit and hurt me into ecstasy. As I stood in front of him, shaking and moaning...he unsnapped my jeans and told me to take them off. When I hesitated, he twisted my nipple, not hard but forcefully.

I stepped out of my jeans and stood in front of him, his hand still active inside my underwear. He told me to turn around, and when I did, he bent me firmly over the dining room table. It was a heavy oak, farmhouse style piece of furniture, and my arms and chest swept the odds and ends and scattered them to the floor. As I stood there, I felt him grab my panties and tear them from my body. The force and suddenness of the movement made me shiver, and it didn't take long for me to find out what was to come next.

## Chapter Six: There's No Such Thing as Original Sin.

As my tits pressed hard into the old oak table, and the top of my pussy rubbed against the edge of it, I felt the remains of my shredded panties slide down my legs, and I came...buckets of hot juice poured out of me and ran down onto the kitchen floor. I collapsed with the effort, and still he waited, this slender man with the quiet, all-knowing smile. I didn't know what he had to offer, but I knew that I wanted all of it, everywhere at once.

As my breathing subsided into a mere flopping gasp, I felt something nudge at the outside of my soaking crease, then it slid gently into the entrance to my wetlands. Then it paused.... It seemed huge...filling and hard...and just out of reach just...almost...but not quite. I thought that I would go crazy with lust. I tried backing up, but he held me.... I tried to reach behind me and through my open thighs, but I could not reach him.... He stroked the entrance to my pussy with the head of his cock, up and down the slit, and over the nub of my clit...again and again....

I thought I would die, simply expire where I was and leave them all to explain why this dehydrated, naked woman, with torn underwear at her feet, had passed away on a frat house kitchen table...but just before I died, he entered me full and hard and fast...it took my breath away, and as I gasped for air, he rammed me again and then again, building to high speed and strong force in the space of just a few strokes. I was gushing again uncontrollably, his entire length was positioned directly on my clitoris, and I rode him as he fucked me silly, fucked me to oblivion, fucked my brains out, fucked me tender—fucked me true. I gripped the far end of the table and hung on for dear life. I could feel him building inside me, feel him swelling as his hot seed raced towards the place where it would escape and fill me. And suddenly, he left me and turned me roughly onto my back.

The table was hard but slick with sweat, my asscheeks hung from the lip of the old wood, and he spread me wide and exposed, wet and dripping. He started tapping me lightly, at the top of my crease, with the hard purple head of his manhood. Rhythmically, and with increasing force...his hardness gradually forced my lips apart until he was directly tapping my clit. He grew harder, and tapped harder, until it became a smack, then a wet slap. Over and over again his cock slapped into my clit...the power of the blows, although not painful, was hypnotic and hugely physical. They resounded throughout my whole body, shaking my nipples and clenching the cheeks of my ass. I could feel the small muscles in my shoulders dance to the tempo and my breathing adjust to fit the strange, building blood rush that surged through my entire being from my toes to my soul.

Then he entered me again, completely, and in the white wave that electrified my skin, I came, a glorious buttshaking, thigh-twitching, clit-clenching, teeth-gnashing, tongue-biting, eye-rolling, toe-curling, back-scratching, hair-standing, mindfuck jesus of a come.... I saw angels on horseback riding his shoulders...they were naked and copulating, and their steeds blew fire from their nostrils, directly into my swollen pussy. I could feel the flames and smell the heat. I saw huge, celestial angel cocks waving in the air before my eyes, row upon row of them, coming in fountains over me, drenching me in golden cherubim come and seraphim climaxes. I was as one with the man, and as one with my soul...this was the sense that I had felt from my very first almost-orgasm...the oneness with a god of love, of harmony...of peace. If only I could still sing.

## Chapter Seven: Peace is Always at the Center of Everything.

These images were still swirling in my head when I heard footsteps approaching the confessional. I hadn't realized that my memories were so entrenched and yet so close to the surface. My breathing slowed, and I waited for the other door to open, for my representative of cozmik justice, for my judge by proxy, my jury by remote. But the footsteps just moved on past, and I immediately swept, in my mind, back to the tabletop....

I can remember looking around me when my flesh ceased to steam. Over Jackson's shoulder, on the kitchen wall behind him, was a small crucifix. It was not altogether out of place in a frat house, although at least a tad incongruous. As he dismounted me, our juices glistening on his cock, I had a sudden flash to that movie, the Linda Blair one where she fucks herself with a crucifix....

I had never seen the functionality of a crucifix before, until that movie...but I had always been intrigued by the idea of bringing joy to the soul with such an obvious symbol of tragedy...and yet isn't that what jesus would have wished for me...even in this extreme? This was not an act of blasphemy in glorifying the body made in his image (although, frankly, I always thought his image had a better ass than me, and wondered why I didn't get that!).

It felt strange, on the table thinking about jesus' ass and of slamming the symbol of his death into my dripping heat...but, after all, if the good lord didn't want us to notice his ass, then why did they have Michelangelo paint the ceiling of the Sistine Chapel, instead of waiting around for Charles Schultz? And if such thoughts were so wrong, so eternally damned, then why were my nipples so hard? I remained fixated on the small wall object as my hands were placed inside open pants around me...apparently my table dance had attracted a loyal and firm following from the living room. My hands were filled with tender, strong young cocks, and others were stroking my cheeks.... Immature, tentative fingers were exploring my insides, shaking with trepidation, like frightened little dildos.

The eyes of the man on the wall were not saddened eyes, and I realized that in very few portrayals of the death of christ was he seen to be sad or unhappy. And yet, surely in Death...?

He looked down at me, enjoying his work, as my nerves raced. He watched me as I opened my mouth and my thighs to the attentiveness of mob youth...we were alike, he and I...we were both subjecting our bodies willingly to the attentions of others, and it was really only a matter of perspective as to which was a real definition of love of mankind, he giving for the sins of many, or me sinning as a gift to many.

By now there must have been eight or ten faces above me, marveling at my intensity of body and calm of spirit. But the face on the cross was the one that counted, and he looked...approving.

In the confessional after the footsteps receded, I could feel the high back of the small pew as it dug into my shoulders...and it was in the same sense as the table edge, all those years ago, my head lolling from one end, sucking and caressing a multitude of meats. Was it the pain of immediate punishment for warm thoughts and actions...or the slight pain of comforting, of congratulations for getting it right?

Sin is, after all, the single most subjective crime. The crime of a thousand definitions and the widest range of punishments saying a few incantations to eternal damnation...let's not give this one to the Simpson jury.

My asscheeks hung over the other end of the table...I enjoyed a succession of fillings. But when I left and, of course, took Jackson's number, I was curiously calm, even after such obvious and technical debauchery...the truth settled on me that I had only really been with one man on that sturdy table...and I hadn't even fucked him. It felt like an audition, like dancing for Flo himself at the follies. I gave it a damn good shot, I knew the part real well, my partners performed passably enough and often enough, so there's a good chance I'll get a callback, at least.

Of course, no one ever really got to dance with Flo Ziegfeld at auditions, but I figured jesus is a man, and eventually he'll want to get him some, and I meant to be ready and at the head of the line when he came lookin'.

## Chapter Eight: He Leadeth Me to Lie Down Beside the Still Waters.

It was well past dawn by now.... I had mused on many of the events in my life and given quite some thought to the memories that they had provoked. I had sought in my heart and in my soul for the betrayal of my faith, for the cancellation of belief which would signify sin. I had searched for new definitions, which befitted my life so as to be able once again to balance my pussy and my pride and my paradise.

But in my eyes I found no memories which could clarify such a definition. I didn't want to get to the gates on the other side of the wall of brilliant white, only to discover that I had never sought total absolution, and yet surely one of the basic requirements for such absolution was to at least recognize one's sins so as even to be able to ask for forgiveness. It's not like one can reasonably expect to say to the lord, "Hey, you know what I did, just go ahead and forgive the stuff you didn't like...." I certainly could take up much of my purgatory just verbalizing it all, if I was supposed to confess everything and ensure that I covered whatever he might consider necessary for absolution.

I had no reason to fear that such a situation was impending...after all, my health was fine, my body was young and firm.... But the small life growing inside of me, my first such life...demanded that I clarify my positions, long before I was called upon to teach the grand lessons of life and its passages. I wanted to know, to be really sure, of where the lines were between my faith and my humanity...between my soul and my body...between heaven and heresy. After all this time, there still seemed little that I had ever done, at least with my body and those of others, which I could view in the spiritual or even religious sense as sinful...as shameful...as wrong—in any sense of the words...although there was strong reason to suggest that some of my actions had probably disobeyed certain local community standards and maybe even bent a few actual laws regarding public indecency and moral aptitude.

I have a small button, in my living room, which has the word "morals" inside the international symbol for "NO". I felt that morals were a religious issue and had always been more comfortable with the use of the word "ethics" and, on this beautiful morning kneeling in the doorway to GOD HISSOWN SELF, I felt no closer to a solution than when I first entered the box. I had no further clues...and yet felt strangely comfortable continuing without that knowledge...and that's when I knew...that's when I became at peace with the definition of sin...with what I would need to ask for, and why forgiveness wasn't any part of the process at all.

I inhaled the majesty of his house and allowed its splendor and quiet peace to fill me, as it had done all of my life in the still, small moments of my thoughts to myself. I felt the harmony that I had captured in the choir and the innocence of a grope at the kids' table...the purity of naïve self-examination and the raw lust of a rising glass room...I felt the sense of sharing the complete physical rapport with my college lovers and the submission to the joy of others that my actions had allowed me....

There was, simply put, no place in my life for sexual shame, and nor should there be, inside the hearts of others. Those who perpetuate such shame, who define the categories of sin in the absence of the lord himself, they are the ones to be forgiven—it is those abstract and malevolent souls who will be milling outside the gates of paradise upon my arrival, and my swift and welcomed entrance through the portals will silence forever the clucking of their disapproving tongues, and still their waving fingers.

And when I reach the throne, the chair of grandness, with my reputation preceding me, and my diaphanous shift swirling around my otherwise naked body, I know what will await me...I know that my lord will look down into my eyes, and touch softly his gentle hands to my cheeks and face, and lead me to his bedding, lead me on his arm, past the singing angels and the rainbow harmonies of heaven, into the place where his creation can be finally given its ultimate test...and in that split second of eternal lust when he finally plants his silver seedlings inside of me, he will smile down into my face...with that same smile that I have seen and worn many, many times...and I will know what I have believed all of my life...that my body is indeed a temple, that the lord my god is a loving god...that words and phrases about sin and judgement days and guilt and forgiveness are not heavenly issues, but merely the attempts on the part of man and womankind to justify their own fears and control others..and the only question I will be left with on that most magical of beds, in that most holy of settings, is, "Does this man eat pussy?"

My guess, today, is that he does.

# A True Account of My Encounter with Dolphins

## Vincent

Eight years ago I had an experience that few people have ever had, and for a long time (actually up to about a year ago) I had never spoken of it to anyone else, thinking that they would consider me perverted. During that time I have lived with the reality that I will most likely never have another opportunity like I had at that time, and, believe me, it has been very hard. I have since had sex with other animals, including dogs, ponies, and most recently horses, but they will never rival my experience with the Dolphins. Here is what *truly* happened. I can offer no proof other than my own word. And for my own protection, I will not divulge locations, names, etc.

Eight years ago I lived in a city that had an aquarium which kept performing Dolphins. By pure chance the aquarium was an assignment I had when I was a security guard for a national security company. Since I was new and had little seniority with the company, I would always get cruddy shifts that no one else wanted...and at the aquarium, the shift was midnight to eight. It really was a pretty cushy place to work since I didn't have to punch clock. (Ever carry one of those security clocks around? They must weigh fifteen pounds!) I just had to wander around and keep an eye on things. It would get pretty boring at night, and after a while I took to playing with the Dolphins. I would come in during the weekends to watch the shows, and eventually I picked up some of the hand signals that the trainers used. With a bit of practice I could get the Dolphins to perform just about any behavior that the trainers had them perform. Dolphins really are quite intelligent. After a while I found myself talking to them, and I swear that if they had vocal cords they would have talked back to me! Their body movements and gestures were extremely animated and very communicative.

After several months I got to the point where the nights I spent with the Dolphins became my own private world. They all knew me and came to know my schedule and habits intimately. It was at that point that I decided it was time for a swim. Now, you have to appreciate the circumstances. I was alone all night with these creatures, I was somewhat of a loner and had no personal life to speak of, and

I had developed a deep bond with at least two of the Dolphins. It was easy to keep the shift since no one else liked the hours.

Finally, one night I brought my swim suit. Around 2:00 a.m. I changed, and after being sure that the place was locked up tight, I eased myself into the pool. At first they simply vied for my attention as they always did, but after a bit, things got pretty rough. I wasn't sure why some of them were getting so excited, when I noticed that one of the males had a hard-on! Now that really fascinated me. They never acted like this around me before, and I was not sure what to do, except I did get out of the pool until they calmed down a bit. While sitting on the edge of the pool, one of the Dolphins swam in front of me on his side. I stroked his belly with my hand and instantly his dick was thrusting in the air. Boy, did I find an erogenous zone.

Before I go on, I should give you a little more background. First, to my surprise, Dolphins do not feel slimy. Their skin feels more like a wet inner tube, and is very soft and sensitive to the touch. They are fiercely independent creatures, and if they don't want to do something, then no amount of prodding will make them change their minds. If you ever go to an aquarium, watch them long enough and you will notice that they spend almost 80% of their time thinking and doing sex. You think humans are obsessed sexually? Believe me, the Dolphins have it all over us, although being in a tank 24 hours a day probably has a lot to do with that kind of behavior.

The night that I first went for a swim was an experience, to say the least. The frenzy that I started unnerved me to the point that I got out, got dressed, and avoided the pool for the rest of the night. Needless to say, the next day I didn't get much sleep. I could not stop thinking about the wild possibility of actually having sex with them. One part of me kept saying what a crazy idea that was, while another part of me created the most wonderful fantasies. My emotions were on a rollercoaster. I don't think anyone will ever appreciate the way that I felt. The bond that I had formed with a couple of the Dolphins was powerful. It was almost as if they had seduced me by pure empathy. In any case, I decided that the next night I would take the plunge.

I could hardly wait for my shift to begin. It seemed like everyone lingered around forever. And then waiting until it was late enough to safely go into the pool was almost unbearable. Finally things quieted down, and I got undressed...this time no swim suit. I sat on the edge of the pool, and, like the night before, the Dolphins gathered around to play a bit. This time I was careful not to get them too excited right away, waiting for most of them to swim off on their own so that just the two that I felt closest to were with me.

As a part of the show, the trainers would have a couple of the Dolphins beach themselves in a very shallow part of the water. This part was just deep enough for the Dolphins to swim in...about a foot deep. It was my strategy to get the two Dolphins into the shallower water. After the other Dolphins left, I lowered myself into the water and very carefully started to stroke them. I eased my way toward the shallow water, and as I had hoped, they followed. Once I was able to sit on the bottom of the pool, I coaxed them alongside of me and carefully rubbed their bellies.

I started with the male first. Just as the night before, I got an immediate response from him. He rolled onto his side, and as I had hoped, he had a huge hard-on. Now my heart was pounding so hard I was sure it could be heard from 30 feet away. I carefully eased my hands down his belly toward his cock. I was very careful. A full-grown Dolphin can weigh from 350 to 600 pounds. And while they can be quite gentle, I was not sure how he would react when I started to rub his dick.

Despite my confidence in his gentleness, I was relieved when his body simply went limp when I stroked his cock. In fact, he went so limp that at first I thought he may have died! But after a moment he opened his mouth about as wide as he could, his tongue doing a sort of aerobic dance. I slipped my hand up and down his shaft, carefully squeezing it every so often. It felt much like the surface of his skin, that is very firm but still soft. It was sort of knife shaped, wider than thick, and I could feel it move in my hands. It was about eleven inches long, about two inches wide, and one and a half inches thick. The tip thinned to nearly a point and crooked down a little. Overall it was shaped much like his own body...very sleek and streamlined.

When not in use, the cock is retracted completely into the Dolphin's body through a long slit just below his belly. The slits in the male and female Dolphin are almost identical, making sex determination tricky. The best way to tell the sexes apart is by looking at the forehead. The male Dolphin's forehead, or melon, is actually a little bigger then the female's. Of course, if the male has a hard-on, then it is pretty easy to tell males from females! When the cock is erect, the slit parts in such a way that it is oval-shaped. It is said that the Dolphin's cock can be used like a finger and has a great deal of dexterity. That may be true, but on this occasion he did not demonstrate that ability to me. Perhaps he was too wrapped up in the experience.

I found that the Dolphin seemed to like having the base of his cock rubbed the best, so I squeezed it regularly. This went on for about five minutes, and then he started to shudder...as if he was very cold. His mouth remained open wide, and every so often I would rub his tongue. (All dolphins love this...I have no idea why.) His eyes remained tightly closed. All the while, he was totally silent.

Assuming that he was about to climax, I rubbed his dick a little harder and faster. His tail swept back and forth really hard, when suddenly he raised his tail high out of the water, and with the first sound that he had made all evening, he shot his load. There was not as much as I thought there would be...perhaps about two tablespoons. It was quickly washed away in the water, but it appeared to be kind of clear and about the same consistency as human cum. What really surprised me most was the pressure of his ejaculation. It came out incredibly hard and fast, his penis contracting suddenly with the ejaculation. He then relaxed and went totally limp. I kept on stroking his penis but after a few minutes he withdrew it back inside of him. It was only at this point that I noticed that I had a real boner myself. Hard as steel and throbbing. Don't think I've had one like that before or since.

I must say that after eight years, the mere act of writing down what happened has rekindled some powerful emotions. While my encounters with other creatures have been strictly on a sexual level, my encounter with the Dolphins was a much deeper emotional experience. It has been said the Dolphins are highly intelligent creatures. That they are. More then anyone really knows.

After resting for a few moments, the Dolphin left for the deeper water. I looked for the female, hoping that she would allow me to satisfy my throbbing dick. Apparently she had gotten bored with the whole affair and was off playing with the others. I slapped the top of the water to try and entice her back, and after a bit of coaxing, I finally got her to come over. My legs were dangling over the edge of the shallow part into the deeper water. When she got close enough, she unexpectedly grabbed my foot with her mouth and pulled hard. I don't think she meant to hurt me, but over eighty short conical teeth can leave quite a bite mark, and my foot ached for a few days after.

When I re-surfaced, I found myself about six feet from the edge of the pool and started to swim for it. She had other plans, though. She quickly swam between me and the water's edge and pushed me toward the middle of the pool. Her actions alarmed me somewhat, and I was getting just a little bit scared. It was at this point that I began to respect the strength of these creatures...something that I had badly underestimated. If she wanted me to stay in deep water, there was damn little I could do about it. I decided to cooperate, and I swam a little ways out and treaded water. In the meantime, she started to circle me, each time her circle getting a little smaller until her beak was almost touching her tail...with me in the middle.

I tried to stay calm, not knowing what to expect next, when she began to scan me with the most intense sound. As you are probably aware, Dolphins use sonar to "see" with. Their eyesight, while not poor, is not their primary sense. Using sounds that range in frequency from as low as 300 Hz to 150 kHz and higher, it is believed that Dolphins are actually able to "see" what an individual is feeling. For example, if you are in a state of anxiety (as I was), then your churning stomach would easily give away your state to a Dolphin's probing sonar. Their sonar has been compared to the sound scans used by doctors on pregnant women, except that the resolution is a thousand times better.

Being scanned by a Dolphin is in itself a unique experience. The sound penetrates and resonates your body in the most peculiar way. While the Dolphin is scanning, you can actually hear the lower frequency sound waves increase and decrease in frequency. When she started to scan me, I noticed that the other Dolphins were swimming around the two of us, and if any of them got too close, she would chase them away. This went on for about twenty minutes. She would scan and probe my entire body. She seemed to especially enjoy nibbling at my ankles.

About this time I was starting to get pretty tired and thought I better try to ease my way toward the shallow water. She made no effort to stop me, but she did continue to swim around and around until I finally felt the ledge of the shallow part of the pool. I pulled myself into the shallow water and rested a bit. The Dolphin, in the meantime, had wriggled her way into the shallow water and lay very still on her stomach. I pet her and rubbed my hands up and down her sides. She just lay there and did nothing.

I decided that now was the time, and I grabbed her pectoral fin and rolled her onto her side. She cooperated completely. From my earlier observations, I had never noticed the folds of the female Dolphin's slit to be all that distinctive. But when I rolled her on her side, her slit was definitely enlarged and had turned a deep pink color. I could only assume that she was waiting for me to mate with her. Now I was really in uncharted waters.

Whenever I watched the Dolphins have sex, the actual act of penetration was always very brief, lasting no more then ten seconds. The pair would be very excited, the water boiling around the mating couple. For Dolphins to mate, it is necessary for the female to roll over onto her back and expose herself to the male. The male then jumps over the female and attempts to hit the mark with his erect cock. Foreplay consists of very fast swimming, both animals crashing into each other, and a lot of biting. And yet, what was happening now was exactly the opposite. Here she was, totally relaxed, quiet, and obviously very cooperative.

I decided not to waste the invitation and initiated some foreplay. I slid my hand along the edge of her slit and kind of eased my fingers into her vagina. The folds of the slit were very soft and squishy. The muscles of her vagina tightened on my fingers and would not let me probe any deeper than the palm of my hand. Not knowing too much about female Dolphin anatomy, I thought that maybe the male's penis kind of ran along the length of the slit. I rubbed her for a while and she continued to simply lay quietly, occasionally taking a breath.

While I had been treading water, my hard-on had mostly withered away. Nervousness over the position I was in probably had a lot to do with that. But after some time with her in the shallow water, my penis was firming up again. I eased myself alongside her belly and slowly began to guide my cock into her. She felt my body draw close to hers, and for the first time since we started foreplay, she moved around a bit, rolling a little further onto her side and arching her back. She obviously wanted me to enter her. Taking a deep breath, I slipped inside of her. To my surprise, my cock went all the way in! She relaxed her vagina and allowed me to move into a more comfortable position. My next concern was the fear that she would roll over on top of me. But fortunately she didn't. Instead, she simply wriggled herself around so that we were both comfortable.

Within a few seconds, my cock had become rock hard again, and she repeatedly tightened and relaxed her vagina. In twenty seconds I was ready to climax. I held back as long as I could, but the pulsing action of her vaginal muscles was just too much. I came hard inside her and was so wrapped up in my own climax that I didn't even notice if she was reaching orgasm, although I would like to believe that she did.

When I finished, I held on to her tightly, wrapping my legs around her tail. My cock was starting to fail me, and despite my best efforts, I could not sustain the erection. She just remained still, occasionally sweeping her tail back and forth. The kneading action of her vagina continued but at a slower pace. I kept splashing water on her side to be sure that her skin did not dry out.

I don't remember how long we embraced, but it must have been for at least twenty minutes or so. Looking back, I am not sure what I enjoyed more, the actual sex act or the time I spent holding her. It was getting close to 4:00 AM, and since the trainers would sometimes come in as early as 4:30, I decided I'd better get changed. It was hard to leave.

# Wedding Night Fantasy

## Sonya

Her name was Amanda, and we were going to be married. She was the gentlest creature I had ever known. Beautiful and quite intelligent, considering her gender.

The last time I saw her alive was the day before our wedding.

I remember it like it was yesterday. We met for breakfast that morning; it was a casual affair for members of the wedding party. She was blissfully happy—laughing and joking with her sisters and friends. While her attention was outwardly focused on them, she occasionally (and discreetly) squeezed my knee underneath the table, her green eyes glancing over at me affectionately.

When we said goodbye that morning, I looked at her and thought, "The next time I see this lovely girl, she will be adorned in her wedding gown and walking down the aisle towards me." I felt like the luckiest man on earth. When we parted, I kissed her softly on the lips and felt her hand slipping into my breast pocket. She gave me a sly little smile and whispered, "Read this after you have retired for the evening."

I don't recall if I told her I loved her.

I probably didn't, and wish now that I had.

• • •

Later that same day, right after dusk, one of the servants from her parents' manor came to the door looking dreadfully unhappy. He told me Amanda had suddenly become ill.

When we arrived at her house, it was surrounded by an aura of gloom. I walked in the door and heard her sister sobbing. I knew something was terribly wrong.

Her parents were away for the afternoon and had not yet returned, so one of the servants took me aside and gave me the grim news. He told me she was dead. Of course, he didn't use those exact words. He used soft, pretty words, but the meaning was the same.

Apparently she had been fine all afternoon. She took a leisurely bath and then complained to her maid that her head hurt. The pain wasn't too severe, and they both assumed it was just a normal headache. She put on a nightgown and planned to lie down, when suddenly she shrieked, grabbed her head, and collapsed to the floor. The doctor was summoned, but nothing could be done. She was dead before he even arrived.

I couldn't believe it.

It simply wasn't possible.

I asked to see her. Since I was her fiancé, naturally I had the right to see her in private.

•••

Her bedroom was dimly lit by dozens of candles and filled with bouquets of white flowers. The thick, sweet aroma was morbid under the circumstances. Of course, the flowers were sent in celebration of her upcoming wedding. She would be receiving many more sooner than anyone expected.

She was laid out on her canopied bed. I walked over and brushed the thin veil aside, catching my breath as I caught site of her.

Keep in mind, she was a proper Victorian woman. As close as we were, I had never seen her in anything but high-necked, tightly corseted dresses. I don't even recall ever having seen her with her hair down.

Apparently the shock of her sudden death had stunned her servants as well. They had not redressed her body, but merely left her laid out on the bed after the doctor's visit.

She looked like a sleeping angel, her head tilted to one side, her arms crossed over her breasts. Her long blond hair unbound, streaming freely across her shoulders and spilling onto the white linen pillow beneath her.

Her face was so pale, yet so beautiful. Long lashes framed the green eyes that were forever closed. Her supple mouth retained a trace of color, her lips pale pink, soft and still as inviting as ever.

She looked very innocent lying there in a white gown and bare feet. I could see the outline of her pale nipples through the thin gauze, and as my eyes moved reluctantly down her body, they lingered on the faintest trace of the golden fleece that was nestled between her legs.

Since I had never viewed her feminine form this way in life, I felt a great sense of guilt as my eyes feasted on her flesh while she lay unknowing in death.

I sat on the edge of her bed and leaned against the mound of pillows, gazing down at her and stroking her hair lightly. Could she really be dead? I thought I saw her chest rise and fall with a shallow breath but soon realized it was merely my imagination. Her body was completely still.

When my hand brushed her cheek, I felt her chill. Her lovely pale skin was cold to the touch yet just as appealing in its velvety smoothness as before. I took her cool, fragile hand in mine and kissed the tips of her delicate fingers. Her body was relaxed. No hint that rigor mortis had begun to claim her as of yet.

Suddenly I remembered the letter in my pocket. I withdrew the envelope and opened it...

To my beloved Groom,

On the eve of our wedding, I want to tell you how very much you mean to me. I love you with all my heart. My desire for you deepens with each passing day.

As I lie here alone in my bed, I think of you and my pulse runs quick. I imagine your warm form lying here with me, your hands running over my flesh, inspiring feelings that I have only fantasized about, yet never experienced.

Dare I confess? I have dreamt of our wedding night for months now. Since nearly the first time I laid eyes on you, I couldn't help but wonder what it would be like to lie beneath you. My virgin body craves your touch, and I shiver in anticipation of our first true union.

Tonight you own my heart and soul; tomorrow you will own my body as well.

With Deepest Love,

Amanda

The words brought tears to my eyes. Hearing her speak to me again made me realize the finality of the situation. But tears were not the only thing her words inspired....

Just one kiss.

I had to feel her lips one more time. I rose to my feet and leaned over, brushing her cheek lightly before I laid my mouth on her soft, cold lips. She was as enticing as ever. If I were to be completely honest—perhaps she was more desirable than ever. Her words had stirred my passion, and her innocent, lifeless form was incredibly seductive.

I ran my hand across her cheek to the smooth, ivory flesh of her neck. She was like an angel sculpted from marble, cold, perfect, still. The difference being marble would not yield to my desire the way her soft flesh would. My hand moved lower, caressing the mounds of her full breasts.

She was almost my bride. Was it truly blasphemy to enjoy her body once before she was encased forever in her tomb? I truly loved her, and the thought of her perfection fading without ever having been tasted was unbearable.

I knew at that moment what I was going to do.

I walked over and quietly latched the bedroom door, then stripped off my clothes.

I crawled into her bed, and somehow it felt natural, even right. I kissed her softly on the lips and let my hand move down her slender form, as if trying to capture her gentle curves, hoping to burn the memory of them into my mind forever.

My hand traced the supple fullness of her thigh and moved to the hem of her nightgown. I drew the gown up to her hips and stroked the inside of her lovely legs, parting them slightly.

I moved on top of her, straddling her as I slowly peeled the gown upwards, over her hips and breasts. I lifted her torso, and pulled her towards me, her head falling against my shoulder as I pulled the gown completely off, then I laid her gently down.

I positioned her arms above her head in a relaxed manner, and she looked as if she were lying back waiting for me to ravish her. I thought, "Yes, my dear, I will ravish you one time before surrendering you forever to the arms of death."

I kissed her deeply. Her mouth was as sweet as ever before. I caressed her neck and cool breasts lovingly with my tongue as my hand slipped again between her legs. Her skin smelled sweet, traces of her bath oil and perfume still lingering. I parted her legs more as my mouth worshipped her stomach and finally the inside of her soft thighs.

My manhood was throbbing, but I knew that in death, as well as in life, she would need to be prepared to accept my shaft. I moved my mouth to her feminine opening and gave her the moisture she could not provide on her own. I probed her softly with my fingers, confirming that her hymen was still unbroken, as I knew it would be.

When I could wait no longer, I moved on top of her and pressed my aching cock against her now-damp entrance. I eased into her slowly, feeling her muscles yielding slightly as her walls were penetrated. When I broke through her hymen, I smiled slightly, knowing it was causing no pain.

She was tight and the feeling was delicious. When I had entered her completely, I stopped for a moment and reflected on the odd combination of sensations. Her body felt wonderful and held me snugly, yet the coolness surrounding my cock was something entirely new. Her flat stomach and full breasts lay against my chest, and they too were delightfully cool against my skin.

I was overwhelmed by the intensity of the experience. This dark pleasure was sweeter than any I had known before.

I moved in and out of her, taking my time, wanting to make the experience last, when something odd began to happen. Perhaps I was not thinking clearly, which would have been understandable under the circumstances, but I swear I felt her begin to get wet. No doubt there are explanations for such occurrences, which I would rather not contemplate; however, at the time it was miraculous. Her body welcomed me, and soon I felt my shaft move easily within her smooth, wet walls.

I made love to her for a long time, stopping occasionally to rein in my passion, shivering on top of her as I slowly regained control, then thrusting into her again. I nuzzled her neck, and whispered endearments softly into her deaf ears, telling her how beautiful she was, how much I adored her, how I wanted to please her as she was pleasing me. I held her face gently and plunged my tongue deeply into her cool mouth, caressing her slack tongue, gently biting her soft, cold lips, moaning my pleasure into her open mouth.

After a long time I turned her over and entered her from behind, kissing the back of her neck and thrusting into her welcoming flesh with ever-increasing passion. I lifted her hips and rose to my knees, ramming into her with greater force, knowing I would not cause her pain, her flesh would not bruise. Her slack body rocked with my motion, arms limply at her sides, face buried in the pillow, covered by her mane of wavy blond hair.

Finally I could hold back no longer, and let myself fall into the chasm of pleasure that was calling. As I began thrusting hard, with complete abandon, I felt her muscles shiver around my cock and that sent me over the edge. I came violently, and I very nearly cried out as my hot semen flooded her cold insides.

•••

I lay on top of her for a little while afterwards, stroking her soft hair and telling her how much I loved her, how much I hoped she would forgive me for what I had done to her. As hot tears came to my eyes, a feeling of peace suddenly immersed me, and I knew she would have given me permission if she could have.

A few minutes later I was dressed, and she was laid out peacefully, just as she had been when I first entered her chamber. I kissed my lovely sleeping angel on the lips one last time and left the room.

•••

That was a lifetime ago; nearly fifty years have passed, and now I am an old man living with nothing but ghosts and memories. I married and had children, and have since buried all of them. Time has robbed me of everything I ever loved and made me realize longevity is a curse.

For many years I shunned the bittersweet memories of Amanda. I lived my life fully and did not allow her ghost to haunt me. Now I spend my days and nights reminiscing. The present is like a fog, yet the past is so clear I can almost touch it. I can still see Amanda's bright green eyes, hear the sound of her laughter, even relive the feel of her cool skin against my own. Her flesh is long gone, her bones have turned to dust, yet in my mind's eye she remains forever young and beautiful. The visions of her comfort me as I wait patiently for a grave of my own.

# True Love

Kurt Hoffman

The day I was to be hanged arrived. A warden called my name, and I shook off a dream of innocent days: impregnating schoolgirls and getting beat for it by my old man. I loved that leather-skinned old alcoholic. I was surprised that I'd gotten any sleep at all, but the previous week of wakeful anticipation must have exhausted my body. We were not meant to know the hour of our own death. Indeed, I'd given no warning to the folks at the liquor store before spraying them with bullets. A mercy I figured.

The warden indicated that he'd be back to fetch me in an hour. My cellmate lay sleeping. A sailor, tough as nails, but prone to every sort of emotional outburst. One evening, a scrap of yellowing bay leaf in his stew sent him on a poignant monologue about a beloved dog he once owned and, apparently, cooked for. His cheeks washed with tender tears, he was nonetheless able to rend a scoffer's throat with a sharpened fork.

I watched his muscular chest drift softly up and down as he lightly snored. I climbed on top of him and leaned my ear against a meaty pectoral. Warmth, the bristle of his thick chest hair, and a thumping heartbeat, the acrid smell of a man. I turned my mouth to his dark nipple and sipped it lightly. It shifted a bit. I noticed a slight change in breathing, and saw his eyes gaze down at me through slits. They closed. Now I preyed on his nipple in earnest, sucking it into my mouth and holding it in my teeth. The sailor grunted and pulled me up to his face. "You're going to die today," he said, eyes going moist. There was nothing to say.

"I want this to be like any other morning for us," I said.

There was a long pause.

He made a gesture. I took my place on the floor, kneeling. I waited patiently, contemplating the familiar smells of our cell, the stale sheets, the rich scent of the sailor's armpits and crotch. The sound of dripping faucets and morning sparrows was joined by the creaking of bedsprings. The sailor stood before me, his heavy, pendulous dick hanging before my nose. Even flaccid, the organ smoked with sexuality, a dark, thick thing, hanging four inches and graced by a pair of large, impossibly low-hanging testicles. It shifted as I watched, and a bit of moisture glinted in the morning light as his foreskin pulled back the slightest bit, sending aloft the strongest concentration of his odor. I lifted him into my mouth and waited.

In a moment, his morning elimination was pouring into my mouth. The amber charge was rank and heady. Rich organic flavors reminiscent of stew and overboiled cabbage vied with the inevitably repulsive sting of digestive juices. It was all from this dear man. I never let a drop fall to waste.

It had been our way. I would relieve him whenever necessary and use the open metal toilet for both of us. Many the nights when I would awaken to his snapping fingers, scuttle out of bed to take my place on the floor.

When this morning's discharge finally dwindled to an end, I spent some time gently sucking out any lingering droplets. He pulled me back into bed.

He drew my mouth onto his, and held me very tight, sobbing. I felt his familiar, thick erection grow between us. He offered his tongue. I parted my lips slightly. The crude, rough-edged muscle slipped into my mouth, probing and tasting, bearing its own ochre flavor of stale tobacco. The organ plunged and twisted, tickling my lips and tongue and the electrified roof of my mouth. Soon it was digging deep into the meat of my throat. As I gagged, my lips struggled to press harder against his stronger ones. My penis billowed to fullness. We ground our crotches together.

He drew his face away and gazed at me.

He made a sudden motion, and managed to roll us both over. I spread my legs, bracing them on the low-hanging bunk above. He gazed into my eyes and took some spit from his mouth. I reached back with my arms to hold the iron bars of the bed and felt his huge meat press into me. He filled me. He reached down to taunt one of my nipples as he began to pump. I pulled his torso down close and locked my lips on his. He picked up the pace. I was not going to last another instant. He planted his mouth over mine, and with one hand, pinched my nose shut. I was suffocating. Come welled up in my balls. I felt his dick, which had seemed rock hard, become harder still, and I knew he too was close. He took his other hand and held my throat closed. I felt a thousand carbon dioxide bubbles effervesce in my bloodstream and a general dimming. I convulsed in orgasm, shooting gust after gust of hot liquid. I could sense his warmth on top of me, in me. Then nothing.

Later that morning I was brought, shirtless and reeking, before a jeering crowd of prisoners. The procedure was unremarkable. The hangman confided to me an anecdote about a sports team. A member of the municipal government gave a brief talk, summarizing the benefits of executing me. I looked forward to the moment I would hang boldly before the crowd, displaying my proud erection. I heard in the distance a hysterical weeping.

## the_Unborn

the Unborn and GashGirl

# *** Connected ***

You join the_Unborn.

Morte
...sideslip... a finely crafted coffin surrounded by mortuary finery...heavy scent of lillies
Mr.Crowe and the_Unborn (slipping away from this reality) are here.

look the_Unborn
the_Unborn
an elegant young man in a ruffled crimson silk shirt and a black leather suit jacket.
He bears a bemused expression as if it were a weapon...

the_Unborn bows, smiling...
the_Unborn intones, "hello there, friend guest... what brings you to this grim place?"

Claude says, "My car's broken down on the road and I was wondering if I could use your phone?"
Claude extends an elegant claw

the_Unborn intones, " .. i am afraid that the phone has been ... out... for some time.."
the_Unborn grips your claw in a friendly manner...
the_Unborn intones, ".. we don't find much need for telephones here... our, um, clients rarely make calls..."

You say, "I could use a bite - I'm starving"

the_Unborn lifts an eyebrow.
the_Unborn intones, ".. hmm.. i don't know if there is much.. it depends on your... tastes.."

the_Unborn pokes at Mr.Crowe.
the_Unborn asks, ".. in the mood to .. eat crow?"

look Mr.Crowe
Mr.Crowe
tall and deathly slim with pale skin and a cruel smile, dressed in a black tuxedo and top hat. In his hands a gnarled wooden cane rests gently. He is sleeping.

Claude says, "Mr.Crowe is a little OLD for my liking"

the_Unborn intones, "i like you, friend guest... we may share some of the same... blood...."

Claude says, "Anything is possible..."

the_Unborn asks, "... i know of a place that you may find to your liking... Would you care to take a walk?"

Claude pierces her neck with her special claw
Claude says, "Tell me where."
the_Unborn peers intently at your special operation...
the_Unborn intones, "let us call it a surprise... "
the_Unborn bows, "... shall we...?"

the_Unborn goes south.

go south
a shimmering doorway
... sideslip ... You stand upon a large disk of dark stone, cracked and worn with age. Light is provided by shining gateways all around you. Beyond these, Blackness... A deep voice whispers in your mind...
Doom...

the_Unborn gestures towards the shimmering <exit>...
the_Unborn intones, "after you..."

Large silver doors seem to float out of nowhere to the southeast. They lead to the Morgue.
You gather your courage and push open the doors to the Morgue.

The Morgue
The smell of ripe bodies inundates your lungs and assaults your senses as you enter the Morgue. The rows and rows of sarcophagi lining the walls don't forebode well, either. It's cold, very cold, and you don't feel very good. You want to leave, but you are drawn. Stay for a spell ... grab a cadaver from Body Bag and have a seat on it... cut it up with the instruments on the table and in the cabinet. Don't forget to leave. Have a nice day.

To the south, you see another pair of doors, also metal. Affixed near the top of the doors are clear plastic windows.
You see Cabinet of Pathology Instruments, Table of Surgical Instruments, and Body Bag here.
Misery (dead) is here.
You have arrived. Welcome.

the_Unborn enters the room with some trepidation.
the_Unborn intones, "you see? we think along the same lines..."

Claude peers inside the body bag hungrily saying, "I always recognise a kindred spirit"

the_Unborn takes a septic axe from Cabinet of Pathology Instruments.
Claude picks up a large syringe and a pair of tongs
Claude is yearning for viscera
A discarded, bloody pancreas starts creeping towards you.
Claude engorges it greedily
the_Unborn tests the edge of the septic axe..

Claude says, "a little crude for my tastes"

the_Unborn intones, "one does what one may with what is at hand.."

the_Unborn drags Spare_Ass_Annie from Body Bag and plops it on the ground.
You can smell the pungent odor of death.

Claude swoons
the_Unborn sinks into the warm flesh of Spare_Ass_Annie.
the_Unborn begins to carve idly at Spare_Ass_Annie...
the_Unborn sighs deeply
Claude straddles Spare_Ass_Annie's face ... the juices mingle

the_Unborn intones, "... the dead *do* become a bore.. one must do all of the work for them..."

the_Unborn drags Lemond from Body Bag and plops it on the ground.

Claude says, "friend of yours? Another guest perhaps?"

the_Unborn intones, "we seem to have no end of playmates..."

Claude says, "Smorgasbord . . . is there a party?"
Claude picks up a saw and looks at it thoughtfully. She likes to play rough with herself

the_Unborn asks, "hmmm... doesn't every good party end up in the Morgue...?"

Claude places a saw on the tattooed black band on her upper thigh. The steel is cold, and merciless. She shivers in anticipation. Claude lightly pierces her skin. Claude's blood drips . . . .
the_Unborn leans forward to get a better view.. he nods in encouragement...
the_Unborn catches a drop of blood on the back of his hand...
Claude's flesh parts to reveal throbbing red wet flesh
the_Unborn brings the blood to his nose, sniffing appraisingly.. he seems a true connoisseur.
Claude licks the blood from the back of the Unborn's white hand . . . so safe!
the_Unborn smiles and nods ".. *very* nice..."

Claude shivers . . . she offers the fine wound in her upper thigh (so soft) to the_Unborn.
Seeing so fine a blood oozing delightfully, the_Unborn stares hungrily..
Claude notices a faint slurping noise as the blood pumps through her open veins..
the_Unborn intones, "... a shame to let such as this go to waste..."

Claude hears a dull rasping as the surgical saw (so sharp) hits the bone of her upper thigh
the_Unborn moves closer to you, a maniacal gleam in his eye...
Claude says, "Be my guest . . . take your time"
the_Unborn bends closer to the ragged wound.. the pain increases wonderfully as he laps hungrily at the warm liquid...
Claude feels an exquisite sensation. She makes a small incision above the_Unborn's left nipple (so hard)
the_Unborn runs a finger expertly over the bared bone of Claude's leg...
Claude shudders with unspeakable pleasure.

the_Unborn whispers, ".. the blood is the life, the flesh is the vessel..."
Claude clamps her full lips to his wound and thinks rapturously of sutures
Claude says, " . . . the spirit is eternal"
the_Unborn murmurs, " .. the blood mingles, becoming one thing..."
the_Unborn intones, ".. we are honoured to carry the liquid, to share in the becoming..."
Claude sucks gently, enjoying the familiar nourishing nectar

the_Unborn is, by now, reddened and glistening over his face and arms... he does wear it well...
Claude . . .in a frenzy . . . grabs the saw and severs her entire leg (so useless) in three swift strokes, saying, "Red becomes you"
the_Unborn, caught up in the frenzy of the moment, bathes in arterial spray...unbridled delight shows in his blazing eyes...

Claude says, "I'd like to offer you a memento ...take this shapely calf and slender foot and do with it as you will, whenever you desire..."

the_Unborn, moving close, reaches to his own face...
the_Unborn plucks forth his own eye in a fluid motion, the squelch of removal and the tiny sound of the nerve breaking sends shivers of wonder through you...
the_Unborn intones, ".. take this.. so that i may always see what you see..."
the_Unborn winks at you with an obscenely gaping socket...
Claude places the eye somewhere safe

the_Unborn offers his wrist..
Claude probes that tantalising tight juncture with her sharpened teeth, irresistable, bites hard
the_Unborn closes his eye and smiles ... the raw remains of his other regards you intently..

the_Unborn tucks your dismembered limb into his jacket, carefully, as if it were as delicate as a butterfly....
Claude strokes the_Unborn's hand with a specially sharpened claw, retracting her razor teeth.
Claude says, "I must go Unborn......"

the_Unborn intones, "... alas... these things must be..."
the_Unborn bows elegantly...
the_Unborn intones, "may you dream of horror unbound, all that may delight your soul..."
the_Unborn winks, "and ... may we meat again..."

*** Disconnected ***

*[Editor's note: "the_Unborn" is not a story. Rather, it is a transcript of a live event as it unfolded. The event is a meeting in cyberspace between two people who call themselves the Unborn and GashGirl (a/k/a "Claude"). This encounter took place in what is known as a MOO. (If I may be allowed to geek out for a minute: "MOO" stands for "MUD Object-Oriented." "MUD" stands for "Multi-User Dungeon," "Multi-User Dimension," or "Multi-User Domain.")*

*Now that you've been overwhelmed with indecipherable acronym-jargon, let's see if I can explain in plain English. When you log onto the Internet and then join a MOO using certain software, you are in a text-based "world." The computer that is hosting the MOO keeps track of where you and all the other people are in this world and gives you feedback based on which direction you walk, what you look at, whom you talk to, and other actions you engage in. You can do all sorts of things, including handling objects, exploring the MOO world, and interacting with other people in the MOO.*

*The Unborn and GashGirl met in LambdaMOO. When they entered commands such as "look the_Unborn" and "go south", the computer responded with, respectively, a description of the Unborn (which he himself had created earlier) and a reference to the shimmering doorway that lies to the south of the room in which their encounter begins. For more info about MUDs and MOOs, check out <http://www.mudconnector.com> or search Yahoo! <www.yahoo.com> for "MUDs".]*

# An Interview with Anna Marti

## Society for Human Sexuality

*Anna Marti is a "sex and spirit" counselor and intimacy coach in Portland, Oregon. Her approach to sexuality is influenced by her knowledge of Eastern spiritual sexuality practices (often collectively referred to as "Tantra"). Although her counseling work is non-denominational, this interview (conducted in her Portland office on 12/26/97) begins with an inquiry into some of her work's spiritual underpinnings.*

Society for Human Sexuality: ***What is Tantra?***

In this country, "Tantra" is actually a catchall word used to describe a number of different spiritual practices that have an erotic component; these practices first showed up in the Taoist tradition, in Tibet, in Nepal, and in India. The word "Tantra" comes from a Sanskrit word meaning "to expand, to weave together." In the cultures that they manifested in, these erotic practices were seen as cults: "You're doing what!?!" It's the same thing any culture says about people who are outside of what they consider the norm.

If you're asking about traditional Tantra, then we're probably going to have to go another direction, because my understanding, from looking at the material for the last fourteen years with the help of teachers, is that there are probably only two people in the Western hemisphere who know traditional Tantra, and I know I'm not one of them. Most people, myself included, simply draw upon the erotic component of what is a huge body of spiritual material.

As far as I can understand, all spiritual systems have their inception with an individual having an altered state experience: the ego boundaries dissolve and there's a connection, there's an acknowledgment, there's a deep knowing of relationship with all things. As I understand Tantra, philosophically it's not unlike quantum physics. I wouldn't purport to be knowledgeable about quantum physics, but my very minimal understanding is that they've broken down matter to a particle which seems to be the same particle. What that translates to is that there's one of us in this room, there's one of us in this floor, there's one of us in this city.

Tantra essentially says there is one energy which pervades the universe, and the pain that I experience in my life comes from my identification with my sense of separateness. I can separate myself in so many ways from the moment I wake up: I'm a woman, I'm older, I'm younger, I have more money, I have less money, I have that kind of car, I'm first in line, I'm last in line, I'm too thin, I'm too short. From a Tantric perspective, that identification with the separation is where my pain is. There's a huge body of material with meditation and practices to purify the mind, the body, and the emotions, so that I can condition my organism to not be in that state of separateness.

There seems to be a part in us which recognizes when somebody else is not in that state of separation and can recognize when someone is in an expanded state instead. There have been individuals who have found that if you hang out in high states of arousal for long periods of time, as well as doing all these other practices to purify the mind and the body and the emotions, that you can enter a room of expanded consciousness—this room of boundaries dissolving.

In this country, we think we've got the copyright on dysfunctional sexuality, but in almost every spiritual system there's a huge schism between body and spirit. What has happened in this country is that because we're a capitalistic society, we've taken that dysfunction and turned it into business. We have so much pain about our ability to connect with another, and so we've got a myriad of books and workshops and audiotapes and videotapes speaking to that part of us which says: "This is supposed to be better!" We've grown up on fairy tales, movies, and romance novels. It would seem that sex has the potential for this union; the ecstatic sense of going into someone else's body, and everything about it implies a real sense of merging and connection, but for most people it's about as far from that as it can get.

I don't think there's a quick fix for us as human beings in connecting with each other; I think it takes a tremendous amount of intention and integrity and commitment and work. But, our culture is not built on things taking time, it's built on, "I want something right now; I want to fix this right now." So it's a perfect market for books and videos and workshops.

I think in some ways we do the public a disservice when we promise they're going to change their love lives and deepen their eroticism with their partners in only a few days.

SHS: ***Is enhanced enjoyment of sex related to enhanced enjoyment of life in general?***

Absolutely. My understanding of sexual energy is that it's a neutral force, like the electricity coming into this room. The electricity doesn't care whether I turn on the lights or the stereo or the heat. And sexual energy is creative in nature; you can create another human being with it. That's about as creative as you can get on the physical plane. Any time we're in a state of arousal, our body is organizing itself to create another human being; that's pretty intense energy. The truth is, for most of us when we're in arousal, that's not our intention: I don't want to create another human being, thank you very much! So what are we doing with that energy, that potentiality, that creativity? Well, for most people there's no consciousness of it at all. From a Tantric perspective, my intention is to remember who I am, to move away from that sense of identification with the individual, and to drop into that state of dissolving into you, of not judging myself for judging you. On a good day it's really cool!

Osho [formerly known as Bhagwan Shree Rajneesh], from my limited understanding, was probably one of the foremost Tantra teachers of our generation. There's red Tantra and white Tantra: red Tantra is the left-handed path which includes the erotic practices, and white Tantra, which is by far the largest body of material, is essentially an ascetic path. In red Tantra people experience all of life as a window of inquiry into consciousness; there are no rules in red Tantra, which is why Osho got into so much trouble (though it wasn't really him, it was the people who were hanging around him). In this system there are no rules about what you drink, what you eat, whom you fuck, whom you do it with. But if your intention is an inquiry into consciousness, then you'd better be awake; you're not doing it any more to satisfy the ego.

My understanding from people who have studied with real Tantric masters is that they had to study for years and years and years before they were allowed to engage in the sexual practices, because you'd better have your ego out of the way in order to come into that union while being clean and pure from an energy point of view. Tantra is being presented as relationship enhancement, erotic techniques, and enhanced orgasms. All those things can occur, but that's not the point. The point is an inquiry into consciousness, and to drop into that state where I can dissolve into you, into the cat, into the trees, and leave behind that pain of separation.

SHS: ***I hear you saying that part of the motivation for spiritual practice is to be able to lose one's sense of separation. Is this because life is more enjoyable from our personal perspectives if we can do that; is it because that is how life would be if it weren't for dysfunction; or is it because we can more easily achieve good things as a species if on a base level that's how we experience our existence?***

I'm going to have to get personal for that one. For me, I've always had a relationship with the divine in some form. In some ways I attribute it to my grandmother, who got out of the camps after the war. What I witnessed for a lot of German Jews was a real separation from any kind of spirituality or religion. My father felt that way for a long time after having lost his sister, and my mother lost brothers and sisters; ours was a very small family as a result of all this. My grandmother got out after being in two concentration camps. Even though I was very young, she was to me an intensely devout person with a very personal relationship with spirit.

Even though I didn't understand conceptually, I witnessed this person who had probably experienced extreme atrocities and was in her 70s when we got her out, but who was like a well of peace. I felt like what I described in the beginning of this interview: when you experience someone in that place, it's like, "How do you do that?" I believe that's what spiritual search is about: that we recognize when someone else is in a place where most people are not. In this culture we're very outer-directed.

I had the great fortune to be in Morocco a year ago. It was the first time I had traveled to a third-world country. Their spirituality is very rich, and their human connection is very rich. In a country where there's no money, time doesn't equal money, so if someone comes to visit your house, everyone stops what they're doing because that's what's of value: the humanity is of value. My brief understanding of religion and spirituality is that we're drawn to those people who seem to be living in those expanded states, who have this deep level of peace and deep sense of compassion.

For some people, the reason they're coming to see me is that they heard they'll have better orgasms. But they have to listen to my rap anyway, because I have a personal responsibility to the integrity of the material. Yeah, I can help you have better orgasms, but trust me: it's not going to make you happy. As David Ramsdale, author of *Sexual Energy Ecstasy*, says: "After a while, even the best orgasm in the world becomes boring."

The way I approach things as far as spiritual practice is that any practice is only as good as its application in my day-to-day life. If I go and have this experience in some monastery or retreat, and it doesn't have its application in my being able to look you in the eyes, or be patient with my kids, or with the people I work with, or when I'm stuck in traffic during the holidays, then it's not worth anything.

Particularly with red Tantra, which says that all of experience becomes my inquiry into consciousness, that means when I'm stuck in traffic, when I'm in line at the bank, when things aren't going the way that I want them to, then where is my practice? It's in allowing myself to come back to present time, because essentially that's what all spiritual practice is. The potential of using the body to be in present time is really what all these practices are about. Every action throughout my day becomes my opportunity to be more fully engaged in the present.

SHS: ***I'm sure that a lot of people do start studying Tantra because they'd like to have better orgasms; in your experience, are these people receptive to hearing about the bigger picture?***

I try to speak to people at the level they come in; it's certainly not my intention to change anyone's belief system. I do have a certain investment in people feeling more integrated. We talked about Tantra meaning "to weave together." I have an interest in at least educating people to know that, although they can have better orgasms, unless they look at other aspects of their life, it's not going to make them happy.

SHS: ***Should couples work to resolve communication difficulties before they start Tantric practice, or does the practice itself tend to resolve these difficulties?***

It can go either way. Somebody who I think is a fabulous teacher—I've studied with him very briefly—is David Schnarch, who wrote ***Passionate Marriage***. He's brilliant. As a psychologist, he has an amazing background in sex and spirit. He does a very funny bit about how "couples don't have problems in communication—they know exactly what their partner's going to say. It's not that they're not communicating, it's that they don't want to hear the message."

SHS: ***In your opinion, what is the single most valuable insight a person can have that will improve their experience of relationships and sex?***

People are not going to be very excited about this, but I think the commitment to your own personal growing up is what is going to give you a better relationship and sex life. That requires a spiritual life; I don't care how you do it, but you need a belief in something that's bigger than your individual ego. Clearing up your emotional garbage, whether that's through individual therapy or group therapy, is also helpful; we've all got it, and I don't know too many people who don't need a little bit of work getting through it—so that when I come into relationship, I'm not bringing my mom and my dad and every lover I've ever had to you. It's just a commitment to be honest with myself and in integrity with myself.

There are a myriad of books and videos about sexual techniques, and if they worked, people would be having a lot more fun than they seem to be having. It really has to do with how I feel about myself, and whether I can be absolutely present in a relationship and in integrity with myself and brave enough to stay with something that's pushing my buttons, to really be in that energy of love and commitment.

Ultimately, what is really healing is sex with meaning; that's a big piece which I try to integrate into my work now. Because you're having functional sex doesn't mean you're having good sex. Functional sex from a clinical standpoint just means you can have an orgasm. I'm shifting my focus away from clinical function. Men, for example, can have an incredibly erotic sexual connection and the best orgasm of their lives and never have an erection.

SHS: ***Do you find differences among various sex-positive communities in terms of their level of interest in spiritual forms of sexuality?***

I would say the S/M community is the most receptive; the S/M community really does seem to be directly interested in altered states of consciousness. My limited experience of swingers is that they tend to be more gender-identified, and Tantra really is about moving beyond gender into an energy experience.

SHS: ***In the S/M community right now there's a lot of interest in using ritualized S/M to achieve altered states of consciousness, spiritual insights, etc. Do you have any tips for people who are using S/M for these purposes, and do you feel that knowledge of Tantra might be valuable to them?***

My experience with people who have a high level of consciousness in the S/M community is that they're essentially working from this perspective, but I think Tantric material could still be very helpful. When I did workshops in Seattle, there were a lot of people from the alternative sex community coming to them, and I thought, "That's interesting, I wonder how I could tap that community here?" So I went to an RCDC [Rose City Discussion Club] meeting, which happened to feature a guy doing a demonstration on caning. He asked for volunteers, and I volunteered.

During the demonstration I just did what I've practiced to do, which is to be in present time. Through this experience I realized this was the same room, just entered through a different door.

SHS: ***For the benefit of people living in or near Portland, Oregon, could you describe your counseling practice and the credentials you bring to it?***

I have a background in hypnotherapy, I've studied with most of the contemporary American teachers of Tantra, and I received my certification in body work through the Body Electric School. Essentially what I tell people is that I support them in creating new maps for how they experience themselves as sexual and spiritual people. There's a huge continuum of people who have sexual dysfunction issues, who haven't done much spiritual work and who could care less about it: it's like, "Fix this problem." My work can be applicable and appropriate for these people, although generally what they get is a lot more than they bargained for. On the other end, I get people who have done a tremendous amount of spiritual and personal work, and who are interested in the erotic piece of that which is not addressed by conventional psychotherapy and certainly not by religion. Most people are somewhere in-between; they have some sexual issues, and they've also been on a personal road or path.

I do a combination of bodywork and sometimes hypnotherapy. I'm really committed to people getting the help they need, and if I'm not it, I'll do my best to help them find someone more suitable as long as what they're interested in is safe, sane, and consensual. I use touch as a modality for people to experience expanded states throughout their whole body rather than just focusing on one part of their body; it's a combination of breath and touch and a vehicle for people to practice communicating about touch. Very few people have practice or are comfortable communicating about touch; how can I tell you what I like if I can't even talk about it? There's the idea that one should endure nothing: if you're touching me and you're touching me wrong, then either I don't say anything—in which case we could be married for twenty years and not learn that when you touch me in a particular way in a particular place, I want to throw up, and build a certain level of resentment that erodes the relationship and trust—or if you touch me in a particular way and I go, "Ouch!! Don't do that!!" what happens is your ego is so involved, you want to pick up your marbles and go home. Realize that the intention we're both trying to develop is connection; even if I have poor skills in communicating that I don't like that touch, you're involved enough to say, "Thank you, of course I want to touch you in ways that are pleasurable."

When I work with couples, there's a kind of dance. Generally I work more on the relationship of the individuals with themselves, because that's where a relationship falls apart—it's when I don't stay in integrity with my relationship to myself. That's what brings breakdown in communication. Generally how it shows up is that what you think of me becomes more important than what I think of me. Schnarch's work is brilliant around this; he sees sexuality as a window to the bigger picture of how you live your life, as a window into individual maturity.

I witness amazing things with people, and sometimes it surprises me. I'm not a clinical psychologist, and I don't have the kinds of degrees that our culture determines as valid, but I witness individuals and couples experience tremendous shift to where I leave my office scratching my head. This goes back to my belief in the integrity of the individual spirit to move itself.

I had one individual I was working with come to that place. He'd done a tremendous amount of work and had stopped drinking before he started to see me. What he said was, "I feel like I have this window open right now, that I could accomplish a lot." I did some hypnotherapy with him—very little bodywork—and in a matter of probably four weeks he was having experiences that he'd never had before. He'd never enjoyed sex, he'd never enjoyed oral sex, and sex was a place that was very uncomfortable for him. In four weeks he was having great sex with his girlfriend all night long, he was enjoying oral sex, all these things were happening, to the point where his girlfriend said, "You must be having sex with her, because nobody could have changed this much." That's not what I do; I'm not a surrogate. I barely touched this person except to do a little breath work with him. It was an interesting side effect; he actually had to stop seeing me because it was problematic for his relationship.

I see both men and women in my practice, as individuals and as couples regardless of gender or sexual orientation. I have done workshops in the past; I would probably do them again, but I need to really feel in integrity with what I've got to say. It's easy to create this really wonderful feel-goody experience for a weekend, but the truth is that people want more of it in their everyday lives. I see it happen in workshops all the time: we can create this very contrived container of love; I can do this exercise with you and be really warm and open with you but have no intention of having lunch with you or going out with you. For certain kinds of individuals, it even exacerbates their sense of isolation.

I do a lot of teaching; we all seem to have been absent on that day of school when they gave out the handbooks for a successful erotic life. Some people come to me just needing a little information to fill in some blanks; they've already done a lot of personal work, and they get to see some lights turn on. With sexual dysfunction issues, depending on what they are, it may require a little bit of time. But I see what I do as Carolyn Mace does, as a boat ticket to the other side of the river; I think any therapy should be a boat ticket to the other side of the river.

SHS: ***What other resources do you commonly recommend to people?***

In terms of workshops, I recommend Human Awareness Institute and the Body Electric School. Charles and Caroline Muir, authors of ***Tantra: The Art of Conscious Loving***, host workshops which are quite valuable for heterosexual-based relational work. I haven't done anything with them for about five years, but for that particular genre I think they do a good job.

My teacher is Bhodi Avinasha, who co-wrote ***Jewel in the Lotus: The Sexual Path to Higher Consciousness*** and who teaches week-long intensives in Mexico through Tantrika International. He has a wonderful level of integrity and closeness to the source of the material. ***Jewel in the Lotus*** is the most concise written presentation of the material I know of. David Schnarch, who wrote *Passionate Marriage* and *Constructing the Sexual Crucible*, also offers ten-day intensives. In my opinion, ten days is just enough time to really go deep with someone.

What I feel I do well is to condense and simplify the material. I always thought that if I were going to write any material—which I probably will—I'll be doing the Cliff Notes of Tantra. Because essentially a simple approach is what people want.

Annie Sprinkle is a friend of mine. I see Annie as a real Tantrika, in that she has an erotic relationship with the planet. That's how I see a true Tantrika; there's this sense of engagement and eroticism that can be expressed in any number of different ways. That's what I explain to people when they first start working with me: we have such a limited range of expression, and my hope is to expand that range of expression. Because if I'm using all of my behavior as an inquiry into consciousness, I may be standing at the checkstand and just drop into the melting cosmos with you standing across from me. The old paradigm would be, "Express it or repress it." The Tantric perspective would be to just drop into the energy; hopefully I will have developed the consciousness to arrive at what the appropriate choice is for that moment, which is probably just to really be in that energy and pay for my groceries and go to my car, which would be neither having to repress it nor express it in a limited way.

Jack Johnston's *Male Multiple Orgasm Step-by-Step* audiotape is also wonderful. I think Jack is doing for men what the feminist movement did for women, as he is redefining male sexuality. The feminist movement has essentially redefined female sexuality, and now says, "Yeah, women have orgasms. Yeah, women can have lots of them. Yeah, women can ejaculate." What Jack is doing, from a Western point of view, is redefining male sexuality so that men need not be limited by one or two ejaculatory orgasms, so that men can access full body orgasms—like women do—which ignite emotional, spiritual, psychological kinds of awareness.

SHS: ***I agree that Jack's work is remarkable. It's interesting to me that in most sexual self-help books very little of the material focuses on how we can enhance our personal experience of sex.***

For both men and women, I think most sexual dysfunction is in direct relation to this. If I'm only focused on what I'm doing to you, I'm not in my body. Men who come in with erection dysfunction or premature ejaculation, especially erection dysfunction, haven't been in their bodies for a long time; this didn't start happening suddenly. Particularly when I work with people who are very outer-directed in their sexuality, it's like pulling teeth to help them realize that they're only going to get as much out of the experience as they're willing to place themselves ***in*** the experience. The most exciting erotic partner is one who is totally wired into themselves and having a good time; they're probably having a good time regardless of who is going to be there. That's an exciting sexual partner! Almost everybody has had a sexual partner who just tries to "do something" to them; it's usually really boring. You see all these books that are focused on this technique or that technique, but it really is about being fascinated with your experience.

For me, the question is how to inhabit my body on a daily basis such that I am totally engaged, because the erotic experience really is about every cell in my body being engaged; the sex cells are not located just in the genitals.

I think Butoh dancing, the Japanese dance form, is incredibly erotic because it's so present. Forget that a lot of times they do it nude; that's not the point. They're so engaged, and that's very Tantric — that sense of engagement. It requires a presence, which is what exalted eroticism requires.

SHS: ***Thank you so much for talking to us!***

You're welcome! It was a pleasure!

## RESOURCES MENTIONED

Anna Marti: (503) 499-7800

Human Awareness Institute: (800) 800-4117

Body Electric School: (510) 653-1594

Tantrika International: (888) TANTRIKA

David Schnarch's Workshops: (303) 670-2630

Charles/Caroline Muir's Workshops: (808) 572-8364

Jack Johnston's Audiotapes: (800) BUY-VIBE

RCDC (Rose City Discussion Club): (503) 650-7052

Tantra website: http://www.tantra.com/

Society for Human Sexuality: http://www.sexuality.org/

# The Lovers
## Akasha

It was the first time I had two victims of the opposite sex at my feet. I'd dominated two men at once before, but this added such a new delightful twist that it thrilled me.

Because not only were they both mine, but they were lovers. Devoted to each other.

And the boy, Derek, was barely submissive at all. He was feisty and defiant, stubborn and cocky. Danielle, his lover, was timid and innocent. She cowered shyly against him when I approached.

They both were sitting on my floor. Danielle's wrists were bound together in front of her with a red satin scarf, matching the pretty color of her nails. She was wearing a thin, light, long dress, and her black hair was hanging around her face, slightly disheveled.

She slid against Derek's chest when I approached, and he looked at me with a cold stare. His wrists were bound behind his back, because he was not to be trusted. And no satin scarves for this boy—no—he was bound with abrasive white twine that I'm sure dug painfully into his skin.

I stood in front of them for a moment, taking stock of my prize. Danielle had her head down against his chest and wouldn't look at me, while Derek tried to soothe her by rubbing his chin against her head.

"If only you could hold her," I said to him, crouching down. "Put your hand in her hair to comfort her." I moved my hand to her hair and she shrunk away, while at the same time he lunged forward, only barely, as if to stop me.

"Back off, pretty boy, or I'll cut that hair of hers right off."

He glared at me and I could hear him whisper to her, his lips to her ear, "It's okay, Dani, she won't hurt you. I'm here."

"So much to learn," I shook my head, running my fingers through the beauty's long, dark hair.

•••

I opened my large chest of devilish instruments and browsed through them, occasionally looking up at my two lovechildren, cuddled against one another and whispering softly. Danielle had her bound wrists up at his neck, and he was kissing her fingertips between words. Such devotion, how badly he wanted to protect her. This was better than I had even imagined.

Danielle was only eighteen. Still almost a child, she was innocent and delicate, but devoted to submission. This had been very apparent to me when she approached me at the club, lowered her eyes, and whispered that she would love to some day serve me.

Derek had come over, pulling her to his chest, looking at me suspiciously. At twenty-three, her part-time Master was too soft to actually command her, so he was immediately wary. And after a few weeks of conversations, I had them both, more because it was what she wanted, and he reluctantly agreed, if anything just to protect her.

I could not have wished for a better scenario.

•••

When I stepped over to them with a leather ball gag in my hand, Danielle peered up for just a moment before letting out a squeak and hiding against Derek's chest.

I crouched down once more, Derek's eyes on me, then the gag. When I reached for her chin to direct her toward me, she started shaking violently against her lover, and he again lunged forward, this time letting her fall over into his lap.

"DON'T TOUCH HER," he hissed.

"But, Derek, she needs this. She needs to submit. Danielle, sit up and take this gag for me like a big girl."

Her fingers were clutching his shirt, her bound wrists fumbling for something to latch onto, and her face was totally hidden in his lap. His shoulders moved with a desperate frustration, and I knew he was trying vainly to work his way out of the ropes that bound his wrists behind his back. Such the protector. And so against submission of his own. His eyes were on fire with such defiance that the most cruel idea came over me, and I even shuddered from the beauty in it.

"Derek," I said with a slight smile, fingering Danielle's hair again and watching him scowl. "I'll show the girl some mercy by not making her wear this gag, under one condition."

He looked at me, sternly, distracted by what sounded like sweet little sobs of fear coming from her.

"I won't put it on her, but you have to wear it instead." He laughed, shaking his head. "Fine, I don't care. I'll do anything, it doesn't bother me," and with that, he opened his mouth and leaned to me, so eager, so brave. But I could see in his eyes that he was hating it, and did not want that big leather ball in his mouth at all.

I pulled it away, out of his reach. His mouth closed and he looked at me. Danielle was peering up from underneath her long dark hair.

"No, Derek," I said softly, lowering the leather ball gag and placing it into Danielle's soft hands. "She will put it on you."

Danielle dropped the gag like it was cursed and without hesitation gasped, "NO!" but Derek hushed her, his lips against her hair, leaning down and whispering to her.

She was sobbing and I heard her say, "I could never do that to you!" His words were inaudible to me, but I sat back and smiled, watching them.

"I will wear it, I don't care, Derek, I can handle it...." she was saying.

"That's enough, Dani; I've made my decision. Now DO IT."

I had to smile. Such a beautiful display of devotion, fear, and sacrifice. They were actually arguing about who would get to wear it.

I stood up, hands on my hips. "Enough arguing. The only solution is to make both of you wear one."

Both of them looked up. Derek had an angry, betrayed look on his face. Danielle sniffled and reached for the leather ball next to her lap and said to me, through tear-soaked eyes, "I'm sorry. I'll do it." It was so obvious at that point her goal was to not displease him. The Master who wasn't even a Master.

So only fifteen minutes into it, I sat and watched her sit up onto her knees, fumbling with bound wrists to hold the gag in place while he urged her when she hesitated, leaning forward because she was frozen in horror over what she was about to do. Only fifteen minutes into it, and she was hesitating and stopping, pulling it away to lean forward and kiss him. How sweet, a farewell kiss that he accepted graciously but broke halfway through to say, "Dani, come on, just do it," because he knew that any more stalling would result in a far worse situation.

Through soft tears Danielle said, "I'm sorry, I love you," and in went the gag, as far as she could get it. She couldn't manage the straps because her hands were bound, so I ordered him to lay down over her lap while I helped get the buckles in place for her. Then I made her buckle it, watching her shaking hands. The slave was forced to be the Mistress, and it was killing her.

•••

When Derek was no longer able to give her comforting words, Danielle seemed more like a lost little girl. She still sat close to his chest, and he still tried to nuzzle her with his chin, but she was afraid to look at him (to see that awful gag), and he was unable to provide those soft kisses against her ear that calmed her.

I reached down, took her by the back of the neck and pulled her to me. Derek moved again, moved to block me or to hold her back, but it was in vain. With a shove to his chest, he was back against the wall, and the entire charade seemed to unnerve his lover even more. When she looked at him with scared eyes, obviously terrified that he was hurt, he just blinked at her, resigned to sit back so she would not get all wound up in a frenzy of fear. If all he could provide was calm, strong eyes of reassurance, that was obviously what he was determined to do.

That is, until I blindfolded her.

•••

Once I got the scarf tied over her pretty brown eyes, it was time to deal with Derek. I had to lock Danielle to the bed so she wouldn't scurry away, ordering her not to pull the blindfold off with her bound wrists. Then I went to Derek, who was edging forward on his knees, and I shoved him back against the wall.

Taking him by the shirt collar, I hissed, "Look, little slaveboy, if you interfere, I will make it more painful for her. I will leave long streaks on her pretty white skin, I will leave her in tears, I will violate her sweet little body in ways that you have never dreamed of."

Danielle could not tell what I was saying but still called out, "Derek??" because she heard me hissing.

I saw his eyes, the pain in his eyes that showed how badly he wanted to answer her, to tell her he was okay. It was killing him that she could not see him, and he could not call out to her. I could tell, by the way he was looking at me, that he was ready to do anything to be allowed to be there for her in some form.

I just shook my head. "You should have thought of this before you were such a miserable bastard to me. Because of that, you can sit here, alone, and she will be calling for you, for your help, for your comfort, and for all she knows you aren't even there." As I stood he looked up at me. Such true pain in his eyes, mixed with anguish and resentment.

"You've abandoned her," I said. And as I turned away I realized that the blow I had just delivered him was by far the most painful thing I had ever done. To anyone.

And I heard him choke back a sob.

•••

I put Danielle on my bed. She was semi-holding me, off balance because she couldn't see. "Is Derek here? Is he okay?" she asked. I knew he could hear her because he shuffled in his little corner, let out a muffled acknowledgment.

She bit her lip. The sound of him like that obviously shattered her nerves. She was used to him being strong and comforting, and he sounded so totally helpless that it killed her.

He must have sensed this too, because from that point on, he kept quiet except for an occasional thump against the wall or the sound of his deep, steady breathing.

"It's okay, Danielle, I'll take care of you now," I said, easing her back against the big pillows on the bed. I untied her wrists and separated them, tying them slowly to each of the bedposts above her. Danielle did not struggle or try to get away. Wearing the blindfold, she looked simply beautiful. Like an innocent princess.

When I moved away from the bed, I stopped briefly to pull up her dress, slowly, and as I did there was quite a shuffle from Derek. I turned and gave him a knowing glare.

He looked menacing. Possessive.

I hiked the dress up a bit more and she squirmed, moving her little hips back and forth. Her lips were parted and she was breathing hard. Her body moved with me, not against me.

I backed off, leaving her dress up right at the tops of her thighs, revealing the pink shade of her panties. But only a little.

•••

I returned to visit Derek for a few moments, bringing over my large case of various pain toys. As I crouched, his eyes were fixed on Danielle on the bed, watching her, as I had just watched her, squirming so helplessly in the bonds. Her dress moved up even more with every shift she made. "Derek," I turned his chin toward me, and he yanked it away but looked at me. I opened the case, and his eyes moved down to it. To the small floggers, the nipple clamps, the sharp little pricking devices, the various pumps and vibrators. The inflatable plugs and things he could not even identify.

I picked up a beaded rubber flogger and held it in my palm, letting the beads drop slowly one at time. "Tell me, Derek, would you trade places with her right now?" My voice was a whisper, so I knew she could not hear.

He nodded without hesitation, nodded and grunted, and then Danielle called out his name and his eyes shot painfully toward her.

"You know, I would be much harder on you," I said.

He nodded and wanted so badly to talk. For a moment I was tempted to take out the gag and make him whisper to me. Whisper how much he would take.

"Or maybe I could make you do these things to her, knowing that if you don't do a satisfactory job, I will do it even worse...that way, at least you could comfort her all the while...."

Derek threw his head against the wall and shook it hard. This was killing him.

"Derek?" she called again, this time her voice shaking a little. "Derek, I'm scared...."

He slammed his head back again. This time hard. Hard, so that the pain would deaden the emotional agony. He was writhing in pure agony, and I was loving it.

"Would you beat her, Derek?" I asked.

He shook his head, his eyes lowered.

"Would you rather I do it?"

He shook his head even harder, then raised his eyes to me and looked at the flogger in my hand. He nodded. He nodded hard.

"I don't trust you," I said as I stood, and he scowled at me, tried to get up, but I pushed him down with a boot to his chest.

"I will do this my way, and you will watch. And maybe learn something. And if you interfere, I will do it twice as long, twice as cruel. If you understand, signify this by putting your nose to the floor right in front of my boot." Even with the gag, I could make out the words this time. It was a very audible "Fuck you."

Without hesitation, I spun around, opened Danielle's legs just a tad, and let the beaded rubber whip fall squarely at the most delicate height on her inner thigh. She screamed, gasped, and the tears came at once, and when I turned to face him, he was nose-first on the floor at my feet, and he was visibly shaking.

•••

I left him on the floor there and moved to Danielle's side, stroking her hair as she cried under the blindfold and the tears rolled down her red cheeks. "Where is he? Is he okay?" she cried.

"He's lying in a puddle of his own drool at the foot of the bed, Danielle. And that swat on your thigh was because he was a miserable prick to me, and had the nerve to tell me to fuck off. I did that to you because of him."

He wailed. Derek lunged up onto his knees, and his eyes were red, red with pain and anguish and tears, and the sounds he made were so unnerving to Danielle that she started shaking in my arms and ended up screaming, "Stop! Stop! You're killing me!" because she couldn't bear the thought of him so broken.

I stood. I picked up the flogger and held it in a threatening position. She sensed it, because she closed her legs, but I opened them for her.

Derek cowered and inched backwards in defeat, eyes begging me to stop.

I moved around the bed and pointed to the floor at my feet. He got up and inched toward me, but I hissed, "Down on the ground, all the way."

With only slight hesitation he crawled to me, stopped at my feet, and held still while I leaned down and pulled his shirt up. I took his bound wrists with one hand (and indeed the twine was ragged from being picked and pulled at, his skin tormented and red) and lifted them out of the way, delivering three hard blows to his back and then dropping him like a heap to the floor. He writhed in the sting of it for a moment, and when I turned back to Danielle on the bed, he struggled to bring himself back to his knees so he could at least oversee what was happening.

•••

I sat next to Danielle, and she turned her head toward me. Her lips were trembling. "Is he okay? Did you hit him?"

"He's fine. He's watching at the foot of the bed. He cares so much about you, Danielle. You should see the look in his eyes." I caressed her hair, and she turned toward my delicate touch.

"Can I see him...please...just take the blindfold off so I can see if he's okay?"

"I can't do that, Danielle, but I can assure you he's fine. He looks so handsome, in fact, in that gag. Strong, yet so tortured. He's looking at us right now. Watching you. Wanting to comfort you."

Derek had eased his way closer to the bed and was near the foot of it, watching me, watching Danielle.

She squirmed in the ropes and turned her lips toward me, almost seductively, "Please, Akasha, can I see him...can I touch him?" I saw a gasp of pleasure from her, of recognition, and turned to see that Derek had put his head against her foot, his hair tickling her naked toes, nuzzling her affectionately, comforting her.

When I stood up he ducked back down, and Danielle gasped, "Please! Don't hurt him—"

I dragged him by the hair to the corner of the room again, growling at him not to fuck with me, and used a metal fishhook to lock his bound wrists to the leg of the vanity, which was bolted to the floor, so I was sure he wasn't going anywhere.

Derek sat up and winced, put his head against the vanity leg, let out his breath, and for the first time looked almost defeated.

•••

As I returned to Danielle's side, she lifted her head to me and said, "Did you put him outside?"

"No, he is on the floor by the door. He can see everything. Are you ready to start, Danielle?"

She shook her head. I played with her mouth for a moment, tracing my fingertip over her soft skin and watching her dampen the bottom of her lips. When I leaned down, her chin in my hand, and placed a very soft surface kiss on her lips, Derek rattled the vanity so hard that hairspray bottles fell over and rolled off.

This time, when I leaned back, I could see a little smile on her lips. She had heard that. She was pleased by how possessive he was. She was more in love with him than ever, beyond all the fear she felt.

That alone seemed to comfort her.

•••

It was time to give Derek the ultimate test before starting in on Danielle. I had taken some time to lay out all of my pain devices on the bed alongside Danielle, and Derek watched me like a hawk. Danielle was mostly quiet during this time, occasionally calling out his name.

I finished and said for both of them to hear, "I'm going to take the gag out of his mouth, but if he talks out of turn or does not answer my questions, it goes back in. Understood?"

Danielle nodded eagerly, and Derek looked steadily at me to acknowledge that he heard me. I moved to him, crouched down, and unbuckled the leather strap behind his head.

As soon as it came free he uttered, "Danielle —" and her face lit up with a big smile behind the blindfold. She writhed a little on the bed to the sound of his voice. Even I watched her. She was — I will say it — so sexy in this way, the way she wiggled around helplessly on the bed, her dress now hiked up almost all the way to her waist.

"Are you okay, Derek?" she asked, but before he could answer I stood up and interrupted them.

"This is the proposition. Derek may decide. I am going to deliver the punishment to Danielle and he may watch, or he will take it for her."

"That's easy — " he scoffed, trying to get up. "I'm ready."

"Nooooo..." Danielle turned to him. "Because she'll make me do it!"

"I don't care, Dani, it's better than putting you through it."

"But!" she tried to find the words but threw her head back, silent. Maybe crying.

"You just don't understand her, Derek," I shook my head at him.

"You don't know anything about me. Let's get this over with."

"Derek," I started with a sigh. "Do you know how much it will hurt her to have to do that to you?"

Danielle interjected, "A lot!"

"The emotional pain is far worse than the sting of the whip to her," I told him. "And for you to want to take her place is an act of pure selfishness, because the pain of watching her helplessly hurts you too much."

Derek stared at me. He was breathing hard. These words did not rest well with him.

"Dani," he said firmly. "I will do whatever you want, angel. You just say the word."

"Let her do it to me," Danielle said firmly. But her voice was shaking. She was definitely scared. It was difficult to determine who was saving whom, even for me.

•••

Danielle took her beating surprisingly well. She did cry, and yelled out his name, and begged for mercy several times, but she never safeworded or urged me to slow down.

Derek sat up against the vanity, gag back in place, unable to do anything but watch and occasionally struggle to show his displeasure.

I used a variety of canes on her thighs and ass, followed by an assortment of floggers and other little pain toys that helped to decorate her soft skin in various shades of pink.

The dress was now pulled up past her waist, and through her soft little sobs she asked me what I was doing as I eased her panties slowly down over her thighs. She wiggled to help me get them off, and the familiar rattling of the vanity behind me signified that Derek was not pleased.

I set down my flogger and walked over to him, his eyes fiercely on his lover as she was sprawled on the bed, her cheeks flushed, her body gleaming with a thin layer of sweat.

I took Derek by the hair, a nice tight fistful, and with the other hand brought Danielle's fragrant panties to his nose. Damp with her arousal, the scent was impossible to miss. He tried to turn his head but I pressed them to his nose.

"She likes it, Derek."

He yanked away.

"Do you feel threatened because I can arouse her this way without laying a hand on her?" My voice was a whisper so Danielle could not hear. She wiggled around on the bed a little and called my name. My name this time, not his, and that unnerved him.

I put a finger on his nose. "I'm not done with you yet. This is the part I have been waiting for. Let's see how brave you are. Let's see how much pain you can take for her."

Derek watched me stand and move to my chest of devices. I sensed the fear starting to well inside of him as I pulled out a series of pulleys, ropes and shackles.

•••

Danielle was restless because of the lack of attention, so as I assembled my torture device, I occasionally reached up and tickled the inside of her thigh with a long feather. She cooed and twisted, trying to get closer to the sensation. Obviously very hot, very turned on. She was dying for pleasure, for the sensations that would put her over the edge. And I don't think it would have taken much.

While Danielle was still bound by the wrists to the bed, on her back, I unlocked Derek from the vanity and brought him over.

He was still gagged, his wrists still bound behind his back.

Getting closer to her, I could tell he was weak, dying to touch her, desperately wanting to hold her. She was squirming in the bonds, and her dampness was visible. Her thighs open, she was grinding even against the sheets, dying for the sensation. Soft little moans escaped her lips.

I took him by the hair and shoved his face between her legs, just out of reach, torturing him with her scent, her arousal. She sensed him there and writhed, opening her legs, wrapping them around his head.

Gagged, he could do nothing. I smirked. He shifted and tried to get closer, helpless, and she was trying to rub against his face, to perhaps feel his breath, to feel anything.

"Ah ah ah—" I hissed, yanking him back and shoving him to the floor. He looked up at me with a glare, breathing hard through his nose.

"No time for that, Derek," I said. "We have to move on."

Danielle was lost, writhing in pleasure, coming down from the endorphins that were a result of her beating. She was oblivious to the sounds of my locking her boyfriend in the chair at the foot of the bed, right under the menacing contraption that he was gazing at.

•••

I bound and chained his wrists behind the chair after removing his shirt and tossing it aside. Danielle, finally aware that he was nearby, was calling to him, confused by the sounds of locking shackles and ropes in pulleys.

"What are you doing to him?" she asked me with concern.

"Just making sure he has a good view, Danielle."

I will admit that at that moment I was very attracted to him, shirtless and breathing hard. Or it might have been the breaking down of his spirit, how his eyes seemed to be showing real fear, or how he was finally distracted enough from Danielle to watch what was about to happen to him.

A rope was hanging down at chest level in front of him. I said nothing to him as I fastened it to a fishhook with several connectors, then let them sway a little in front of him while I walked over to my chest to find a few more devices.

As I dug through my toys, I watched him looking at the rope, the pulley, then at his half-naked girlfriend before him as she twisted in her ropes, her arousal still so obvious.

I returned and tossed a few metal things that I'm sure he would not recognize onto the bed, then turned to Danielle. "Time to move you into a new position, my dear."

•••

Danielle didn't resist. In fact, she was quite cooperative, almost in a daze, a weak, sort of drugged state from the various feelings rushing through her. Her hair was wet with sweat, and her body was trembling only slightly when I moved her, still blindfolded but wrists unbound, so that she was lying on her stomach, facing the chair where Derek was sitting facing her.

I stretched her arms and bound them together at the wrists so they almost reached the foot of the bed. If Derek were free, he could lean over and probably touch her fingers. If he were free.

I spread Danielle's legs apart and wrapped soft rope around each ankle, binding them to the corners of the bed where her wrists had previously been secured.

With her dress hiked up almost all the way, I moved my hands over her naked ass, smiling at Derek as he struggled, watching, giving me a look of combined anger and desperation.

"I'll have plenty of time for this," I smiled as I got up, leaving Danielle wriggling face down on the bed.

I took the slack from the rope that bound her wrists together, stood on the edge of the bed to feed it through the pulley, then locked it to the rope that waited on the other side.

I think Derek started to understand, vaguely, what the purpose of this contraption was. Only vaguely.

•••

The clover clamps looked menacing enough to Derek that he turned his head and squirmed a little. "Don't worry," I whispered right into his ear so that Danielle could not hear. "They aren't too bad when they're on loose. It is when they are pulled that they tighten...and keep tightening...until it's unbearable...."

Derek winced and twisted when the first clamp went into place on his left nipple. The right one made him let out his breath.

Danielle lifted her blindfolded head toward us. "What are you doing?"

"Put your head down, Danielle, or I will hurt him."

Her head went down at once.

Next the chain choke collar went around his neck, and his eyes were still shut tight from the bite of the clamps. When he felt the cool metal, his eyes shot open and he looked at it.

I intertwined the loose link of the chain with a cord that was locked to the clamps, then attached both of them to the rope that hung right in front of him.

The way his eyes moved over the device showed me that he understood. He understood all too well.

• • •

"Danielle, honey," I said softly, sitting beside her and moving a hand down her bound wrists, over her arms. "What I'm going to do to you is going to feel really good. In fact, better than anything you have ever felt."

I was watching Derek but he was examining the device before him, looking for a way out, a way to move his body, a way to wiggle free.

"And to show me how much I am pleasing you, as opposed to punishing you, I want you to pull your hands toward your body like a good girl."

Derek looked up at once, letting out quite a startled, muffled yelp.

I chuckled and stroked her hair. "Don't mind him, you know he's jealous. Aren't you Derek? Are you jealous about the pleasure I am going to provide her, is that the problem?"

When I stood up and moved toward him, Danielle innocently tested the slack on the bonds, and when the pulley turned, tightening the clamps that assaulted Derek even more and taking up the slack on the collar around his neck so that it was firmly against his skin, he felt every inch of it.

"Oh dear," I whispered to him, standing behind him as we both watched Danielle innocently fumble with her hands. "Can you imagine what it's going to do to you when she cums, Derek?"

My hands were on his shoulders, and he was shaking, trying to hold so completely still as to not put any more strain on the rope, but his eyes wanted so badly to find mine. He was truly ready to beg.

I wondered which would be worse for him. Seeing her cum as a result of my doing, or the body-wracking pain combined with the total inability to take a breath.

•••

I suppose the most sinister aspect of all was that the more Danielle writhed, the more he whimpered. And blindfolded as she was, she thought the whimpering was merely his painful jealousy and helplessness. She was not attuned to the differences between whimpers of pain and whimpers of frustration.

She didn't notice that the whimpers became more strained because it was harder for him to breathe. Of course, she was busy writhing under my touch, under the feel of the vibrator pressed under her naked crotch, the soft feather up and down the crack of her ass. She squirmed and gasped, lifting her head right toward him, her bound hands wavering, wavering, threatening to jerk up at any moment in the heat of passion.

Derek watched, somewhat mortified, his eyes moving between her, in desperation, and me, pleading.

Such big, defiant eyes turned now to pleading desperation. I stared right at him, absent-mindedly sliding the slimline vibrator toward her most sensitive of areas.

Derek was sweating, trying to squirm into a more comfortable position. He looked so helpless at that moment that I definitely wanted him, I wanted him on the bed and her in the chair. I wanted to be pushing him to the edge while she watched helplessly.

"Do you want to cum, Danielle?" I asked. Derek shook his head hard. He shook his head at me, his eyes saying please, please, please let me go. I dangled the vibrator just out of reach. Her body tried to get to it but she couldn't.

"Please, Akasha," she begged. "I need to cum, I'm so close."

"I think it would only be fair if you asked your lover for permission," I smiled as I stood up. She heard me get up and moaned at my leaving her side, the stimulation stopping.

"Derek, honey, my love, please let me cum," she said, lifting her head toward him, toward where she knew he was sitting. But with no idea what situation he was in.

Derek watched her, his eyes glazed over. Tears maybe, or just a painful delirium.

I was behind him, unfastening the gag slowly. Taking my time so he would be able to think about what he would say. I wondered myself how he would explain this to her, and how she would react. Would the arousal vanish with her breaking down into choking sobs of horror?

Danielle turned her head back and forth, waiting to be acknowledged. "Derek? Are you there? Are you going to let me cum? Please?"

The gag came out of place and I set it on the bed, then walked around in front of him. His eyes were on her, wordlessly staring at her half-naked frame. He was wincing at the mere shaking of the rope as a result of her shifting her hands anxiously. The collar so tight around his neck, I'm certain breathing was not entirely easy.

His eyes moved to me.

"Go ahead, Derek," I said quietly. "Answer your love. Tell her what's on the tip of your lips."

Derek hesitated. "Danielle...I..." he stopped when her head raised to the sound of his voice, the huge smile coming over her face. "I give you permission," he said, and he closed his eyes.

Startled, I turned to him. His eyes were shut. He lowered his head. He took a deep breath and muttered to me, "Get it over with, please." Danielle's body tensed in anticipation and excitement as I sat on the bed beside her. "I underestimated you, Derek." I said. "You're braver than I thought."

He shook his head slowly, not looking at me. I saw his body tense up when she moaned, and he knew better than anyone what sounds she made right before she came.

And when she came, his screams drowned out hers.

•••

It took some quick maneuvering to get from her side to the pulley in order to release it before he choked, to disconnect the clamps before her curling up into a little ball resulted in his nipples being torn right from his body. I muffled his wailing with a damp cloth so she wouldn't go into hysteria, and in her half-dazed post-orgasmic state, she just writhed on the bed.

With the cloth half over his mouth, half over his face, I could feel him sobbing, really sobbing, biting into it to release tension, his body going into involuntary shudders that shook the whole chair.

Her voice came soft, innocent. "Derek...? Are you there?"

When I unlocked his wrists from behind the chair and removed the shackles that held him down, he did little more than slump down and hold himself by wrapping his arms around his chest, careful to avoid his nipples.

I scooped up Danielle from the bed after freeing her ankles and directed her into his lap, where he put his arms around her as she clung to his neck, still blindfolded.

"Do you want some water?" I asked him, a hand on his shoulder, soft, trying to be somewhat reassuring. I was coming down from my own high, I will admit, shocked at my own level of cruelty.

He nodded at me, then nuzzled Danielle, and their nuzzling turned to kissing as I walked away.

•••

In the kitchen I pondered whether or not I had gone too far this time, but reassured myself that neither one had used their safewords, even though they had both had the opportunity. I heard them talking in the next room, and he sounded calm.

When I arrived at the door and went to open it, I stopped. The distinct sounds of eager lovemaking were impossible to miss. Standing against the door, drinking the water, somehow it didn't seem quite fair. But I smiled anyway.

# Clean, Safe, Totally Shameful

Susie Day

Women come, they go. All kinds. Tall, dark, fat, thin, manic, depressive, we get 'em. Women in shaky relationships. Women solidly celibate. Women with incest memories. Women sick of listening to incest memories. They all been cutting slack, stepping back, taking crap, giving in. They all want to *get*, for a change. And they're all lesbians. Whew. Women got a lot of needs, you know? But lesbians need the most, if you ask me.

Me? I'm a working girl. Down near I-95 at the Lesbian Cuddle Brothel. I'm what you might call a "happy hugger." See, cuddling is lesbians' dirty little secret. It's clean, it's safe—and it's totally shameful. The ideal '90s turn-on. We got this blinking woman's symbol out in front of the house, with a neon sign that says, "Unconditional Love for Sale," in big, magenta letters. Draws 'em like flies, too. I got three kids to feed, and these gay ladies are paying my bills.

Let's say a bunch of hotsy dykes comes in here, fresh from the bars, their Avenger meetings. They look slick and fine, and they're oh, so liberated when it comes to back rooms, lesbo porn, cordless appliances and all. But inside they feel sliced up and alone, because, really, how much can you tell your vibrator? None of our clientele will even look at us in broad daylight, but at night they come here. Just to be held, just to be heard by another woman.

And baby, they want us. They want us bad. They spot us nice, old, lumpy dames, all available and snuggly like Mom shoulda been, hanging out around the upright piano in the parlor. We're tricked up in our fuzzy bathrobes and floppy slippers, see, hoisting our mugs of cocoa, some of us with curlers in our hair. Couple of us are knitting, maybe, or playing a hand of Old Maid. To make it homey-like, we're singing soothing Enya songs for the young ones; Holly Near for the '70s crowd. Me, I got my leg up on the coffee table, with my support hose unhooked, giving my varicose veins some downtime. I exude comfort. Hot, steamy, forbidden comfort. Hey, I admit I got a special appeal for these ladies, 'cause I'm straight. They all want raw intimacy with a matron. Oo la la, come and get it, girls.

One by one, they pick us out. I get one of my favorites, a little transgendered gal. We go upstairs to the rooms with them. We loosen our robes to show a hint of maternal cleavage. We open up our arms, and let the girls inside. No sex; no therapy. We listen. We witness the fact that they survive. And we hold them. "There, there," we occasionally say. "There, there." In a rocking chair, singing Tu Ral Lu Ral Lu Ral, I can project a hell of a lot of warmth, for the right price.

Oh, you hear the stories, the reasons why they come around. "My girlfriend doesn't satisfy me," says one, pointing to her heart, "down here." Somebody else tells me she "wants to die" because yesterday she picked up the phone and overheard her lover on the extension, discussing birth control options with her secret boyfriend. Yeah, I've heard it all. They cry, they sob, then they quiet down and listen to our hearts beating patiently through the terry cloth of our bathrobes. And pay by the hour. We also get Union benefits. A health plan. Dental.

Some of them goddam '70s lesbians have been at us to use a sliding fee scale. Huh. They're the ones with the dumb "special requests," like asking us to dress up as famous historical nurturers. Eleanor Roosevelt, Joan Nestle, Shari Lewis, they're standard. The needier ones want to see the Mother Goddess or Glinda the Good Witch. But we gotta draw lines: no Virgin Mary impersonating, and no cuddling cops for free. We run a clean house.

Someday, when I save up enough, I'm going to get out of this one-horse town, take the kids, and open up cuddle franchises all over the map. Later, after I get to college, I plan to design the first-ever virtual intimacy machine. Then I'll be able to lay off most of my staff and watch while my stock shoots up. What can I say, it ain't a perfect world, you know? Not just lesbians, people everywhere are begging to be touched. You just gotta watch they don't screw you, is all.

# Poems

## Ernest Slyman

### Gonorrhea

Human disease blessed degradation
so sweet call in the long lyric cry
of the gonococcus germ,
wolf bay at the moon, lovestruck germ,
worm of the body's temple dark, love-lit,
quoting the Bible, grinding its tiny teeth on the impulses
of joys, singing an old blues song,
lapping up the inhibitions of an age,
and dancing with vigorous wild merriment—
its bizarre thoughts centered on the inner self
and secret the life, scarcely audible
the dance of the spirit, where moonlit
in microscopic snatches
blue red green high stars spiraling
toward the outer galaxy—
the disintegrating infinities
shriek like monkeys burning.
The red stones hurled upward, the mouth
of penicillin clamoring after it,
and gulping it down,
sweet as mother's apple dumpling

### Honi Soit Qui Mal Y Pense

In the dark,
tremble up the unknown unholy pleasure,
as he was a young man
and finding himself passionate,
lusting for the touch of a woman,
Christ masturbated—
and sudden the queer sin
shocked the holy spirit within
unsteady flesh come of praise,
the bland unsatisfactory joy
torn of facile senses, intended for mortal
common man taken good or bad,

spat out the stink of lust,
stained the holy age, quarreling
with the sweet scent of flowers,
devotional sleep and Christ dreamed—
angels about bursting with anger,
red-faced and shouting recriminations,
hideous light, madness about heaven,
thumping on the golden streets
and weeping in the cathedrals.

*(Title Latin translation: "Shamed be he who thinks evil of it.")*

## Mother Teresa's Vagina

Unearthly things
the foolish secret kept delights
these whispers at night
the linen heard the shimmering cool surface
of sin's pale blue moonlight
Stretching out like a virgin sea,
And the giggling fish
Recall the day Christ slept
with a whore,
suckled at her breast like at fish.
The face of one who devoted and zealous
counted his virtues like the stars.
She in the dark sees him on the cross,
she feels the tingling deep within,
guilt changes the world.
Ruthless temptations and the hungry mouths
come and nibble her as she sleeps

# Cum Pigs!!

## Brian

I arrived home from work and found my lover, Mario, already home and naked. Both of us are almost always naked at home. He was lying on the couch reading the paper. I gazed at my lover's Italian beauty as I greeted him. Mario is 29 and a stud at six feet, with dark blond, slightly curly hair and a beautifully hairy chest and torso leading to his lush pubic bush, which surrounds a thick nine-inch (six-and-a-half inches soft) meaty penis with a huge, beautiful mushroom head enveloped by gentle folds of brown foreskin. His penis hangs down over his left thigh and a large, full, hairy ballsac holding his overproductive sperm glands. His beautiful legs, covered by that same curly, blond hair from his crotch, spread gracefully, one down to the floor and the other over the back of the couch, giving a full view of his beautiful hairy, large and delicious butthole surrounded by his lightly furred cheeks.

"Glad to see you're home," Mario said, getting up while I started to undress. Once I was naked, we hugged and I felt his hairy body against mine, my hands caressing his furry butt. "Dinner's cooking," he said, as he looked at my dark-haired, six-foot frame which also boasts a hairy chest and a line of hair leading to a nice bush, crowning an eight-and-a-half-inch (six inches soft) piece of thick meat which, like his, also has a big mushroom head surrounded by folds of meaty foreskin hanging over an equally productive spermbag that crowns my long, hairy legs. With that, he gave our hairy sacs a gentle squeeze and winked that nasty wink and flashed that nasty smile I love.

You see, we're both sperm pigs. We love sperm. Eating it, smelling it, feeling it, playing with it and making love with it. The fact that we love eachother makes us practically worship eachother's sperm. Of course, the sex we have in order to get the sperm is fantastic, but once we gush our cream, the real fun starts.

We have developed many ways of eating eachother's semen. One of my favorite ways is with dinner. Sperm dressing over salad has become a staple of meals at our house. After getting eachother as excited as we can, we hold our oozing, bloated mushroom heads over eachother's salads, watching strands of our juices drip onto the lettuce. I'll insert my finger into Mario's hairy butthole and wiggle it while he jacks off over my bowl. Then *SPLOOSH!* Streams of sperm gush from his swollen cock. You can hear it splash onto my salad. Like me, he shoots huge loads, about eight or nine forceful squirts. My salad is covered and dripping with Mario's sperm.

Now it's my turn. Mario gets behind me, spreads my hairy cheeks and dives his tongue inside my hairy hole. Mario loves feeling my anus spasm on his tongue when I cum, and soon I'm flooding his salad with my sperm. We kiss as we milk the last drops of semen from our semi-flaccid, fleshy foreskins onto eachother's plates. Then it's time to feast. You don't know how sexy it is to sit down to a bowl of salad dripping with sperm, the smell of semen filling the room. I mix up the salad to make sure all the leaves are coated with Mario's sperm. We lovingly look at eachother as we lift forkfuls of sperm-dripping salad into our mouths.

Besides salads, ice cream à la semen is delicious, and bananas or grapes soaked in a bowl of our sperm is fantastic. Sperm instead of ketchup is great on hotdogs, or instead of mayo on a turkey sandwich, mmmm. We love adding sperm to a lot of dishes. Mario takes lunch to work and is sometimes surprised to open his lunch and notice the smell of cum wafting from his food. At home we usually follow our sperm dinners with a thirst-quenching drink of eachother's piss, which we get either by sucking on our fleshy hoses or by pissing in glasses and watching eachother gulp it down.

Both of us are monogamous and have been tested several times. Therefore, we indulge in the most intimate of acts, inseminating eachother by cumming inside eachother's buttholes. We can both cum at least three times a night, and we do. We fuck eachother slow and easy, enjoying the feel of our swollen rods deep inside. Then we wrap our arms and legs around eachother as one and get into a beautiful rhythm as we moan "I love you" into eachother's ears, swapping tongues and finally swallowing eachother's tongues as Mario floods my insides with sperm. I do the same to him, and after we're full and leaking, we get into a loving, ass-eating 69 and slowly eat the sperm from our dripping holes.

Another favorite is when just before bed we stand in front of eachother and jack off into a saucer. We fill the little bowl with sperm, then get into bed and hold eachother tight as we scoop up sperm with our fingers and feed it to eachother, then kiss and swap it back and forth in our mouths as our ballsacs rub together and our dripping foreskins kiss.

Our ultimate sperm feast was the time we each saved our cum for two months in a tupperware bowl in the freezer. We noted each time we added another load of sperm into the bowl. In two months we collected 154 loads of sperm! I had never seen that much semen at once. It was beautiful. We heated it up by letting the bowl float in hot water for thirty minutes. The whole house smelled like a sperm factory. Anyone walking in would've felt like they were suffocating in sperm. It was wonderful and made us sooooo horny. We spent that half hour in the tub pissing all over eachother, and once the sperm was warm and sticky, we took the bowl to the tub and covered eachother with our sperm from head to toe, including soaking our hair with sperm. We each dipped our faces into the bowl of cum (a big bowl FULL) and filled our mouths with sperm and ate it. We slid our sperm-slippery bodies against eachother and poured more semen over our faces as we kissed and took gulps of more sperm, then spit it into eachother's mouths. We fingered eachother's holes with our sperm-covered fingers, then as a finale, we fucked eachother like animals as we scooped sperm into eachother's mouths. With jism dripping from our faces and hair, we kissed and moaned while I flooded Mario's hairy anus with the biggest wad of cum I had ever shot. Mario then fucked me as we wallowed in the tub full of sperm, the smell driving us crazy. Soon Mario ejaculated into me a load so big he almost fainted.

We caught our breath as we lay against eachother and slowly massaged the sperm into eachother's skin and hair. Watching it get all frothy in our hair was great. Mario's penis was still inside me, and as we kissed, I realized he was pissing inside my ass. One more time we sucked eachother off until we came in eachother's mouths and ate the last load of sperm for the night. We were so exhausted we slept naked in the tub full of sperm and let it dry on us until morning.

The next morning, we were getting cleaned up, and as we showered, I slid my cock into him standing up from behind. As his hair got wet, it became gooey with sperm again, and it drove me crazy eating it out of his hair while I fucked him and filled him with my morning cream. Mario did the same to me, and we had a mini-pig session that morning.

Mario and I are no longer together, but I have several other hot stories to share, like the two other couples we met on the Net who were into sperm as much as we were.

As for now, I masturbate like crazy, eating my cum all the time. Even now it's hard to eat salad without sperm on it. So I jack off at dinner quite often. Actually, jacking off at breakfast is becoming more common. Ever try corn flakes and sperm? I even managed to save 74 loads of my cum in a tupperware bowl and relived those incredible nights of wallowing in sperm and feasting on it by myself. I usually go to bed with fresh sperm somewhere on my body and face, often in my hair since I shoot so far. My room always has that cum smell to it, and so do my sheets.

# Baby, Tell Me, Does She Love You Like the Way I Love You?

R. T. Bledsoe

Call it the dignity of solidity, the triumph of flesh over air. Call it the Vargas versus the Crumb model. Vargas's ***Playboy*** pinups, all sleek lines and hollow tummies and streamlined legs, resemble the fantasies they are. Robert Crumb's Amazon women, on the other hand, with their bird-frames, big butts stuck way back, tits held proudly forward, and their thumb-thick nipples, are drawn by a man who, for all his misogyny, genuinely loves the sight of real women (note the famous photographed French kiss he shared with Janis Joplin; who, other than Janis, could lay better claim as the embodiment of his caricatures?). Not only do Crumb's women look sexier than Vargas', they are shown having a lot more fun in bed.

Plumpness, you see, is neither sin nor indulgence. Sometimes it's just fun. Sometimes there's a correlation, an inverse proportion in the amount of fat on a person's body to the amount of pleasure that same person is willing to give. But this isn't that old saw about fat chicks appreciating it more.

Chita, you see, is a large woman, taller than me by a good six inches, which makes her almost six feet tall. She's hefty and weighs around 200 in her usually-stockinged feet. She's one of those Hispanic women who are especially feminine. Who wear dresses and skirts and stockings and a little scent. Who wear just enough makeup to highlight the natural attractiveness of their round, apple-shaped faces, framed by short, black hair. With her mestizo skin and her glasses, her cornflower earrings, and her multicolored dresses and vests, she is a bespectacled kachina doll.

I was only the second man she'd been to bed with. In our society we tend to determine each other's desirability based on muscle tone and weight. A potential partner's resemblance to Leonardo DiCaprio or Sharon Stone. This is really too bad. Because in our quest for the socially-sanctified good fuck, we often pass up the naturally sexy in favor of the artificially hyped.

Chita, you see, was not a Latina Sharon Stone. I met her at a party at the house I share. I recognized her on sight. There are few Hispanic women in Minnesota, and

Chita, in her flowing, flowered, pleated dress, is a redwood in a stand of birch. Talking with one of my housemates, she saw me looking at her. She closed her mouth and gave me the stare right back.

I went over. Asked her to dance. She danced me into the hallway. Pressed me against the wall. Kissed me with a tongue that drilled for oil. I put my hands on her. She was thick. Her fat didn't hang on her but was solid. Like mutton. I put my hand between her legs and she gasped. Her hands found my dick. Squeezed it.

I insisted on leaving the lights on in my room. I took off her glasses and then undressed her slowly, moistening every newly uncovered part with kisses and little bites. I unsnapped her bra. Her tits flopped out like playful whales. Her nipples were large, brown doorbells. I licked them and she grabbed my belt and threw me to the bed. She didn't undress me so much as declothe me. My briefs in the next day's early light dangled from the top of the curtain rod.

She went down on me first. She told me later, "You don't stay a virgin at 21 without learning a few things." She'd taken good notes and made steady use of tongue and lips and fingers. I watched her dark, parted-on-the-side hair bobbing up and down over my cock, haloed by her big, cocoa ass. When I pulled her on top of me, she didn't seem entirely sure what to do. But we soon settled into a rhythm that kept us happy. She hunkered over me like a nurse. I suckled at her luscious tits. Made happy-baby noises. She stared down at me with dark, shiny eyes. When she came the first time, she closed them, and a shudder ran through her that sent a bolt of lightning to the tips of my toes.

I turned her over and covered her mouth with kisses. My hips were an oil derrick pumping past overtime. I slipped one meaty thigh over my shoulder and she cried out at the sensation. There was a sudden odor of hot, meaty juice, like a pocket of trapped air had opened in a broiling steak. Another spasm passed through her, and it touched off one in me. I groaned and spewed warm, wet life into her. She pulled my ass harder to her, as if she wanted to wring every drop out of me.

I rolled and she grabbed my cock, which stayed surprisingly hard. Her hair was askew and her lipstick smeared. Her face was blotchy and the broad expanse of her dark chest covered with small, red marks. While she stroked me, I glanced at the clock. It seemed like only minutes since we'd entered my room, but it had been two and a half hours.

We dozed. My hand on her cunt. Her fist holding my cock. In my dreams I was holding back a delightful, never-ending ocean, and when I woke I spread her body out and played like my tongue was a measuring stick. When I reached the black growth of her cunt, slick with salty lubrication, her hips shifted and her lips opened, and I knew she was awake. I lapped at her clit until she begged me to stop. I made her swear, and she did, laughing, to do anything I asked of her. Then I positioned her with her wide ass humped into the air and pumped her until our groans brought my housemates' nasty pounding on the door.

• • •

Well. All this sounds wonderful. Naturally it didn't last. I wasn't in love with Chita. I was more involved in finding my pleasure in other female and some male beds. But it became painfully obvious in time that she was in love with me.

We spent afternoons having pumping contests to see who would come first and make the funnier face. The loser had to serve the winner food without using hands. We discovered there are many parts of the body uniquely suited for use as utensils. Then she started cooking for me. It began with irregular meals prepared, I thought, just because she was there and wanted something to eat herself. Then she started to call and make plans for us to have dinner together. Then she stopped calling and simply showed up. She came by my house at odd hours, sometimes while I was entertaining some other lover in my room, and left little notes signed "nada."

Still, it was something more than pity or guilt that kept me returning to her bed. She was completely involved in obtaining her own pleasure, and that is a sensuality hard to ignore. Chita was, bluntly, fun to fuck. Our lovemaking was all touching, licking, and sounds. The slap our flesh made when it came into contact was an impetus to greater, harder contact. Her sighs and moans filled my ears. She bathed with lotions and rosewater, softening her skin until it was almost a fragile film that covered her like sausage wrapping.

But I'd never limited myself to one partner, despite the best advice of friends and the government, and I didn't now. I was consistently on the make and brought to my bed an assortment of females and males who shared two qualities: they attracted me at that moment and satisfied me, and I did not return to them afterward.

Instead, I'd find myself knocking at the door of the dorm room that Chita, as a Residential Assistant, had to herself. She'd answer wearing only a nightshirt that reached to the tops of her brown, hairless thighs. She was barefoot and barelegged, the crotch of her colored silk panties visible where the shirt stopped.

I didn't need to say anything. She'd take my hand, guide me inside. Then to the spot between her legs where the color of her panties was darkest. Then press me against a wall or her desk or onto her single bed. Then proceed, with her mouth and hands and cunt, to make me wonder why I ever left there in the first place.

You understand that this struck me, at first, as absurd. I am a well-built, rather handsome young guy, a runner and a cyclist, who stops at windows for minutes at a time, just to check my image. I was, I confess, extraordinarily shallow, the type to make a point of being seen on campus and at the movies with lithe, lovely young things several times a week. Don't think, however, that they didn't satisfy me or were somehow wanting, or, worse, that I failed to satisfy them. On the score of mutual gratification, I am a natural. My cock fits every orifice it comes up against, and I am the type of lover to make certain his partner comes first. (I've often wondered what a night with my twin might be like. Would we both hold off spasming, wondering when the other would shoot off?) But I always ended up in Chita's bed. And I loved every moment of it. And then it was time to get dressed and go someplace else.

• • •

I'd been in Minnesota for a year, and one day I received a phone call. A previous one-nighter, who'd since evolved into a regular stopover on cross-country trips, was coming my way. And she wanted nothing more than a few days with me. Alone.

Lise is a large woman, too, but smaller than Chita. The fat on her is beer bloat, but that isn't the only difference. Chita is a fastidious, feminine dresser. Lise is an androgynous biker chick in jeans and leather boots. Our first night was the result of a misunderstanding. Drunk in a bar in Hartford, I tugged on the rat tail dangling from her short, red hair. At that moment it seemed like the thing to do. She spun on her heel and slugged me. When she saw my genuine mystification, she softened and said, "Poor baby." Offered me a ride on her bike.

We ended up on the beach near Mystic. I was astonished when she took her shirt off. Her tits were huge; but she had no nipples. I prodded the tip of her pale, speckled breast with my finger and then with my tongue. Presently the errant nubbin woke up and poked her head out. Lise laughed and said she had a pair of "innies." I asked if she'd thought to pierce them, so her lovers could tug them out by the rings. She said she'd thought of that, but was afraid the rings might disappear inside her.

She had a nose stud and another diamond stud through the left lip of her labia. She said it identified her as bisexual, although I figured anyone who had the opportunity to see it was pretty sure of her sexuality. The stud glistened in the moonlight when I licked around it. I was surprised it wasn't uncomfortable when I slid into her, although that could have been the condom. When we fucked, her cunt stud demanded she sling a beefy leg over my shoulder so we wouldn't dislodge it. I was a little conscious of something wearing a slight groove along the right side of my cock. But it wasn't unpleasant. When she came, the knob of it actually pressed against me and held me in place.

She slipped her phone number in my pocket when she dropped me off at the bar. Said, "Use that when you come back," and gave me a deep soul kiss. When I found myself near Hartford six months later, I took it out and called. I was at a bar called McCrary's. She said to wait right there.

She roared up to the bar on her bike and swept in, trailing looks as she went. Dressed to the nines in dusty leather. Boots and trousers and jacket. They rode her thick form like a second, black skin. She came up to me and kissed me. She sloshed her tongue around my mouth like she was panning for gold, and she leaned into my body on the stool, slipping my proto-erection against the groove between her leather breasts. She took my hand and led me through the bar of gawkers to the back of her bike.

We went to her place this time. Lise lived in a small house on a very back street in a quiet neighborhood. Once inside, she kissed me again, and her hand trailed from my chest to my cock. "Get naked," she ordered into my ear. I quickly complied, and she pushed me on the bed. There was a mirror, an old, gilt-edged thing, fixed to the wall. I leaned on my elbows and looked up at my reflection. Two Lises rubbed their leather-clad bodies over me, rolling on me like a dog. They grabbed my erection and stroked it. Their thumbs flicked the tip like a lighter. They bit my nipples, drawing blood.

I looked great. All tan thigh muscles, butt scoops, and ribs. Upward-straining cock to which Lise now was attached by the lips. She looked up in the mirror and gave herself a wink.

Lise stood and tugged at the zipper of her jacket. Her very white flesh stood out from the lustrous blackness. She pulled the zipper down just far enough to show me her deep cleavage. Then the freckles on her tits. Then she hung those massive breasts above me. I breathed in the hot odor of road leather and sweat. I licked the sweat from her chest and slipped one fat tit out of the jacket. Her nipple pouted on her breast, and I teased it to erection.

Pretense at seduction or who dominated whom was gone now, and lust flushed out its floodgates. We were a sweaty, black and white-fleshed lump now. Hands everywhere. Lips following hands. For good or ill, we didn't take time with a condom. Lise tugged her trousers down her hips and got on her knees, and said, "Fuck me." She was positioned at the edge of her bed, and I stood behind her and slid the length of my cock into her warm, wet cunt in one stroke.

I have never felt as close to premature ejaculation as I did at that moment. She grabbed my cock with muscles that could have strangled it. She reached back with one hand and held me still until she came in a long shudder. She closed her eyes and a beatific expression came over her face, like those of supplicants contemplating God. The sight of this face in the mirror was enough to send shockwaves down my spine and into my balls, and I unleashed a torrent of come that would've drowned Egyptians. Later, naked and four of us touching under the mirror, she said I came so deeply inside her she could taste it. And the next morning, stumbling on jellied legs, I put on my smelly clothes and, making certain not to lose that number, I went off to make the acquaintance of other lovers in other places.

• • •

Lovemaking with Lise evolved over the years into something occasional and satisfying, that sort of magical, scientific impossibility of two bodies occupying the same space at one time.

All day I thought about how to tell Chita that Lise was coming to visit. I had no doubt that ultimately she would accept it. But, call it maturation, I was becoming conscious of the effect my sexuality had on my partners. One girl, when I mentioned another lover's name, a boy, had burst into tears. I made excuses and left quickly, with her still huddled sniffling on a chair. Over beer bought by someone else, I recognized with a pang of guilt the responsibility I had to those I'd bedded: I wanted to make them happy and I didn't want to hurt anybody. Sometimes this led me to return to beds I hadn't really enjoyed, or even to sleep with someone I wasn't attracted to—the purchaser of that beer, for example, a pretty frat boy with silky blond hair whose hips shook and pounded his narrow bed, but when it came his turn just pumped up and down on my cock like a sailor on leave. It always ended the same, though, with hard words and tears and slamming doors.

This isn't to say I couldn't have had the same problem—too many cocksuckers spoiling the bed—with Chita. But frankly, I didn't, and here is where the real difference between Chita and everyone else stands out. Not only did I fuck Chita more regularly, but I told her everything, the good and the bad. She was a part of my life—a large woman, looming, in some small way, at the door of my life.

Sometimes that wasn't just an overwrought metaphor. One night Chita and I attended a party together, and I ended up walking home with an eighteen-year-old virgin. We began making out on the lawn of my rooming house, and when it progressed to my sucking on her small breasts, we went inside for condoms. There was a knock at my door in the middle of my sucking between her legs. I lifted my face just enough to say, "Yes?" Chita opened the door and stood there, taking in the girl and me. The girl on her back with her legs luxuriously spread on either side of me. Her cunt thrust up. My hands supporting her ass. Her virgin's eyes hidden behind long, black hair.

And in that scene all I could think to say was, "This really isn't a good time."

The next day Chita barged into my room after the girl left. I'd been on my way to the shower and wore just a towel. Chita made short work of that.

"Is she gone for good?" Chita demanded.

"I can't say," I lied. "She might be back." I was sweating. I still wore the scent of the girl, whose name I can't recall.

"Is she gone for now?"

"That I'm sure about."

"Good." Chita kicked off her high heels and pushed me onto the bed. She lifted her skirt. She had no panties on, and the spot where her legs met glistened. She straddled my bare chest and rubbed her cunt across my nipples. "I want you to do to me everything you did to her." An oil-slick of scented juice formed on my chest hairs.

"This is the first thing I did," I lied again. I grabbed her ass and pulled her cunt to my face, sticking my tongue out and in. The girl became a distant, warrantless memory.

I didn't want to hurt Chita. At the same time, of course, I didn't want to miss fucking Lise. A quandary? Well, there are worse, and I'm not so wrapped in myself not to realize that, frankly, I had it pretty goddamn good. But the day was looming when Lise would pull up on her bike, and I would have to let somebody know something tout de suite. So that night, when I mentioned Lise's visit to her, Chita said, "That's the biker girl, isn't it?" Then she said, "Is she staying with you?"

I nodded. Chita, who was cooking pasta for our dinner, smiled and reached into the cooling pot. She flung a handful of the stuff against the wall. Our lovemaking that night was all bites and slaps. Afterward, she slept turned away from me.

• • •

Lise's bike has a loud deathrattle. She cut the engine and kicked the bike up on its stand, then took off her helmet. She smiled at me and pounded some of the dust from her jacket before enfolding me in arms that felt like ten-inch cable. I kissed her, and she put her tongue down my throat. She broke off and said, "I've had nothing but that machine between my legs for so long, I'm going to take you apart."

I whispered in her ear. Her face fell a little and she said, "When does she leave?" But Lise was secure in whatever it was that was our relationship. I took her hand and led her inside, where Chita stirred a pot of chili paella.

She'd decked out for meeting Lise. She wore a blue and gardenia chiffon dress, with a pair of red cornflower earrings, and white stockings. She wore pumps, too, which made her even taller. Her legs were a mare's. Hard, heavy. The muscles on her calves stood out.

Lise, on the other hand, wore all leather, and it was dusty and smelly at that. Her boots were leather, her jacket and pants. She looked like a tall bowling ball, with a red-haired doll's head stuck into one of the holes. She smiled and shook Chita's hand and then kicked back into a kitchen chair. Chita was gracious enough to get her a beer and herself another gin and tonic.

I wore shorts and drank juice.

That they were nervous around one another goes, I think, without comment. Chita's hands shook when she ladled paella onto plates, and Lise kept slipping her long, acid looks whenever her back was turned. They did not trust each other, that was plain. Both took up some part of my life that the other, consciously or not, craved. I'm sure Lise regretted Chita's presence right there, right then, when all she wanted was a fast, hard bodyslam, followed by more leisurely ones. And I think she envied her, in some little way, Chita's having me to herself for long periods. She waited out the meal, after which Chita had said she would go home.

Chita, for her part, probably regretted Lise's presence altogether.

I don't want to give the wrong impression. It wasn't a silent meal. There was too much to fill each other in on. Lise and I hadn't seen each other in almost a year, and a lot had happened in that time. And Chita and Lise, for all the undercurrent of anxiety and anger that might have been going on, were not about to allow that to mar their self-visions as polite, unselfish women. Chita, at least, was too much the gracious hostess for it, and Lise, who has a self-image as the fast-riding androgyne, knew that there's no place in there for wayward testosterone.

The paella was good, and we layered on waves of hot sauce and bit the tiny heads off shrimp and shoveled forkfuls of rice into our mouths. I looked at Lise. Her red rat tail bobbed each time she lowered her face closer to the plate before her. There was a piece of red pepper stuck on her lower lip, and I wanted to lean across and flick it off with the tip of my tongue. She looked at me and winked broadly, then turned to Chita, sitting on the other side of me, and stared openly at her, until Chita glanced at her and Lise's eyes returned to her plate.

I looked at Chita, who was involved in mirror exercises to my right. She had an open napkin on her lap. She sat straight against the back of the chair, one hand to her lap, and closed her eyes as she placed each careful forkful of the dish in her freshly rouged mouth. The tiniest flash of her tongue accompanied each bite, and suddenly I grew hard. At that moment, Lise reached under the table to lay one beefy, proprietary hand on my nearest leg. She squeezed my thigh above the knee, and then traced her finger along the network of hairs there. Chita, in the meantime, slipped off the high heel from one foot and rubbed it against mine.

When we finished the meal and they'd finished their gin and beer, it was dark. It grows dark quickly in the Midwest, even in the summer. We piled the dishes in the sink, and I submerged my arms in warm, soapy water. I washed, Lise dried, and Chita put them away. This was a point, it seemed, she was scoring against Lise: she knew the layout of the kitchen. Lise, to mitigate it, stood under my arm, which made it hard to wash and rinse, but her large, still leather-clad body was pressed against me in the most pleasurable spots. Chita sometimes leaned across for a plate, and her fat tits brushed against my shoulder.

• • •

I am not stupid, but I took a long time to figure out where all this was going. I think the first clue came to me when, after we finished the dishes and more polite conversation, we walked into my room with a trio of glasses of white wine and a joint. Chita would not leave. We sat on my bed and smoked. The potsmoke eased lazily from Lise's mouth when she pressed me to her to shotgun it into my lungs. She had had enough. Her mouth was hot and her tongue thick from beer and seafood. Immediately on my release, Chita grabbed the joint and me. She'd made her decision too, and she pushed me down while inhaling a huge hit. Lay over me and released a cloud of the stuff into my mouth. My hands shook at my sides.

Lise cupped my growing erection while Chita shoved her tongue far back in my throat. In a moment the tip of my cock nudged from under the bottom of my shorts and popped its pink head out for a look. My right hand went to touch Lise's thick breast while my left went around Chita, whose tongue was still lodged somewhere near my esophagus. Now she released me, and her hand swallowed my cock where Lise's didn't. They looked at each other across me, both of them with a hand around my cock, my hands on two unrelated breasts. Then they looked at me. I said, "Am I the only one here who wants to fuck?"

In response Chita stood and pulled her dress over her head. She was wearing white panties and a white bra, and her warm, Brazil-nut flesh stood out, pressed hard against the fabric. She was nervous, and she slipped out of the underwear quickly. Lise caught her breath as Chita's fat tits popped out. Her hand tightened around my erection. When she was naked, Chita wrapped the blanket at the foot of the bed around her. I reached under it and fondled her cunt to ease her down a little, while she and Lise tugged my cutoffs off. When they were on the floor, Chita leaned over and swallowed the shaft of my cock.

Lise, meanwhile, was peeling the leather from herself. It came away, leaving indentations on her body like river silt. She turned, and I saw she'd gotten a tattoo, a spread-winged eagle, on one shoulder blade. It was bisected by her bra strap, and then that, too, slipped from her milky skin.

I took Chita's bobbing head in my hands and said, "Look at this." She stopped sucking me and saw Lise's nipples, or their absence, for the first time. Chita has hard, thumb-sucking nipples, with aureoles that are almost as wide. The sight of tits without nipples was strange for her, and she stared while I teased them out with my tongue and teeth. Lise pushed me down on the bed and straddled my face. She'd recently shaved her cunt, and the stud pressed against my nose. She spread her pinkness with her fingers. I took a lavish lick. The juices welled up. Spread across my mouth in an oily ooze.

I told Chita, "Watch her face, isn't she beautiful when she comes." All Chita could do was to sit back and stare. Lise rode my tongue to a delirious orgasm, which she conducted in tongues no one had ever heard. She had her hands spread wide on the wall above my head, her hips pounding me like waves against the surf. Her body jiggled in a half-dozen places when she moaned, and her mouth opened, and her cunt lips opened and smeared a pint of her wetness across my face.

Chita wasn't a spectator for long. When Lise had come down and moved away, she took advantage of the opening to straddle my hips and slide the full length of my cock into her in one clean, decisive stroke. Her knees pressed painfully into my hipbones, and she thrust down on me like a rocket in reverse. She hunched over me, and I rolled her nipples between my thumb and forefinger. She rode forward just far enough to let my cock almost slip out of her, and then swooped back to engulf it to the hilt. When she came, gently as rain in the summer, the drum of her cervix was pressed hard against the tip.

The room smelled the way paintings of lavish, Elizabethan banquets look: ripe, heavy with the aroma of a multiplicity of dishes and diverse tongue-pleasers. Lise rolled onto her knees and her plump, white ass bobbed in the air. She looked over her shoulder at me. The eagle seemed to mimic, with its wings, the spread of her legs. I tucked my cock into her, and we made the sounds sump pumps make on rainy days.

Chita lay on her back practically under us to watch. One hand worked between her legs while her eyes never left the sight of my shaft emerging and reentering Lise's thick, swollen pussy. Lise, for her part, watched Chita intently. More specifically, she watched Chita's tits, which jiggled with every thrust of our hips on the bed. She rimmed the closest nipple with the flat of her tongue, and its tiny bud unfurled. Chita stared with glassy eyes at Lise's rat tail bobbing at her shoulder.

Lise came up for air. Chita was looking her straight in the eye. Lise gave her the look right back. Licked her lips. Chita closed her eyes and opened her mouth, and Lise let one of my thrusts carry her directly onto that open mouth. Their lips met in a harsh, foamy soul kiss that sent a shiver through me. Lise pressed her hand to the hot dark cleft of Chita's cunt. Two of her fingers disappeared between the folds, and the sight was an electric prod directed at the base of my cock.

"I'm gonna come," I moaned.

Chita broke off their kiss long enough to murmur, "Come inside me. You haven't come in me for so long." She spread her legs impossibly wider. Lise gave her another couple swabs for good measure. The red-haired girl released my cock. She made a popping sound as she let go. Chita's cunt was soft and wet and wide, and slipping into it was like sliding a straw into the Grand Canyon. I pumped into her, and Lise kissed me passionately, and her tongue snaked around my teeth and gums, and Chita's chubby fingers explored the redhead's shaved cunt lips hovering inches from her face, and suddenly I felt a dull weight lift from my balls and shoot out of me to splash thick and wet against the inner surface of somebody's belly.

• • •

I guess you know what happened next. Chita and Lise and I didn't leave the bed for days except to shit and piss and shower. When one went away and came back, it was always with a few pieces of fruit or a drink for the other two, who were always involved in play or naps.

But here is what you might not have figured. Lise didn't leave. She unpacked her trail bags, sublet her house in Hartford, and parked her bike in the backyard. Chita dropped her RA position and school and moved in with us. We took day jobs, and with our pooled first-week's wages we bought a king-size bed. We drift our nights away alternately sleeping and exploring other bodies. In the year that's followed, Chita and Lise have determined that we need a child in the house, but neither can agree who should get pregnant. In the meantime, I practice with both, and they practice breast-feeding each other.

On occasion, I still sleep elsewhere. I am content with both of them, but sometimes I still get the itch for someone different. Sometimes I just want to suck cock. Neither woman has shown interest in anyone except each other. One weekend I went camping with a man I'd found attractive. I came back home with him and found Lise spread-eagled against the bedroom wall, pumping her hips over Chita's open, red mouth. Her tongue was stuck so deeply into the other girl's cunt I couldn't make out where it left off. The boy had stayed in the living room, and I asked if he could join us, and they agreed. But once we were all naked he sort of fell out of the picture. We tried hard enough, taking turns sucking his engorged knob, and the sight of him on his back while Lise hunkered over him, her slick pussy straining with him, was satisfying. But after about an hour the boy was forgotten and drifted off to sleep on the floor while the three of us kept at it. I wasn't awake when he left.

It's as if Lise and Chita, who have become inseparable, companionably as well as sexually, open their new-found relationship for me alone. What feeling this may be out of, I honestly can't say, although they are always telling me how they love me. I never feel the odd man out, but sometimes, after I have pumped one or the other or both full of come, and am leaning back watching Chita's lips vacuum Lise's pussy clean, or watching Lise pressing her thick fingers into Chita's newly-shaved cunt, I wonder if I'm only being kept around as a warm fuck-stick, and could just as easily be replaced with a good dildo.

But then I need to ask myself, in what may be the objective correlative to this situation: when I am munching on one cunt, my fingers in another, is it myself I'm really touching? When I slide my cock into one and slurp for all I'm worth on another, slipping from one sex to the other, often within seconds, am I fondling my own imaginary but bountiful cunt, living out my dreams of being totally androgynous? The idea is not unwelcome.

Then Chita or Lise notices my face getting a little cloudy and stretches luxuriously across me, kisses me, nibbles at my cock, and offers her beautiful and heavy body up to my mouth and fingers. Bodies, you see, are designed for meeting, bellies for slapping together, asses for holding, lips for kissing. At times like this, who cares about the theory or what our situation might be? At times like this, I even love them.

# Ronin

## Ronin

Nobody knows whether I am male or female, not even myself. I am a masterless warrior, roaming the cyberjungles of imagination. Like the waves for which I am named, I surge restlessly in search of fulfillment and fate. I would serve, if an honorable master would have me. And I would reign, if honorable men would submit.

I am not unique. There are many ronin, wave-men, restless and yearning, wavering between the edges of the sharp-sided world. We are shadow people, unseen and pointless, lacking the context of reality that binds ordinary people and gives them significance.

Our freedom is our curse.

We will never give it up for the lesser options of one or the other; but we will never fulfill it either, for the world is so ordered that we fall within the interstices. Between male and female, gay and straight, between top and the bottom, dom and sub. We are not switches, not bisexual, not hermaphrodites, but something altogether Other, a new kind of being, a being without a name. I call us ronin; I call myself Ronin.

Do you need to know my gender? Do you need to know if I have a cunt or a prick? What if I have both, or neither? What if my sex rages in my brain and my nimble hands build whatever organs I need to express whatever it is that I am feeling at the moment? Do you need to know if I am flesh, or am I fantasy? I am plastic and blood and metal and meat, building myself out of the materials that are at hand. Some of the materials are exotic and sensuous, some of them are old and worn. I am a matrix of being, self-assembled out of spare parts and improvisations.

Do you need to know my color? I am chameleon. White people call me white. Brown people call me brown. Grey people see me as grey. The color blind don't see me at all. I am whatever color I put on today. Black or green or rainbow. These are the colors of my moods.

Sometimes I am an angel, with a breathtaking beauty that would stun you, if you ever happened to look out the back of your eyeballs. Sometimes I am a demon, with grinning tusks and slanted eyes, giant ears and horns and a boneshaking laugh. Most people don't find my jokes funny.

I desire you, desire to hold you down and plunder your soft flesh. Male and female I plunder you, your shivering thighs parted by my thrusting flesh. I bite you, leaving my mark upon your skin, bitter caress of my angry pleasure. I hurt you, twisting your nipples to the point of excruciating pleasure, your body bucking and heaving beneath me. I ride longer than you have ever been ridden. I have made myself, and I am invincible and inexhaustible. Your rape is my pleasure—the men especially—struggling to answer the ronin in themselves—fighting the belief that men are impenetrable and secure—wanting to be open and desirable. They yearn to be taken even as they fear it.

I know what you feel, every ronin knows it. We were once like you. Once we had two choices, male and female, dominance and submission, gay and straight, until we discovered the abyss beneath our feet and having once seen it, found ourselves eternally plummeting into the chasm between conventional truths.

We cannot straddle the chasm, choosing when to cross from one side to the other. We cannot put on and take off masculine and feminine, they are melded inside us. We desire the freefall of imagination, and our orientation is fusion, confusion, and delusion. Yours, not ours. We know what we are. We want you to become like us. We want to people the planet with restless surging minds that shape their bodies in accordance with their will and whim. We desire imagination in all things; the escape from straight jacket of either/or.

We want new. We want you. We want true.

Let me frighten you, please you, take you, tickle you, suckle you, hurt you. Let me explode your mind so that you will never again be able to grasp the sharp edges that make me bleed. Let me hurl you into Beyond so that you can never find your way back to what was. Renew. Be you. Be more, be other, be Self. Be surprise and pain and curiosity. Be kind.

Be me.

# Kicked Out Again

## Nadyalec

Sometimes Felix could be so embarrassing to be around. Why did he have to talk about anal sex in Denny's? I really wasn't in the mood to get thrown out. I just wanted a chance to finish my strawberry cheese blintzes for once.

"It has been so long since I have been fucked!" he was proclaiming dramatically. "I really think I've become a virgin again. Do you think it's possible my hymen has regenerated?"

"You don't have a hymen, Felix. You're a boy."

"Beast!" He threw his napkin at me and it landed in my lemonade.

"Great. Now I get to drink all of your germs."

"Honey, I hate to break it to you, but anything I have, you have. You have already encountered to my germs. They are now your germs as well." He batted his eyelashes at me. "Men. How quickly you forget."

"I'm not a man."

"Say it's not so! Have you taken me under false pretenses? Have I been molested by a—woman?"

"I don't know that I'd say that, either."

"Then what could you be?" He began fanning himself. "My binary views of gender are collapsing around me! Whatever will I do? And when, oh when, will I experience penetration again?"

"I don't know why you like it so much."

"Clearly you are not a woman. The exquisite pain—the intensity of sensation—the way a man's balls feel as they slap up against my ass while I cry out to be taken harder and faster!" He was fanning himself more quickly as he spoke. "Feeling my loved one come inside me, his love juice dripping down my legs when I can finally bear to rise again! Not being able to shit properly for days!"

"Yes sir, we're on our way out," I told the gentleman who had appeared, scowling, behind Felix. "Why do you always have to do that? I didn't get to finish my meal," I whined as we left.

"Yeah, well, you didn't pay for it, either, did you? Come on—there's one more store I want to experience."

"Felix, I'm sick of this mall. And I'm sick of getting kicked out of every place we go into. Why can't you just chill out and shut up for awhile?"

"I may never recover from the bruise those words leave on my soul. Come on—just one more store." He took my hand and pulled me through a set of doors before I had a chance to read the sign.

Great. It was a sex store. I should have known. I stood looking at a wind-up walking penis while Felix vanished into the back. I didn't want to go back there—I truly did not want to look too closely at the dildos I could see out of the corner of my eye. Not in front of Felix. I hate it when he sees me blush.

The guy behind the counter didn't like me at all. He probably recognized me as that dork who lurks around and never buys anything. He followed me around the front of the store as I looked through the X-rated greeting cards, novelty condoms, and plastic breasts. What was taking Felix so long? This was one store I'd be glad to get thrown out of—quickly.

Finally Felix appeared, grinning, and beckoned me away. "To the ladies' room," he said, "to try out my new acquisitions."

"Damn, Felix, have you been shoplifting again?" I lowered my voice at his warning glance. "I hate it when you do that. Do you know what they'd do to you in jail?"

"I can hardly begin to dream of it!"

"OK, do you know what they'd do to me in jail? I don't want to be some scary person's boyfriend. You know they'd arrest me, too—hell, they'd arrest me first. Cops do not like me. I do not like cops. I don't appreciate—" He was leading me into the women's room. "This isn't legal, either, you know."

"Don't worry about it, nobody ever uses this bathroom. They all use the one at the front of the mall. And I need to touch up my lipstick." Quickly he dabbed at his eyes, put on some more lipstick, then pulled me into the large handicapped stall. "There. Now no one can see us. Happy?" He hung his trench coat on the hook on the door, and a collection of things fell out of it. "OK—now shut up and put this on."

It was a dildo. I had to fight back the urge to club him over the head with it, but I had to admit it was pretty. "Now turn your back like a gentleman so I can change," he was saying, and I did. Once I was facing away from him, I looked at it more closely.

It was honestly quite lovely. Long, and smooth, almost matching the tone of my hand when I ran it against my skin. There were even delicate tracings of blue veins.

"Don't you have that on yet? Now come on and zip me up," he said, and I turned around to wrestle with the cheap zipper in shiny fabric.

He turned around before I could scold him, and then I lost the chance because I couldn't breathe. He was the most beautiful girl in the world, looking at me with huge green eyes while he smoothed down the wrinkles in the dress. His hair had grown out while we'd been on the road, and he hadn't dyed it black in awhile; a rebellious tendril was in his eye, glinting red under the fluorescent light. "Now it's your turn," he said, and took the cock from me very gently. He bent down to pick up another object, and I was riveted by the sight of him straining out of tight, tight fabric. Felix is so skinny—where did he get all that flesh?

I rebelled when he tried to unbutton my pants, though.

"What's the problem?"

"I don't want you to see me without my pants on!"

"Well, are you wearing underwear?"

"Yeah. Boxer shorts."

"So what's the problem then?" Suddenly he looked much less confident, biting his lip and using those huge eyes against me. "Will you wear it for me? Please?"

I mumbled something and let him unbutton my pants.

He was in my space now, easing my jeans gently down, and working them over my boots. I looked down at his graceful neck, at the place on the back of his neck where the hair was shaved. I wanted to run my lips all over it.

Now he was kneeling to buckle leather around me. It was awkward, creaky with being new, and seemed to involve millions of buckles and straps that hung terribly loose on me. I glanced down, wincing at the sight of my skinny legs under the boxer shorts. There's a reason I don't wear shorts even in the summer. I looked all wrong. This was a really bad idea.

When he had the leather arranged to his satisfaction, snug but not tight, and fitted in the cock, everything changed. I looked down at my body, baggy shirt tenting down over my erection, Felix, kneeling lovely before me, making some minute adjustment, and I was almost frightened by how good it all looked. He was watching my cock with an expression I hadn't seen before. Hungry.

"May I suck your dick, please, sir?" he asked, that low throaty voice gone a little bit breathless, and I put my hands on the back of his head and pressed him forward in assent.

He closed his eyes and put his tongue on me, lightly, at the tip, and I felt a little ripple. Then he closed his eyes and took me in his mouth, all at once, struggling a little with my size in a way that made me feel mean and tender all at once. He slid me out again, and ran his tongue along me. I swear I could almost feel his tongue, watching him was so powerful. I had to lean against the wall to steady myself, watching him take me inside himself.

Very soon he opened his eyes and looked up at me again. "Please, please," he said, "will you come inside me?" I smiled down at him. This was a new sort of power, this saucy creature turned shy, this beautiful girl, wanting me so badly. "It's been such a long time!"

"I don't think so," I said, watching his face. "Not yet! Maybe later, though. I've heard it's possible to come from wearing a dildo. Why don't you try? That might make me more receptive."

He smiled at me a little, then, though his eyes were still huge. "Tease."

I grabbed his hair and pulled him down on me until he choked, tears running down his face and his whole mouth filled with my cock. Beautiful, and frustrating; my whole body flushed with heat, and I wanted to fuck him. "Turn around," I said, and helped him, shoving him a little as he turned so that he fell forward onto his hands. I pushed the dress up and ran my hands over his ass. He was panting, and when he looked over his shoulder at me, his face was flushed. "Please?"

"Make me want to," I said, running a finger along his face, along his dark lips, and he pulled the finger into his mouth, closing his eyes, and drew me in and out. I shut my eyes and sank into the feeling, then opened them and smiled into his worried face. "Oh, all right," I said, and he grinned an enormous grin. "Just this once."

I took my finger from his mouth and ran it along the crack of his ass. His shoulders drew up and tensed as I touched him just inside the opening, feeling the muscle press back at me. I made little circles, marveling, while he panted and whined, and then suddenly he pressed up against me and I was in.

Feathers, and silk; everything wet and warm; I wished I could crawl inside him. I wished my finger was longer. I wanted to pour myself inside. I put another finger beside the first, pressing into the place where he curved on the inside, listening to his breathing as he made way for me. For a moment I lost myself in the sensation, pushing in and pulling out, the warmth on my fingers. His breath caught in almost a sob and his voice was high when he said, "Your cock...."

"But I love how this feels!"

"Oh, please," he panted, fumbling for a little package from his trench coat, and coating me with lubricant. He couldn't meet my eyes.

Giving up on the notion of sensation, I pressed my dick up against the fingers I was still fucking him with, and very slowly pushed. It wouldn't go in, so I had to guide it with one hand and press against the finger inside him, and then I was in, just inside the opening. He made a surprised sound and jerked forward. "Didn't think I'd do it?"

His voice was shaky as he told me, "I hoped you would." I pressed in a little further, looking down at my cock against him, inside his asshole, and I almost did feel it. He was making little noises, and it made me push further, halfway in now, and he said shrilly, "No, stop, please, it's too much." I stopped moving immediately. Moved my hands over his back, then up to his face and said gently, "You can take this, and you know you want to."

"I know," he said, voice sounding lost. "Just give me a minute, please, wait and let me get ready for a minute."

I reached beneath him, he lifted as he realized what I wanted to do, and I got my hand around his cock. It moved a little in my hand, and I played with the moisture at its tip, making little circles with my fingers and he said, "Now..."

One slow, easy push and I was in. Felix shuddered beneath me, saying something I couldn't understand, and I was perfectly still, continuing to rub his silky cock. I pressed my lips against his ear and told him how good he was being, how good he was making me feel. His shivering calmed, and he pulled forward a little, drawing me out of him, pressing back against me again and making a small soft sound of pain. I let him fuck himself, tentatively, on my cock for a few minutes. Then I put my hands on his hips and started drawing him against me, first gently, but then with more and more force. The base of the dick rubbed against me, caught against my pubic hair; it hurt and felt good, and the mixture made me a little crazy. I stopped paying attention to him at all for awhile and just concentrated on how it felt for me, the strokes that almost reached my clit, heating up and starting to go liquid. Listening to all the different sounds I could get him to make.

"Touch yourself," I told him, and he slid his hands over his cock, more and more quickly in time as I fucked him. I felt him orgasm, shudder, and convulse under my hands, and I kept fucking him through it, then slowed, and stopped. And very, very slowly, I pulled out of him.

He collapsed on the floor, looking up at me while I pulled up my pants. "Hurry up," I said, but gently. "We need to get out of here before we get thrown out." He was staring at the bulge the dick made under my jeans. I gave him a hand up and helped him out of the dress and into his clothes, since he seemed a little out of it.

By the time I held the door open for him and for two women who looked at us curiously, he had revived enough to say, "So when is it my turn?"

"In your dreams," I laughed, and took off running.

# The Bet
## Phil

My friend Carol and I are having our usual bet. We're sitting in my car outside the club. She's wearing a boob-tube and microskirt; I'm wearing a camisole top and microskirt.

"Ten minutes, OK? Last back to the car pays ten pounds."

"You're on, let's go!"

It's nine minutes, thirty seconds by my watch as I leave the club and head for the car. Shit, Carol's already sitting in the passenger seat!

"I don't believe it," I say as I get in. She pulls down the top of her tube to show me the globules of creamy cum between her ample breasts. I can't argue. She touches the streaks of whiteness on my neck and cleavage.

"You got more, but I was first. I win!"

"Hmm. Double or quits?"

"Straight?"

"Yes."

We grab the tissues and clean each other up, then head for the club again, pausing at the door to synchronise watches.

This time it's eight minutes, and I'm back at the car first, and Carol owes me twenty pounds. She runs up panting at the ten minute mark, cursing.

"Trust me to get a romantic one. Come on then, evidence!"

She pulls up my skirt and spreads my thighs. I can feel the cum trickling down into the crack of my ass. She admits defeat with a good grace, and we spend a few enjoyable minutes wiping each other clean.

"That's twenty you owe me."

"Double or quits again?"

"Doing what?"

She tells me.

"OK, you're on!" I know I'm the favourite for this one.

It's eight minutes, thirty seconds when I'm walking back to the car, feeling a little tender. Holy shit, Carol's already there.

"You bitch! I don't believe it!"

She turns and kneels on the seat, hiking her skirt up to her waist. Her anus is still red and dilated, a trickle of white runs down onto her fat lips.

"OK?"

"OK," I sigh. "Forty quid. I don't know how you do it."

"Charm and personality," Carol grins. "Never mind, I'll let you lick me out when we get home. That's worth forty quid of anybody's money."

# Bonkin' the Buddha

## E. Terry

My intention was no intention. But that wasn't good enough. The white zendo wall blurred in and out of my consciousness. The lines in the wainscott swirled like silk ribbons. The zafu under my ass was a round laughing belly tickling my cunt. Counting breaths...counting moments. If only enlightenment would cum soon.

And if so, what then? Would it grunt and roll over and go back to sleep? Or would it offer me a smidgeon, some good thing to eat? A grain of rice, perhaps, with my name written on it.

The Buddha was big as an armoir, but not as heavy, his robes being ashes of incense and his food dots of sun under closed lids. He invited me to lighten up.

"Nah," I told him. "Your dry rice kernels stick in my teeth. You could pour rains of grains and I'd never be filled. Give me fresh cut tomatoes slid down in olive oil; love me with watermelon and bing cherry cider. Tattoo my name on your ass and the shape of my left tit on your thigh. Don't do me any favors."

I sketched the ridges of his roundness with my little finger, making him quiver, making seconds quiver like pond circles, making great quivering oceans of hours. Someone else's ocean. Someone else's beach party; we were only minding moments here, after all. Those moments that wound down into some small wet thing, the honey in the cactus pot, the pussy in the basket, the Buddha's cunt.

Now, the Buddha's cunt was no small surprise. Not the fact that he had one, but that it was so tight, so insignificant, so crack-in-the-sidewalk. I wanted juice. I bowed to the wall. I wanted hot Buddha fire. God forgive me, I wanted to fuck him with a bloody cross and turn his piss into wine.

I put my fist in a glove and forced it up him. "Beg me for lube!" His Buddha smile thinned and his Buddha teeth bared. I put my foot in a boot and made him bite it. "Give me some drool!" But he was silent. I slapped his ass with a broken yard rake and made him bend for his marks the way I had been taught; but the only liquid that emerged was my own sweat dripping onto his back. "OK, fine," I gasped, "you do it."

He took my cheeks in both hands and straddled my head. He covered my face with his belly and said, "Breathe." He smelled raw like an open gutter. He put my mouth to his cunt and said, "Drink." I drank kernels of dead things and dry things and rust. His pussy was rank with the dust of neglect.

I gathered spit in my mouth and drooled it in him. His vaginal walls were like bitter slime. I tasted small children eating cereal while being fucked by their babysitters. I tasted ulcerous old men spitting bile out train windows. I tasted women at sinks with splitting heads and broken glass. I tasted the inside of my own pussy and it was nothing.

So did I lighten up? Well ... no. But I got through another session without the cane on my back, which is more than I can say for counting breaths. And the Buddha flavor is not too bad, once you get used to it.

# The Girl Behind the Fantasy

## Mary Anne Mohanraj

Hey, boy. You listening? 'Cause I have a story for you, oh yes I do. It's the story you've always dreamed of—it's your story; it's every story. It's your favorite fantasy—'cause that's what I am, a fantasy, and I can be whatever your heart desires.

I was a nurse once, remember? In a short, crisply starched white dress, and I said, "Good morning, sir," and asked you to please undress. And I slipped out the door, and when you were down to your undershorts I came back in. Instead of apologizing, I stood there by the door, watching you finish, pulling down those shorts to reveal your hard cock. And I said, "That looks like it needs some medical attention," and I walked up, slowly and deliberately, and sank to my knees in front of you, and tilted my head with its little nurses' cap, and licked my lips before licking your cock, up and down, caressing its length, and you knew that you were one of a hundred men who passed through the doctor's offices, and I was down on my knees for every one and that turned you on, oh yes....

...or maybe you'd rather remember a quite different type of doctor. When I was seven and you were eight, and we were playing hide and seek and wandered far away from the other kids. We ended up beneath a willow tree, and you asked me if I wanted to play doctor and I said, "Okay!" So you said you needed to examine me, so I pulled up the skirt on my pink polka-dotted dress and pulled down my panties, and you looked very carefully to make sure that I wasn't sick. And then I was the doctor, and you pulled down your shorts and underwear and I stared, amazed to see how different you were....

...or perhaps you preferred a more knowledgeable sort. You were seventeen and I was the professor's wife—a little bored and a lot tempted. When you came over for special tutoring on Saturday afternoons (you were such a bright young boy), I'd keep you after your lesson for tea and sympathy. My sedate skirts would somehow slide up my thigh, and you could only imagine what lay beneath them, and we would talk of adult things, and I would enjoy being a little shocking, and you would try very hard to be grown-up until the day when your sweet young body would be really too much to expect a rather deprived woman to resist. I would take your head in my hands and draw it down to my breast and slide your hand under my skirt and between my legs....

...and do you remember your hand between my legs when I was your childhood sweetheart and we were necking in the back of a '57 Chevy? I was a good Catholic girl, so we never had intercourse, but after a lot of petting and promises, you could pretty much touch me wherever you wanted, though I never took my clothes off. Your hands would slip beneath my white blouse and push my bra off my firm young breasts, and sometimes I'd let you unbutton the blouse so that you could suck on the dark pink nipples while your fingers slid beneath white cotton panties to the thick swatch of blond hair and then up and inside me, and we were trying so hard to be quiet even though we were up at Lookout Point and the only people around were other couples in other cars doing exactly what we were doing....

...or maybe you like more people around? I was the town librarian, with granny glasses and my hair pulled back tight in a bun. You cornered me in the stacks one day and threatened, laughing, to steal a book unless I gave you a kiss. I resisted at first but then gave in, tentatively kissing you between Shakespeare and Chaucer, and the children's room is right below us, and if the kids look up, they'll see right through the grated walkway and see the librarian kissing this handsome stranger, who slips his hands up behind her neck and pulls out the pins holding her hair so it tumbles down, a heavy blonde mass down her back....

...or maybe you don't like me as a blonde. Maybe you prefer me as your wife, with sweet brown curls and a surprisingly wicked streak. You like me whispering suggestions in your ear, "Let me touch you, let me suck you, let me lick your cock, your balls, your asshole...call me your little girl and I'll call you daddy...call me your slut, your whore, whatever you like but please fuck me now—I'll beg you if you want, oh yes..."

...or would you prefer to beg? Me with flowing auburn hair down to my butt and green eyes and all in black. A black leather bodice laced tight so my breasts overflow at the top, and black leather pants with the crotch cut out and black boots with five-inch spike heels and a nine-tailed cat in my hands, its soft leather aching for your back. I'd have you on your knees beneath me, begging for a chance to please your mistress, and I'd slap your face saying, "Who gave you permission to speak, little boy?! You only open your mouth when I say you do, understand? And now I want you to use it, crawl over here and lick me like you mean it." And when you do, I will get angry and say you aren't doing a good job, and the cat will rain blows on your naked back, and you will kneel there, silently begging with your eyes and trying not to scream....

...or is the screaming the shriek of the speakers at the neighborhood club? I'm a stranger in a tight black dress and copper curls, blue eyes laughing at you across the room. You make your way through the heaving mass of bodies on the dance floor to pour a drink between my lips and pull me close, our bodies sliding then slamming together as the dance swirls around us. A muscled man stumbles into us, and his eyes slide up and down my body, appreciatively. "Nice tits," he says to you as the tide of the dance carries him away, and you grin smugly, pressing those tits into your chest, pushing me up against a speaker, your cock a hard lump in your jeans pressed against my hips, and your hands everywhere on my sweating body, sliding up the dress with your thigh while the speakers shriek in our ears....

...or maybe you just want me screaming beneath you, the office slut who's desperate for a fuck and takes you into the file room and locks the door. Me with too much makeup and too short a red skirt, stripping quickly for you, and you don't even bother to take off your clothes. You just unzip and push down your pants and shorts and pick me up and push me up against a wall. And the boss is outside so we're silent, and I'm biting your shoulder as you shove your cock into me, over and over, harder and harder, and when you come you shove so hard that my shoulder knocks into a shelf and papers tumble to the floor. You pull out and leave me dripping there. You zip up and say, "Clean that up," as you open the door and walk out....

...or perhaps you're more discreet. Perhaps you have to be. You're having an affair with the boss's wife, and it's so satisfying to be screwing her when he's been screwing you for so many years, but you wouldn't want your wife to find out. So we meet at sleazy motels, and I have curves to die for, not like your skinny little stick of a wife, and you bury your head between my breasts or thighs and I love your body, the long length of it, and I spend hours kissing it, tasting it, sucking your cock and nibbling your balls and doing whatever you desire and afterwards asking you to run away with me and you shrug and say, "Sorry, babe...."

...but maybe that's not the type of woman you want. Maybe you prefer a little East Asian girl, less than a hundred pounds and five feet tall, with porcelain skin and straight black hair. Almond-shaped eyes staring up at you as I lay naked beneath you, my tiny body smelling faintly of jasmine and musk. Your broad hands enveloping my small breasts, squeezing them hard, and I shiver, holding almost motionless except for a thin shaking sheen of sweat. I'm completely shaven, hairless like a small girl, and when you slide into my cunt it's so small, so tight that it's like a Western woman's ass, and you think you must be hurting me, but I don't care, I'm arching beneath you, begging you for more more more....

...or I could be one of a harem of such girls, remember, all of us waiting for your command...a harem of women from all over the world, collected for your pleasure, trembling with love for you, and each one of us hoping that she'll be the one chosen tonight to share your bed, to spend the night devoting every second to pleasing you, taking your cock in cunt and ass and mouth, sliding it between her breasts, so that when you spurt, your jism spreads across her neck and face until you call one of the other girls in to lick it off....

...or isn't one at a time enough? Take three or four of us, all of us crawling over you, sliding against you, our bodies slick with exotic oils, a blonde, brunette and redhead—slim, medium and extra curvy...I can be all of them at once, begging and screaming for you as you fuck us, your proud cock slamming into us over and over as long as you want, as long as you can keep paying for it....

...I can be everything your heart desires—everything your groin demands. And all I ask is that you never ask me if I like my job

# Neighborly Neighbors

MIKE HUNT

## Foreword

*I've decided technology is fucked up. Like computers, for instance. I don't like them. Did I ever tell you about the time I mixed up my folders and started sending my stories to people who had just written to say "Wow" and didn't really want the stories showing up on their machines at work? Funny thing is the people who wanted the stories and didn't get them were even more pissed!*

*Hey, and how about the time I mixed up folders with my neighborhood garden club newsletter? I don't even want to talk about it!*

*Computers. Except for this free smut, who needs them? Like spreadsheets are fun or something. Like they make you smart or something. I'm sure you know the richest guy on the planet is a nerd who runs a Seattle software company that's trying to take over the world. And sometimes he even smells bad! Hey, Bill! It's easy! TAKE A SHOWER! You'd think his computers would tell him how to fix his dandruff if they're so fucking smart.*

*At the very least these machines should be able to tell me your age, and if you're over eighteen. You're supposed to be if you're reading this stuff. Over eighteen? Computers can't tell me shit about you. Hell. They don't know shit about me! I just got my AARP card.*

*Computers are fucked up, you know?*

•••

Some of our best friends in the neighborhood are Pete and Mary Sikes. They live about four doors up in the little green house on the corner. We've been friends for a few years, ever since we moved into the neighborhood. Pete and Mary stopped by to introduce themselves on the second or third day we were in the house, I think. They thoughtfully brought over some pizza and a few beers; I guess it was obvious that we weren't exactly ready to entertain yet. Hell, we'd barely found the silverware.

Over the past couple years, we've gotten to know them pretty well. We see each other every couple of months for a movie, or to go bowling, or to rent a video, or just for dinner. We know they've been trying to have kids for several years. June and I don't want any of the little buggers, but Pete and Mary are just the opposite. They'd make great parents, you can just tell.

It was last Friday when I stepped in it. I mean, I didn't know. I casually asked how "the project" was going. That's how we referred to their attempt to have kids. The four of us had talked about it for many months, and they weren't shy about telling us what was going on. They had progressed from making love whenever they felt like it (no pregnancy) to making love on the day when she expected to ovulate (nope) to taking her temperature to know when the egg dropped (nada) to going to a fertility clinic (nothing).

We hadn't talked to them since their appointment last week. And that's when, as I say, I stepped in it. We had Pete and Mary over for cards. The four of us sat in the game room. June was across the table from me; Mary was to my left. "So how goes the project?" I asked. Silence. Suddenly I noticed Mary's eyes welling up, a tear pooling at the pocket at the bottom of each eye socket. She waited for a moment to try to regain her composure, then excused herself and walked into our kitchen.

"Oh, shit," Pete said.

"Whad I say?" I asked. "Hell, I'm sorry, I...." Mary was dabbing at her eyes in the next room. June pushed back her chair to get up and help, but Pete motioned her to stay.

"We went to the clinic on Friday. They checked both of us out. It seems, ah, we can't have kids. Ever."

"Oh, no," June exclaimed. Her hand fluttered to her mouth. "What did they tell you?"

"Well, she's fine. It's, ah, me. They tell me I'm shooting blanks. A natural born, perfect vasectomy poster boy, that's me. Sperm count, minus fourteen or something."

"I don't understand," June said. "You had a vasectomy and you're trying to have children?"

I turned to my wife, who can be a little thick at times. "No, dear, he didn't have a vasectomy. It's just *as though* he had a vasectomy, but it's natural." I didn't want to say it, but I wasn't sure she understood. "He's sterile." I turned to Pete. "Isn't there anything they can do?"

"Oh sure. For $7000 I can have an operation which has a 10% chance of being successful, and a 10% chance of leaving me impotent. No, thanks. For $15,000 we can get in vitro fertilization, five tries. If I have $15,000 lying around somewhere, wop me in the head, OK?" Pete was bitter.

Mary returned to the table. Her eyes were reddened. Now we knew why. "Isn't it terrible?" she said. "No children."

"You could adopt," June said, trying to be helpful.

The tears came back in Mary's eyes. This time she stayed in her seat and dabbed at the moisture with a napkin. "We've talked about that, and we probably will. But we really wanted to have our own. Now we never...." Her voice trailed off.

"How can it cost that much to get some sperm from a sperm bank and, uh, put it in, or, I mean, do whatever they do to, you know...." I was fumbling my words.

Pete answered me. "It's not the sperm. It's all the fucking doctors, and the tests, and the hospital, and the lab, and the specialists. It's ridiculous. If I had the money, you know, I'd probably do it. But I don't. So now our option is to let her loose on the street and hope she gets lucky."

"Peter," she screamed in mock anger, "stop that!" She slapped him on the arm, but at least she cracked a little smile. "Anyway, I couldn't just 'do it', you know, with a stranger. I mean, what if he had some terrible hereditary disease, or his father was a serial murderer or something? I'd have to know the guy and be comfortable with him. And know his medical history, and all."

"I have my records right upstairs," I said gallantly. Mary blushed a deep red and let out a little yelp. June kicked me under the table. "Hey, hey, it was a joke. For God's sake, take it easy, you all. Where's your sense of humor?"

It was Pete who thought about it and spoke up. He said, "You know, Mike, you may have something there." Mary's blush became an even deeper shade, if that was possible. "No, no, listen to me. I don't mean that you, uh, you know, I mean, you could be a sperm donor. You could be the father, sort of. I mean, we do know your medical history and your personality...but we can overlook that...and, well, it sort of makes sense on a lot of levels."

It was my turn to be uncomfortable. June looked at me with that "What the fuck is this?" look in her eyes.

I didn't respond. I didn't say anything. I couldn't. My wife was going to kill me after they left, I just knew.

Mary said, "You know...." and her voice trailed off.

I tried to change the subject, but both Pete and Mary wouldn't allow it. Grasping at straws, I thought. Desperate, I thought. Crazy, I thought. They talked about it for the next hour, back and forth across the table. I sat quietly, only speaking when directly spoken to. June didn't contribute much either. But Pete and Mary were transfixed with the idea, and a short sixty minutes later were practically begging me to help them. June nodded, giving me permission.

The plan was that I would jerk off in a cup, give the sperm to them, and they would, uh, apply it. No doctors, no hospital, no lab tests. Just neighbors helping neighbors. Sort of like the United Way.

A week passed, and June and I went over to their house. This was going to be weird. We socialized, and the subject of our mission for later that evening scarcely came up. We joked about all the things we usually joked about, drank a bunch of wine, and had a good time. About 11:00 Pete announced that it was about time to "get started."

Mary said her goodnights, and went into their bedroom to change. Pete followed her, and returned a moment later in his PJs. He had a plastic cup in his hand. "Here, fella," he said, offering it to me. "The bathroom is just down the hall."

June just smirked at me, as if to say, "See what your big mouth has gotten you into." I knew she'd never let me live it down. I walked to the bathroom. I unzipped my pants and let them drop. Pete had thoughtfully provided some pornographic magazines, and I leafed through them as my tool began to enlarge.

Dicks in pussies, dicks in mouths, dicks in assholes. Pretty girls with cum on their face. Girls with two guys fucking them. I turned page after page of porno pictures, getting an erection and stroking myself. But I wasn't here for pleasure, I was here to do a job. And I had practiced for this since I was twelve! I came in the little cup, cleaned myself up, and pulled up my pants.

I knocked on their bedroom door. Pete cracked the door open and looked out at me. I offered him the cup. I could see Mary sitting on the bed in a see-through nightgown, but I couldn't see all that much in the dim bedroom light. I tried, but I couldn't tell if she had her panties on because the blankets were bunched up in front of her.

"Wow," Pete said, looking at the cup. "Good volume. Good job." He winked at me. I didn't know if he was going to use a turkey baster or what. I didn't want to know.

"I feel like an idiot," I said. "And you're welcome."

June chimed, "We'll see ourselves out. You guys have fun." We left.

A couple of weeks went by, and June called Mary. Nothing yet. We got together the following weekend, and everyone decided it was too soon to tell anything. But as more weeks passed, it became apparent that the experiment had failed.

We repeated it a month later, again on a day when Mary was scheduled to ovulate. With the same results. Now June had relaxed with the idea, and so had I. In fact, the idea of Pete dripping my cum into his wife's cunt was kind of a turn-on for me, although I wouldn't say anything of the sort to my own wife, of course. Mary and I seemed to form a closer bond than just neighbor to neighbor, as well. I suppose it was only natural. Here we were sharing the most intimate of experiences. Sort of. The experiment failed again. And failed again another month after that.

Mary and Pete and June and I were at our house. The Bulls were on TV again, and we had a big screen and they didn't. We all had a few beers as we watched the game. The subject of the experiment came up, of course, and we talked in some detail about it.

"Maybe we're doing something wrong," Pete said. "Maybe you pay for all those specialists for a reason. Maybe there's some special technique, or something...."

"Don't be silly," June said. "People have been making babies for thousands of years. How hard can it be?" I guess she realized the insensitivity of her remark just as the words left her mouth. "Oh. I'm sorry," she said softly. She was talking to a couple for whom it wasn't just difficult, it was impossible.

I tried to backpedal and lighten the conversation. "It's hard," I said, with a leering emphasis on the word "hard." I smiled at no one in particular.

"Oh, Mike, you're incorrigible," June said. "Still. Maybe there's something else we should be doing that we're not doing."

Mary spoke softly. Her eyes were cast down, averting contact with anyone else in the room. "There is," she said, almost in a whisper. "I've been thinking about it." She paused. We were all silent. "Maybe we should just try, you know, the old-fashioned way. I mean, sort of, well...." The words hung in the air.

It took June a moment to realize what Mary was saying. When she did, her eyes got wide and blinked rapidly. Then she said, "You don't mean...I guess you do mean...I mean...." She was at a total loss.

It was Pete who spoke next. He also looked down as he talked. "Mary and I talked about it. Maybe, you know, maybe it would work.... I mean, we would understand if you don't want to. Or if June would object," he added quickly. "Totally understandable. It's just that this is so important to us."

It was so quiet in the room you could have heard a sperm swimming. June broke the silence. "This is bizarre," she said.

Mary spoke quickly. "See, Pete? I knew it. It's too much to ask." Her eyes welled with tears. It was pitiful. "I'm sorry. I don't mean to cry. And I understand. Really." A tear dripped down her cheek.

June must have been deeply touched, because she said, "I suppose it could be OK. I mean, only for the experiment. You know. Not for sex." She paused. "I would at least think about it." She thought a moment. She looked into Mary's reddened eyes. Then she said, "If it's OK with Mike."

Yahoo! Whoopee! Zowie!

I kept my composure as best I could, and although my voice cracked as I said it, I said, "I could do that." I smiled at Mary, who smiled back. I figured we'd set up a "date" and consummate the dirty deed later in the month. I asked, "So how do we set this up? I mean, when, and where, and... uh, you know?" I paused. "When's the time, I mean when's she ready?" I asked Pete. I stumbled over the words. Big surprise.

It was Mary who answered the question. "Actually, today's the day," she said. "But I know that's rushing things, and you guys probably want to talk it over and all. So we can wait till next month, if you want." I shrugged. June said, "It's really OK with me. Sort of. Might as well get it over with."

"You mean, tonight?" My mouth dropped open. My dick began to get erect inside my pants.

"Yes, tonight, lover boy," Pete said. "You guys can just, uh, retire somewhere, and June and I will wait here."

"Oh no," June said. "If this experiment is going to happen, I'm going to be part of it. I have a stake here, like not letting my husband get involved with another woman."

I didn't see the logic in it, since she had just given me permission to fuck Mary. But what was I going to say? "What do you mean, hon?" I asked.

"I mean I'm going to be in the room. I want to make sure that it's just for procreation, not for recreation."

"You're what? You're going to be in the room?" You could have knocked me over with a feather. I lost my erection.

"That's right. Or no deal. Deal?" she said.

I looked at Mary, then at Pete. June was driving a hard bargain, so to speak. "It's OK with me if it's OK with you guys." They had no choice. Neither did I.

We all finished our beers and headed for the bedroom. June gave Mary a nightgown that didn't reveal much. She decided that I would wear pajama bottoms.

Mary and I climbed onto the bed. June took one of the two reading chairs at the far end of the room. Pete waited outside. I sat next to Mary and waited for my body to take charge. Nothing happened. I mean nothing. No problem, I figured. I thought of a dirty movie I had just seen. Nothing. I remembered the time I got jerked off by a nurse. Nothing.

After several minutes June called out, "What's going on?"

"Nothing." I said. "Nothing."

Mary added, "Boy, I'll say."

Thanks. As if I didn't already feel the pressure. I guess that must have been it, that and the fact that my wife was at the foot of the bed, waiting for this to be over. "I need a little help, here," I said. "Do you mind, hon?" It had been long enough that she could see I wasn't lying.

"Go ahead," she said.

I took my flaccid penis out of my pants. Mary stared at it. I reached up and cupped her tit. She had a nice set; they were still round and firm. I felt her nipple become aroused. I wished I could say the same for myself. I said, "Maybe if you touched me...."

Mary's hand reached for my tool. She took hold of it as though it was a month-old banana. Nothing. She stroked me up and down. Nothing. I reached for her pussy, and her legs parted. Nothing.

"What's going on?" Pete called in through the door.

"Nothing." June shouted back. "Absolutely nothing."

"Why not?" he asked.

"Do you want to tell him?" she asked me. I shook my head. "My wonderful husband, who gets horny at the sight of a bagel, can't get it up."

"Jesus," I exclaimed. "Give a guy a break."

"Really?" Pete said. "I think I'm insulted."

"You're insulted?" Mary said. "How about me?"

June got up and walked over to handle the situation. Or at least try. She came over to the side of the bed and knelt to get a better view. With one hand she reached up and cupped my balls, keeping her hand away from Mary's, which still held my limp dick. With the other, she unbuttoned her blouse. She knows that I love to look down women's blouses. It's one of my biggest turn-ons. One of 592 that I've cataloged so far. Nothing.

"Maybe if I helped," she said. She pushed Mary's fingers away from my penis and bent over me. She took me in her mouth and began to suck. Nothing. Really nothing. The stress was just too great.

"Anything?" Pete's voice came through the door.

"Nothing," Mary said. "Shit," I said. "Would you people stop it? I feel like I'm a blue-light special at the Kinsey Institute. What pressure!"

Pete appeared in the doorway. "Can I see?" he said. I thought to myself, "What're you, the fucking doctor? You can't even knock up your own wife." But I stayed silent.

He came in to survey the situation. He looked down at my paltry pecker, then at his wife. "Well, I can get turned on," he said. Mary leaned over and hugged him. Since she was sitting on the bed and he was standing, her head went into his crotch. She could feel him through his pants. "God, you're hard, at least."

This was humiliating for me. Me! MIKE HUNT! Dirty story writer. Sex fiend. Pervert.

"Would this help?" Pete said, lowering the zipper on his pants. "I know you like pornography. At least I know you used it in the bathroom when you were jerking off in my cup." He withdrew his dick. He was a good eight inches, nearly two inches longer than me. About seven inches longer than me at the moment.

"As if I'm not feeling insecure enough, you take out your schwantz and you're a lot bigger than me," I pouted. June, who had her eyes pointed down as she continued her efforts with her mouth now released me and turned her head. She gasped.

"Oh my God," she said. "Mary, you are so lucky!"

"Holy shit," I thought. "I'll never get it up now."

Mary's hand had reached out and she was grasping Pete's dick, softly stroking it. He pushed his midsection forward, and she leaned toward him. He wanted her to put him in his mouth, and she was complying. Now, do you think that was enough for me? No. Nothing.

I watched her work on him orally for a few moments and realized that nothing was happening. To me, I mean. It was obvious that a lot was happening for them. June, with her hand still on my dick, knew my predicament. She didn't know what to do.

"Listen guys," I said. "This isn't working. I don't think I'm going to get it up, here. No hard feelings, you know what I mean? No hard anything, apparently."

Mary made some little sucking noises. Pete moaned. June released me and turned toward the couple, now engaged in sex just a few feet away. She was looking at Pete's dick with awe. "We weren't supposed to be having sex, anyway," she said. "This was just for, you know, to make a baby."

But she couldn't take her eyes off his dick. "I am feeling a little flushed, though," she said to no one in particular. The way she was twisted, her unbuttoned blouse was no longer open to me. But it was to Pete, who I realized was staring down at her chest. I felt my dick twitch. When she suddenly figured out that Pete was looking down her blouse, she involuntarily jerked back and straightened her shoulders.

"No, hon, lean forward," I said. She looked at me. Pete pulled his rod out of his wife's mouth, and we could all see its angry red head bobbing in the open air. June was mesmerized. She bent forward, and her blouse opened. Pete stared into the gap in the material. I felt my dick twitch. "Uh, good," I said.

Mary wanted to put her mouth back on his member, but he pushed her away. She grasped his manhood and began pumping it with her fist. He pointed at June's chest and wiggled his finger. Her hands involuntarily went up to the front, and she undid another button. My dick twitched again.

"Hey, guys, I'm getting something," I said. Everyone's eyes turned to look at my dick. It didn't look much different than it had minutes earlier, but I knew something was happening. "This is a turn-on, having Pete look down June's blouse."

Now she unbuttoned the final two buttons on her shirt. The front hung open, and the sides of her breasts were clearly visible. She wasn't wearing a bra; she rarely did. But in spite of the size of her tits, there wasn't a sag or stretch mark anywhere. I knew. I had plundered that real estate hundreds of times over the years. June had larger breasts than Mary, and Pete was enjoying the view. I felt some movement in my penis.

June never looked at me but continued staring at Pete's pole. "Glad to help, hon," she said. Her hand reached out for him, and she cupped his testicles in her upturned palm. I felt a major twitch. He closed his eyes. Mary looked over at me and shrugged. I bent my finger and told her to come to me. She moved away from her husband and crawled along the bed.

She reached me by crawling on all fours, and I reached into her top and grabbed one of her tits. I looked down the top and saw the other one swinging free, its red tip pointing down. I looked up and saw that June's free hand was no longer free. She had grabbed Pete's hard-on and was stroking it. She turned slowly and looked at me. I looked into her eyes and gave permission. She turned back to him and lowered her mouth.

Pete reached for her shirt and pulled the sides apart, releasing June's pendulous breasts from the loose confines. She momentarily released his dick so that she could take the shirt off. My cock slowly continued to grow. Finally Mary had decided to help and reached for me. As she made contact with my member, it jumped up slightly. I was now perhaps half-erect. Not exactly home-free, but getting there.

Mary brought her mouth down to my midsection and licked my balls while she stroked me. The soft piston action of her hand, coupled with the wetness of her mouth, soon brought more hardness to that instrument that had malfunctioned just minutes earlier. June was now eagerly sucking on Pete's dick as well. I could tell she liked it because of its larger size. I watched as her mouth sank down on him, and I knew his mushroom head was pushing against the back of her throat. June does that for me all the time, and even occasionally deep throats me, but I only reach about an inch into her throat. Pete was a good two inches longer than I was. Would she even try?

I motioned Mary to turn around. She got up on her knees and faced away from me. I didn't plan it, but we were both pointed directly at Pete and June. I found the crotch in Mary's panties, pulled it to the side, and rubbed my dick against her pussy lips. I found the opening. I pushed. As I did, I watched my wife also push, trying to get Pete's entire penis into her mouth. Judging from his length, he was already part way down her throat, and I knew there was more to follow.

"Oh, god, look at that," Mary said. She too was entranced by the activity on the other side of the room.

I began bouncing against Mary's ass, finally fucking her with abandon. My dick was now fully erect, and her love juices covered it from top to bottom as I slid in and out of her hungry box. Pete stopped his moaning long enough to say, "You really should be lying on your back, hon. That way, the sperm will have a better chance to travel—"

Mary cut him off with a grunt. I said, "Let's not push it, OK, Pete? I'm just lucky to be here."

"You sure are," Mary giggled. "But I feel lucky, too."

June backed off of Pete's throbbing dick. She turned to me and said, "He's right, you know. She should be on her back."

Christ. Technical details in the middle of a fuck session. Jeez!

"Fine," I said with a trace of frustration in my voice. "Mary, if you wouldn't mind?"

"Oh, I don't mind at all," she said. As she rolled onto her back, she whipped off the rest of her clothing, then lifted her legs straight up in the air and split them, presenting her cunt as the target. I leaned forward and presented my arrow. Talk about a bulls-eye! I sank into her, her cunt folds again wrapping themselves tightly around my cock. Her warmth enveloped me, and I leaned on my elbows above her looking down into her face.

I felt so tender towards her. I leaned down and gave her a little kiss on the lips, which turned into more, then into a passionate embrace.

"Hey," June exclaimed. "What are you doing? This is supposed to be for sex. Don't do that." Like it was OK to have my dick in my friend's wife's cunt, but I wasn't allowed to kiss her. Still, there is an intimacy to a kiss that just fucking doesn't have, as any hooker will tell you. "This is unfair, anyway. You're getting fucked. She's getting fucked. Pete is getting a blow job. I'm the only one not getting any."

"Go ahead, hon," I said. I never took my eyes off Mary's face. "It's fine with me." Mary gazed into my eyes as the tempo of our rhythmic coupling increased. June was on her feet in a millisecond, shedding her clothes. She pushed Pete down onto the edge of the bed, and as he sat there, she sat in his lap. I turned my head to watch. I could tell by her contortions that she was lowering herself onto his erection. I saw the passion in her face that told me when she had hit bottom.

"Don't get too used to a dick that size," I said. "I wouldn't want you to be disappointed when you get home."

"I don't think she'll be disappointed," Mary said, bouncing against me. "You're pretty good at this. I like having your dick in my pussy."

"I'll bet he doesn't mind it either," Pete said. He leaned back and lay down on the mattress, and his head came to rest just inches from my leg. June was bouncing up and down on his lap, and I could see that his hands were busy grasping at her tits as they bounced in front of him. June had her arms outstretched, her palms open against his chest to use for leverage for her bouncing. Up and down. Up and down. With Pete lying on his back, I could see the juncture of their sexes, and watched his fuck tool slide in and out of my wife's cunt.

"This is great," June said. "I have a nice big dick inside me, I have my husband's permission, and I don't have to worry about becoming pregnant. This is just great."

"Yeah," I said. "And my job tonight is to deliver a load of sperm into this lovely lady's pussy." I looked back into Mary's eyes; they fluttered with my compliment. Her hips bucked. "This is not a bad job at all." My hips returned the favor.

My head slid down, and I grasped her breast. Even though she was smaller than June, her tits weren't quite as firm, and I had to hold my hand around the outside to get it to stick up in the air. I licked the nipple, bending my head down as far as I could in the process. I heard Pete start to moan.

"Oh, I'm going to cum," he said. "I'm there already."

"Go ahead," June told him. "I'm close myself. And one thing that gets me off is feeling a nice hard dick in my pussy when it erupts. It's the ultimate turn-on. Come on, big boy." She was bouncing up and down with abandon; his hands continued to grab at her tits, twisting and squeezing them like they were some sort of Nerf toy.

"Ahhhh," he said, and I knew he was peaking. "Ahhhh," he said as the second wave passed him. "Ahhhh," he said more slowly this time.

"Ooooo," June said. I knew that sound. That was her cum sound. Her hips were bucking violently against his, she slammed herself down on his pulsing dick, and moaned again. "Oooooo," she said. I knew there would be another four or five of those, but then I felt a rush of my own, taking over my body and my mind.

I looked down at Mary. I softly said, "Get ready, the delivery man is here." She looked up at me and pulled me close. I felt her legs spread even wider as she tried to sink me as deeply as she could. I didn't know if it was passion or just her attempt to get my sperm closer to her egg, but she bent her legs and surrounded me, pulling me as far in as I've ever been inside a woman. I felt the buzz of my orgasm begin in my loins.

I thrust forward, shooting my first load into her hot cunt. I pulled back a little, and then pushed forward again, delivering my second spurt into her. As I pulled back again, I felt the flush of heat deep in her cunt that told me she was about to join me on the roller coaster, and I bucked forward mightily, as my third wave crashed over my head. She cried out, "Yes! Yes! Yes!" Her own orgasm overtook her, and her cunt gripped my dick with a series of contractions that squeezed out the last precious drops of my spunk. I collapsed on her even as her cunt continued to grip me, our sweaty bodies now slipping and sliding over one another.

Finally, we were done. I gave her a peck on the lips and started to get up. She pulled me down, and we stayed that way for several minutes. June did the same with Pete. Finally the four of us were sitting, standing, walking around completely nude and exhausted. Then somehow our modesty got the best of us. Mary dressed quickly. Pete followed. June climbed into the bed and under the sheet. I just walked around in a daze, my spent dick hanging low between my legs. I walked them to the door; Mary just said, "Thanks." June glanced back at my exhausted penis as I walked back into the bedroom.

I said a silent prayer of gratitude. What a way to end the evening.

But the story doesn't end there. About two weeks later Mary called to give us the news. She had missed her period. She had a doctor's appointment the next day. As the days turned into weeks and the weeks into months, the news came in rushes. She was pregnant. It would be a boy. The baby was healthy. She was due in October.

Finally the big day came, and she had a healthy baby boy after a fairly routine delivery. She was in labor just seven hours, pretty good for a first-timer, I've learned. Pete told me they were naming him Carney. It's Irish for "victorious." But his nickname was going to be "Hunter," in honor of me. Pete wanted to know if I would be the child's godfather. Of course, I said yes.

A few weeks after Mary returned from the hospital, she felt good enough to socialize and let us coo over the baby. We sat around, reminiscing about the "experiment," as we all called it. I spoke up.

"Anytime you want little Carney to have a baby brother or sister, you just call." Neighbors helping neighbors, you know? Like the United Way. "I'll be glad to help out again."

"So will I," said June.

•••

## Afterword

***So help me, it's all true. Except the part about Carney. His name's actually Dave. He's now 26 and drives a truck. I hope he doesn't read this, because then he'll know I fucked his mother, and he'll probably get a gun and kill me. He's a weird dude. It's probably hereditary.***

***Speaking of weird dudes, you are too if you're not getting these swell stories by e-mail, all in one piece, and early delivery to boot! Almost everybody else is. Except Dave, of course. I took him off the list last week.***

*To get 'em by e-mail, send me a note. Make sure you say something like "I'm over eighteen" or another witty saying. To protect your identity from other recipients, the stories are sent out as "blind" carbons. There's actually no carbon used, of course. I think it's all done with electricity. If you print the story on your laser printer, there IS carbon in the toner, which if you put in your eyes can make you "blind". Be careful. Also, if you get it on your hand and play with yourself, it can turn your dick black. But this will NOT fool most women into thinking you have a big black dick, I've learned.*

*Casual conversation and other drek at M1KE@hilarious.com. Please note that the 2nd character in M1KE is a "one" (1) not an "eye" (I). Thanks. Yes, the mailing address has changed. But I still can't spell M1KE very well.*

*As a friendly and neighborly service, I've made my older stories available at my website: <http://baird.pair.com/mrm1ke.htm/>. Some of my older stories are about me when I was younger. I have no older stories about me when I was older, because I'm not older yet, but by next week I will be older, and then some of my older stories will be even older. However, I'll still be younger in my older stories.*

*I've also added "M1KE's Graffiti" to the website. If you've ever wanted to peek over someone's shoulder and read their mail, this is the place. In fact, if you've ever sent me an e-mail, it might be posted here. Maybe I posted your return address. Maybe I even included a credit report and the information I got from the FBI about you. You never know. Please don't try to sell this story. You'll embarrass me when nobody wants to buy it, and you'll experience a painful disfiguring death when I get Dave to kill you by running over your head with his truck and squashing you like a cantaloupe. You can give the story away if you want. Good luck. Some people won't even take free shit.*

*This story is Copyright © 1997 by M1KE HUNT. Like somebody would steal it or something. Although I do think it has potential as an NBC mini-series, don't you? Maybe in the next episode we could all watch little Carney smash his tricycle into a fire hydrant and be rushed to the hospital and get 47 stitches. Maybe he could even get tuberculosis or some other horrible disease, or maybe a wacky doctor could cut off his foot by mistake. Oh, the possibilities are endless!*

*Does anybody know anybody at NBC? I hear it works better if you have an inside connection. I think that's how Seinfeld got started. Supposedly he was fucking the top guy's wife or something and got caught and they made him do a TV show to make up for it. At least, that's how I heard it.*

# dollspace
## GashGirl

*@join doll yoko*

*You enter deep doll space zero.*

*doll yoko swims up from crater mud pond of dead girls. She places her moss damp lips on yours and kisses you tenderly. Her pale hands perform gentle inquisitions upon your fleshform as she haunts your imagination, bruising your skin with her words.*

**gash ripped split bleeding slit**
**ice in her veins**
**totally fucked up on bad E**
**screen dump**

**<it's over baby and you know it>**

He fucks her as if she were already dead, shoving into her sweet rotting mango flesh.

cunts smooth as mirrors reflect her terminal gaze
taking her silver blade she cuts a line
real fast real slick fresh young slit
mirror site tight

**river boys wail: she's dying man, who's gonna kill us now? who's gonna fuck our pretty corpses? who's gonna suck our cooling dicks?**

**genderfuckmebaby says: sex and sudden death is totally too boring**

**shu lea says: all animals are sad after fucking**

**orphan slut snarls: the only good slit is a dead slit – shut your slit bitch and get on with it**

petrol_hed **says:** boring sex life of an infidel

snakeboy retracts his forked tongue and keeps silent

profanity declares: laws are made by men who fuck their daughters

Madame.de.Clairwil yawns loudly

*a pack of hungry ghosts hovers over the bridge of winter dreams*

*whispering: all history is pornography*
*whispering: trust no-one*
*whispering: to kill is to forget*
*whispering: a doll is forever*
*whispering: all women are ghosts and should rightly be feared*

*doll yoko, ghost girl tender and dirty, claws her way out of ragged gash skin. She slithers through the slit, translucent grey tentacles teasing her momma's lips.*

*Eyes soft watering holes, ghost ponds, sad salty holes. Sour plum lips. Octopus in her cunt, giving doll formidable grasp on human nature.*

*doll is the infinite spaciousness of zero, haunted by deep doll hunger and the impossible.*

eagles swooping over river, mountains surround

paper red lanterns line impossible narrow laneways

old man in bath-house peers through bamboo blind, touching himself to luminous gaijin display

sailormoon softmoan pantyporn peepshow in every convenience store

cocks permanently soft with self disgust

mothers fuck sons while husbands go down on their daughters

incest to neon pain pachinko surround sound

pork fat pig piss demon stirs cauldron with shovel
doll baby born of charcoal demon in filthy ramen bar
on edge of floating world

she's a ghost but she doesn`t know it
damage courting danger

doll rides subway
seduces softskin school boys mangahard in prussian uniforms

she`s a 7-11 ghost girl,
a modern convenience

doll plays with wealthy wives who never suspect she's a cunt
her exquisite stiff formed from the dreams of mad women

she`s a salary ghost
ghosting for a living

doll plays with crones' sagging sento bellies,
taking their wispy secret hair between her stay-sharp serrated teeth,
tugging insistently until the old women`s fingers stray, remembering the future,
dreaming the impossible

soft accidents, haunted fucks

holding breath

doll dives deep into snow pond

brown stem like forest mushroom held firmly in pale hand

blood sharp knife cuts oysters from luscious salty bed

sea demon doll hole sailor moon

slow surface

taste stempearls on moss

zero swallows one

one becomes three

demon eats ghost

ghost drinks moon

lips touch lips

skin codes skin

stemmoon in ghostgash again

deep doll space

*a ghost never tires*

*and a doll is forever*

**haunt me**

**fuck me**

**again and again**

# Appendix A

# "Ream Me Up, Scotty" or "Mulder, Do Me" A Look at Erotic Fan Fiction on the Net

Russ Kick

Right now, in a parallel universe, Captain Kirk is fucking Mr. Spock. FBI agent Dana Scully is sucking agent Fox Mulder's cock. Wilma Flintstone and Betty Rubble are licking each other's bodies. And Dorothy is being gangbanged by Munchkins before having sex with the Tin Man while the Cowardly Lion watches.

This certainly isn't what the owners of these TV shows and movies would like to see happening, but the human libido refuses to be dampened by anything—even intellectual property laws—so our culture's best-known characters have been freed from their sterile worlds and are being allowed to hump with gusto. It is the fans of these works of pop culture who have provided the liberation. Not content to merely be spoon-fed the action, they make these worlds and characters their own.

The officially unrecognized genre of fiction known as fan fiction (or "fanfic" for short) is surprisingly voluminous. From the mid-1970s until recently, its main mode of distribution was through amateur zines which were sold at conventions or offered through classified ads in the back of fanzines. Then came the Net. Just as it offered instant worldwide exposure to every other form of information, the Net brought fanfic to the masses. As more people discovered fanfic, more of them began writing it. Even if you only selected the absolute best stories, there is easily enough material to fill an anthology larger than *Hot Off The Net.*

Naturally, not all fanfic—probably not even most of it—is erotic. Much fan fiction describes situations that the creators of the mythos—be it *Star Trek* or *Superman*—would themselves create. But that's not the kind we're interested in. No, we want to see what happens when sexual reality descends upon characters created by conservative corporations.

According to general consensus, the first erotic fanfic appeared in the mid-1970s. It was based on the original *Star Trek* series and usually featured sex and/or a romantic relationship between Kirk and Spock. (This type of story was known as Kirk/Spock or K/S. This form of denoting which two (or more) characters were having sex led to this type of story being called "slash". Inexplicably, slash only refers to fanfic in which characters of the same sex have the hots for each other. Although slashes are also used to signal hetero and bi relationships (e.g, Picard/Crusher, Mulder/Krycek/Scully), slash only refers to gay (and, usually, lesbian) fanfic.)

Kirk/Spock slash paved the way for sex among the denizens of almost every TV show that has a devoted following and attractive characters, including all the ***Star Trek*** series, ***The X-Files, Babylon 5, Highlander, The Sentinel, Xena: Warrior Princess, Hercules, Due South, Buffy: The Vampire Slayer, Miami Vice,*** and ***Starsky and Hutch.*** (The recent Net-fueled popularity of fanfic explains why most of it is devoted to current shows.) Although these shows have the most material written about them, it's possible to find isolated examples of erotic fanfic concerning just about any show, including ***Home Improvement, Party of Five,*** and ***Friends.***

Cartoons are also the subject of erotic fanfic, with the Japanese ***Sailor Moon*** apparently the most popular. Comic book characters get a chance to explore further uses of their super powers. The bulk of such fanfic involves DC superheroes—such as Superman, Batman, and Wonder Woman—with the notable exception of Marvel's X-Men. For some reason, movies don't generate a lot of fanfic, erotic or otherwise, though there are some scattered examples. Books generate the least amount, with Anne Rice's ***Vampire Chronicles*** being the only ones I've seen that have led to fanfic.

The rest of this article will present a sampling of some of the best erotic fanfic on the Net. I'd actually prefer to have published one or two stories in their entirety, but that could be legally problematic. You see, fanfic is truly an outlaw form of writing. Its very existence violates trademark and copyright laws, since the characters, settings, and universes in general belong to multinational corporations. For example, ***Star Trek*** and everything having to do with it are the property of Paramount Communications.

So far, the corporate behemoths have quietly tolerated fanfic—even of the erotic variety—probably because they know that the writers and readers of fan fiction are the biggest supporters of a particular show. Cracking down on fanfic would alienate and enrage a very vocal, loyal fanbase. Also, no one is making much, if any, money from fanfic. The zines don't sell very many copies, and the stories on the Net don't earn any money at all and even cost the writers and collectors who pay for Webspace. But if a for-profit, (hopefully) popular, aboveground book were to run fanfic, it could easily incur the wrath of the multinationals. Therefore, I have decided to present this overview of the genre with healthy excerpts. Please don't let the fact that I am only presenting juicy parts of these stories cloud the fact that many of them have good plots and characterizations along with the steamy sex scenes. (Also bear in mind that all typos in the original stories have been preserved.)

## *STAR TREK*

The ***Star Trek*** universe has inspired far and away the most fanfic. As noted earlier, the original series probably fueled the creation of erotic fanfic in the first place. In a typical example—"Crazy Fingers" by Greywolf the Wanderer—Kirk and Spock are taking some R&R, kicking back in a pool on Risa. The Captain gets horny watching the Vulcan floating face-up, displaying "that lean and powerful body." Kirk gets touchy-feely with Spock and asks him if he'd like a back rub, the answer obviously being yes. Moving to a nearby massage table, the interspecies fun begins.

***He drew the towel down to Spock's narrow hips, draped another across his shoulders, and poured some more oil into the hollow just above the Vulcan's tailbone. Using his thumbs first and then his whole hand, he spread it across the lightly-furred skin there — pausing once to encircle the other's waist with his hands and murmur, "Mmmm..." He felt Spock's breath catch, for just an instant, and he smiled even wider.***

Soon, Kirk has rid Spock of the towels and is kissing and licking the back of the Vulcan's body.

***Starting at the back of one knee, he began to lick and kiss his way upwards, to nuzzle and nip at the heavy furred sac, and lick his way up that sensitive cleft.***

***Spock moaned. The Vulcan's head was thrown back. His eyes were closed; the silky black hair was tousled, disheveled. He shivered each time he felt Jim's mouth on him — and the human felt all of it.***

[...]

_The human slid one warm, oiled finger down into that cleft, and felt the other push back against him. Jim refused to hurry. He was waiting for something, and diverting himself, while he waited, with lips and fingers and willing, quivering flesh. Finally he heard it..._ <<t'hy'la — *please*...>> _He licked at the tight-puckered skin, spread more oil there..._ <<...ahh... yes — *please*, t'hy'la...>> _And those slim, powerful hips lifted towards him again, and this time he let his finger find its way inside — so tight there, so hot... Slippery with oil, it slid in easily, to be followed by a second — and he found it, that small tender place, right *there*..._ <<Yes!! *Please*!>> _A sharp little wave of pleasure ran through both of them..._

_Jim was so hard it was almost painful; very gently, he pulled his fingers out, and touched the tip of his cock to that well oiled place. He pushed, very gently, felt himself begin to enter — and the other arched up towards him, again, and he was *in*, surrounded, engulfed. The link between them opened up wide. They *burned*..._

Kirk reaches around, playing with Spock's nipples with one hand and stroking his cock with the other.

_He felt it begin in Spock, first — a series of little shudders, a wave of pleasure that grew, and built... Then in him, the same, getting stronger, hotter, brighter. He couldn't breathe, couldn't stop; he was burning, both of them were — on fire, out of control... One flesh — one mind, one heart... One soul. And the wave crashed..._

In the sub-subgenre of erotic fanfic concerning *Star Trek: The Next Generation*, the pairing of the commanding, bald Captain Jean-Luc Picard and the mischievous, practically omnipotent Q is quite popular. "From Q with Love" is Varoneeka's tale of Q's pursuit of Picard. After some well-written verbal sparring and cat and mouse games, the two are having dinner with each other. Again, things start with a massage, this time the target being the Captain's aching tootsies. For some reason, it takes Picard this long to pick up on Q's lust, and the human throws a fit, telling Q he feels nothing but anger and contempt towards him. He questions whether Q intends to rape him, to which Q replies:

_"If I were interested in forcing you, we'd have come to this room years ago." His voice dropped. "And don't think I wasn't tempted, Picard, sorely and deeply tempted. How do you think it's been for me, knowing I could simply wish it and you'd let me fuck you on your own bridge, while Riker applauded and Data took notes?"_

Eventually, Q wears Picard down.

_"So long," Q moaned softly. "I've wanted to do this for so long."_

_And then their lips came together, just a faint brush at first, and then more pressure, and then a bit more, and Picard felt Q's lips, soft and warm and trembling just a bit, twist around his, and something jolted him. He opened his mouth in surprise and Q's tongue breached him, moving over his teeth to slide along his tongue, teasing it, curling under it, then retreating to thrust back in again._

They end up on the floor, with Q peeling off Picard's clothes.

*Flushed a deep red, rising from a thick nest of grey-black curls, Picard's cock rose straight up, with a thick teardrop of fluid at the tip. Q breathed in deeply, and here was that new smell, sweet and erotic, and, not stopping the movement of his hands over Picard's body, Q leaned forward and licked that fluid from the crown of Picard's penis. His hips jerked in response, and the man moaned, "Q."*

*He began to bob his head, sucking hard and then licking with his tongue, around the crown, along the underside — Picard gasped very loudly at that, Q noted for future reference — then sucked again, moving up and down as Picard's hips thrust involuntarily. They quickly found a rhythym, and Q used his left hand to trail patterns on Picard's stomach while his right hand cupped his balls, and he felt the man's scrotum tighten even as Picard grunted a warning.*

*"Q, I'm going...ooooh...I'm coming...ahhh. Oh!"*

*And with that, Picard came in Q's mouth, hot spurts that Q sucked in and swallowed greedily, wanting every drop, every taste of this man. He drew the orgasm out as long as he could, sucking and licking until the man was completely spent, and lay there bonelessly on the carpet, gasping, eyes unfocussed.*

The two end up in the sack, where Q rims the Captain, then slowly slides into him.

*Q went completely still for an instant, then shuddered and thrust deeply, deeply into the body of his beloved captain and came, screaming. Picard felt the hot liquid moving even deeper into his body, and his own eyes rolled back as he came into Q's hand, blacking out and collapsing to the soft bed, Q's body holding him so that he didn't melt into nothing.*

Written in a more humorous vein, "Yada, Yada, Yada" by Cameron Burnell involves characters from *Star Trek: Deep Space Nine*. Specifically, the changeling Odo—who can mold his body to any form—and Major Kira Nerys, the impish Bajoran Liaison Officer, have some *really* wild sex while Dr. Julian Bashir watches.

*Kira's head was thrown back in absolute ecstacy. Odo was on top of her, arms and legs holding him up - *other* arms and hands touching her everywhere. Three cocks were sliding in and out of her, one in her pussy, the other in her rectum and one tiny one going in and out of her belly button.*

*Then there was the three mouths ... besides Odo's regular mouth that was sucking at Kira's neck. Two more were sucking on her nipples and another seemed to be latched onto her hugely swollen clit.*

Kira notices Bashir spying on the plastic, fantastic lovemaking, and Odo invites the doc to join in.

*He pulled his clothes off and headed for the bed. "All right so... what do I—?"*

*Before he could finish his question, a tentacle from somewhere on Odo's body swept him into the fray, between Odo and Kira.*

*He found himself being grabbed by Kira, too, who slid him on home. "Err..."*

*Then he felt a very large, pulsing cock sliding on in and a very warm naked changeling pushed up against his back. His eyes widened, but Kira's tongue was busy licking each of his tonsils. Besides, he decided, he was finally fucking. And being fucked!*

Odo gives Bashir a hard time by asking Kira whether the doctor is as talented a lover as he.

*"Does he do *this*, my tulip?"*

*Julian felt a bit of changeling slide between them and start sucking on both of Kira's tits at once. Before he could complain, two more little mouths began sucking on his own hard nipples.*

*"Ahhh...."*

*"And does he do *this*?" Odo murmured in Kira's ear, another bit of changeling sliding between them lower down and sucking on her fat clit. As Julian waited for Kira's answer, that bit of changeling began sucking on his balls.*

Bashir can't take much more ectoplasmic ecstasy and comes soon after, but he's not out of the picture. While continuing to hump Kira, Odo fills Bashir's booty and mouth with two of his shape-shifting cocks.

Nova D. has created an impressive body of fanfic titled *The Secret Logs of Mistress Janeway.* It turns out that the Captain of the *USS Voyager* in the series *Star Trek: Voyager* is a domme who likes to provide some of her crew with a form of discipline that Star Fleet probably does not condone. She dominates and has sex with several members of her crew (as well as some characters from the other series), including Ensign Harry Kim, Lieutenant Tom Harris, Captain Picard, Dax, Lieutenant Uhura, the luscious Seven of Nine, and, of course, her long-suffering second banana, Commander Chakotay.

In the second chapter, we witness Janeway's first three sessions with Lieutenant Paris, a notorious ladies' man. Upon entering her chambers, Paris is overly eager to get his hands on the Captain, but she has other plans. She shackles his arms and feet while he is standing, then cuts off his uniform.

*I picked up a lightweight paddle since corporal punishment was what frequently came to mind with Mr. Paris. I spanked his Irish ass until it was bright red and very hot. How will you address me in this room, Mister? It took him a few whacks before he gritted it out minus the hesitation. He took about thirty before I stopped. Paris was gulping air and looking at me warily when I came around him. He was also quite erect. Perfect.*

*Eyes down, Mister. You look at me when I tell you. He lowered his eyes, but didn't answer. What are you to say when I talk to you? Yes, Mistress. I hope your not trying to humor me, Mr. Paris. It would be an insult to me, and a disservice to you. I touched him again, gently. The time had come to show him some of the pleasures of proper service.*

Janeway sucks Paris for a minute but stops before he comes. "I just wanted his attention." After letting him hang for a few minutes while she sips water, Janeway returns to Paris, gently stroking his cock. He creams all over her.

*I started to wipe the cum off, then thought better of it.*

*I held my hand out and told him to lick it off. He knew from my tone that I wasn't kidding. Mr. Paris was startled by the taste. He didn't seem to like it. However, he was fascinated by the texture of the gloves. He had a good tongue. The sensors were telling me that I would enjoy feeling it on my bare skin. He cleaned the glove.*

Janeway puts a gag on Paris, then whips him viciously with a cat-o-nine tails. Thus ends their first session.

In "One-Upsmanship", the tables are turned as the dashing Chakotay makes Janeway strip, shackles her in a standing position, whips her back, inserts a buttplug, and has sex with her. He then restrains her face-up on a bed.

*He was in between my legs running the whip along my thigh.*

*"You'll have to guide me," he murmured.*

*"Yes, Chakotay," I replied.*

*He smacked my inner right thigh. It was nearly perfect.*

*"Harder," I whispered. He complied. I gasped at the next smack. He had the touch. My thighs were throughly reddened. My breathing was very labored. I was suspended in sensation awaiting his attack on my clit. When that blow finally fell, I nearly levitated off the bed. Chakotay looked concerned about the sound I made.*

*"Don't stop," I gasped.*

*By the sixth smack I was begging for release.*

*"Please, Chakotay, please..."*

*He tossed aside the whip and began sucking the sensitive nub he'd just been swatting. I arched toward him seeing stars in an endless, colorful array.*

*Chakotay let me rest for a moment only a moment. When my head cleared. I felt him sucking on one nipple while tugging the other. Then he was inside me. He was kissing me moving with slow controlled strokes until I was coming once again. He reared back with a roar then collapsed on me. I never thought I would move again.*

In one of the latest additions to the saga, Janeway succumbs to the inevitable, bringing the Borgalicious babe Seven of Nine into her fold(s). The Captain and Seven go to Janeway's quarters, where Ensign Harry Kim is already prepared—"shackled to the bed naked, spread eagled and blindfolded."

*Seven positioned herself on her hands and knees over Harry's torso. I was surprised when she removed the blindfold. When she kissed his eyelids, I unpinned her hair and allowed myself to run my fingers through the gold silk of her hair. Seven licked Harry's lips then kissed him. During that searing kiss, I removed her shoes then unzipped the jumpsuit. The woman hardly noticed she was so intent on Kim's mouth.*

*Seven moved her mouth to kiss Kim's neck. She licked it and sucked at the skin.*
*"Let me bring this jumpsuit down to the waist. Lick and suck his skin down his torso then run your nipples along the same path," I said.*

[...]

*Seven was kissing him again as I deftly shimmied the luscious woman out of the jumpsuit entirely. I was almost mesmerized by those rounded muscled cheeks, but Kim brought me back to the matter at hand.*

*"Let me show you how to taste him where he wants it most," I whispered.*

*Seven heard me. She lapped her way down to Kim's cock. I licked at his testicles letting the woman see what I was doing. Silently, I urged her down beside me.*

*"Lick him," I murmured.*

*She complied licking his right testicle as I licked his left. Her eyes were riveted on mine as we tongued him thoroughly there then moved up his ridged shaft together tonguing and sucking together until we got to the head. I was pleased at how she lapped at the liquid already seeping from the head. Our mouth's met at one point causing Mr. Kim to nearly scream and raise off the mattress in ecstasy.*

Janeway turns her full attention to Seven, sticking her tongue down the Borg's throat. Janeway releases Ensign Kim's restraints, so he can boff her while she goes down on Seven.

*Her taste was glorious, her responsiveness was astonishing. I was able to work her into a frenzy without real effort.*

*"You want to know who taught him. It was me," I said with a gasp when Kim thrust into me. "Look at us, Seven."*

*She gasped then moaned loudly. She was letting go. Feeling her come sent me over. My orgasm pushed Kim over the edge. We all ended up in a tired heap on the bed.*

*I was waiting for Seven to emerge from the bedroom less than an hour later. She looked flushed and disheveled and lovely and delicious.*

### THE X-FILES

Featuring two eye-pleasing leads who are obviously mutually attracted but who have yet to become romantically or sexually involved with each other, *The X-Files* has teased its fans mercilessly. The fans, naturally, have responded by creating a huge amount of work in which FBI Agents Dana Scully and Fox Mulder finally "investigate" each other.

In "Midwinter Thaw" by Lydia Bower (who is one of the most talented erotic fanfic writers), Mulder and Scully are in Wyoming, tracking a serial murderer/rapist who lets his victims freeze to death in the arctic temperatures. Mulder leaves their hotel room to experience for himself what it's like to be so bone-chillingly cold. When he comes back in, Scully—who is narrating the story—warms him up. Perfectly capturing Mulder's weirdness and Scully's hard-on-the-outside, creamy-on-the-inside personality, one thing leads to another until the agents are getting down to it for the first time.

*I am the one who loosens the cuffs of my blouse as Mulder slips the last of the buttons free. I have become an active participant in this drama playing out in a lonely motel room in the middle of a frigid hell.*

*The blouse is eased over my shoulders and falls into a snowy pile at my feet. My hands come around to free the button on my slacks, but Mulder catches them and holds them gently. He brings first one and then the other to his mouth, baptizing them with feather-soft kisses across my knuckles. His eyes beg for understanding and permission.*

[...]

*In the space of a second, the clasps of my bra are unhooked and Mulder quickly removes it. My hands fly to the front of his shirt as he buries his face in the valley between my breasts. His hands move in lazy strokes up and down my back. He pulls away and I watch as he opens his mouth and his tongue slips past his lips.*

*In strokes that last an eternity but are over in fractions of seconds, Mulder laps at the taut peak of my breast. He licks in long circular strokes around the nipple before finally taking it into his mouth.*

[...]

*I cover his mouth with mine. Lips speak without sound. Tongues whisper secrets, one against the other. And Mulder tastes of all the things I imagined.*

[...]

*I rock my hips against him in small, instinctual thrusts and then gasp as his hand slips into my panties to cup me. With gentle desperation his fingers slide into me and back out, spreading new moisture over already slickened and swollen folds. Fingertips find my clitoris and I buck against him, grinding into the heat of his hand.*

Scully starts squeezing Mulder's cock through his pants. He disrobes and pushes her onto the bed, then mounts the sultry redhead.

*His hands slide under me and lift my torso from the bed, drawing my back into a bow as he pulls himself upward, sitting with his legs folded beneath him. His mouth finds my breasts as his hands land at my hips, lifting me up and away before slamming me back down. I can do nothing but cling tightly to him, my fingers digging into his shoulders, my head thrown back in glorious surrender. I ride him with a fierceness and a passion I didn't know I possessed.*

[...]

*Mulder gently eases me back to the bed. And then all gentleness leaves him as he begins to slam into me, thrusting in short violent strokes. Sweat drips from his face and clings to his chest. We grasp and cling to each other as friction becomes heat becomes melting fire. My legs are wrapped around his hips with incredible strength. I can't let go. I can't let go.*

[...]

*I bring him over the edge with me as the tiny muscles of my vagina contract around him, milking his essence as we kiss and swallow down the sounds of one another's joy. The last thing I remember is Mulder's fingers moving softly over my face, trailing warmth and contentment and hope.*

In "Abstract Expressionism" by Nicole van Dam, the agents are visiting the studio of Jo, a Brazilian painter, who conveniently has to leave for about an hour to pick up some paint.

Displaying a silly side that seems implausible, the agents get in a playful fight, smearing each other with paint.

*Dana's breath became shallower as he continued, feeling the gentle strokes. She watched his eyes follow his hands, tilted her chin and closed her eyes when she felt the cool paint on her neck. His fingers trailed down to the top button of the shirt she wore. Dana watched him, keeping her eyes on his the entire time. She could feel his fingers undo the first button and it made her suck in a short breath.*

*"Mulder..."*

*He glanced at her with dark eyes, his hands stilled. "If you want me to stop, Scully, tell me now."*

Naturally, she doesn't want him to stop, and eventually things get quite heavy.

*With one last look up at him, she lowered her mouth over him. Fox moaned and arched his hips at the feeling. This hadn't happened in such a long time, he'd almost forgotten what it felt like.*

*Dana's mouth lifted, taking only the tip inside. She sucked on it gently, running her teeth around it lightly. Fox twisted his head back and forth on the canvas, she was driving him crazy.*

[...]

*Dana brought her hands up to place them on his thighs. The muscles tightened as she lowered her mouth on him again. She raised periodically to talk to him.*

*"How do you want it, Mulder?" she purred. She ran her tongue along the length of him. "Like that?" Mulder moaned, his eyes closed. She repeated the same action again. "Talk to me, Mulder."*

*"Oh, God..."*

*Scully sucked on him gently. "How about that?" Her tongue stayed on the nerve right under the tip of him, stroking it gently.*

*"Oh... yes... oh, God...." He sucked a breath through his teeth. "Harder."*

*"What was that?" she asked, looking up at him. He gazed at her with dark eyes.*

*"Harder," he repeated. "Please..."*

*She smiled and lowered herself over him. His hips jumped forward as he felt the heat of her mouth engulf him. Her head bobbed up and down, applying more suction.*

*"Yes.... oh, yes... harder..." His hips moved with her as she continued. Her hand found his balls and fingered him, causing him to jerk slightly. "Ahhh... Dana..." She kept up the pace, sucking him and milking him for all she was worth. "Oh, God... Dana... I'm gonna come.... oh, yesss...." His hips pounded her face and he could feel it. He was right on the edge.*

*This, Scully knew, and she stopped.*

From there, they finish up in missionary position and declare their love to each other during the post-coital relaxation phase.

In quite possibly the most unusual specimen of *X-Files* erotica, the not terribly well-written "Scully's Secret XXX-File" by latoro, Scully has an erotic encounter with singer Melissa Etheridge. Turns out that the two knew each other in college, and it was Scully who gave Etheridge her first kiss from another woman. They had made out one day, but things had gone no further. Luckily for us, thirteen years later Etheridge's tour bus is followed by a UFO, allowing Scully to go to the rock star's penthouse for an interview. Before you know it, the two are flirting with each other, Etheridge's hand on the agent's knee.

*Dana crossed her legs over Melissa's hand trapping it between her legs and gazed lustily into her eyes. Melissa dropped her head letting her mane of hair fall on Dana's lap. Dana heard Melissa moan into her skirt. She raised Melissa's face and pressed her mouth to her lips. Melissa hungrily sought Dana's tongue with her own as Dana unbuttoned Melissa's silk blouse. She carefully removed the blouse and cupped and kneaded an exposed breast. Melissa moaned loudly into Dana's mouth as Dana tweaked a hardened nipple. Melissa reached for Dana's camisole groping under the material to get at her tits but instead she found Dana's gun holster. Dana abruptly stopped kissing Melissa and let her pant into the open air.*

[...]

*Dana watched with delight as a topless Melissa swaggered in her tight leather jeans. She removed her jacket and withdrew Dana's dildo out of the gun holster and inserted it into her portable harness. Melissa almost dropped the serving tray when she viewed the erect dildo laid across Dana's lap. She rested the tray on the coffee table and offered a glass to Dana, her hand shaking noticably. As they slung back their shots, Melissa repeatedly glanced sideways unable to avoid the seduction of the Dana's dildo. She massaged Dana's exposed thigh in an effort to hint at what she wanted.*

[...]

*"I want to find me a bar with a blue light on,"*
*"Dollar shot specials, a bartender named Dawn........."*
*"All the way to heaven is heaven............"*

*Dana thought, this must be heaven. She lifted her face and guided her dildo into Melissa's steaming cunt. Melissa bucked and growled under her and the women rocked to the slow beat of the music. They picked up the tempo to the incessant plunging as their pussy muscles gyrated in unison. They cried out, overwhelmed by the tingling sensation. The blue light glowed stronger as it pulsated in a rhythmic beat to the womens' cadence. They rocked in time to the beat as they burst into an orgasmic explosion. Both women's bodies jolted as if struck by lightening as an electric current coursed through their spent bodies.*

## OTHER TV SHOWS

While *Star Trek* and *The X-Files* have the most erotic fanfic, other, newer shows are coming on strong. The medieval fantasy *Xena: Warrior Princess* is a natural for such treatment, given that its two main characters are an unconventionally beautiful, ass-kicking Amazon (Xena herself) and her younger, more nubile sidekick, the blonde bard Gabrielle. The possibilities are just too ripe to leave unexplored.

In "The Labrys" by Patricia L. Ennis, Gabrielle is supposed to meet Xena at a tavern but doesn't know which one. She ends up in a lesbian inn, the Labrys. When Xena doesn't show, Gabrielle continues to search and finds her quaffing ale in another tavern. Xena has to open a can of whup-ass to keep men from pawing pretty Gabby, so the two decide to room at the female-run Labrys. Once upstairs, Gabrielle puts moves on Xena, who resists at first but understandably caves. The two engage in a liplock, then Xena takes charge.

*She lifted the smaller woman into her arms and carried her to the bed.*

*Laying her down, she removed her shirt, brushing her fingers across swollen nipples, but just lightly, causing Gabrielle to shake. Then she pulled off her skirt, her eyes drawn to the pale patch of hair at the joining of her legs. She could smell Gabrielle's passion, a good, clean musk that caused a slight dizziness in her head. Her tongue moistened her lips unconsciously, something that made the muscles in the bard's abdomen tighten.*

*Standing, she pulled off her leathers, sliding them down her body, the friction almost sweet on her flushed skin. She threw her wrist and arm bands across the room to join her boots and knee guards. Kneeling on the bed, she looked down at Gabrielle, whose eyes had gone wide and her mouth dry at the sight of the woman kneeling before her. If Xena needed any more convincing, she had it in her eyes. They were bright with her need and something else as well. A tenderness that she knew was reflected in her own. Love.*

[...]

*"Please," She [Gabrielle] whispered. "Not slow...not this time. I need to feel..." She let the words trail off as she could not describe what she needed. Could not explain how she could want something so badly that she had never even noticed was missing before this moment.*

*Xena nodded and broke away, trailing kisses down her chest until her lips found Gabrielle's nipple. The bard arched against her, her breath coming in gasps and Xena knew she wouldn't be able to take much more. She slid her hand down a silky hip and into the soft hair between her legs. Her eyes closed as warm wetness covered her fingers.*

*"I ...I told you." Gabrielle tried to smile, her head falling back to the pillow when Xena's fingers found her swollen bud and ran over it, pressing lightly.*

*Unable to wait, she slid down the bard's body and lifted her thighs to wrap her arms around them. With her scent driving any thoughts from her head, she opened her mouth against Gabrielle's swollen labia and began to stoke her softly with her tongue.*

*Gabrielle cried out, unable to believe that anything could make her feel better than how she had felt a moment ago, but somehow, she did. She could feel each stoke of Xena's tongue, each movement of her lips. Searching for something to do with her hands, she reached down and placed them on her lover's head, which seemed to drive the warrior more. She tried to control the wave rising within her, but it was useless. With a resounding cry, her hips lifted off of the bed and came down shuddering as her climax rolled through her. She reached down and pushed away Xena's still questing mouth. "Please...let me rest...I can't.." She heard the warrior chuckle.*

*"You were the one that said 'not slow'."*

*Gabrielle smiled as her lover rose to lay on top of her. "I know, I know. It's just that it's too much ri...oh.." Xena's legs had spread, straddling her thigh, and Gabrielle could feel her wetness against her skin. Her eyes widened when the warrior began to move slowly against her, pushing harder with her hips, her head hanging low, hair covering her face. She raised her head, reaching up to kiss her. Her lips stilled at the first taste of herself on Xena's tongue, and then quickened when she found it to her liking. A few moments more and Xena's movements stopped, her body shook silently and she laid her head against Gabrielle's breast. With a soft laugh, she brought her hand up and caressed the warrior's hair.*

*"What's so funny?" Xena demanded.*

*"For someone who makes so much noise in battle," Gabrielle grinned. "I would have expected more of a finish."*

A show doesn't have to currently be hot to receive the fanfic treatment. The 1970s cop-buddy show *Starsky and Hutch* has a smaller but no less devoted following. "Fifty-Five Cents" by Alexis Rogers, who has one of the most distinctive voices in fanfic erotica, shows what happens when the young lovers are on a stakeout at a practically deserted LA bus terminal. They each stand at the opposite ends of a row of phones, talking to each other. Starsky tells his blond beau how much he wants him.

*Hutch turned to face the wall, pushing himself against the booth. The image was distorted by the glass. "Don't."*

*"Don't what, blondie?" He loved the power he had over the man. Great golden lion tamed by his touch.*

*Soft cough, forced sigh. Stern command. "Don't tease. It'll keep until we get home."*

*"I don't think so. Not if you think about it. Us. Together on the bed, my fingers tugging at your jeans. Think about my mouth, lover boy. Think about what I do to your beautiful cock with my mouth." Starsky smacked his lips. "You taste so good."*

*"Starsk!"*

*"It's too late, babe. You're ready for whatever I want to do."*

*He watched as Hutch slammed the receiver on his phone, heard the loud click in his ear. He watched Hutch slump against the phone booth. The man would not look at him.*

Eventually, the two talk on the phone again, and the power shifts. Hutch is in control now, and Starsky knows it as he pleads:

*"Hutch, don't leave me like this. Do something."*

*"Unzip your pants and I'll tell you what to do."*

*Starsky stared at phone booth number seven. "No." He replaced his receiver.*

*Another dime.*

*"Okay."*

*"Slip your fingers inside your shorts. Feel the shock run through your body. Think about what my fingers do to you. How they know every inch of you — inside and out. That's right, babe, move your hand, stroke your cock. Think about my ass and how good it feels when you shove your cock*

*inside me. Feel the muscles tighten, hold you, milk you dry. Think about fucking me, babe. Your body moving in mine."*

*Starsky swayed against the glass. He tried to fight the words, the emotion. Failed. He tried to hang up the phone and could not. He was trapped in the web he had woven. Hutch had control now.*

*"Harder, lover, harder. Feel yourself climb higher, higher. Now."*

*His body responded to Hutch's voice and his commands. White fluid splattered onto the blue glass, trickled down. He felt sick and lightheaded. "Hutch!" There was no sound. And no dimes. "HUTCH!"*

## MOVIES

The *Star Wars* series has inspired probably more fanfic—erotic and otherwise—than any other movies. Strangely, it's much harder to find erotic *Star Wars* fanfic now than it was a couple of years ago when I first discovered it. I wonder if George Lucas has anything to do with that. Nevertheless, the *Star Whores* trilogy of stories still survives on a website in Sweden. The first episode of this screamingly funny series doesn't contain much actual sex, but there is this great scene between Luke Skywalker and Han Solo.

*Han slapped his thigh. "Today's your lucky day, kid. You ever make it with a Corellian?"*

*"Can't remember."*

*"What are you waiting for, a writ from the Emperor?"*

*Luke strode over and gripped Han's shaft, which seemed to squirm in his hand like an exotic fish. It swelled with blood, as if it was taking a breath.*

*"You're hung like a ewok, for Christ's sake. The Sarlacc wouldn't swallow this."*

*Han smirked. "You've sucked off so many Womp Rats, you don't know a real dick when you see it. I've made Tauntauns blush."*

*"No wonder they call you 'Hand Solo.' I've got a bad feeling about this." Luke held Han's cock between thumb and forefinger, examining it clinically.*

*"What did you expect, an ion cannon? If you can't make it to hyperspace it won't be my fault, kid. You've been stretched by every Snaggletooth and Stormtrooper in the sector. Show me one toy in this bay that wasn't bought with some lonely Imperial fruit's per diem, and I'll eat a bowl of Wampa shit. They've got your biography up in the cantina bathroom. You should read it sometime."*

*"I wrote some of it."*

*"Is it true you can ride a Bantha through your ass?"*

*"On a warm day."*

The most straightforward sex scene occurs in the third installment, *Sperm of the Jedi.*

Darth Vader encases Han Solo in carbonite, but something goes wrong and (conveniently) Han's crotch and mouth are not covered. He convinces Princess Leia to give him a blowjob.

*Han's penis began filling with blood. Leia shrugged. "What the hell." She began flicking at it lightly with her tongue, letting it grow upward to meet her lips. Han groaned.*

*"You're one of those chicks with a thing for pirates, aren't you?"*

*Leia licked her lips, tasting Han's pre-ejaculate. "I happen to like nice men."*

*"I'm nice men."*

*"We'll see." Han's cock was fully erect now, and she took it languidly into her mouth, covering most of its length. She twisted her head from side to side, biting down slightly and gently washing it with her tongue.*

*"Oh, baby. It's kinda nice bein' frozen. Oh, yeah..." He gritted his teeth at the sensations.*

*Leia's head bobbed up and down rhythmically over his cock. With her hand she played with his balls, which were soft and pliable from the heat. Slowly, she lifted her mouth away from him and began working his cock with her hand. She slid down with her tongue and began sucking Solo's testicles. She went from one to the other, letting each pop into her mouth from the suction.*

Leia invites Chewbacca to take her from behind while she's sucking his friend. Han warns her that Chewie has a humongous schlong, but she's sure she can take it.

*Chewie lubricated his cock as best he could and inserted it, half-erect, into Leia's cunt. She gasped at the sensation.*

*"Jeeezus Christ! How much of you is there?"*

*"Reearrreeuhhgh rawarr." (You don't want to know, honey.)*

*Chewie began pumping his hips rhythmically, driving himself into Leia as far as he could go. Half of his cock was still outside her as it continued its merciless expansion. He leaned forward and bit Leia on the shoulder viciously. She let out a muffled cry of pain, climaxing at the same time, and momentarily forgetting about Han's cock, which was still pressed enthusiastically against her uvula. Blood began to stream from the wound in her shoulder.*

*Chewie withdrew his fangs and settled into an easygoing stroke, starting to enjoy the sensations of Leia's vagina (which was of course remarkably small by wookie standards.) Leia panted and moaned desperately, sweat flying from her and spattering Han's lips.*

*"Hey, Chewie, what the hell's going on back there?" Han's mouth turned down at the edges, frowning.*

*"Reearrahrhra roooooaaruaur reeeaaarrhghh." (I could develop a taste for this. Forgive me, Malla.) He continued stroking, the tension steadily mounting. Leia's eyes fluttered as she teetered on the brink of unconsciousness.*

*"Oh God, Oh God, Oh God..."*

[...]

*With a spasm that seemed to shake the entire floor, Chewie climaxed, expelling a thick load of semen into Leia. He roared mightily as it overflowed her cunt, squeezing out past his cock and splashing onto the floor.*

*Leia exhaled, exhausted. "I'm glad he's not multi-orgasmic. I can practically taste it. Remind me never to do this again." She began kissing Han's cock gratefully. "Thank God for the average. Now let's get him out of me so I can clean up."*

*Han chuckled. "'Fraid not, your Worship."*

*"What?"*

*"Well, you see, a wookie's penis expands inside the vagina during intercourse. Barring an episiotomy, there's no way we can get him out of you for at least the next 8 hours."*

*"You're kidding, right?"*

*"Nope."*

*Leia rubbed her forehead, exhausted. "My mother warned me there'd be days like this."*

Of all the classic movies, one that certainly seems among the ripest for erotic treatment is *The Wizard of Oz.* With its assortment of strange characters revolving around the beautiful, freshly-scrubbed Dorothy, it cries out for steamy sex action, which is what Shelby Bush amply provides in "Dorothy Does Oz". With humor, imagination, and style, he takes us down the Yellow Brick Road as Dorothy engages in all kinds of sex with Toto, the Munchkins, the Scarecrow, the Tin Man, the Cowardly Lion, the Soldier, two women in the Wizard's castle, the Monkey King, the Wicked Witch of the West, and the Witch's entire army.

As in the movie, Dorothy starts out an innocent farm girl, but, unlike the movie, that quickly ends when she finds her corn-fed self in Oz. After Dorothy accidentally kills the Wicked Witch of the East, a Munchkin clusterfuck ensues, with our Little Miss Innocent in the middle. She happily mounts a Munchkin.

*Before she could object, she felt something pressing against her anus, insistently.. and then she felt her anus open as the new cock slid into her. She was surprised at how good it felt to have two cocks inside her. The new Munchkin behind her squeezed up to rest his hips against her ass, while her asshole relaxed around the intruding member.*

*Another Munchkin male approached her, offering his cock to her face. She took it into her mouth; he pressed it deep into her mouth, until she felt her airway threatened and pulled back. The Munchkin sensed how far he could go, and began to fuck her face gently, as she sucked on the little man's member.*

Having discovered the wonders of sex, there is now no stopping Dorothy. Her encounter with the Scarecrow is particularly memorable. Once the Scarecrow is liberated from his post, he munches Dorothy's muff. She reciprocates the orality.

*She fumbled with the buttons on the Scarecrow's fly, then reached inside. She pulled out a corncob and held it in her hand. It was not attached to the Scarecrow's body.*

*"Is this your..."*

*The Scarecrow pushed himself up on his elbows and nodded. "Not much, is it?"*

*Dorothy smiled. "It's so smooth."*

*"Well, I've polished it a lot."*

*"I see. Does this feel good?" Dorothy touched the corncob to her lips.*

*"Wait..." the Scarecrow said. He reached up, took Dorothy's head gently in his hands, and pulled it forward, until the end of the corncob touched his groin. "Now I can feel it. It has to be touching me."*

*Dorothy slid her lips down the length of the corncob, taking as much of it into her mouth as she could.*

*"Oh gosh," the Scarecrow moaned. "I never imagined it would feel this good!"*

*Dorothy slid the corncob back out of her mouth. "It tastes like a corncob, though," she said softly.*

It turns out that the Tin Man also has some unusual equipment. After Dorothy oils him, he grins and says,

*"Take a look at this!"*

*He opened the small door in his groin, and out slid a shiny tube, studded with rivets.*

*Dorothy stared. "How come that's not rusty?"*

*"Stainless steel," the Tin Man grinned. "I knew what parts were most important to keep in operation!" He stepped toward Dorothy. "Touch it."*

*Dorothy reached out a tentative hand, and grasped the appendage. Instantly, the angle shifted, becoming more upright. It began to warm in her fingers, throbbing... vibrating... then it began to rotate in a slow spin.*

*"Oooooh!" Dorothy moaned. "You've got all the extras!"*

Later, the Tin Man rogers Dorothy while the Cowardly Lion—who is impotent at this point in the story— watches.

*Dorothy rolled over, and the Tin Man slid over her, his mettallic cock sliding deep into Dorothy's cunt. It began to vibrate and rotate. Dorothy began to moan softly.*

*The Lion sat up and watched interestedly as the Tin Man moved slowly, pushing his manhood deeply into Dorothy's pussy and then withdrawing just as slowly until just the tip rolled against her clit.*

*"It's toys like that make a guy feel inadequate," the Lion whined.*

*Dorothy moaned. "But it feels so gooood," she breathed.*

*She began to writhe under the Tin Man. The Lion and Scarecrow watched as she began to work her hips with the Tin Man's movements, meeting each pelvic thrust with one of her own.*

*"Ohhhh," Dorothy gasped, "I'm coming, I'm coming!"*

*"So am I," grunted the Tin Man. "Just one more... Unnngh!" He thrust deep into Dorothy's cunt, practically lifting her off the ground as he ejaculated silicon grease into her.*

*Dorothy's body quivered with the force of her own orgasm. She felt her cunt fill with grease.*

*"Just let me keep it inside you a little bit," the Tin Man whispered. "The better to grease the joint."*

*Dorothy smiled through half-closed eyes. "As long as you keep it buzzing on 'low'," she whispered back.*

Naturally, everything ends happily. The Scarecrow gets a foot-long schlong, the Lion is no longer impotent, the Tin Man gets access to the Wizard's harem (because, the Wiz explains, "it is not how much you love that counts, it is how much you are loved"), and Dorothy returns to Kansas, much more experienced and ready to take on the farm hands.

## OTHER EROTIC FANFIC

Creations in other media have their erotic fanfic followers, too. Considering that many of us went through puberty while viewing the adventures of perfectly muscled people in tights, it's not surprising that comic book characters often find themselves in sexual situations. In "Superman Suck Slave" by Hector Oppenheimer, Lex Luthor weakens Superman with Kryptonite, then forces him to perform 136 blowjobs. The final recipient is Luthor himself.

*"This just won't do," exclaimed Luthor, "I have to give you the final proof that you truly are an unrepentent cocksucker, and that your only hope for relief is to have a stiff dick in your throat." With a dramatic sweep of his hand, Luthor unzipped his fly and pulled out his own sizeable piece of meat. "You see, Superman, or should I say 'Semenman'", this is the cock that made Lois Lane happy after all of those years that you neglected her, and this is the cock that is going to finally give you the release that you so desperately desire."*

*With a quick step forward, the archenemy of Superman thrust his turgid rod deep into the mouth of the kneeling Man of Steel. "Suck on it baby, this is THE cock that will finally give you release! And this is the dick that you will have to suck from now on. Eat it! Cocksucker."*

[...]

*"Well, Superman," laughed Luthor, "Now its time to prove my point. To prove that only this cock can give you true satisfaction, and that you will only find true happiness between the thighs of a man. I'm going to cum in your mouth now, old buddy. Yup, Lex Luthor is gonna shoot a load down your throat, and when I do, your dick is finally gonna shoot its load. Are you ready, cocksucker? Here it comes!"*

*Grabbing the back of Superman's head, Luthor impales the Man of Steel on his hot, spewing cock.*

Unlike a real Superman adventure, the Man of Steel does not find a way out of this predicament and, indeed, remains Luthor's suck slave.

Similarly, cartoons provide lots of fodder for the dirty mind. Japanese animation (called anime)—particularly ***Sailor Moon***—has inspired fanfic. Characters in American cartoons, such as ***He-Man, Transformers***, and ***Scooby Doo***, have likewise been getting it on.

In "Wilma and Betty", Anne Douglas—who usually writes non-fanfic erotica—gives us her take on the secret relationship between two ***Flintstones*** characters. The more adventurous Betty Rubble is complaining that her husband, Barney, and Wilma Flintstone's husband, Fred, are lousy in the sack. "They take more time polishing their bowling balls than getting us off," she laments. To help remedy the frustration, Betty gives Wilma her polished nine-inch tooth from a sabertooth tiger and instructs her on how to use it. When the boys go out bowling, Wilma takes it for a test drive.

*Laying back against the pillows, Wilma spread her legs and ran the point of the polished tooth across the outline of her mound. Gently she brushed the tip against the tight opening and eased it slightly inside. She sighed as she applied a little more force and felt it rise up inside her. Wilma had to admit to herself that it felt good.*

[...]

*"Yaba Daba Doo!" She screamed as her cunt gushed all over her hands and the saber tooth. It was the first orgasm she'd had in months.*

Betty hears her neighbor yelling and comes over to "investigate". Soon, the two friends are going at it hot and heavy.

*Betty guided Wilma's hands, placing one on each breast. She smiled as Wilma squeezed each one, playing with the large aureoles. Moving downward, Betty took a hold of her breasts and guided them to Wilma's waiting mouth.*

*Betty let Wilma take her time, enjoying the feeling of her wet mouth as it took a turn at each of her breasts. Many nights she had dreamed of this moment, and now that it was here it was meant to be savored. She ran her fingers through Wilma's red hair, undoing the small hair-bone, letting the long hair fall free around her shoulders.*

[...]

*Parting the wet walls with her fingers, Betty drove her tongue deep within Wilma. An electric spark ran up through Wilma's body at this first touch. Betty then began to cover the entire area with her probing tongue, savoring the taste of her friend.*

[...]

*But Wilma wasn't to be disappointed as a new rush of girlcum filled Betty's mouth. Rather than swallow it, Betty tried to hold as much of it as she could in her mouth. A small stream of girljuice ran down her jaw as she moved from between Wilma's legs and kissed her new lover as hard as she could. Using her tongue she pushed Wilma's own juices into her mouth, letting it mix with what was left of Betty's own.*

The scene ends shortly thereafter, with Wilma upset that she didn't make Betty come. Betty promises her inexperienced friend that she'll have more chances.

One of the most interesting forms of erotic fanfic is the crossover. In this subgenre, characters from different shows, movies, comics, etc. get to sample each others' wares. In what seems like the perfect match, the two weirdest FBI agents on TV—Fox Mulder of *The X-Files* and Dale Cooper of the defunct *Twin Peaks*—find in each other solace from a strange, hostile world. The story takes place after the events in the final *Twin Peaks*. Cooper had been possessed by a homicidal entity, but it is now supposedly gone. Mulder has been sent to investigate Cooper, who is recovering at a hospital, to see if he is mentally stable. The two are immediately attracted to each other, and the inevitable occurs.

*Fox and Dale wrapped each other in arms and legs, eagerly exploring the symmetry of their bodies and spirits. For every Samantha Mulder, there was a Laura Palmer who could have, should have been saved, if only it hadn't been impossible. For every Wyndham Earle there was a Cigarette Smoking Man, for whose crimes there would never be any revenge, let alone any satisfaction. When they finally wrapped each other in tongues and throats as well, Dale sucked him down deeply, taking in Mulder's smooth, slender cock as if re-absorbing something that already belonged to him. Fox's delicate fingers and agile tongue were driving out everything but the tenderness Cooper had come to feel for the younger man in the past few days, rising up in him like a tidal wave. His orgasm, when it came, was both shocking and soothing, like being ducked suddenly under cool water, and Dale couldn't help laughing aloud. *Fire walk with me.... I had no idea I needed this so badly. It was still burning in me, until today.**

Later in this long story, the two continue to break the Agency's rules about fraternization.

*When Dale unexpectedly took Mulder completely into his mouth and then slowly pulled away, it was more like being propelled into the stratosphere. Mulder yipped in an undignified manner as the cool air hit his wet and hardening cock. It was all Mulder could do to observe common courtesy and not grab hold of Cooper's ears.*

*Cooper pulled his fingers fully out of Mulder's mouth and rested them against Mulder's ass. His tongue was flickering up and down Mulder's erection. Mulder pulled his legs up and apart until the pants around his legs caught tight. "I'm ready," he said through clenched teeth, the polite version of *What in the holy hell are you waiting for?**

*Two fingers eased inside him, and Dale's tongue was lapping briskly at the underside of his head as Dale's fingers searched systematically. When they found what they were looking for, Mulder's hips came up off the floor. Screw flying; this was what a head-on collision would feel like if his brain were a hood ornament.*

*The pleasure quickly absorbed him, until Mulder's consciousness only existed as a flicker of sensation scrambling crazily between the erogenous zones that Dale was carefully stimulating. When orgasm hit him, Mulder suddenly understood why people talked about orgasms "hitting" people. It felt like two fists slamming into the small of his back, the pressure driving breath and noise and semen out of him all at once.*

## THE FUTURE: THE SHOWS MEET THE FANFIC

Evidently, the creators of television shows are partially responding to erotic fanfic's popularity by implying or all but showing sexual action between characters, even those of the same sex. According to *Xena's* producers and stars, the show purposely teases its audience with hints of desire between the two female protagonists, including an on-the-lips kiss (which admittedly took place in some sort of alternate reality after Xena's death). Debate rages concerning whether Xena and Gabrielle have a sisterly relationship or whether the closeness indicates the two are lovers. Several websites and a Usenet group are devoted to chronicling the "subtext" (lesbian innuendo) in each episode.

While it's highly obvious that Mulder and Scully of *The X-Files* dig each other profusely, it's also evident from the glances and double entendres that Agent Krycek covets Mulder's ass, although this appears to be unrequited lust. In one episode, Krycek even kisses his would-be beau on the cheek.

*Star Trek: Voyager* has perhaps gone farthest down this road. Janeway and Chakotay have an unconsummated Mulder/Scully attraction towards each other. We are outright shown that several characters are in romantic relationships, which include on-screen kissing and nuzzling but, so far as I'm aware, no bed action. The most brazen event thusfar has been Seven asking the smitten Harry Kim if he would like to "copulate". Faced with such a blunt offer, the Ensign freezes like a deer in headlights, thus missing his chance to be temporarily assimilated by the swank Borg.

Given the direction things are headed, not to mention the desire to hold audience interest and keep ratings up, it's probably only a matter of time before we see a sex scene between characters on one of these shows. At that point, erotic fanfic will lose some of its forbidden appeal, but it will always serve a purpose by letting us see all possible carnal pairings among our culture's most popular fictional icons.

•••

*You can find links to all of the above stories on my website at <www.mindpollen.com/hotn/reamme.htm>. For general sources of online erotic fanfic, see "Online Erotica" in the back of the book.*

*All titles, characters, and other aspects of these shows, movies, and comics are the property of their respective corporations and are presented here to chronicle the existence of a genre of writing.*

# Appendix B
## Where I Found These Stories

*For your further edification—and because several authors wanted me to list this information—here is where I found the stories. This may or may not be where they were originally published online (I know that many of them first appeared on Usenet). I haven't listed the addresses for every author's webpage, because not all of them wanted me to. Check the capsule biographies at the back of the book to see if your fave authors listed their sites. If not, you can probably still find them by doing a Web search.*

Anna Marti interview: Society for Human Sexuality Website <www.sexuality.org>
"Baby Tell Me, Does She Love You Like the Way I Love You?": Other Rooms <www.other-rooms.com>
"Beach Slut!": author's webpage
"Bloody Grunge Love": K-WEB <www.kweb.org>
"Bonkin' the Buddha": Fishnet <www.fishnetmag.com>
"Clean, Safe, Totally Shameful": Sapphic Ink <www.lesbian.org/sapphic-ink>
"CobWeb Years—Aspects": Sauce*Box <www.guillermobosch.com/saucebox/sb.html>
"Cum Pigs!!": Club Stroke <www.bmcg.com/clubstroke>
"Grizzly": Diana the Valkyrie <www.TheValkyrie.com>
"James/Joyce": Nifty Erotic Stories Archive <www.nifty.org>
"Kicked Out Again": roughriders <www.netgsi.com/~listwrangler/roughriders.html>
"Mother's Sons": roughriders
"Neighborly Neighbors": author's webpage
"Ripe": author's webpage
"Ronin": roughriders
"Taking a Bow": author's webpage
"The Bet": author's webpage
"The Fence": author's webpage
"The Girl Behind the Fantasy": author's webpage
"The Lovers": author's webpage
"Threesomes": Society for Human Sexuality's mailing list
"A True Account of My Encounter with Dolphins": The Ultimate Zoo Page <psg.com/~jimd/uzp>
"True Love": author's webpage
"Wedding Night Fantasy": Femmes Obscure <www.blackplague.org/femmes>
"Wineskin": author's webpage
Guillermo Bosch's poems: author's webpage
J. J. Campbell's poems: Wanton <www.wanton.com>
GashGirl's work: author's webpage
Ernest Slyman's poems: Juicy Britches <www.juicybritches.com/Ezines.html>

# Appendix C
## Online Erotica

### Sexzines, Archives, and Other General Erotica Websites

***The following sites contain loads of erotica (and other sex writings) from various authors, usually covering a wide variety of practices, positions, permutations, relations, situations, etc.***

**ASSGM** <assgm.com> The official archive of the Usenet newsgroup alt.sex.stories.gay.moderated.

**Clean Sheets** <www.cleansheets.com> An online erotic magazine coedited by Mary Anne Mohanraj, author of "The Girl Behind the Fantasy" in this book and *Torn Shapes of Desire* from IAM Press.

**Erotasy** <www.erotasy.com> An online publisher selling previously unpublished literary erotic stories for $2 each. The publishing wave of the future.

**Erotica Readers Association** <www.erotica-readers.com> Houses the material from the ERA mailing list, which features listmembers' stories, poems, discussions, and reviews. Leans towards "literary erotica infused with a woman's view of sensuality."

**Fishnet** <www.fishnetmag.com> Created by the people behind the mail order sex emporium Blowfish, Fishnet contains lots of strong writing. The daring fiction is the best part, but the essays and reviews hold their own, too. Fishnet has been on hiatus for a year now but will hopefully start swimming again soon.

**Juicy Britches** <www.juicybritches.com/Ezines.html> A promising but so far not spectacular webzine of erotic stories and poems.

**K-WEB** <www.kweb.org> Kinky Women Expanding Boundaries: "A Perverted Playground for Penisless People."

**Nerve** <www.nerve.com> The reigning online sex magazine. Intelligent, gutsy, insightful essays, articles, fiction, and reviews, plus a wide variety of daring erotic photography. Also in the mix are roundtable discussions, a chat area, online events with contributors, and a regular look at the sexy bits from works of literature.

**Nifty Erotic Stories Archive** <www.nifty.org> A humongous collection of gay, lesbian, bi, trans, and zoophile/furry material, mostly from Usenet.

**The Official Lady Cyrrh Website** <members.aol.com/ladycyrrh> Lady Cyrrh reviews erotic websites and individual stories, mostly from the alt.sex.stories newsgroups on Usenet.

**Other Rooms** <www.other-rooms.com> Started by erotic writer Marilyn Jaye Lewis, this ever-expanding site contains loads of great writing from published and unpublished writers, including Mark Pritchard (of *Frighten the Horses* fame), Michael Hemmingson, R.T. Bledsoe, and Marilyn herself.

**QZ** <www.qz.to/~eli> A massive, uncensored archive of stories posted to two Usenet groups— rec.arts.erotica (which is now pretty much dead) and the heavily-trafficked alt.sex.stories.moderated. From the execrable to the enlightened, it's all here.

**Sapphic Ink** <www.lesbian.org/sapphic-ink> A defunct journal featuring lesbian fiction and poetry that's high on literariness and low on sex action (not that this is a criticism or anything).

**Sauce*Box** <www.guillermobosch.com/saucebox/sb.html> Mostly featuring work from unpublished or underpublished authors, Sauce*Box is one of the best sources of erotic writing on the Net.

**Seumas** <www.seumas.com> Home of the Authors of Erotica Webring.

**Sex & Sensibility** <www.sexsense.com> Created by Marcy Sheiner (erotic writer, editor of *Herotica* volumes Four through Six and *The Oy of Sex),* this site contains stories and essays by Sheiner and others. You can also subscribe and receive a new erotic story via email every week.

**Sex Fiction** <www.sexfiction.com> Fairly large collection of Net smut.

**Society for Human Sexuality** <www.sexuality.org> The Net's largest repository of sexual information. Not much, if any erotica here, but so important and enjoyable that I'm listing it anyway.

## Websites for Special Tastes

*These sites focus on more specific practices, kinks, and turn-ons, some of which were previously unrecognized.*

**Breast Expansion Archives** <www.bearchive.com> Stories (and visuals) relating to women who undergo extreme, often rapid enlargement of their breasts.

**Diana the Valkyrie** <www.TheValkyrie.com> A collection of female heavy domination/wrestling/brutality stories. Because "a hard man is good to beat."

**DsKiosk** <www.cuffs.com> BD/SM fiction, essays, poetry, and an ongoing diary.

**The Erotic Mind-Control Story Archive** <www.mcstories.com> Hypnosis, drugs, subliminal tapes, and other methods are used to turn people into willing sex partners.

**Erotic Vox** <www.eroticvox.com> A collection of BD/SM stories, poems, and even novels.

**Femmes Obscure** <www.blackplague.org/femmes> A collection of high-quality snuff, torture, and cannibalism stories.

**roughriders** <www.netgsi.com/~listwrangler/roughriders.html> Female-to-male transerotica for people of all sexual persuasions. Besides breaking new ground and trashing taboos (two worthwhile endeavors all by themselves), roughriders contains enough superb writing to make it one of the best sexzines on the Web.

**Zeta World** <209.241.214.18> An extensive zoophile site with stories and essays regarding attraction to animals.

## Erotic Fan Fiction

**The Adult Fan-Fiction Webring** <www.jadzia.demon.co.uk/fanfic/xxxring.htm> A group of over 40 websites devoted to erotic fan fiction.

**Fantasies: Adult Fanfiction** <www.geocities.com/SoHo/Cafe/9123/fant1.htm> Headquarters of a Webring devoted to all types of erotic fanfic.

**Fan Fiction on the Net** <members.aol.com/ksnicholas/fanfic> The be-all and end-all of fan fiction. Info on mailing lists and links to hundreds of sites, including ***beaucoup*** erotica/slash.

## Collections of Erotica Links

***The above websites are just the tip of the iceberg when it comes to Netrotica. The following websites are collections of links to hundreds of other websites, including those of individual authors. The specific addresses I list will take you to the sections that link specifically to sites containing sex writings.***

**Catalog of Text Archives** <php.iupui.edu/~jewest/catalog.html>

**Eroscan** <www.eroscan.com/links/le>

**Gayscape** <www.manquest.com/gayscape/erst.html>

**Jane's Net Sex Guide** <www.janesguide.com/links/fiction.html>

**NAUGHTY Linx** <naughty.com/Arts_and_Entertainment/Fiction>

**NerveLink** <www.nervelink.com> Click on "Sexy Texts"

**Persian Kitty** <www.persiankitty.com/index2.html#ERO>

**Yahoo**
<www.yahoo.com/Arts/Humanities/Literature/Genres/Web_Published_Fiction/Adult_Fiction>

## Usenet Groups

*Although the Web is the most well-known part of the Net, there are other areas, including Usenet. Each Usenet "newsgroup" (there are over 25,000 of them) is devoted to a particular topic and can be thought of as a global bulletin board to which anyone can post a message. There are many newsgroups devoted to erotica. Most of them are completely flooded with ads for adult websites and scams, but the moderated ones filter out this garbage (referred to as "spam"). If you don't know how to access Usenet groups, you can read them at some websites, including Deja News <www.dejanews.com> and Supernews <www.supernews.com>.*

alt.sex.stories
alt.sex.stories.moderated
alt.sex.stories.gay
alt.sex.stories.gay.moderated
alt.sex.stories.bondage
alt.startrek.creative.erotica.moderated

# About the Contributors

**Akasha** is the webmistress of Akasha's Web (www.akashaweb.com), a compilation of over 250 stories about her real-life experiences with female domination.

Zigzagging the country grown tiresome, **R.T. Bledsoe** now makes his home in a western Wisconsin town of 500, not counting eagles, bears, and trout. He's joined by his wife, two dogs, and a cat. His work appears in a number of journals, and he's published two long-out-of-print books. His erotica—among which are the novels-in-progress *Sally Can't Dance* and *The Last Small, Good God*—appears regularly at the other-rooms website.

**Guillermo Bosch** (http://www.guillermobosch.com) is the editor of the erotic E-zine, Sauce*Box, an artist, poet, and the author of the highly acclaimed novel, *Rain*. Bosch was born in a small town, but his political views forced him into exile. Bosch eventually returned and became a successful editor and writer in Hollywood. Today he lives in a small village overlooking the ocean with his beautiful second wife and a wonderful little dog.

**Brian** I am 30 yrs. old 6' 170 from California. Recently moved to Chicago. I have been "out" since high school. My first sexual experience was with my first boyfriend when I was 16 years old. We were together for 3 1/2 years. I developed my addiction to sperm as a teen, starting with my own and then taking my boyfriend's. I see eating and taking my lover's sperm inside me as the most intimate and erotic joining between two men.

**Bronwen** is a professional writer/designer. And a contented ex-lush. Oh, and English. Having sworn that marriage was a trap she'd never fall into, she did. She lives in domestic delight with the love of her life and their two little boys. Surprised but happy sums it up. Her erotic writing has been such a kick, and she's grateful to readers and friends for their generous feedback. Just a feel-good sorta woman, really.

**J.J. Campbell** I was born Jan. 21, 1976, in Ohio, where I still reside and work. I began writing poetry at age 16. Then, one day, I discovered Charles Bukowski and had some foolish notion that I, too, could be a poet. So, fueled by alcohol, cigarettes, some luck, and a dirty mind, my dabbling in words has brought me here.

**cbratb** has been publishing erotica on the web for almost three years. The author's description of the work is to refer to it as philosophical erotica with a dash of humor, on the irreverent side. There is a concentration on the spaces between the words

**Airyn Darling** is a 28-year old woman living in Ann Arbor, Michigan, where she works as a UNIX system administrator for the University of Michigan. Although she received her degree in Sociology & Criminal Justice, she figures computers are as good a refuge as any until she figures out what she wants to be when she grows up. Airyn invites you to peruse her website: http://www.umich.edu/~airyn

**Susie Day** lives in Brooklyn, where she writes for queer and lefty publications. Because of her writing and her politics, she is fabulously wealthy.

**GashGirl** usually works collaboratively, investigating the poetic potential of film, video, email, virtual communities, and web-based narratives. She was a founding member of the prolific cyberfeminist art group VNS Matrix. Through a process of cross-fertilization of communication forms and contexts, she has created a number of personae, netspaces, and texts. *FleshMeat*, a novella based on her online lives, explores identity, desire, and deception, and will be published by Shake in 1998. http://sysx.apana.org.au/~gashgirl/arc/index.html

**Kurt Hoffman** was born in New York City in 1957. His small contribution to the genre of Net Porn is available for inspection at The Fucker Page (http://www.bway.net/~supine/y.html). Mr. Hoffman works as a graphic designer, and as a musician. He currently resides in Williamsberg, Brooklyn.

**Mike Hunt** An autobiography in 75 words or less: I was born, as most people are, and uh, I guess no further clarification is needed. Anyway I grew up and then I was a grownup. I had a career, made money, had dinner a few times, too, I remember. Recently I wrote some stories, of which this is one. Not THIS, I mean the thing with my name on it in the main body of the book. THIS is an autobiography, as I said at the beginning. OK?

**Raven Kaldera** is an intersexual transgendered female-to-male activist, organic farmer, parent, pagan minister, and pornographer whose myriad writings are scattered hither and yon. (Do a web search, we dare you.) His life is an open if kinky book. Enjoy.

**Lord Malinov** <malinov@mindless.com> has been posting erotica to the Net since 1990.

**Anna Marti**, an intimacy coach and certified hypnotherapist, is director of Body Moves, Portland, Oregon, one of the nation's leading body/mind movement studios. She works privately with individuals and couples, drawing on material that views life as a sacred marriage between sexuality and spirituality. Featured in the film "Masturbations Memoirs, Vol. II," distributed through House O' Chicks, she hopes to leave the earth a more 'pleasurable' place than she found it.

**Mary Anne Mohanraj** (http://www.iam.com/maryanne) is the author of *Torn Shapes of Desire*. Other stories of hers will be appearing soon in *Herotica 6* and *Best American Erotica: 1999*. Her newest project is editing an erotic webzine, Clean Sheets (http://www.cleansheets.com). She moderates the Internet Erotica Writers' Workshop, co-moderates the newsgroup, soc.sexuality.general, and is a graduate of the Clarion West 1997 Speculative Fiction Workshop. She has received degrees in English and Writing from Mills College and the University of Chicago.

Whenever he isn't taking dictation regarding the exploits of Amazon women, **Montrose** enjoys quiets evenings under the bleachers at the local college during football games. He turned to writing about strong women on the web after failing as a speech writer for Ms. America finalists.

**Nadyalec**. queer arab american slacker geeky freak who likes porn sex love crushes & other life-affirming activities, currently located in the suburbs of washington dc but spending way too much of my time online working on this: http://www.erols.com/nadyalec/

**Phil** is an Englishman who writes erotica purely as a hobby. He doesn't live in London and is not married to an interior designer. He loves: Women, Wilderness, and Mahler. He hates: Bigots, Background Music, and Caravans.

**Ronin** would just like to say that "Ronin" *is* hir autobiography.

**Jordan Shelbourne** is a technical writer for a Silicon Valley startup. He is occasionally astonished by the apparent normalcy of the life he lives with his wife, his daughter, and his dog. His fiction has appeared here and there on the Web, but is mostly collected at his website, http://www.compu-diva.com/IvoryGates/index.htm.

**Suzie SleaZe** Hi! Im Suzie SleaZe. I write to pleaZe! I love writing sex because it makes me so horny. I've been writing sex since age sixteen—I remember it well because Mom found some of my scrawled filth and I got a beating! I also write because I love the reaction (e-mails) I get in return from you lovely NetWankers out there! "BeachSlut!" is one of many stories I've written for the Net, and what you see here is an edited version. ENJOY! Luv and kisses, Suzie xxxxxxxxx

**Ernest Slyman.** I was born in Appalachia—Elizabethton, Tennessee. I have been widely published in over a hundred zines. I am a member of the ***Alsop Review.*** I have over ten books online on the World Wide Web. Three novels. HomePage: http://www.geocities.com/soho/7514. My print publications include ***The Laurel Review***, ***The Lyric***, ***Light:A Quarterly of Light Verse*** (Chicago), ***The NY Times***, ***Reader's Digest*** and ***The Bedford Introduction to Literature***, St Martin's Press, edited by Michael Meyer, as well as ***Poetry: An Introduction***, St Martin's Press, edited by Michael Meyer.

**Society for Human Sexuality**, through its free website at http://www.sexuality.org, seeks to archive and expand the quality and scope of sex information on the internet. Through our all-volunteer chapters in Seattle and San Francisco, we offer inexpensive and diverse educational events that offer a gentle introduction to sex-positive community. Our history dates back to March 1995, when we first started out as a student organization at the University of Washington.

**Sonya.** "Wedding Night Fantasy" has to be the mildest tale I have ever written. It is part of a large collection of dark, twisted stories dealing with sex and death by various authors with strange tastes and vivid imaginations. Our literary site, Femmes Obscure, exists thanks to the generosity and protection offered by our host, The Black Plague (http://www.blackplague.org), a domain dedicated to free speech and forms of artistic expression generally shunned by the mainstream public.

**E. Terry**, a.k.a. Jerusalem Cricket online, lives in San Francisco, where she is a bookkeeper by day and a writer after dark. When she grows up, she wants to be Madonna.

**Davis Trell.** Ex-patriate Britisher living in US. Has problems, as America and England 'separated' by common language. Problems arise, as I can 'twitter' in English, but have lost contact with life on the streets there, so can't write contemporary. American is a second language, but not 'grounded', so apt to put Britishisms in US story. So write fictions set nowhere....and everywhere.

**Mat Twassel.** I'm an ordinary middle-aged guy who lives in a middle-class, midwestern suburb with a lovely wife and two adorable children, one cat, and thousands and thousands of books. I enjoy music, reading, sex, writing, and watching my children grow up. Most days I run two or three miles. I'd rather play golf. I'd rather be strolling a lonely beach with my wife, our special little place just two hundred yards ahead.

The corporeal Emanation of the **Unborn** in this Realm studies English Literature at the University of British Columbia, in Vancouver, Canada. This creature will claim that the Unborn is one of its Internet Personae; the Unborn allows this delusion. When the Veil between Worlds parts, the Will of the Unborn gains primacy. the Unborn seeks . . . .

Nothing is known about **Vincent.**

**Matthew von der Ahe** is a business owner in the Seattle area. His priorities are (1) to facilitate his two older kids' (and his own) survival of their teenagehood; (2) to play alliteration games with his younger kid; and (3) to reach 40 years of age without having to buy pants with a 40" waist.

# ORDER FORM

*Return to: Black Books, PO Box 31155-HN, San Francisco CA 94131-0155, or call (800) 818-8823 to order with a credit card, or fax (415) 431-0172 with credit card info. We accept checks, MOs, cash, Visa, MC, AmEx, and Discover.*

**Hot Off The Net:** erotica and other sex writings from the Internet, edited by Russ Kick
*Taboo subject matter. Brutal honesty and candidness. Experimental forms and styles. From personal confessions to the most outlandish fantasies, witness the future of erotic writing.*

- ❑ Please send me ____ copy[ies] of *Hot Off The Net.* Enclosed is $17 ($14 + $3 s/h), or $18.20 if I am in California (includes sales tax), or $20 US if I am in Canada/Mexico, or $23 US elsewhere for each copy ordered. ISBN 1-892723-00-X.

**The Black Book, 5th edition,** edited by Bill Brent
*The foremost directory of sexuality resources for all orientations, gender identities, and lifestyles in the U.S. and Canada. Over 2,500 listings.*

- ❑ Please send me ____ copy[ies] of *The Black Book.* Enclosed is $20 ($17 + $3 s/h), or $21.45 if I am in California (includes sales tax), or $24 US if I am in Canada/Mexico, or $28 US elsewhere for each copy ordered. ISBN 0-9637401-5-6.

**Pathetic Life,** by Doug Holland (available spring 1999)
*Doug's popular zine about life in the slimy cracks of sidewalk society is now a novel! Post-modern urban life: drug-crazed rommates, stalkers, cockroaches, and more. Unpretentious but affecting.*

- ❑ Please send me ____ copy[ies] of *Pathetic Life.* Enclosed is $12 ($10 + $2 s/h), or $12.85 if I am in California (includes sales tax), or $15 US if I am in Canada/Mexico, or $20 US elsewhere for each copy ordered. (no ISBN)

**Make A Zine!,** by Bill Brent
An indispensable how-to guide for those producing zines, newsletters, and other smaller publications. Completely addresses the nuts and bolts in detail. ISBN 0-9637401-4-8.

- ❑ Please send me ____ copy[ies] of *Make A Zine!* Enclosed is $12 ($10 + $2 s/h), or $12.85 if I am in California (includes sales tax), or $15 US if I am in Canada/Mexico, or $20 US elsewhere for each copy ordered.

**Black Sheets:** Our magazine of sex and popular culture. Kinky, queer, intelligent, irreverent.

- ❑ Please send me 4 issues of *Black Sheets* for $20, or $32 Can/Mex, or $36 elsewhere.
- ❑ Please send me a sample issue. Enclosed is $6 / $7 Can/Mex / $8 elsewhere.

I am 21 years of age or older. ________________________________
(signature required!)

________________________________________________________
Name

________________________________________________________
Address

________________________________________________________
City State Zip

________________________________________ ____________
card number expiration date

In case of a question about my order:

tel. number ______________________ email address: ______________________

I heard about *Hot Off The Net* or got this copy at: ______________________________.